FIRE AND FORGET

ANDREW WARREN

Boldwood

First published in 2017. This edition published in Great Britain in 2025 by Boldwood Books Ltd.

Copyright © Andrew Warren, 2017

Cover Design by Head Design Ltd.

Cover Images: Alamy and iStock

A CIP catalogue record for this book is available from the British Library.

Paperback ISBN 978-1-83703-867-1

Large Print ISBN 978-1-83703-866-4

Hardback ISBN 978-1-83703-865-7

Ebook ISBN 978-1-83703-868-8

Kindle ISBN 978-1-83703-869-5

Audio CD ISBN 978-1-83703-860-2

MP3 CD ISBN 978-1-83703-861-9

Digital audio download ISBN 978-1-83703-862-6

This book is printed on certified sustainable paper. Boldwood Books is dedicated to putting sustainability at the heart of our business. For more information please visit https://www.boldwoodbooks.com/about-us/sustainability/

Boldwood Books Ltd, 23 Bowerdean Street, London, SW6 3TN

www.boldwoodbooks.com

FOREWORD

The events of *Fire and Forget* take place near the end of the South Sudanese Civil War, prior to the current (time of writing) conflict in Sudan.

FOREWORD

1

Nhial walked at a steady pace, ignoring the infernal sun that beat down on his back. He kept his eyes on the long dirt path ahead of him, watching for potholes or debris. Rockets and mortar fire had long since blasted away the road's chipped pavement. Fragments of rusted metal and deep holes now gouged its uneven surface. The debris was a dangerous reminder of the town's bleak past.

The sunbaked mud road stretched through what was once the town center and led past the charred remains of the old colonial structures. Crumbling churches, dilapidated manor houses, and the burned, desecrated shell of the once-pristine town hall – the old buildings seemed like relics of a fantastical era. A forgotten paradise, long since abandoned by whatever strange inhabitants once lived there.

A white stone plaque remained standing near the ruined buildings. Soot and ash covered its carved surface, but the writing underneath was still legible. It marked the town's name as Kanfar, but Nhial knew the place had gone by other names. From European colonists to Sudanese armed forces, and finally to the warring factions of the newly independent South, this tiny scrap of land had changed hands many times in its bloody, war-torn history.

Other people traipsed along both sides of the dirt road. Like Nhial, they carried supplies in scavenged backpacks or thread-bare sacks. A few of the town's inhabitants had set up makeshift stores along the route. They sold food, purified water, oil, and other valuables. The produce was bruised and insect-ridden, but Nhial knew he had to grab whatever he could find. Food of any sort had become a priceless treasure, despite the efforts of the United Nations and other charitable groups.

He crossed over the invisible boundary that separated the old town from the new encampment. The packed, hardened clay of the road became softer, soaked with sewage and refuse. The sun blasted down on the shanties and tents, baking the inhabi-tants and the filth surrounding them. The air itself seemed to thicken into a miasma of decay and suffering.

As he maneuvered between the narrow rows of tents and carts, Nhial listened to the chatter and voices around him. Despite the aura of death and despair, the town's inhabitants did their best to keep their spirits up. He walked past a row of chil-dren, all lined up in the street, books and bundled lunches balanced atop their heads. A group of mothers, draped in mud-stained sarongs and other rags, kissed the children on their cheeks. They sang to them in a hodgepodge of languages and dialects. He could make out smatterings of Nuer, Dinka, French and English, among others.

The children would soon begin the long hike to Bentiu. The tiny town, nestled near the banks of the White Nile River, was in better shape than Kanfar. Its buildings had been renovated by gas and oil companies, and the local orphanage had a fence with a lock. The children would be safer there at night than they would in the tents and hovels of the camp.

And night was when the raiders came.

It had been many months since the last raid. After he and his family had arrived in Kanfar, the fighting between the South Sudan armed forces and the rebel groups to the east had died down. Nhial's wife, Aya, began to speak of better times and impending peace as she served tea to the elders outside their shack.

But Nhial and his family had fled their hometown in the dead of night after armed men had ransacked his village for supplies. He had seen the flames of hatred and cruelty in the invaders' eyes as they lined the town's men up against a wall. Then they blindfolded the male children in the village and ordered them to execute their fathers. Those who complied were taken as soldiers or slaves. Those who refused, or cried too much, were mutilated. Nhial heard the gunshots echoing one by one through the sweltering, dark night as he and his family fled.

When the men were dead, they moved on to the women and the young girls. Their screams and wails of despair carried for miles. Nhial could hear them all through the night as they ran.

After that night, his heart had changed. He knew the violence and bloodshed that engulfed these lands could not be erased by time or words. Perhaps his son might live long enough to see an end to the fighting. But for Nhial, hopes of peace in his lifetime were not worth the saliva he spat onto the muddy, stinking road.

Up ahead, set apart from the other tents and huts, was the shack that gave him and his family shelter. He had built it himself, using sheets of corrugated plastic provided by a nearby UN refugee camp. An older man, his beard and hair white as ash, sat outside in a folding chair next to a battered old table. He sipped hot tea, admiring the young women as they sauntered by.

A tall, healthy-looking local woman emerged from the shack carrying a chipped porcelain jar. She set it down on the tiny table. 'There you go, sir, all the sugar we have left. Sorry for the wait.'

One of the old men reached for the spoon. 'No worries, Aya. Tea is good as it is. Red. Dark.'

'Gondolosi tea,' she said, refilling his cup. 'Good for the blood.'

Nhial could not help but smile as he ducked under the plastic tarp that shaped the tiny porch. 'That's not all it's good for, Aya. You trying to give old Talak's wife here a surprise?'

Aya beamed at Nhial.

'You're back!' She set down the teapot and rushed over to him, wrapping her arms around him in a tight embrace.

'Don't you listen to him,' she said over her shoulder to the old man. 'That's just old wives' tale!'

Nhial set down his sack and removed a few items, setting them down along the sides of the tea house. 'Here, I got you more sugar. Only one bag though.'

Aya took the tiny brown paper bag and refilled the sugar bowl on the table. 'Price go up again? Soon they will want a drop of blood for an ounce of sugar.'

Talak laughed and set a collection of crumpled notes on the table. 'Thank you, Aya. Maybe I come back tomorrow. See if wife wants me to drink more tea. And share more war stories with your guest.' He chuckled as he ambled out into the street.

'You better come back,' Nhial called after him. 'Or Aya tells your wife you flirt with all the girls.'

As the old man wandered into the street, Nhial continued

unpacking his bag of goods. He turned to Aya. 'And how is our guest?' he asked in a low voice.

She glanced at the street, then whispered, 'Better, I think. The tea and food seem to have helped. But the neighbors saw him bathe early this morning.'

Nhial nodded. 'It cannot be avoided. Talak was a soldier, he can be trusted. But the others will gossip. Word will spread. We have repaid this man's kindness. Tomorrow, he must leave.'

Aya bit her lip, then put her arm on Nhial's shoulder. 'His wounds have not yet healed. Maybe he stays a few more days. If he had not found Buri on the outskirts of camp, before nightfall...'

Nhial nodded. 'You know I feel the same, but it is dangerous keeping him here. If word gets out—'

Before Nhial could finish his sentence, an explosion tore through street. He threw Aya to the ground, shielding her body with his own. He felt fire lick his back, and an immense wave of heat rippled through the air.

His ears were ringing. He had not even noticed the sound of the explosion, but the aftereffects left him almost deaf. He could just make out people screaming and the crackle of nearby gunfire. Everything was muted, muffled by the incessant buzzing that filled his skull.

Aya was crying and screaming. Her voice sounded far away, like she was trapped in a deep well. Nhial staggered to his feet. He took a tentative step towards the shack, but his body swayed like a drunk. Another explosion rocked the town. He saw fragments of burning plastic and corrugated metal cascade into the air.

Time seemed to slow to a crawl. Nhial had only managed to take a few steps towards his shack, but all around him the destruction and bloodshed seemed to grow. Gunfire crackled and sprayed in all directions. Bodies collapsed in the streets. Another shack exploded into debris as a barrage of rocket-propelled grenades screamed through the air.

He realized he was walking in a tight circle, stunned by the chaos erupting around him. Hot liquid stung his eyes. He reached up and touched his forehead. He felt fresh, sticky blood spilling from a jagged gash.

'Buri! Where is Buri?' Aya cried out. She ran into the shack.

Nhial started to follow her, but he stopped and stood in the doorway. The sound of a powerful engine roared towards him. He turned to see an armored truck barreling down the street. The vehicle plowed through the scattered debris, crushing the bodies of the fallen villagers into the mud.

The Ural 63099 Typhoon armored vehicle was painted in khaki and brown camouflage. A heavy machine gun turret protruded from the roof. Nhial saw no gunner manning the weapon, but its barrel flashed and roared. It spat a barrage of slugs towards a squad of SPLA soldiers who had taken cover down the street. They returned fire, but the massive weapon cut them down in seconds.

The vehicle screeched to a halt in front of Nhial's shack. His jaw dropped in surprise. He knew the armed forces of Sudan used such vehicles north of the border. But they were far too expensive for the raiders and rebel forces that caused trouble in the White Nile region.

The rear door swung open, and Nigerian music blasted from the truck's dark interior. The thumping bass of the song seemed even louder than the gunshots and explosions that continued to decimate the camp.

A tall, slim East African man stepped out of the vehicle. He wore a navy pinstriped suit, and a leather bolo tie hung from the collar of his pressed white dress shirt. He sniffed the air and nodded, as if oblivious to the violence that surrounded them. A bullet ricocheted off the truck next to him. He turned and looked at the mark the bullet had left. Then he looked back at Nhial, his face devoid of all expression.

Two more men flanked him, dressed in scavenged military uniforms. They carried assault rifles and wore red sashes tied around their right arms. More armed men poured out of the truck and took up positions behind them. Their lanky bodies were draped in tattered rags and clothes, and they all wore similar red armbands.

The man in the suit walked over to Nhial and looked him up and down. He grinned, revealing a set of yellow, mangled teeth. His left front incisor was missing. A tiny, polished diamond sat in place of the missing tooth. Unlike most stones, this one was not clear. It held a pale, red tint, and glowed with an inner fire as a beam of sunlight struck the man's face.

'Your name is Nhial. Do you know who I am?'

The stunned younger man nodded. He swallowed.

'Yes. I know. We... we want no trouble,' Nhial stuttered. 'Please... take whatever—'

The man did not stop grinning. 'We are not thieves, my good man. I am told you have something that belongs to me. Dis is true?'

'Leave them alone,' a man's voice called from inside the shack. He limped out into the light. His Caucasian skin was flushed, and beads of sweat dotted his forehead beneath short brown hair. His tan, sunburned skin crinkled around his eyes as he squinted at the other men. He took another step and winced in pain. His shirt was unbuttoned, and a dark stain soaked a cloth bandage that was tied around his abdomen.

'I'm the one you want.' He glared at the man with the red diamond tooth. 'Isn't that right?'

The uniformed men surged into the cabin. Nhial heard screams from inside. One man dragged out a struggling Aya and a slim, young boy.

'Buri! Don't you hurt him or—'

'Why you come here?' the boy cried out. 'Why you take him? He help us, he bring medicine, from America.'

The other soldier emerged from the shack carrying a canvas rucksack. He handed the bag to the man with the diamond tooth. 'His things, Commander.'

The commander took the bag. He stepped over to the boy and rubbed his head with rough, calloused fingers.

'This stranger is not who he seems to be, young one,' he said, nodding toward the injured man. 'He is no angel. He is a demon, an evil spirit. His kind do not care about you. They care only for what they can take... what they can steal from our home. Isn't that right, Mr. Galloway?'

The white man shrugged. 'You must have me confused with someone else. My name's Carter. I work for the World Health Organization. You and your dogs are the only demons I see around here.'

The man with the diamond tooth rummaged through the rucksack and pulled out a small, silver metal case. He dropped the bag and flipped open the case. An icy white mist crept out, evaporating in the morning heat. He peered inside the case for a moment, his eyes wide and searching. Then he snapped it shut and handed it to one of his men.

'Your name is Josh Galloway, and you work for the American CIA,' he said in a singsong voice. He tapped the side of his skull, next to his left eye. 'You see, I have my own demons, my own spirits. They see through your lies. You stole two of these cases from me. Where is the other one?'

'I told you, I don't know what you're talking about! I was carrying medicine samples, and—'

'You anger the spirits, Mr. Galloway. Soon enough, they show us both the truth, I think. Yes, you will be begging to talk, once they start to whisper in your ear. Put him on the truck.'

One of the guards prodded the man called Galloway with the butt of his rifle. Josh winced in pain. He glared at the two soldiers for a second, then allowed himself to be led to the back of the truck.

'I'm sorry,' he whispered as he stumbled past Nhial. The men shoved him into the back of the idling vehicle.

'Very good, very good,' the man in the suit said, clapping his hands. 'Now, Nhial my friend, you have taken two things from me. This man, Mr. Galloway. And the property he has stolen from me. So I will take two things from you. First, I take your family.'

'No, please, I give you anything, take me, take—'

The man in the suit held up his hand and looked away. Two more men grabbed Nhial. They kicked and pummeled him, forcing him to the ground.

'Have no fear, they will help us in our glorious purpose. They will serve us, just as we serve Almighty God.'

The second soldier dragged Aya and Buri, kicking and screaming, towards the truck.

Two of the other men grabbed Nhial's right arm and held it over the wood table. The man in the suit slipped open his blazer, revealing a long silver machete hanging from a leather sheath under his arm. He slid out the blade and held it up in the morning sun, admiring the way the light glinted off the sharp edge.

'Please,' Nhial moaned. 'Please, you can kill me, do whatever you want to me, just leave my son.'

The man smiled again. His tooth reflected red beams of light, like lasers dancing across the interior of the shack.

'Don't worry, good sir. I'm not gonna kill you. But this man, this Mr. Galloway, he take a great treasure from me. So I must take more from you. Otherwise, people everywhere, they think they can steal from me. They think they can steal from our glorious cause, and nothing will happen to them. And our country, our home... We have enough thieves here, don't you think? Thieves from outside, and thieves from within. But now, maybe all these thieves see men like you, and they know better.'

Nhial looked up as the man raised the blade. He stared into his eyes, expecting to see the same hate and cruelty he had seen in the men who raided his village. But instead, he saw nothing but pale, white orbs. The man's eyes had rolled back into his head, as if he was having a spasm or seizure of some kind.

Then the blade descended. And Nhial screamed.

2

A hot breeze cut across the waters of the Louisiana bayou, and the late afternoon sun cast dappled waves of golden light over its choppy surface. Rows of black cypress trees lined the banks on either side of the wide expanse of water. Long trails of Spanish moss hung from their lower branches, kissing the dark water's surface.

John Blayne eyed the thick vegetation from the rear seat of the airboat as it roared across the water. A flash of motion caught his eye. He turned his head and spotted a lumbering six-foot alligator slide down the muddy bank into the water. The huge reptile disappeared beneath the rippling surface.

Predators, Blayne thought.

In the world outside, Blayne considered himself a powerful man. He was the Director of National Intelligence. He coordinated and assessed intel from the CIA, NSA, FBI, and others. Operations, personnel, budgets, planning, and execution... all aspects of America's vast intelligence apparatus felt his influence. And in addition to his personal status, he had the ear of the most powerful man in the world... the president of the

United States. It was his job to brief the president on all intelligence matters relating to national security. His recommendations held tremendous sway in the White House.

But that was back in Washington, back among the secure tree-lined streets and pristine white government buildings. Great Falls, McClean, Arlington... The high-priced suburbs with their malls, mansions, and five-star restaurants. As DNI, his actions affected the entire world. But the further he ventured from the capital, the more he felt his own sense of personal power begin to crumble.

Out here, he found himself surrounded by an endless expanse of black water and dense groves of gnarled trees. A beautiful but lonely sunset burned across the sky above. Here, he could sense that he had fallen even lower on the food chain.

You're not a predator, he thought as the airboat drifted around another bend in the river. Predators are pure, of single mind and purpose. You're not pure.

You're compromised.

How had he allowed this to happen? How had he fallen so far?

Up ahead, a massive bird exploded from the vegetation and took flight. Blayne watched, stunned, as a pair of four-foot white wings flapped through the air, their powerful beating driving the large bird up and over the airboat. It screeched and swooped low over the deck. As Blayne ducked, he spotted a patch of red pigment decorating the black skin of the animal's throat.

The bird spiraled up into the sunburst sky. It beat its wings, then disappeared into the shadowed canopy of gnarled trees and moss.

'Big fucking bird, right?' the pilot shouted behind him. Blayne turned around and looked up. The pilot sat in an elevated seat that gave him a better view of the waterline and floating vegetation. A sly grin was plastered across his lean, hawkish face. 'I couldn't believe it when I first saw one of those things myself. It's called a jabiru. South American crane, believe it or not. Been spotted around these parts recently.'

'Fascinating,' Blayne snapped back. He raised his voice, shouting over the deafening engine noise. He turned to the man next to him. 'How much farther are we going? I can't be gone all day. Sooner or later, I'll be missed.'

The man, a beefier, taciturn hunk of sinew and muscle, pointed ahead. 'Right around the next bend, sir.'

'And how long is this ridiculous rendezvous expected to take?' Blayne asked. He hoped the roar of the engine would cover the quiver of fear hiding behind his words.

The bigger man shook his head. 'No idea. Our orders are to bring you to the meeting, but we'll wait outside while you have your conference.'

Blayne nodded. 'Very good.'

Although they acted as bodyguards, Blayne knew these men were not loyal to him. They were handlers, assigned to make sure he followed instructions with a minimum of fuss. If he made things difficult, if he refused to obey his summons... they, in turn, would make things difficult for him.

The pilot reached down from his perch and manipulated the twin control sticks mounted to the boat's deck. The left stick tilted the rudders behind the massive aircraft prop at the rear of the boat. The right stick controlled the throttle. The pilot pushed forward, increasing their speed across the water. He powered the boat into a long, graceful turn. The small craft circled around a lump of forested land that emerged from the swamp ahead.

Blayne squinted. In the distance, a tiny shack came into view, nestled between the drooping branches of a cypress grove. The dense foliage blocked out what little sun was left, hiding most of the shack in shadow.

'You've got to be fucking kidding me!' he shouted over the noise of the propeller. 'Here? He wants to meet here?'

The pilot eased back on the throttle. The propeller slowed. The boat drifted towards a rickety dock that extended from the shack.

The lean man shrugged. His eyes were impossible to read behind his mirrored aviator sunglasses.

'Can't put a price on privacy, I guess. If I were you, I'd head on in, sir. Not wise to keep him waiting.'

The beefier man stepped out of the boat and lashed it to the dock with a yellow, frayed nylon cord. He extended his hand, but Blayne ignored it. He stumbled a bit but managed to step out of the listing boat and onto the dock. The wood creaked beneath his weight.

The man nodded towards the shack. 'We'll wait out here to take you back when it's over. Shouldn't be long.'

Blayne grimaced. 'It's already been too long.'

He forced himself to turn his back on the men and took a few steps toward the shack. Behind him, the sun dipped lower on the horizon. The patches of light on the water shifted to orange and blood-red, mirroring the thick, painted clouds in the sky.

* * *

The door to the shack creaked open. Inside, Blayne found a tiny room with rotted wood flooring and boarded-up windows on each wall. The roof sagged in the middle, warping the room like a circus funhouse mirror. No line in the structure seemed to be straight. A small wooden desk sat at the rear of the room, but there was no other furniture in the dark, cramped space.

Blayne turned and gave one last look at the two men waiting for him on the dock. They stood motionless, staring back at him. Blayne exhaled and shut the door, cutting off the sliver of light from outside.

The glowing screen of a laptop computer cast a square of light on the rear wall. Blayne spotted a thick orange power cable running from under the desk. It snaked through a hole in the wall. Must be a generator outside, he thought. They were miles from civilization and any source of power.

Blayne walked to the desk and sat down. A logo filled the screen: Delta Blue Security. No other information was displayed on the monitor. He picked up a small Bluetooth earbud from the desk and slipped it into his ear. Then he removed a tiny USB key from the pocket of his khaki pants. He inserted it into the computer.

The screensaver dissolved, replaced with a video conference panel. The screen split into three windows. Three faces stared back at him, each one masked by shadow and distortion filters. The secure conference software masked their identities in case the signal was intercepted.

But Blayne knew each of the men behind those blurred faces... he knew how dangerous they could be.

'Christ, Blayne, can't you ever be on time?' The voice distortion could not mask the impatient, arrogant tone, nor the thick Southern accent of the man in the center window.

'Blame your men. They were my chauffeurs for this meeting. I'm all for security, but isn't this taking privacy a bit far? When I told you I would be available to meet in New Orleans, I didn't think you meant the middle of the swamp. You know who I am, I can't just disappear for hours at a time.'

'Watch your tone, son. It's thanks to your fuckup that this level of security is necessary.'

Blayne narrowed his eyes. 'How do you figure that? Lapinski was your asset. I warned you that running ops in China in the middle of the president's talks could blow up in your face. And I also warned you—'

'You an Elvis fan?'

Blayne blinked. 'What?'

'Elvis. The King? He's got a song that's apropos in this situation. "A little less conversation, a little more action, please".'

'I don't—'

The voice interrupted him again. 'Warnings are well and good, but it doesn't take much to cry that the sky is falling. Hell, even a broken watch is right twice a day. Question is, what are you going to do to fix it?'

Blayne swallowed. 'Fix it? Lapinski is in FBI custody with CIA oversight. He's set to testify before a senate committee in Washington.'

'Lapinski was NSA. Last time I checked, you were the DNI, correct? You coordinate intel from the alphabet soup that serves our great nation's intelligence community. Oxymoron if ever I heard one. Now, I know I'm an ignorant yokel compared to a fancy DC suit like yourself. But that is your job description, yes?'

'Yes, but—'

'So there's a question on my mind, John. How the hell did you coordinate this into such a colossal goddamn shit-show on wheels?'

Blayne could see no features on the shadowy figure's blurred face, but he could feel the man's eyes burning into him, observing his powerlessness, his fear.

'Rebecca Freeling, the new D/NCS, she had an asset in

China,' he stammered. 'Someone the CIA didn't know about, someone who—'

'I know all about her asset.' Another voice this time. The head on the right. Blayne could make out the shape of wire-rim glasses resting across the blurred, gaunt face. 'A mistake,' the man said. 'One that should have been rectified long ago.'

The man in the center grunted. 'Mistakes. Well, we've all made 'em. Lapinski, did he know you were involved?'

Blayne's words tumbled from his mouth as he struggled to regain control of the conversation. 'No, he never knew. I made sure to push him in the right direction, but I played dumb about his China asset, about you, about everything!'

The man laughed, a deep, low guffaw. 'Played dumb, huh? Yeah, you got that down for sure. Okay, I think we can get this under control.'

The man on the right nodded. 'I agree. I can handle Freeling's asset. In fact, he may even prove useful to us.'

The man on the left finally spoke. His voice was higher pitched than the other two men, with a lilting accent. 'What about the operation? We already set things in motion, committed manpower, acquired the necessary materials.'

The center figure's voice was firm and held the snap of a man used to being obeyed. 'The operation moves forward. We all have too much invested at this point. I'm not gonna let some pansy ass NSA rat take us down now. Even if he doesn't know anything, I don't want Lapinski to take the stand. I want a total blackout on this, understood?'

'Understood.' The man on the right again. 'We have an asset of our own who can take care of that problem for us.'

'Good. No more mistakes.'

Blayne stared at the screen and drummed his fingers on the

desk. He realized he was no longer an active part of the conversation. He had been left out of their plans.

He was not part of the solution.

'And what about me?' he asked. 'I take it I'm free to return to New Orleans for my lecture?'

'Gentlemen, why don't you give Mr. Blayne and myself some privacy here.'

The two other faces disappeared, and the center face swelled to fill the screen. Blayne leaned back in his chair as the face loomed before him. Once again, he could feel the man's unseen eyes burrowing into him. He knew the man could sense his weakness, his fear, even from across the digital gap that separated them.

'John, maybe I've been too hard on you. Hell, like I said, we all make mistakes. I've made my share as well. I should have ridden you harder. Made sure your head was in the game. Let's face it... you're a pencil pusher. A suit. You were a lawyer, right?'

'Now wait a minute here, I've served my country same as you, I—'

The man on the screen waved a hazy, shadowed hand and his voice softened. 'Now now, calm down. I don't mean offense. Just telling it like it is. Smarts, intelligence, political savvy... Those qualities have value in the right circumstances. But I'm afraid we've gone beyond those circumstances now. Do me a favor, John. Open that drawer to your left. The little one on top.'

Blayne slid open the drawer. He reached inside and his eyes widened.

Inside the drawer, his fingers wrapped around the butt of a pistol.

He lifted the gun up and examined it. It was a smooth, nickel-plated Ruger SR 1911, chambered in .45 ACP. The walnut grips were polished to a high sheen, but a single scratch marred the wood on the right side. Blayne recognized the mark. He had caused it when he had dropped the gun once, during cleaning.

This was his pistol. Taken from his home.

'How did you...' His voice trailed off as he realized his initial fears had been correct. There was blood in the water. His blood.

The predator was moving in for the kill.

'Son,' the man on the screen said, his voice smooth and soft as velvet. 'There comes a time in all our lives when we outlive our usefulness. It will come for me, sure enough. But today, it's come for you. I'm counting on you to do the right thing here.'

Blayne narrowed his eyes at the screen. The tiny red light next to the web camera blinked on and off, as steady and unchanging as a heartbeat.

'Wait, you mean... You can't expect me to...'

'I can and I do. Life is full of shattered expectations, John, but I warn you, do not let me down here. There're more lives on the line now than yours.'

Blayne turned his eyes from the screen and stared at the gun in disbelief. He wanted to put it down on the desk, but somehow his arm and fingers refused to comply.

'I can't... I'm the Director of National Intelligence, I'm—'

'John, do not test me!' Once again, the cold snap of steel filled the man's voice. 'So you're the DNI, so what? You think that means anything? You think you have power? At the end of the day, you have the same power any man has. Kill or be killed. You botched things with Lapinski. He's a loose end now. And that makes you a loose end as well. I can't have that, John. I don't expect you to like it, but you must understand what has to be done.'

'No! No, I won't!'

'You do this for me, I'll make sure your family is taken care of. Just like I promised. Your wife will never have to know the ugliness of need. Of poverty. Of fear. And your daughter will go to that expensive prep school you had your eye on. She'll live out her charmed life, spend her trust fund on sports cars and vacations with her friends.'

Blayne turned his eyes back to the screen. The voice paused. The shadowed figure leaned closer, filling the webcam's view with his warped face. Blayne heard the man tapping some keys on the other end of the digital call. The distorted mask disappeared. Blayne found himself staring into a single, enormous blue eye. Craggy peaks and valleys of wrinkled skin surrounded the brilliant iris.

The sudden clarity of the image was unsettling. Blayne was half-aware of a noise outside, some kind of muted commotion. But he paid it no mind. He was unable to tear his attention away from the man on the screen. The eye rotated in its socket as the man stared at him.

'Blayne, look into my eye. You know what I've seen, what I've done. I've killed men. In war. In peace. Sometimes far away, sometimes up close and personal. I've felt hot blood on my hands, John. Do you know what that feels like? To feel a living thing lose that spark, go pale as the blood drains from its body? And then to look into their eyes and watch as that spark goes out for good? Permanent, John. There's a peace in that, knowing it's permanent. Their death is forever. And you're still alive. Have you ever felt that?'

Blayne shook his head. His lips mouthed words, but no sound came out. The commotion outside was louder. He heard wood splinter and crack. He looked up at the door, dragged from his hypnotic trance by the noise outside.

The man on the screen continued speaking. 'You deny me now, John, and my men outside will come on in and do the job for me. Won't look as good. Murder instead of a suicide. But it's still manageable. But John, if that happens, I swear to you, your family will find out what it feels like to see that spark go. They'll see it in each other's eyes. And then they'll see ugliness. Ugliness like I've seen. Decades of it, all compressed into a few short, painful days. And when they go, John, they'll know. They'll know it was your cowardice that made them suffer. I'll make sure of it.'

Blayne looked back at the screen. 'You... fuck, goddamn you!' he whispered.

'Grow up, John. And grow a pair. Let's get this done. I don't have all day.'

Blayne swallowed. He imagined his wife and daughter. A family vacation to Disneyland, years earlier. His daughter playing in the pool, learning to swim. His wife smiling at him. Making love in their room, laughing, trying to keep their voices down. That was before. Before he fell.

He raised the gun to his head.

'That's it, John. You're doing the right thing, I promise. I thank you. And so will your family.'

Blayne pressed the barrel of the pistol against his temple. 'You motherfucking piece of...' He continued to whisper a stream of curses. The man on the screen did not show any reaction, if he even heard them at all.

'Almost there, John. Come on, let's finish this and move on. No point in drawing things out.' Again, the voice was velvet smooth, like a man speaking to a beloved pet.

Suddenly, the shack's door crashed open. Blayne jumped out of his seat and took a step back.

A body flew to the floor and rolled to a stop. It was the heavyset man from outside, one of the men who had brought him here. One of his handlers.

A second man charged into the shack. Blayne had never seen

him before. He was tall, and his body was lean, taut, and muscular. He moved with the grace of a natural athlete, keeping his shoulders low to present a smaller target to any potential threats inside.

Blayne watched as the heavier man reached down and slipped a tiny Smith & Wesson M&P pistol from a holster strapped above his ankle.

He aimed the weapon, but before he could draw a bead, the other man lashed out with a powerful kick. The tiny pistol fired, but the kick threw the man's aim off. The bullet thudded into the shack's wooden roof.

The other man raised a pistol, a Beretta PX4 Storm compact. The gun's roar was deafening in the tiny space of the shack. He fired twice, sending two bullets into the prone target's chest.

The man's body spasmed as the bullets struck his flesh. A third shot opened a brilliant red circle in his forehead. He ceased thrashing.

The shooter looked up at Blayne. A fringe of short brown hair swept above his tan, chiseled face. Streaks of sweat and dirt covered his skin, as if he had crawled through the swamp and surrounding brush. The man was half-hidden by darkness, but Blayne found himself staring into a pair of the greenest eyes he had ever seen. They looked like emeralds blazing out from the man's shadowy, haunted features.

Blayne yelped as the man swung the gun in a two-handed grip and fired again. The laptop exploded into a shower of sparks and plastic shrapnel.

'Drop the weapon! Do it now!' the man shouted in a commanding voice.

Blayne released his hold on the gun, letting it fall and clatter to the warped wood floorboards.

'Kick it towards me. Gently!' The mysterious shooter kept his distance from Blayne. He held the Beretta in a steady grip. Blayne kicked the pistol towards him. The shooter bent at the knees and picked up the weapon, never taking his eyes off Blayne.

'Whoever you are, we have to get out of here, we have to—' Blayne tried to inject some authority into his voice, but he could barely speak above a terrified whisper.

'Bernatto,' the shooter said in a low, firm voice. 'Where is Allan Bernatto?'

Blayne blinked. 'What? Listen, who the hell are you?'

The man charged forward, flipping over the desk with one hand. The fragments of computer crashed to the floor as Blayne backed away in fear. Blayne found himself pinned against the wall by the man's powerful forearm. He snatched and clawed at the vice-like arm, but he could not pry himself from the iron grip.

'I've been following you, Blayne. For over a month I've been your shadow. Allan Bernatto, former D/NCS. He was one of the people on your little conference call, wasn't he? Tell me where he is!'

'More men... coming. Have to... get out of here!' Blayne hissed, struggling to form words.

The man cocked his head toward one of the boarded windows and listened.

'Look, I'm the Director of National Intelligence, I can help you, I—'

'I know who you are. Shut up!'

It was a faint, distant buzzing, almost inaudible against the sounds of the insects and birds in the swamp. But it was growing louder. Closer.

'Airboats. Two or more. Friends of yours?'

Blayne shook his head. 'With... them. The men who brought me here. Men you... killed.'

The man released his arm, and Blayne slumped to the floor.

'Then you have a choice to make. My name is Thomas Caine. You can come with me and tell me everything I want to know. Or I can leave you for them.'

The DNI stumbled to his feet. 'Caine? Wait, I remember the reports. You... You're supposed to be dead.'

The man named Caine glared at him with his emerald-green eyes. To Blayne, he looked like a tiger, guarding a fresh kill.

This was a true predator.

Blayne swallowed, then nodded.

'Get me out of here and you have a deal.'

'You hold out on me, and I swear, Blayne, I'll make you wish you pulled that trigger yourself.'

'I'll tell you everything. Bernatto, the others... all of it.'

Caine stared at him for a second, then slid his Beretta into his waistband. The buzzing grew louder. He stalked towards the door, thumbing the safety on Blayne's Ruger as he moved. He racked the weapon's slide a quarter inch, checked the load, and then released the slide with a soft, metallic clack.

'Good choice. I came here on a fishing boat. My ride's long gone now so we take the airboat on the dock. I'll cover you. Move, now!'

The two men exited the shack and charged towards the docked boat. The noise of the motors echoed between the dark groves of trees.

3

As they ran down the dock, Caine reached into his pocket and grabbed the key he had removed from the pilot's corpse. He leapt onto the bobbing deck of the boat and took a seat at the controls. He made sure to keep Blayne in the corner of his eye.

'The mooring ropes, cast them off, now!' He slid the key into a yellow plastic ignition socket.

Blayne hurried to untie the frayed nylon ropes at the stern and bow of the long, flat craft. 'What happened to the pilot?' he asked as the loose cords slipped off the dock and into the boat's hull.

'I left him for the gators,' Caine said. 'Same thing that will happen to you if you hold out on me. Now sit down!'

The noise of other airboats grew louder. Caine turned the key and the rear-mounted propeller sputtered to life. Caine guided the boat away from the dock and pressed the throttle stick forward. As the engine roared, two shimmering metal boats sped around the riverbank.

The airboats were unmarked, but they looked brand new. They were long, sleek, and built for speed, sporting carbon-fiber propellers and nitrous tanks mounted next to the engines. Each boat held a pilot in a low-slung, front-mounted seat, and a two-man team seated in the rear.

They wore black polo shirts, jeans, and gray Kevlar vests. The men in the rear carried small bullpup assault rifles. Caine recognized the design: IWI Tavor. The weapons were Israeli-made and chambered for 5.56 NATO rounds. They were compact, reliable, and capable of burst and full automatic fire.

The guns, the clothes, the boats, Caine thought... Money. Private contractors.

Mercenaries, like the men who had brought Blayne into the swamp.

Caine had scouted this area of the swamp days before. During his surveillance of Blayne, he had noted the two men from the dock tailing the DNI. He shadowed them as they followed Blayne throughout the city of New Orleans. Then he followed them into the swamp and observed as they had prepped the area in advance of the meeting. He watched while they rigged power from a generator, set up an antenna for satellite internet coverage, and secured the grounds around the shack. Then he waited, taking shelter in a hunter's hide until the men reappeared with Blayne.

The shack was on the outskirts of land owned by Delta Blue, a private military and intelligence company. Their main training facility was a twenty-four-acre compound a few kilometers northeast of the shack. But if these mercenaries worked for Delta Blue, who had hired them?

Caine pushed the questions from his mind. There would be time enough for answers once he questioned Blayne... assuming they lived that long.

As they sped away from the dock, Caine turned the boat to starboard and circled back around the little island. Outrunning the pursuers' boats would be difficult. The airboat that had transported the DNI was a civilian model, a far cry from the high-tech craft that were now closing in on his wake.

As their pursuers moved closer, Caine slid Blayne's Ruger from his waistband. He looked back over his shoulder. The massive propeller, and the wire safety cage that surrounded it, blocked his line of fire. There was no way to get a clear shot at their pursuers.

Blayne stood up and reached for the pistol. 'Give me the gun! I can shoot!'

Caine slammed the butt of the pistol down on Blayne's face. The DNI crumpled back into his seat, a trickle of blood streaming from a gash on his forehead.

'I'm not stupid, Blayne,' Caine shouted. 'Stay down!'

A barrage of automatic gunfire erupted behind them. Caine ducked low in his seat as sparks flew off the safety cage... the shots had missed the propeller by inches.

Keeping a loose grip on the gun, Caine wrapped his fingers around both control sticks. He jerked them in opposite directions, gunning the throttle and forcing the rudder full to port.

As the boat pivoted, Caine eased up on the throttle. The boat sped sideways across the murky water, skipping across the river like a stone thrown from the shore.

Now sideways, Caine had a clear shot. He twisted his body to the left and let go of the sticks. He used a double-handed grip to steady his aim as the boat bounced across the water. The gun roared in his hands as he sent a stream of bullets towards the lead airboat.

Sparks flew from the boat's hull. Two of his shots ricocheted off the metal, but the third struck the pilot. His body jerked backwards. Caine set the pistol down on the arm of his chair and pulled back on the sticks. A hail of return fire cut through the humid swamp air around them.

'What the hell are you doing?' Blayne shouted. 'You're gonna get us killed!'

The boat straightened out. Caine pushed forward on the throttle again, speeding away from the boats behind them. The lead boat pursuer slowed down as one of the mercenaries pulled the injured pilot from his seat. The other boat surged forward. The two armed men onboard fired short, controlled bursts into the rear of Caine's boat, causing a plume of smoke to billow from the propeller housing.

Another lump of dark, forested earth rose from the swamp ahead of them. Caine pushed the boat to starboard, hoping the smoke would throw off their pursuers. But the roar of the other boats soon caught up to them. More gunfire nipped at the water's surface. Stray branches and bits of moss clattered onto the deck as bullets tore through the surrounding foliage.

The engine noise behind them grew louder. Their airboat lurched sideways and shuddered. The Ruger pistol flew from the chair and slid across the hull towards the back of the boat.

One of their pursuers had managed to pull up along the starboard side of the boat and rammed them. The thick roots and gnarled trees of the island loomed to their port side. The boat's hull scraped against the raised land.

Dammit! Caine cursed. How did they catch up so quickly?

Then he remembered the nitrous tanks.

The two men in the rear raised their weapons to fire. Caine gunned the throttle, slamming into them again. The impact threw off their aim, sending the burst of bullets thudding into the deck.

A stream of water sprayed from one of the holes in the hull of his boat. They were taking on water.

Caine looked to his right and spotted a small metal tool bin bolted to the deck.

'Blayne, make yourself useful. Open that toolbox. See if there's a bilge pump!'

Blayne eyed the stream of water filling the hull, then scrambled towards the bin.

Caine yanked back on the stick, once again slamming into the other boat. More gunfire sliced through the air above them. The engine of the second boat roared closer. One of the other men must have taken the pilot's position, and now it was gaining on them.

Blayne shouted over the loud prop wash. 'There's a hammer, a box of nails, a flare gun... no pump!'

Caine glanced to his right. The setting sun cast a golden glow through the trees and vines. The dying rays of light reflected off the steel propeller cage, and the silver nitrous tanks of the attackers' boat.

'Grab the flare pistol and hold on,' he shouted.

He swung the boat again. The metal hull groaned as it slammed into their attackers. Blayne tumbled across the deck and thudded into the sidewall. Water continued to spray through the holes in the hull.

Caine reached behind his back and drew his Beretta. As the men on the other boat recovered their balance, he locked his sights on their nitrous tanks.

Blam! Blam! Blam!

The gun barked three times. A high-pitched metallic twang screamed through the air as the bullets struck their target. A pair of dark holes erupted in the middle of the tanks. Twin streams of liquid nitrous oxide spilled out onto the deck.

Blayne struggled to sit up. He turned and aimed the flare pistol at the attackers' boat.

'No,' Caine shouted, jerking the control stick to the right once more. 'Wait, not yet!'

The two boats clashed again. As they drifted apart, the men in the other boat ignored the ruptured tanks and opened fire. More slugs tore into the deck of Caine's boat. A two-inch pool of swamp water now filled the bottom.

Blayne gasped as a bullet struck his thigh. A thick cloud of blood mixed with the water as he fell backwards.

'Blayne, get up! Shoot, now!'

Blayne groaned and leaned over the side of the boat. Their attackers steadied themselves and prepared to fire again. Blayne extended his arm and aimed the flare pistol. His face was pale, and blood continued to pump from his wounded leg.

Caine rammed into the attackers' boat one more time, struggling to keep the men off balance. 'Fire!'

Blayne pulled the trigger. A blinding red light sizzled from the barrel of the gun as the flare streaked out. For a split second, it lit up the dark trees and vines, surrounding them with a sinister crimson glow. Then it bounced onto the deck of the boat and exploded into a shower of sparks.

The liquid nitrous oxide, on its own, was not flammable. But mixed with the oxygen in the air, the vapor became a highly flammable gas. In a fraction of a second, it accelerated the burning flare into a hellish inferno.

The men shrieked as the flames licked at their flesh. Caine accelerated and sped past them as the flaming pyre that consumed their boat reached up into the sky. Then, with a loud whoosh, the remaining nitrous oxide in the tanks ignited.

Caine looked back and saw a massive fireball erupt behind them as the boat exploded. His lips twisted into a grim smile. The burning fragments of the boat splashed and fizzled as they pelted the surface of the murky water.

Blayne collapsed into the muddy puddle that was rising inch by inch, filling the inside of the airboat. Another round of gunfire erupted behind them. Caine ducked and cursed as more sparks ricocheted off the propeller cage. The second boat was still in pursuit.

Caine worked the controls, weaving the boat back and forth across the river. The smoke trail that followed in his wake grew thicker and darker. He was not sure how much more punishment the engine could take.

More gunfire screeched off the metal hull and sliced through the foliage on either side of them. The river was narrowing, and the two boats found themselves forced into a tight channel. The strip of water cut between two islands of mud-streaked land and gnarled trees.

Caine squinted in the dim light. He could see a dark shadow blocking the way farther up the river. As the boats charged forward, the obstruction came into view. A rotted tree had toppled and hung suspended between the two riverbanks, cutting off the channel. There was only a foot or two of clearance beneath the enormous trunk. The airboats, with their top-mounted propellers, would not be able to pass under it... They were on a collision course!

4

Caine jerked the boat to starboard, smashing into his attackers as they pulled alongside him in the channel. From the corner of his eye he could see the injured pilot lying across the deck. One of the other men had taken the controls. The third man knelt on the bow, aiming his rifle at them.

Caine slipped his Beretta from his waistband and sent a burst of gunfire across the bow of their craft. His shots didn't hit anything, but they had the desired effect. The lone gunman scrambled for cover, ducking down below the edge of the metal hull.

As the boats split apart, Caine spotted a dark clump rising up from the water off their bow. A thick, twisted column of roots jutted out from the shallow, muddy swamp.

'Blayne, hold on!' Caine shouted. There was no time to avoid the obstacle. He pushed the throttle forward and the engine roared louder. A metallic thunk rattled through the hull as they hit the roots. The impact launched the boat up and out of the water.

Caine gripped the handles of the pilot's seat as the airboat sailed through the air. For a split second he felt weightless. Then his stomach lurched as they fell, crashing back into the river with a tremendous wet slap.

As he wiped the spray off his face, Caine heard his pursuers' boat splash down next to them. Then he felt his boat shimmy and tilt in the water. One of the men from the other boat had jumped onto his deck!

Caine saw the mercenary standing at the bow of the boat, swinging his rifle towards him. He yanked on the throttle, causing the man to stumble. Dropping the rifle, the mercenary charged forward as Caine slid out of his seat and raised his pistol.

Before he could fire, he heard another loud thunk. He grabbed the side of the boat as they lurched into the air again... the boat had hit another clump of roots. The channel was getting shallower.

A wave of muddy water sprayed through the air as they crashed back into the river. The boats continued racing forward. The merc lunged towards him. Behind him, Caine could see the fallen tree looming downriver. The rotting trunk still blocked their path.

The man closed in before Caine could fire. He slapped Caine's pistol aside with the open palm of his left hand. Caine instinctively knew what was coming... he had used the same move many times himself.

These men have had training, he thought. They're good.

The thug wrapped his fingers around the barrel of the weapon and pushed it down. He launched a right hook towards Caine's face. Caine ducked and raised his left elbow. His forearm deflected the punch, and the man was thrown off balance.

Grabbing the shoulder strap of the man's rifle, Caine yanked him forward. He slammed the top of his skull into the bridge of the man's nose. The mercenary grunted in pain.

Caine wrenched his pistol from the stunned thug's grip. The man staggered backwards, trying to put some distance between himself and Caine's fists.

The airboat bounced across the water as it continued charging forward at full speed. It drifted right, scraping hulls with the other boat. The mercenary stumbled and fell, splashing in the muddy water that filled the airboat.

They were racing closer and closer towards the fallen tree. Caine saw a long stretch of mudflat speed by as the bank of the island flattened out and dipped down to meet the river. A row of wooden shacks jutted out from the desolate swampland.

He turned and pushed both sticks backwards, forcing the vehicle into a quick turn to port. The airboat spun in the water and flew up onto the riverbank. The prop wash generated by the massive rear propeller blasted behind them at over one hundred miles per hour. It was powerful enough to push the boat across the slick, mud-covered earth.

Caine fell backwards as the boat surged across damp ground. Behind them, the other boat raced forward, continuing down the river. Caine heard the shriek of twisted metal and a loud crash as the craft collided with the fallen tree at full speed. He turned and saw the boat's hull flip up and spiral through the air. The impact tore the propeller housing away from the stern of the craft.

Looking back towards the bow of his boat, Caine saw they were still speeding across the muddy plain, heading straight towards one of the abandoned shacks. But before he could adjust their course, the mercenary stumbled to his feet and raised his rifle.

Caine rolled behind the pilot's seat as gunfire burst through the air above him. He kicked out with his right leg, striking the throttle stick and driving it forward. The boat shuddered as the propeller drove it even faster across the wet terrain.

Caine grabbed the side of the boat, bracing for impact. The mercenary narrowed his eyes, then spun around, raising his arm in a defensive gesture. It was too little, and too late...

Crash!

Once again, the boat launched into the air. It flew up a muddy embankment and tore through the rotted wood of the shack's walls. Caine felt the boat tip. He flailed his arms, grabbing for anything he could find to steady himself. His fingers grasped one of the loose mooring ropes. He wrapped it around his arm as his body whipped through the air.

The metal hull groaned in protest. It tipped over and spun, tearing through the remains of the shack like a wrecking ball. It exploded out the other side, sending a rain of wooden planks and debris flying through the air. Then it crashed to the ground and rolled over, landing upside down in the mud.

The engine continued to roar. The top of the propeller housing was wedged into the mud. The blades still spun inside, sending a fine mist of water and earth into the air. The hull sloped back at an angle. The bow faced the remains of the shack and sank into the soft ground.

Caine groaned and lifted his face out of the mud. The roar of the spinning propeller drowned out all other sound. He paused, taking a quick mental assessment of his injuries. Some bruises, some pain, but nothing broken. He felt pressure on his left leg. Looking back, he saw it was wedged between the muddy earth and the overturned hull of the boat. He tugged at it, but the metal hull was too heavy... he could not pull free. He looked around for Blayne... no sign of him.

Through the spinning blades of the propeller, Caine saw a

blurred landscape. Twisted, desolate trees silhouetted against the setting sun. Then, in the distance, he saw the mercenary, thrown clear from the crash, stagger to his feet.

The man wiped dirt and blood from his face. He shook his head, then turned towards the roaring boat engine. He stared at Caine through the blur of the spinning blades. He took a step forward and winced in pain. Then he took another step and continued moving towards the overturned boat. Based on his lopsided gait and grunts of pain, Caine guessed the man's leg was broken.

The Tavor automatic rifle, crusted in dirt and mud, still hung from his shoulder.

Caine looked left and right. His fingers clawed at the mud, searching for his pistol. The Beretta was nowhere to be found.

'Jesus, looks like you took care of Blayne for me!' the man called out, shouting over the noise of the spinning propeller. 'That man does not look good. Guess it's only fair I take care of you in return.'

Gunfire ricocheted off the rear of the boat. Caine winced as bullets thudded into the earth next to his face.

The rifle clicked empty. The man stopped walking. Caine watched as he ejected the spent magazine from the rear of the weapon.

'Goddammit!' the mercenary cursed as he slipped a new magazine from a pouch mounted to his vest.

Caine examined the hull of the overturned boat. He needed a weapon... something, anything. Once the mercenary reloaded his rifle, Caine knew he would not get another chance. His eyes darted to the tool bin mounted next to the driver's seat.

He reached up and flipped the latch. The upside-down lid flew open, and a barrage of tools pelted his head. He remembered Blayne going over the contents... the words played back in his mind.

Some epoxy, a hammer, flare pistol...

Caine looked back and saw the mercenary slam the fresh magazine into the butt of the rifle. He pulled back the charging handle. The weapon was ready to fire. He continued stalking towards the boat.

Caine's grasping hands wrapped around a small plastic case. He yanked it out of the mud and popped the lid open.

Box of nails!

The mercenary raised the rifle again and stared at Caine from behind the flip-up sight mounted on the barrel. He took a step to the left, beginning to circle around the propeller for a clear shot. 'You know, some of those men were my friends, you son of a bitch,' he shouted.

'No accounting for taste,' Caine snarled.

He tossed the open box at the propeller. A cluster of four-inch galvanized nails struck the spinning blades, piercing the air with a high-pitched shriek. Caine covered his head with his hands and dropped back down into the mud. Several nails ricocheted off the hull of the boat, knocked backwards by the immense force.

Sparks popped and flew from the engine as the whirling blades melted some of the nails into slag. The remaining shards of metal shot out from the back of the engine with the force of bullets.

The mercenary's body jerked as the barrage of high-powered projectiles slammed into him. He dropped his rifle and took a step backwards.

The propeller coughed and groaned and finally sputtered to a stop. Caine looked up... The other man was only about fifteen feet away, and he was still standing. It seemed like his Kevlar vest had managed to deflect most of the impacts. But three crimson streams dripped down his face and spattered into the gray, muddy earth at his feet.

A pair of nails protruded from his forehead, and one jutted from his right eye socket. The man opened and closed his mouth, but only a low, quiet groan escaped his lips. His remaining eye blinked twice, then rolled back. He fell to his knees and tumbled forward into the ground with a wet thud.

Caine watched the man for a few seconds, but he did not move. Using all his strength, Caine managed to rock the heavy metal boat hull back and forth. Finally, he was able to slip his leg free. He rolled out from underneath the wreckage of the airboat and staggered to his feet. He stood still, panting for breath. Then he used his shirt sleeve to wipe the muck from his face. He looked up and examined his surroundings.

Blayne lay motionless in the mud several yards away. The man's leg bent backwards at an unnatural angle. Caine walked past the mercenary's corpse and knelt down next to Blayne. Grabbing the body's torn shirt, he rolled him over and placed two fingers on the man's neck.

He felt no pulse. Blayne's skin was pale and streaked with blood and dirt. His chest did not rise or fall. He was not breathing.

He was gone.

Caine stood up and took a deep breath. He stared at the dead body before him. He felt no sympathy for Blayne. The DNI was corrupt... dirty. But the man had been in his custody, however briefly. He was an asset. Assets had to be protected.

Caine had failed to protect him.

Ted Lapinski, a compromised director at the NSA, had implicated Blayne in a conspiracy that reached the highest levels of the intelligence community. Caine had gone rogue to track him down, hoping the DNI could lead him to Allan Bernatto, and others like him. Men who had betrayed him. Men who had hurt Rebecca, his former lover, and his superior at the CIA.

But now the trail was cold. Lapinski was in CIA custody. Blayne was dead. There were no more moves left on the board.

The hunt had come to a dead end.

Or had it? Caine squinted. In the dim light, he noticed a cell phone clenched in Blayne's left hand. He knelt down again and pried the fingers open.

The phone's screen glowed white. Blayne must have unlocked it before he died. Caine knew that a dead finger could not activate the sensor in the phone's fingerprint scanner. He slipped the phone from the corpse's hand and held it up.

He scrolled through the contacts app. It was empty. The same was true of the call log, the email, text messages... all data on the phone had been erased. There were certain techniques that might retrieve the lost data, but right now, Caine had no access to such technology. He was in the country illegally. He had disobeyed Rebecca. And thanks to Bernatto's treachery, the rest of the CIA believed him to be a traitor... a man who had murdered his partner and sabotaged a crucial operation for his own personal gain.

Caine continued searching the phone. There had to be something, some reason why Blayne had unlocked it. Finally, he opened a note-taking app. At first, it too appeared to be blank. But then Caine scrolled down and found a single file. It was unnamed, marked only by a date. Today's date.

He opened the file and found a single phrase typed into the memo... two words: PUFF ADDER.

Caine gritted his teeth. Those words... A jumble of memories flooded his brain, like sand rushing through an hourglass. Hot, humid wind blowing through his hair. Endless green plains, blood-red sands... and her. The girl. Those eyes looking up at him, pleading. Begging.

Someone else he'd failed to protect.

He snapped his eyes shut tight. It's a coincidence. That mission, that girl... Puff Adder. All dead. Ancient history.

He banished the ghosts of memory from his mind. Coincidence or not, it would have to wait. He had to get out of here. Even this far out in the bayou, the gunshots and explosions might attract attention. He had to get clear, get to safety. Buy himself some time to investigate the phone, decipher exactly what that file meant.

Whatever the cryptic phrase referred to, Caine knew one thing: it was another link in the trail. His hunt had resumed.

The last burning embers of sunlight sank behind the black horizon. The chirping rasp of insects and the screech of bird calls filled the air. Caine slipped the phone into his pocket and trudged into the dark, twisted trees. The shadows seemed to embrace him as he disappeared into the night.

5

A shadow descended across Rebecca Freeling as the motorized stretcher hummed to life. She closed her eyes and exhaled. The mechanical bed began to move backwards, sliding her into the dark interior of the MRI machine.

She felt naked and defenseless despite the blue hospital gown draped over her body. Her sleek designer suits, her expensive jewelry, even her makeup... all had to be forsaken so as not to interfere with the sensitive magnetic resonance imaging machine.

She kept her eyes closed as she lay still on the sterile white surface. Her fiery red hair cascaded around her shoulders. A specially shaped pillow positioned her neck and spine at the optimal viewing angle. The curved, pristine white ceiling of the machine hung a few inches above her nose.

Her heart began to race. She imagined becoming trapped in the tight, claustrophobic tube.

She knew her fears were groundless. The MRI technician had given her a small remote that acted as a panic button. She could stop the session and remove herself from the machine at any time. Of course, doing so would ruin the series of pictures the machine was taking. That would mean another session in the machine, thus prolonging her restless captivity.

Just get through it, she told herself. Get it over with.

She tried to relax her jaw and stop gritting her teeth. A pair of Sennheiser headphones covered her ears. The hospital pumped in music of her choice to make the experience more pleasant. At first, she had limited it to a selection of classical compositions... Mozart, Beethoven, Vivaldi. But the light, relaxing melodies were unable to mask the harsh, grinding noise the machine's camera made as it rotated around her. So she had requested a change. Now, soothing but fast-paced electronica played through the headphones.

But even the deep bass and pulsing rhythms of her new music could not completely mask the disturbing sounds the machine generated. It sounded like a jackhammer was pummeling the tube. It vibrated through the curved white walls, drilling its way towards her skull...

She took a series of rapid, shallow breaths. Her chest heaved and beads of sweat broke out on her forehead.

'Please, try to breathe normally,' the technician's voice crackled through her headphones.

She forced herself to calm down, slow her breathing. She kept her eyes closed and focused on the music. As she relaxed, a memory crept across the empty canvas of her mind. A hot, sweat-soaked night in a private gym. A late-night sparring session... the crinkle of smiling eyes. Rippling muscles, arms wrapped around her, embracing her...

Josh Galloway.

She had to get through this, had to get back to work. She had to find him.

She lay still as the machine buzzed and clanked around her.

Then, with another electronic hum, the table slid back out into the light of the examination room.

'That should just about do it. Sorry, I know it can get to you inside there,' said Isaac, her MRI tech. He wore blue scrubs, and thick glasses covered his kind brown eyes. He helped her sit up, then rolled her wheelchair over to the table.

Rebecca took a deep breath. She ran a hand through her copper hair, pushing it back behind her ears.

'Ninety minutes sliding in and out of a two-foot-wide dark tube? Sounds like an enhanced interrogation technique to me,' she said. She shimmied off the table and lowered herself into the chair.

Isaac grabbed her charts from the wall. He walked alongside her as she rolled out of the MRI chamber. They moved through a short corridor towards the administrative wing of the hospital.

'It's a lot less invasive than sticking a camera up your spine. And magnetic resonance imagining is safer too.'

Rebecca shook her head as they entered a small, pristine office. 'I don't know. Any machine that sends all my atoms spinning in the same direction doesn't sound that safe to me.'

'What is it with you CIA types and hospitals?' a booming voice called out as a door at the end of the room swung open. A tall man with a shock of white hair and a neatly trimmed goatee strode towards them. He wore a white doctor's coat over a light blue Oxford shirt and slim jeans. A stack of papers and folders were tucked under one arm. The name tag on his coat read 'Paul Corrigan.'

Rebecca saw a flash of golden sunlight and green foliage through the window in his office. Then the door shut behind him. It was a refreshing jolt of color, a break from the hospital's cold, sterile surroundings. Corrigan gave her a gentle hug, kissing the air next to her ear.

'You're trained to withstand extreme pain, solitary confinement, and mind-altering drugs,' he said. 'And yet, you make the worst patients.'

She laughed. 'You're not exactly selling the hospital's facilities, Paul. I doubt Medstar Georgetown would appreciate being compared to a black site prison.'

Doctor Corrigan glanced up as Rebecca's MRI data began to fill a series of large monitors mounted to the wall. 'Luckily I don't work for Medstar, I work for you.'

Rebecca couldn't resist a smile. The CIA Office of Medical Services had vetted and approved dozens of surgeons and spinal specialists. Corrigan was the one she felt most comfortable with. Other doctors spouted meaningless statistics and case studies. Safe, approved information designed to avoid lawsuits and malpractice claims. Corrigan told her the truth, good or bad.

As far as Rebecca was concerned, she was fighting for her life... to regain what she had lost. She was fighting to run again, to walk... even to crawl.

Safety was the last thing she cared about.

Corrigan worked in Boston, but he flew in to oversee her case based on a request from the director of the CIA himself. Rebecca didn't know what pull the so-called 'God on the Seventh Floor' had over the talented and respected surgeon. But whatever it was, it had worked. Although she was still confined to her chair, her prognosis had improved since Corrigan had taken over her treatment.

'Isaac, can I see the next set of images please?' Corrigan focused on the screens with laser-like intensity. Rebecca moved next to him as Isaac sat down at a desk and tapped a computer keyboard.

'Sure thing. Series B-154 through 175.'

Rebecca glanced over at Corrigan. 'Jeans and work boots?

What is this, casual Friday? I thought doctors always wore bad ties and cheap khakis.'

Paul smirked. 'Maybe you've been hanging out with the wrong doctors. Like the ones who removed the shrapnel and bullet fragments from your spine. Sloppy work. They missed the bone splinter that was causing swelling in the surrounding tissue.'

She nodded. 'Good point.'

They both examined the new series of images that flashed across the screens. 'So, what exactly are we looking at here?' she asked.

Corrigan pulled a small laser pointer from the pocket of his white coat. He aimed the pinpoint of light at a hazy gray mass, near what Rebecca assumed to be the small of her back. It was difficult for her to tell exactly what she should be focusing on in the black and white haze of the MRI image.

'I'd say we're looking at significant improvement,' he replied. 'After removing that bone fragment, the swelling at the impact point seems to have gone down quite a bit. The remaining scar tissue here... That looks like nerve damage to me. Damage that should be treatable.'

Rebecca swallowed. She felt her heart leap in her chest. For so long, words like 'improvement' and 'treatable' had been dreams, fleeting hopes that she tried to control, to keep hidden, lest disappointment crush her if reality failed to live up to her optimism.

But this was Corrigan. She trusted him. And if he believed there was a chance...

She closed her eyes and brought a hand to her forehead. She had expected to feel joy, or excitement, at such news. Instead she felt light-headed and nauseous.

Corrigan looked down at her and smiled. He turned to Isaac.

'Hey bud, could you grab us a couple waters from the cafeteria? This is good news, so go for the sparkling stuff.'

'Uh, yeah, sure thing.' Isaac stood up from his post. 'I'll be right back.'

Corrigan watched him leave, then turned to Rebecca. 'You okay?'

She nodded. 'I am. I mean, I'm better than okay, this is... this is amazing!'

'Yes it is. But I know it's a lot to process.' He smiled and turned towards his office. 'Follow me... I have a special prescription for you.'

She followed behind him as he opened the door to his private office. Inside, the colors were warm and natural – khaki curtains, a tan carpet, dark brown leather sofa. He removed an unmarked bottle of amber liquor and two crystal tumblers from the desk. Outside, the late afternoon sun cast dappled pools of light amidst the shadows of the trees.

Rebecca closed her eyes. For a moment, she could feel the wind at her back, streaming through her hair. She could almost hear the metronome of her feet pounding across packed earth.

She remembered running... The freedom.

'We must accept finite disappointment but never lose infinite hope.'

Corrigan's words pulled Rebecca back to reality. She opened her eyes. The tall man sat down front of her on a leather ottoman and held out one of the glasses. He stared at her for a second. His brow furrowed as a look of concern filled his eyes.

'Sounds a bit poetic for you,' Rebecca said. She brushed back a strand of fiery hair as she accepted the glass.

'The quote isn't mine. Neither is the scotch, for that matter.' He took a sip and eyed the glass. 'I'm borrowing the office from Doctor Rothman.'

Rebecca took a long drink, then nodded. 'Doctor Rothman has good taste in single malts. So where's the quote from?'

'Martin Luther King, Junior. Rebecca, some of that scar tissue I saw... it's recent. Post-trauma. It didn't happen during the incident in Thailand, did it?'

A shiver ran down Rebecca's spine. It was an involuntary reaction as she remembered recent events. A kidnapping attempt in an alley, the assault in a Virginia farmhouse. Ted Lapinski's efforts to clean up loose ends, including her. And a battle with a professional mercenary named Wallace Ganda.

Rebecca stared at her hands. She had trained in self-defense as part of her CIA orientation. But it had been Josh Galloway who had taught her to fight in the chair. Her lower center of gravity, the weight and bulk of the wheelchair... Under his guidance, things she saw as weaknesses became weapons. But the critical thing he taught her was that no matter how scared or broken she felt, she was not helpless.

'Paul, I... Does this mean—'

He raised a hand and cut her off. 'Everything's fine. I still think your recovery is on track. But what the hell happened?'

She paused for a moment and stared at the scotch in her glass. Then she threw her head back and swallowed the remains of her drink.

'I'm sorry, that's classified. But trust me, it's not something that's likely to happen again.'

Paul grabbed the bottle and refilled her glass. 'Okay, fine. Let me hit you with another quote. This one's from the Dalai Lama. "When we meet tragedy in life, we can react in two ways. Either by losing hope and falling into self-destructive habits, or by using the challenge to find our inner strength."'

'I didn't know philosophy was one of your specialties.'

He shook his head. 'Rebecca, you're closer than ever before...

closer to walking again. Maybe even running again. But with hope comes fear, and sometimes guilt. And those things can drive good people to make bad decisions.' Paul stood up and walked to his desk. He flipped through her charts. 'I'm recommending you for spinal decompression surgery in thirty days. It is vital that your swelling continues to go down before that time. That means easing up on the exercise. You're in physical therapy, not training for the Navy SEALs.'

She took a deep breath. 'Got it. I'll be a good girl, Doc. Promise.'

'And may I remind you, your physical therapy regime does not include parkour or hand to hand combat. Leave the fieldwork to your Special Operations Group. That's what they're for.'

Rebecca cocked her head and eyed the handsome surgeon. 'You and the director must be closer than I thought. What's the deal with you two? How did he convince you to come out here, anyway?'

Corrigan shut the file and smiled. 'Sorry, Freeling. My turn to play the classified card.'

Rebecca laughed. 'I guess the CIA Medical Service wouldn't have cleared you if you couldn't keep a secret.'

A loud buzzing erupted from her taupe leather Hermès purse. She pulled out her phone and checked the display. 'It's my security detail. Are we good here?'

Corrigan nodded. 'I'll have the hospital make the arrangements with your staff. Thirty days, Freeling. Take it easy. Focus on your recovery. Doctor's orders.'

'How about we call it a doctor's recommendation? Following orders isn't my greatest strength.'

Corrigan nodded and set the glass down on the desk as Rebecca headed towards the door. 'Your director mentioned that to me as well.'

The beams of sunlight from outside played across the scarlet and copper highlights of her hair. She turned to give him one last smile. Then she left the office.

As she navigated the long, sterile corridors of the hospital, Corrigan's words echoed in her mind, over and over.

Thirty days. Fear and guilt...

She made up her mind. In thirty days she would walk again. But if she was going to free herself from fear and guilt, and focus on her recovery, she knew there was one thing she had to do first.

She had to find Josh Galloway. Find him and bring him home.

6

There is blood on his hands. Caine stares at them, holding them up to the flickering glow of the campfire. The stain is pale, almost pink in the firelight. He remembers the feel of the knife in his hands as it sliced through the assassin's neck. The cascade of blood over his fingers, the dark puddle on the floor of the mosque in Khartoum. The blood glowed white-hot in the lenses of his night-vision goggles. It faded to gray, then black, as its residual heat dissipated into the stone floor.

Caine leans forward on the wood bench and holds his hands over the fire. Other men carrying rifles and machetes walk past him. Loud rap music blasts from a radio somewhere in the camp. Some of the younger men dance and pump their fists in the air. The lyrics are all in an African language. Caine doesn't recognize the dialect.

Jack Tyler steps out of a hut and walks towards him. Caine clenches his hands into fists to stop them from shaking. Jack is a former Delta Force operator, trained in demolitions, sniping, and hostage rescue, among other things.

Jack is his partner.

The man is holding two unmarked brown bottles in his left hand. Caine recognizes them as a local beer, brewed in Sudan from fermented sorghum grain. Jack sits next to Caine on the bench and slips a Leatherman tool from a pouch on his belt. He pops open the two beers and hands one to Caine.

'This round's on me. You did good out there tonight. Sorry I let one slip through.'

Jack was perimeter security for the operation. Caine was on the ground, spotting targets and picking off strays. The asset they have been assigned to protect is a man codenamed Puff Adder. He was granted safe passage into the city by Sudan's intelligence service. Puff Adder represents a rebel faction in South Sudan. This splinter group has formed in opposition to President Kiir. And in Sudan's view, anything that sows discord in the fledgling southern government is something to be encouraged.

Caine sips his beer. He winces as the foul liquid burns his throat.

Jack laughs and takes a swig from his own bottle. 'Damn,' he sputters. 'That's the second most dangerous thing we've done tonight. You know, this shit's illegal in Sudan. The wives brew it under the sink in old bleach bottles.'

Caine looks at the grass huts and collapsed buildings around them. The village is in a no-man's land, disputed territory.

'We're not in Sudan,' Caine mutters.

Jack looks around, then squints as he stares into the fire. 'Yeah. Guess anything goes here.'

Caine looks up as two men exit another hut. One of them, a man with graying hair and wire-rimmed glasses, is his handler, Allan Bernatto. Bernatto's voice was in his head earlier that night, crackling through a micro-earpiece.

Bernatto gave the kill order.

Bernatto's dark, beady eyes dart towards Caine as he speaks

to the other man, Khairi Abboud. Khairi is shorter, but his chest and shoulders are powerful and athletic-looking for a man his age. His thick, gray hair is brushed back from his face. The wrinkles around his deep-set brown eyes look like smiles in the dim light of the fires.

Bernatto paces towards them, his shirt stained with dark patches of sweat. Droplets of perspiration roll across his forehead and cheeks. He wipes them off as he stands over them.

'Nice work tonight.' He turns towards Jack. 'Too bad you let one slip the net.'

Jack glares up at him. 'Hey, had to let Tom have a little fun.'

Bernatto frowns. He peers at them over the rims of his glasses and is silent for several seconds.

Finally, Jack sighs. 'I messed up. He must have come in from the side entrance. I was too focused on the street.'

Bernatto nods. 'Don't make the same mistake twice. Tom, is the site clean?'

Caine keeps his eyes on the fire. 'Body's in a dumpster a few blocks down the street. Knife's at the bottom of the Nile. There's some blood in the mosque. Nothing to tie the body to me. Besides, the assassins were from South Sudan. I don't think the police in Khartoum are going to look too hard for a suspect.'

Bernatto glances at the watch on his wrist. 'Sounds adequate. I have to report in. We're wheels up at 0600. Don't be late.'

He turns and walks towards a black Land Rover. The rugged vehicle sits among the battered pickups and dusty vans surrounding the rebel camp. As Bernatto drives out of the camp, Khairi joins them by the fire.

He pulls a silver flask from the rear pocket of his linen pants and takes a long swig. He offers the flask to Jack.

Jack shakes his head and swigs his beer. 'No thanks, Khairi. Thought you weren't allowed to drink that stuff.'

Khairi laughs. 'It is true. In Sudan we have Sharia law. No alcohol, no relations between men and women – unless, of course, they are married. But, then again, this is not Sudan. Yesterday, perhaps it was. Tomorrow, it may yet be again. But today, we are in purgatory.'

'Why are we here, Khairi?' Caine asks.

Khairi takes another swig. 'Look who has become a philosopher.'

'I mean, what does Sudan get from facilitating an arms deal for this asshole?'

The older man shrugs and stares into the fire. 'Ah. Well, I'm not sure we should be discussing such things. Let's just say it's a joint effort. I'm sure it has to do with oil and money. And, of course, cooperation with your government's counter-terrorism efforts. It benefits both our countries to work together on these things. Either way, I promise you, in a few years, no one will even remember. Everything will have changed. Everything but the fighting.'

Khairi takes another swig, then looks around at the desolate village. Small groups of rebel soldiers laugh and dance to the blaring music. They cheer and fire their rifles into the sky, but their eyes hold a haunted, watchful look.

The older man sighs. 'In Zambia, they have a saying... It makes no difference whether you are a lion, or an impala. In Africa, when the sun rises, you must wake up running.'

Jack takes a long sip of his beer, then wipes his mouth. 'You know, it's times like this I like to remind myself of some advice a colleague of mine once gave me. Guys like you and me... we're weapons, Tom.' He points his fingers at the fire, like a gun. 'There's a job to do, you aim us at the target, and bang! We get it done. Bernatto, his boss, his boss's boss... Those guys have to sort out all the puzzle pieces. They have to untangle all the knots and see where the strings lead. Me? Just tell me where to go. Point and shoot. Nice and easy.' He slaps Caine on the back. 'Sooner or later, you'll learn, bud. Only way to keep your sanity in this business. You have to be a weapon. You have to fire and forget.'

A cloud of dust approaches the camp from the north.

Khairi squints. 'Here he comes.'

A battered pickup truck swerves into the camp. Its lights cut through the dusty air and sweep over the rubble and collapsed buildings. A radio in the cabin blasts more rap music, and a pair of speakers thump in the pickup bed.

A man jumps out from the back of the truck. Rebel soldiers exit the front doors and stand by his side. 'There he is!' the man bellows. 'The one who saved my life. The man who helps me save South Sudan!'

Simon Takuba walks over to Caine, holding his arms wide. His diamond tooth shimmers in the flickering light.

Caine stands but does not embrace the man. He takes a step back and gives him a wary smile.

'I did my job, Takuba. That's all.'

Takuba cocks his head and gives Caine a strange look. His smile flickers for a second, then returns. His curled lips once again reveal his blood-red tooth. 'You too modest, man!' Takuba turns to his soldiers. 'This man, I tell you, he slayed the Dinka assassin like a dog.' He draws his finger across his throat, and the men cheer.

'Were your negotiations successful?' Khairi asks.

Takuba gives the man a small bow. 'My movement is in your debt. With the weapons your friends will provide – guns, rockets, tanks – we will rain fire on our enemies and take back what is ours.'

Khairi nods. 'And we too will remember, Mister Takuba. Your

current president has been threatening to lower the oil transit fees on our pipelines. If this cannot be resolved, your government may shut down oil production altogether. No one wants that.'

Takuba laughs and shakes his head. 'Yes, yes, good sir. We talk business later. Now, it is time to celebrate!'

Another dust cloud kicks up in the distance. Caine's hand drops to his pistol.

'Khairi, you expecting friends?' he asks.

Khairi shakes his head. 'No. My people will be staying far away from here. They wish to keep our involvement in tonight's activities... discreet.'

Takuba watches the new vehicle approach. He waves off Caine's concern and laughs. 'It's okay, my friend. You can stop protecting me. These are my men. They bring us the spoils of war.'

'What are you talking about?' Caine mutters. 'What war?'

The vehicle draws closer. It is a battered old school bus. Ripped and torn camouflage netting hangs from the roof. It flaps in the breeze like tattered wings.

Takuba walks towards the approaching vehicle. 'The arms dealers we meet with tonight, they came bearing gifts. Samples of their wares. My men take the weapons and drive south, to the nearest Dinka village. The home of those dogs who tried to silence me tonight.'

The bus circles around the camp and comes to a stop. The rear door creaks open. A pair of armed rebels hop to the ground. Over the din of the thumping rap music, Caine hears sobs and screams from the smoking vehicle. Tiny figures are herded out the rear door.

Children.

The armed men fire their rifles in the air and circle around the huddled mass of bodies.

Takuba shouts to his men. They leap up, grabbing the children and dragging them away from the bus. The boys line up in the dirt. One of the rebel commanders paces back and forth in front of them, leering and yelling.

'What the hell is going on here?' Caine snaps.

'Tom...' Jack's voice sounds hesitant.

Takuba watches as a group of girls are led out the front of the bus. His men drag them off to nearby huts. One of the soldiers holds a girl by the wrist and tugs her across the dirt. She looks up, wailing and crying in a dialect Caine cannot understand. Tears stream down her face.

Caine looks into her eyes. They are wide with fear and terror.

The man flings her at Takuba's feet.

Takuba kneels down in front of her. 'Shhhh. Hush, my lovely. Tonight, I make you my wife. As for tomorrow... Heh, we shall see, eh?'

The girl crawls away from Takuba, but he grabs her foot and yanks her back. His laughter is high-pitched and carries across the night breeze like the barking of a hyena.

'That's enough!' Caine steps forward, his pistol clutched in his hand.

Two of Takuba's men raise their AK-47 rifles. They shout at him, but he does not understand their words.

Another man leaps up from the fire and charges towards Caine, reaching for his pistol. Jack steps in front of the man and swings out his arm, striking him in the throat. The clothesline blow knocks the rebel to the ground. He rolls in the dirt, gasping for air.

'Everybody just chill,' Jack says, his voice low and dangerous.

'This wasn't part of the deal, Takuba,' Caine mutters. 'Let her go.'

Takuba lets go of the girl. She jumps to her feet and bolts away from the men.

Without taking his eyes off Caine, Takuba shouts an order.

One of the men spins around and opens fire with his rifle. Caine's eye twitches as he watches the girl drop into the sand.

'You son of a bitch!' he whispers. The girl wails in pain.

Caine raises his pistol and lunges forward. Jack loops an arm around his neck. A pistol appears in Khairi's hand as well, and he brandishes it toward the nearest group of rebels.

'Get back,' he hisses.

'Go get her,' Takuba snaps. Two of them trudge towards the fallen girl.

Jack tightens his grip on Caine's throat and pulls him away from the men. 'Khairi, get his gun, dammit!'

The older man grabs Caine's gun arm, pinning the pistol by his side. He struggles to wrench it from Caine's grasp, but his fingers clutch the weapon with a white-knuckled grip.

'Let me go, Jack! I swear I'll—'

'You're not thinking right! This is not what we're here for!'

'Thomas, you cannot do this,' Khairi whispers. 'Or all of this was for nothing!'

Takuba slides a long, silver machete from a leather holster strapped to his side. He points at Caine with the weapon.

'Tonight, I will forgive you, my friend. You save my life, so I owe you that.'

He takes a step closer. His lips curl up, and his teeth look like fangs in the firelight. 'But if you ever point a weapon at me again... I don't kill you. I do worse. The spirits are my allies, Tom. They protect me. And they will curse you!'

The men drag the girl back to the fire. The fierce glare of anger melts off Takuba's face, and once again, he cackles.

'You know what, I think you jealous, huh? You want her for yourself, is that it?'

Caine grunts in rage as he struggles to break free from Jack's chokehold. He bucks and claws at Jack's arm, but he cannot loosen the man's grip. Jack pulls his forearm tighter, cutting off Caine's air supply. Khairi wrenches the gun from his fingers. He staggers back, panting for breath.

Jack glares at Takuba and pulls Caine away from the fire. 'We're leaving. Everyone stay calm. Things got a little out of hand, that's all.'

He turns to Khairi. 'Get the car.'

The older man nods and fishes a set of keys out of his pocket. Takuba raises his hands in surrender.

'It's okay, my friends, I understand. Jealousy is a powerful beast. It can slay the strongest man. But I will fix this. You watch, we be friends again now.'

Caine's eyes bulge and he gasps for breath. Again he looks into the girl's eyes. She is panting. Blood drips from her abdomen and thigh. She moans in pain, a low, guttural howl.

The men let her go, and she falls to the ground. Takuba stands over her and raises the machete into the air.

'Now, there is nothing to fight over, eh?' He smiles at Caine, but his eyes are blank, emotionless. Empty.

Caine's vision blurs. Jack drags him back from the cluster of armed men. Behind them, Khairi starts the truck. The headlights flare to life, bathing the grounds in harsh white light.

'We can't fix this, Tom. This isn't why we're here,' Jack whispers into his ear.

A curtain of black fogs Caine's view. Between the light and

shadows, all detail is lost. He sags in Jack's arms as he begins to lose consciousness.

He reaches a hand towards the struggling girl, but she is like a ghost now. All he can see are her eyes. They look up at him, pleading...

He hears the machete whistle through the air, hears the girl scream.

'Allah yaghfir lana,' Khairi whispers. Allah forgive us.

'This mission is over, we're gone. We're out of here,' Jack intones, his words soothing and calm.

'Fire and forget, kid.'

Fire and forget...

* * *

Caine's eyes shot open. The muscles in his abdomen and throat ached, and his tongue felt thick and dry. He had been panting, gasping for breath. The haze of dreams and memories lifted, and his body lay deathly still. The air around him was thick and damp with humidity.

It had been a six-hour bus ride from the bayous surrounding Lake Pontchartrain to the city of Alexandria. Caine had chosen to base himself in the area due to its proximity to Alexandria Airport. Commercial flights did not use the small municipal airport, but he knew he could get a charter there to Mexico, or Central America. From there, he could get to wherever he decided to go next. It was the only other international airport in the state, aside from New Orleans. Caine didn't want to risk venturing into a major metropolitan area if he could avoid it.

Officially, the CIA believed him to be a traitor. A rogue agent who had sabotaged an off-books black op meant to expose extremist group ties to the White Leopard drug cartel in Afghanistan.

Allan Bernatto was his handler at the time. Bernatto's hired mercenaries stole the Leopard's heroin and the shipment of arms meant as payment. Then he set up Caine to take the fall.

In the aftermath, Jack Tyler was killed. Trapped in a collapsed well in the middle of nowhere, Caine watched his partner, his friend, bleed out in his arms. There was nothing he could do to save him.

Caine went off the grid. The world believed he was dead. After the sting of betrayal, Caine saw no reason to disprove that assumption.

And, of course, there was Rebecca.

Bernatto was promoted to the Director of the National Clandestine Service. He was her boss. Caine knew it was safer for her, safer for anyone he cared about, to disappear.

Caine thought of the last time he had seen her. The sun gleaming in her fiery red hair. Her eyes, wide and concerned. The disappointment in her voice after he lied to her and disappeared again, to continue his hunt.

And the chair... the chair Bernatto and his mercenary killer had put her in.

Caine sat up. He rubbed his hands across his face as if to scrub away the taint of his dark memories. He grabbed his watch from the nightstand. The luminous hands showed that it was three in the morning. He stood up and stretched. It was still dark outside. Neon lights from the fast-food joints clustered around the interstate cast a dim glow beyond the curtains.

He dropped to the ground and began a series of exercises. Push-ups, sit-ups, jackknives... He performed each set of repetitions without pause, then moved on to the next exercise. When he finished one circuit, he started the routine over. After a while, his pace began to slow. The tight, lean muscles of his body shimmered with sweat.

Finally, he stopped. His muscles ached and his body was exhausted, but his mind remained focused and restless. Thoughts of the past continued to tumble through his consciousness.

Puff Adder. Was he still alive, after all these years?

Caine opened the mini-bar and removed a bottle of water. He took a long sip, then sat down at his desk and flipped open his laptop. He googled 'South Sudan civil war.'

There were dozens of articles and videos. The death and destruction that consumed the region was perfect news fodder. No matter how many atrocities they reported, there was always fresh blood being spilled.

He found the most recent news footage and pressed play.

'Founded in 2011, after decades of conflict with the Muslim government to the north, South Sudan is the youngest nation on the planet.' A British voice narrated the report. The video showed rows of people walking through the blasted remains of a war-torn village. The crowd of dark figures seemed to stretch forever into the distant horizon. There were hundreds, thousands even...

'But only two years later, forces allied to President Salva Kiir found themselves engaged in yet another brutal civil war. Rebel forces loyal to former Vice President Riek Machar took up arms against them. The result has been years of bloody conflict. Many fear the killing is inevitably sliding towards genocide.'

Caine took another sip of water and stared at the screen. The images of refugees dissolved, replaced by soldiers wearing tattered makeshift uniforms. They were firing battered AK-47 assault rifles on full auto. They swept gunfire across burning houses, schools, and medical clinics.

'Despite a peace treaty signed in 2015, the violence shows no sign of abating. Thousands of lives have been lost in the region, and over 2.3 million people are displaced from their homes and villages. Rape and torture of civilians have become commonplace. Children as young as six years old have been forced to fight on both sides. Oil, water, food, and other vital resources provide the spark in a war that has reignited old tribal tensions. The conflict has escalated into a massacre. It is a crisis the United Nations seem unable, or unwilling, to quell.'

The footage changed to the aftermath of a skirmish. Dead bodies littered the barren fields surrounding the decimated town. Their limbs were askew, their bodies bent in unnatural, twisted positions. Some were missing arms, others legs.

Land mines, he thought. They killed hundreds that tried to flee from the conflict zone.

Men. Women. Children...

He slammed the laptop closed.

Caine was no stranger to death and murder. He had seen things, done things... things that were the stuff of nightmares. But the carnage he had witnessed years ago, the bodies sprawled across those barren, blood-red sands... That place was its own special hell.

If the man known as Puff Adder was still operating in the region, if Bernatto was there with him...

Caine took a long, slow breath. Coincidence or not, this clue was the next link in the chain. If Puff Adder was still alive, then he was living on borrowed time. Time gifted to him by Caine, years ago.

The cheap mattress creaked as Caine slipped back under the covers. He did not sleep. His unblinking eyes pierced the darkness like twin verdant suns. He watched the dusty blades of the ceiling fan spin round and round until the first light of dawn.

7

'Director Paulis, you can't be serious!' Rebecca slapped her palms down on the conference table. 'Josh Galloway has not filed his latest call report, he has not responded to any of the pre-arranged code phrases we have left for him. Local assets have confirmed he hasn't been seen at any of our pre-arranged dead drop locations. How much more do you need to declare the man is missing!'

Michael Paulis, a heavyset African American man dressed in a gray suit, with salt and pepper hair and a neatly trimmed goatee, glared at Rebecca. He took a sip from a glass of water. 'Are you finished, Director Freeling? Because this is beginning to sound an awful lot like insubordination to me.'

'With all due respect, Director Paulis, I'm not trying to be insubordinate. I'm trying to follow standard procedure. We haven't even begun to assess extraction plans, and you're telling me this is a non-starter? Since when do we leave our people to the wolves without even trying to—'

'There's nothing standard about this situation, Rebecca.'

The director stood and leaned over the table as his voice rose in volume to a deep, angry rumble. 'I don't expect you to like it. I don't like it myself. But by presidential order, Sudan and South Sudan are off-limits to all operations for the time being. I trust you've read your briefings? There's been a civil war raging in the South for years, with atrocities committed on both sides. Now their government has finally agreed to negotiate another cease-fire with the rebels. The United States has a checkered past in that area, and the president doesn't want us anywhere near this thing in case it blows up in our faces.'

Rebecca pulled her hair back and exhaled. 'I know the situation there is volatile, I just don't understand why—'

'You don't understand because you don't want to understand!' Paulis gathered the photographs and papers she had presented him. He slid them into a file folder and tossed it across the table to her. 'If you would stop for a minute and think about this rationally, you'd come to the same conclusion I have.'

She looked up at him as she grabbed the folder. 'And what conclusion is that, sir?'

'That you're letting this situation affect you on a personal level. You're putting your feelings for Galloway ahead of your responsibilities as the D/NCS. Just like you did with Thomas Caine.'

Rebecca blinked. 'I beg your pardon? Sir, how can you say that after reading my report? My instincts about Caine were correct. Bernatto framed him for Operation Big Blind. If it wasn't for Caine, Bernatto could have succeeded in sparking a war between China and Japan. And God knows what would have happened if Ted Lapinski's cyberweapon had fallen into the hands of—'

Paulis raised his hand and nodded. 'Yes, Director Freeling, I've read your report. And for what it's worth, I believe every word of it. But without Caine coming in to debrief, the quality of this intel is always going to be questioned. That limits my ability to act on it. Instead, he's running wild on his own private vendetta. FBI Counter Intelligence received a lead that he was sighted in Louisiana. You know who else is in Louisiana? The DNI. Who, I might add, has also gone missing.'

'You can't think Caine would—'

'Until he turns himself in and is properly debriefed, I don't know what to think.'

Paulis turned around and took a few steps from the table.

'I take it this meeting is over?' Rebecca asked icily.

'Follow me. I think we both need a change of scenery. OPSEC is all well and good, but I can only sit in a room without windows for so long.'

Rebecca moved her chair away from the table. 'I thought that was what the paintings were for.' Her eyes drifted to the paintings that hung along the walls of the conference room. A kaleidoscope of geometric cubes by Alvin D. Loving, the neon splatters of Jackson Pollack, bold blue and red gingham patterns of Thomas Downing...

Paulis cast an admiring eye over the canvases, then continued towards the exit. 'When I took over the office, I requisitioned them from the Intelligence Art Collection. Some folks would be surprised to know the CIA covertly funded many of these artists at the height of the Cold War. Back then, we saw it as useful propaganda. A showcase of American creative freedom versus the rigid dogma of the Soviet Union.'

Rebecca followed him out into his office, a large square room filled with soft muted shades of gray. 'Is that how you see them, sir?'

Paulis sat down behind a massive desk. Like the rest of his furniture, the slab of dark stained wood was simple, clean, and modern.

'I see them as a reminder that there's more than one way to skin a cat. And that sometimes the reasons why we do things are just as important as the results themselves. Besides, I happen to appreciate modern art.'

He leaned back in his chair. A bank of windows stretched behind him, looking out over the dense green Virginia foliage. Rebecca saw the white domed roof of the Headquarters Auditorium nestled in a grove of trees. The structure was known as 'the igloo' by CIA employees due to its bubble-shaped construction.

Paulis rubbed his temple. 'Look, it's obvious that you and Galloway were... close. Not the first time it's happened, and it won't be the last. Now, I could quote agency regulations all day long, but where would that get us? It's not like I can say I've always made the best decisions when it comes to that area of my life. So let's leave that alone for the time being. But I promoted you to D/NCS for a reason, Director Freeling. Do you know what that reason is?'

She uttered a short, bitter laugh. 'To clean up Bernatto's mess?'

Paulis's dark brown eyes did not blink, but a frown creased his lips. 'Bernatto crossed the line. He used our people as his own private army, to progress his own agenda. But men like Bernatto aren't created in a vacuum. Did you ever meet Bernatto's superior, Walter Grissom?'

'No, sir. I was working under Bernatto when Grissom was the D/NCS. He resigned a few years after my orientation.'

Paulis chuckled. 'Resigned. Interesting story there. I worked with Grissom when I was with the JSOC. The man was intelligent. Ruthless. Toughest SOB I ever knew. Second man in history to be awarded all four of our nation's highest honors. Medal of Honor. Distinguished Service Cross. Distinguished

Service Medal, and the National Security Medal thrown in for good measure.'

'That is impressive. Funny, I never see his name turn up on the speaking circuits.'

Paulis shifted in his chair. 'Despite the awards, his record doesn't make good speech material for the Ivy League crowd. Before he resigned, Grissom was laser-focused on China. At the time, we had our own little cold war going with Beijing. Their Ministry of State Security effectively dismantled our intelligence network there. Grissom was convinced we had a mole. One of the men we had planted inside the US Ambassador's Office. Grissom believed that China had turned him, that the man was a double agent. He claimed this man was selling out other operatives we had in place there. Giving China decryption keys for our communication network.'

'Was he right?'

Paulis smiled. 'The D/CIA at the time didn't think so. But we'll never know for sure. The suspect's apartment exploded. Gas leak of some kind. Grissom's supposed mole died in the fire. Along with his wife and daughter.'

'Oh my God.'

'A Senate Intelligence Committee investigation tied the explosion to Grissom. He'd ordered an unauthorized assassination, based on his own suspicions. No hard proof. No authorization from the D/CIA, or anyone else. Our ambassador to China was furious. He was well-connected, and the committee wanted Grissom's head on a plate.'

'I'm surprised they let him resign.'

'Like I said, Grissom was smart. He wasn't just using agency resources to spy on China. By the time the committee called him in to testify, he had dirt on every single senator sitting at that table. Sex scandals, payoffs, shady deals... He knew where all the bodies were buried. The committee was forced to accept his resignation, or deal with the fallout. After that, Grissom did some light consulting work – Homeland Security advisor, private intelligence contractor, that kind of thing. Then he dropped off the face of the earth. Man would be in his late seventies now, if he's even still alive. So as you can see, Bernatto's apple doesn't fall far from the tree.'

Rebecca leaned forward in her chair. 'So what does all this have to do with me, Director?'

Paulis sighed. 'Grissom and Bernatto tarnished the reputation of this agency. That hurts our credibility, and that's dangerous. To fix it, I need someone I can trust, someone who can get the job done the right way. Someone who can put their responsibilities ahead of their personal feelings.'

She nodded. 'You mean someone who follows orders.'

'That's a cop-out, Freeling. We both know this job is never that simple. Sometimes you have to make the tough call. But I need to know that I can trust you to make those calls for the right reasons. And that you know where to draw the line. Guys like Grissom, and Bernatto... they lost sight of that. I need to know you won't do the same.'

'Sir, putting aside any... personal feelings I have for Agent Galloway, there's still the matter of his mission. He may possess critical intel concerning a stolen biological weapon.'

Paulis flipped open a report that sat atop a stack of folders on the side of his desk. 'Yes, the Syria thing. As far as I can tell, you can't confirm that the missing materials are in fact a weapon of any kind. There's no clear indication of exactly what was being manufactured in that lab.'

'Sir, I realize the intel is not conclusive, but this is too important—'

'Yes, it is. Too important to risk your personal feelings

blinding you to facts that don't fit with what you want to see. I'm reassigning this to your deputy director. He'll have an independent team confirm this report. If the situation warrants it, I'll brief the president. Until that time, his order stands. You are not to send any operatives of this agency into Sudan, for any reason whatsoever. Is that clear?'

She met his stare for a second. Then she lowered her eyes and nodded. 'Clear, sir.'

'Good. Now, in the meantime, I want you to liaise with FBI counter-intel. They're moving to incept this rogue operative of yours. After they take Caine into custody, I want you on hand to advise during his debriefing. You know him better than they do. Let's use that to our advantage.'

'I thought I was going to handle Caine's capture and—'

Paulis shook his head. 'Not a chance. You already got away with running one illegal operation on US soil. You try to take this on yourself, and I'll have the FBI, the Department of Justice, and an Oversight Committee camping out in this office for days. And trust me, they won't be here to admire the art.'

Rebecca nodded again. 'Understood.'

'I'll have my office send you a report on the agent in charge. I understand they're also responsible for ensuring Mr. Lapinski makes it to his own Senate Intelligence Committee hearing. I want you on site when they move him. You'll only be an observer of course, but I'll feel better if you sign off on their security protocols. It's their party, but that doesn't mean we can't help set the table.'

'Got it.' Rebecca turned and began to move away from his desk.

'And Rebecca?'

She stopped near the double doors that led to the anteroom outside the office suite. 'Yes, sir?'

'I spoke with Doctor Corrigan.' His voice softened. 'After you meet with the FBI, I want you to take some time off. Focus on your recovery.'

'Corrigan's a good doctor. He wouldn't tell me how you two met though. Said it was classified.'

Paulis chuckled. 'Not exactly. I was suffering chronic lower back pain after my last marathon. It was Boston. Corrigan treated me there. Told me to take it easy for six months.'

'I didn't know you ran, sir.'

Paulis smiled. 'Something else we have in common, Director Freeling. Thing is, I didn't listen to Corrigan's advice. Ran a 5K two months later. My back gave out halfway through. I ended up with a lumbar stress fracture. By the time I was through with physical therapy... Well, let's just say I won't be running any more marathons.'

He tapped his desk with a pen and stared at her over the rim of his glasses. 'I hope you'll be smarter than I was. Listen to the doctor. Get better.'

'I'll try, sir. Thank you.'

She exited the office and past the pair of secretaries. They were both busy answering the phones and filing reports. They didn't even look up as she exited the director's suite.

She took the elevator down to the first floor and exited the southwest corner of the Old Headquarters Building. Once she put some distance between herself and the OHB, she slipped her cell phone from her purse and tapped the screen.

A man's voice answered. 'Director?'

'He said no. We're on our own.'

The man on the phone grunted in acknowledgment. 'FBI is on him. I have a narrow window to extract the asset. You sure you want to do this?'

Rebecca was silent for a moment. A light breeze picked up.

Her fiery hair whipped behind her. She bit her lip. Then she brought the phone closer to her face and lowered her voice.

'Code green. Do it.'

'Understood.'

The man hung up.

Rebecca slipped her phone back in her purse and continued to head away from the building.

8

Josh coughed and spat up a mouthful of blood. His body tensed as he watched the muscles ripple under the shoulders of the big man standing in front of him.

The hulking brute's fist slammed into his gut again, and he felt the muscles around his ribs spasm in pain. The wind expelled from his lungs in an agonized gasp, and his chest heaved up and down. Each panting breath shot a lance of white-hot pain down his side. He winced and tried to slow his frenzied breathing.

Gotta be a cracked rib, he thought. Add it to the list.

The muscles in his shoulders throbbed in protest. His arms were pulled behind him and cuffed to a thick metal pipe that ran up the wall and snaked along the ceiling. The room was dark, but he could make out clusters of other pipes and valves, hidden in the shadows. They had hooded him before leaving Kanfar, and now he had no idea where he was. It had been hours since his last sip of water, and days since his last meal.

The big man grabbed a tuft of Josh's short brown hair and yanked his head up. Josh's face was a mess of cuts and bruises, and his right eye was swollen half-shut. But he could still make out the features of the man standing before him. Tall, broad shoulders, a wide snarling mouth, and small beady eyes.

A white paste-like paint covered his face, drawing the shape of a skull around his eyes and nose. Long painted fangs curved down his cheeks. The paste smelled like a mixture of ash and clay, mixed with the pungent odor of the man's sweat.

Josh forced a whistle though his battered lips. 'Hey, man. I think you got something on your face.' He began to chuckle, but his laughter transformed into a painful spasm of coughing.

'You think this is funny, eh?' the big man snarled. 'I give you more to laugh about then.'

He drove another fist into Josh's stomach, cutting his bout of coughing short. Josh groaned and tugged against his chains. He looked up and glared at the man, rage simmering behind his battered eyes.

The big man smiled. 'You think you die here in Africa, eh? You wrong. I won't let you die. Not yet. Not until you tell me what I want to know.'

Josh spat another mouthful of blood and watched it pool on the dusty concrete floor.

'Where is Mister Takuba's property?' the brute demanded. 'Is it still in Kanfar? Did you leave it in Malakal?'

Josh looked up and panted for breath. 'Wait, please. Just... there's something I need to know first.'

The big man focused his tiny eyes on Josh. He took a step closer. 'What are you talking about?'

'Does that scare people? You know, painting your face? The whole skull thing? 'Cause where I come from, we have a word for people who do that. We call them clowns.'

The man grabbed Josh's forehead and slammed his head

back against the pipe. His skull hit the metal tube with a loud clang. The sound echoed through the room.

'I don't hear you laughing anymore,' the man shouted. Josh's eyes fluttered and rolled back into his skull. His head lolled forward, and a black mist began to creep in around the sides of his vision.

He forced himself to chuckle, despite the pain that burned through his body.

Footsteps echoed across the concrete floor. Someone was walking towards them.

'That's enough, Yiel. You let him get the better of you. He must be awake to feel the pain, yes?'

Josh recognized the voice.

Takuba.

'Huh,' Josh grunted. 'We got the clowns, now here comes the ringmaster.'

Takuba smiled. Josh saw the glint of red, the diamond, glowing between his curled lips.

'Let him down,' Takuba said. His voice was calm, almost serene.

The man called Yiel walked behind Josh. There was a click as he twisted a key in the handcuffs. They snapped open, and Josh tumbled forward onto the floor. He moaned in pain as his battered flesh struck the concrete.

Takuba shook his head. 'So much pain, Mr. Galloway, so much ugliness.' He kneeled next to Josh. 'And for what? What are you fighting for?' He looked around the dim room and gestured towards a cluster of pipes. 'You think you fight for your country? No, my friend.' He thumped a fist against his chest. 'I fight for my country.'

He pointed at the brute, who stood under the single

dangling light bulb. White sweat dripped from the man's face paint and ran in streaks down his neck.

'Yiel there, he is one of my warriors. He is a Ghost Jackal, favored by the spirits that give me power. He also fights for his country. But you? You are nothing but a dog, sent to gather scraps for your master.'

'Yeah?' Josh wheezed, lifting his head to stare into Takuba's eyes. 'I guess that makes you the latest scrap.'

Takuba stood up and brushed the dirt off his trousers.

'I have some entertainment for you, Mr. Galloway. Come, you will find this most interesting, I promise.'

He turned to the man he called Yiel. 'Bring him.'

Josh winced again as Yiel yanked him to his feet.

'Move!'

Yiel shoved him forward. A pair of rebel soldiers stepped out of the shadows behind him.

Josh wiped a streak of blood from an old cut on his cheek and glared at them for a second. Then he followed as Takuba led him out of the dim room, into a long gray hallway. The air smelled of rusting metal and chemicals.

'Where the hell are we?' he demanded.

Takuba looked around. 'This place? This place is a cancer, a tumor on the flesh of my home. It sucks the blood from the ground and leaves only death and desert behind.'

'You mean oil?'

They walked past a row of slim, dusty windows. Josh caught a glimpse of men training outside. He looked closer, but he could not make out the weapons and equipment they were using.

'Yes,' Takuba continued. 'Oil. The great addiction of the civilized world.'

'Your country sold the oil rights,' Josh muttered. 'No one put a gun to your head.'

Takuba stopped. 'You are wrong. When I was six years old, a man did put a gun to my head. Not for oil. Not for money. I had neither, of course. No, this man said he was a soldier. He fought for the Lord's Resistance Army. Have you heard of them?'

'The LRA are a bunch of thugs led by a psychopath,' Josh said. 'Just like you.' He glanced out the windows as a pair of big rig trucks pulled up outside the building. He saw the men rush to the trucks and begin unloading long black cases.

'Yes, the LRA are very bad men. Raiders and thieves masquerading as freedom fighters,' Takuba continued. 'This man, he told me I was to become a soldier, and fight for his glorious cause. Then he said I must give him my loyalty. Or he would give me a bullet.' Takuba laughed. 'I was just a boy, I was terrified. I said yes, of course. What choice did I have?'

Josh was silent as they marched past the windows. The men behind them prodded him again with the barrels of their rifles. They turned left and entered a larger room filled with metal chemical tanks and more pipes. A massive plate glass window was set in the far wall. On the other side, a series of long pipes and valves ran across the ceiling. A catwalk ran along the top of the room. Panels of instruments and controls lined the walls of the second floor. Shadowy figures moved along the catwalk, monitoring the gauges and screens above.

'To prove my loyalty, that man ordered me to kill my own parents, Mr. Galloway.' Takuba grinned. 'I remember my father looking up at me as I held a bloody machete in my hands. It was so heavy, my arms were shaking. He smiled at me. He said, "It is all right, my son. I will feel no pain. It is all right, as long as you live."'

Takuba shook his head and paused for a moment, then

continued. 'Can you imagine the strength? The strength it took to face death like that?' He shook his head. 'I was small. I was not strong. My father did his best to hide it, but he was a liar. It took him many hours to die. He suffered great pain.'

Josh looked around the room. A squad of rebel soldiers herded a group of men through a door into the room with the glass window.

'You think I am a monster. A... what did you call me, a psychopath?'

'If the shoe fits,' Josh snarled.

Takuba nodded. 'We all have our scars, Mr. Galloway. But today, the life of these men is in your hands, not mine. Let us see what decision you make.'

A woman's cries echoed from down the hall. Josh tensed as a pair of soldiers dragged Aya, Nhial's wife, into the room. Her sarong was torn and bloody, and angry bruises marked her face. She was sobbing, muttering in her native tongue, but when she saw Josh, she shouted in English, 'My son, they have my son! Please, don't let them hurt Buri!'

More soldiers entered the room, dragging the young boy by the wrists. He looked up at Josh with wide, terrified eyes as they led him towards the prisoners in the other room.

'What the hell is this, Takuba? Look, you've already beaten me senseless. I don't have your missing property, whatever it is!'

Takuba sighed. 'A shame. That is too bad for the boy then.'

As Aya continued sobbing, a group of men wheeled in an industrial dolly, carrying a large, blue steel barrel. The men opened a valve on the lid of the barrel and clamped on a metal hose. The hose ran along the floor and up to one of the larger tanks. One of the men turned a dial on the valve. A needle on the tank's pressure gauge began to climb.

'What is that?' Josh asked, his eyes darting to the glass window and the men behind it.

Takuba stared through the glass at the beaten, hunched bodies of the prisoners. 'That is crude oil, Mr. Galloway. To the rest of the world, that is all my country is worth. They poison my land, and kill my people, all to extract her black blood. Now, the land shall fight back.'

A low electric hum rose in the room. The needle on the tank shot higher.

'This building was once an oil refinery,' Takuba said. 'Just a small one, Canadian-owned. A few years ago, they claimed they could no longer tolerate the human rights abuses the Sudanese government inflicted on us here in the South. They divested all their holdings here. It was acquired by a Malaysian petrochemical company. That company has changed hands several times now. But they had a small problem... all the men who worked here died.'

Josh watched as Buri's wide eyes darted left and right behind his glass prison. The noise of the machinery grew louder.

'What the hell are you doing to them?'

Takuba turned and stared at him. His face was frozen and emotionless, as if carved from black onyx.

'I thought you would enjoy seeing a test of what you stole from me, Mr. Galloway. When the oil in that barrel finishes cycling through the tank, it will be pumped up there.' Takuba gestured to the ceiling. 'To the fractional distillation column, where it will be refined into various products. Gasoline, kerosene, tar... I don't understand the science behind it all. But I do know that the process will happen quickly. It will only take a few minutes.'

Takuba turned and stared into Josh's eyes. 'And I think you know what happens then. It will not be the pollution that kills these men. You know as well as I, something hides in the oil. It is waiting to be set free. Gemini...'

Josh grabbed Takuba's shirt. 'Stop it! He's just a kid!'

The soldiers behind him clubbed his head and shoulders with the butts of their rifles. As he fell to the ground, Yiel stomped towards him. The big man snarled and lashed out with a powerful kick. Blood spattered the floor as Josh's head snapped back.

Takuba nodded, and Yiel hefted Josh in the air. He grabbed his hands and pinned them behind his back as the other men covered him with their rifles.

Takuba stood next to him and whispered into his ear. 'I had to face death when I was but a child. Now, everyone in that room must do the same, Mr. Galloway. I told you, you cannot stop me. The spirits are with me. You are nothing, a mosquito nipping at a hyena. And that boy will pay the price for your interference. But I will give both of you one last chance. Where are the samples? Where is my property? Who did you give it to?'

Aya threw herself against the glass. She raised her hand to the window. On the other side, Buri looked up and raised his hand against hers. The woman looked back, tears streaming down her cheeks.

'Doctor Vasani,' she said. 'This man, Galloway, he came from Malakal.'

Josh glared at her but said nothing. He couldn't blame her. What else could she do?

One of the men stormed over to her and spun her around. 'Tell us what you know!'

The woman looked back at Buri for a second, then turned to face Takuba. 'There is a doctor, Nena Vasani. She lives in the north, in Khartoum. She has a clinic in Malakal. She sometimes comes to Kanfar to treat the sick and injured. When we found him, he said he had seen Doctor Vasani, in Malakal.'

Takuba smiled and gestured to his men. They opened the door and beat back the crowd of prisoners as the desperate men rushed towards the exit. One of soldiers grabbed Buri and pulled him out. Then he shut the door to the room, sealing the others back inside.

The child ran to his mother and embraced her.

'Get them out of my sight,' Takuba hissed. A pair of soldiers dragged them from the room and down another dark hallway.

Takuba turned to Yiel. 'Find this Doctor Vasani. Check Malakal first but alert our people in the north. Go there if you have to. Anyone who has come into contact with the samples must die!'

'Yes sir!' The big man bowed, then threw Josh back to the ground. 'What about him?'

Takuba glanced down at the battered man. 'We no longer need Mister Galloway. Take him outside. Let the men use him for target practice. Shoot him down like the dog he is.'

'Negative,' a gruff voice called out from overhead.

Josh looked up. A tall Caucasian man stood above, leaning against the railing of the catwalk. He glared down at Josh, peering over the rims of a pair of wire-framed glasses. His features were gaunt, and a spidery burn covered one side of his face.

Josh squinted at him. 'Allan Bernatto?'

Bernatto ignored him. 'We may still need him. Keep him alive for now,' he said to Takuba.

Takuba glanced up at the catwalk. 'I don't take orders from you, old man.'

'They're not my orders,' Bernatto snapped. 'I think we both know I speak for the man who's funding this operation of yours.'

Takuba stared up at him for a moment, then looked away. 'Do it,' he muttered. Yiel nodded and dragged Josh back towards the hallway.

'Bernatto!' Josh shouted, struggling to free himself from Yiel's meaty fists. 'You goddamn traitor! What the hell are you doing here? Takuba's a madman, you can't—'

But Bernatto had already turned around and stalked away from the railing. As he disappeared into the shadows above, Josh heard the hiss of gas. He turned and saw the men behind the window begin to choke and cough.

As Josh was pulled out of the room, he saw a gray mist fill the test room. A bloody hand reached up and slapped against the window. It left a crimson print where Buri's hand had touched minutes before. Then it slipped away, leaving a streak across the glass.

9

Seconds after the yellow taxicab pulled out of the motel's parking lot, Caine felt a familiar tingling on the back of his neck. Years of living in the shadows had honed his senses. He knew when something was off, when something felt wrong. In his line of work, the smallest detail could mean the difference between life and death.

He glanced at the rearview mirror and scanned the road behind them. A dusty blue pickup truck and a rusted white Toyota sedan followed them down Highway 498. On either side of the cracked pavement, farmhouses and grasslands stretched into the distance, until the lonely, flat terrain met with the brilliant blue sky at the horizon. There was no sign of pursuers. Nothing to explain the nervous energy that crackled through his body.

The cab's tires thumped a soothing rhythm over the sun-bleached pavement. Everything seemed fine, peaceful even.

But Caine knew better.

He knew it was usually the enemy you could not see who

fired the bullet with your name on it. He knew this because for many, he had been that invisible enemy.

He also knew the capabilities of his pursuers. Drones, satellites, helicopters... Just because he didn't see them, didn't mean they weren't watching. It could be paranoia, and maybe he was being too cautious. But whatever it was, that tingling sixth sense of danger had kept him alive so far. Now, as always, he would trust his instincts.

He leaned forward in his seat. 'Hey, you know what?' Caine asked the driver, putting a slight drawl into his voice. 'I never did make it to see downtown. Is it far from here?'

The driver cocked his head and looked up at him in the mirror. His skin was pink from sunburn, and beads of sweat dripped from his wrinkled forehead.

'Downtown Alexandria? Nothing there to see. Airport's only a couple miles down the highway, I can have you there in five.'

Caine peeled a twenty from the money clip in his front pocket and handed the crumpled bill to the driver.

'I'm in no rush. Plenty of time to see the local sites. Let's turn around.'

The driver shrugged and took the bill. 'Whatever you say, mister.' He stuffed the money in his shirt pocket and turned the wheel. The cab made a U-turn across the highway and headed back the way they had come.

Caine looked out the rear window. None of the scattered cars behind them matched the turn. They continued down the highway, disappearing in the distance. Caine was about to turn away when he spotted a cloud of dust to their right. A black SUV pulled off a dirt road and kept pace behind them.

Might as well have an FBI bumper sticker, he thought.

He hunched lower in the seat. So far, only the lone vehicle pursued them. There had to be others. Caine was a rogue CIA operative, believed to be a traitor. He was in the country illegally. And now he was linked to the disappearance of the Director of National Intelligence. That would fall under the jurisdiction of FBI Counter Intelligence.

And that meant things were going to get messy.

The SUV maintained a discreet distance. When Caine's taxi turned back onto the I-49, it sped off, appearing to leave them behind.

But Caine was not fooled.

Another car pulled out of a nearby gas station and took up the tail position behind them. The new car was a white Toyota with a dent in the front bumper. The same car that had been behind them earlier.

They were rotating vehicles. But why the Toyota? He had just seen it only a short time ago.

The airport was only a couple miles from the motel, he reasoned. They anticipated my exit point. Set up there to take me down. Now, they need time to re-deploy. They sent the closest car they had to keep tabs on me while they coordinated.

Another question flashed through his mind: If they followed me to Louisiana, why didn't they intervene when Blayne was killed?

The answer came just as quickly. They didn't follow me. Someone must have tipped them off. Someone tried to take me off the board.

He had to keep them off balance. The longer he stayed in the taxi, the more time they had to communicate with local law enforcement. They would position roadblocks, lay down spike traps, add tail cars. He could only flee in one direction at a time. They could come at him from all sides and force him into a choke point. He had to change the dynamics of the situation before they got that chance.

Caine watched the exit signs rushing past them. He saw the turnoff for Route 71 growing closer in the windshield. He thought over the map of the area that he had committed to memory.

'Hey, is there a mall around here? Someplace I can pick up a present for my wife?' he asked.

An annoyed look flashed across the driver's face. 'Now you want a shopping mall? Well, Alexandria Mall isn't too far away. Route 71's coming up, but we—'

'Do it!' Caine snapped. 'There's an extra hundred in it for you.'

The driver swore and jerked the wheel to the right. The wheels of the cab chirped as they skipped over the ridge of the divider. The yellow cab wobbled, then straightened out and pulled into the exit lane. Caine turned his head and watched the white Toyota pass by.

He slipped the driver a hundred-dollar bill. 'Let's stick to surface streets from now on, if you don't mind.'

The driver shook his head. 'You spend a little too much time in the titty bar or something?'

Caine tilted his head. 'What are you talking about?'

The driver spat out the window, then looked at Caine in the rearview mirror. 'Man who wants to buy his old lady a present that bad is a man who done fucked up.'

Caine forced himself to laugh as he turned to look out the rear window once more. 'Yeah. I'm sure she'd agree.'

* * *

Caine's taxi cruised through the mall parking lot. It was still early, and although a few cars dotted the expanse of pavement, the lot was far from full. Caine's eyes darted left and right behind the gray lenses of his aviators. He had hoped for more people, a larger crowd to throw off pursuers.

As they drove past a row of department stores, Caine spotted a blur of motion at the other end of the parking lot. Two more black SUVs, identical to the model he had spotted earlier, swerved into the lot. They were coming from the opposite entrance, off North Mall Drive.

Must have followed us onto the 71, Caine thought.

Time to move.

'This is fine, you can let me off here.' Caine shoved a wad of bills at the cab driver as they slowed to a stop. The driver looked out the window as Caine exited the vehicle.

'Sears? You think that's gonna cut it with the missus?' he drawled, a crooked smile plastered across his sunburned face.

Caine ignored him and entered the store, keeping his head down. He doubted his pursuers would have tapped into the mall's surveillance cameras yet, but best to be sure. He kept moving, making his way deeper into the store. A few shoppers ambled around him... housewives checking out the sales, some old timers traversing the hardware aisle. Mirrored columns rose up from the floor. As he walked past, he kept an eye out for the shifting reflections of pursuers, but he saw no one.

He knew that would change soon.

He headed towards the sporting goods section. As he made his way through the aisles of football equipment and hunting gear, he spotted movement to his right. He clocked a man in a blue blazer, walking towards him. Thick legs, broad shoulders... He looked like he worked out. As Caine eyed him, the man veered off to the next aisle. He could hear the man's footsteps, clicking across the floor. He was keeping pace with him.

Here we go.

As he walked towards the end of his aisle, Caine snatched a

basketball off a nearby rack. He listened for the footsteps on the other side of the shelves. He could hear the tapping of the man's heels, moving in time with his own.

Cradling the ball in his left hand, Caine stopped short, just a couple feet from the end of the aisle. The other man's footsteps continued. As he rounded the corner, Caine slammed the basketball down to the ground.

'Catch!' he bellowed. The man's arm darted towards his jacket. Before he could draw, the sudden, erratic movement of the ball and Caine's booming voice distracted him. He froze for a split second, hesitating. His eyes tracked the ball as it bounced in his direction.

As the ball flew past, he slipped a pistol from a shoulder holster under his jacket. But Caine was already moving, pivoting his body out of the line of fire. Continuing his fluid motion, he reached out and grabbed the barrel of the gun. He jerked it up and back, twisting it around in the man's hand. He heard the crack of the snapping bones; the sudden twist broke the man's trigger finger.

The man yelped in pain. His other hand flew up as he struggled to regain control of his weapon, but Caine was not finished.

Reaching across the aisle, Caine grasped the hilt of a field hockey stick. He yanked the pistol from the man's weakened grip and swept low with the hockey stick. The curved head of the stick hooked round the man's ankle, sweeping his foot off the ground.

He tumbled to the floor. Caine dropped the hockey stick and kneeled beside him, then clubbed the back of the man's head with the butt of the pistol.

The man groaned and lay still. Frisking the body, Caine slipped a leather badge case from the inside pocket of the man's blazer.

The card inside identified him as 'Special Agent Christopher Nash.' The gold badge, stamped with the embossed wings of a bald eagle, left no room for doubt – the Federal Bureau of Investigation was pursuing him. Caine slipped the badge into his pocket and examined the pistol. He recognized the chunky black polymer frame of the weapon as a Glock 19. Standard issue for FBI special agents.

He stood up, tucked the gun into his waistband, and continued down the aisle.

Turning left, he stepped onto an escalator and began climbing up the moving steps. He stopped behind an exhausted-looking mother dressed in a loose T-shirt and jeans. Caine smiled at her as she did her best to comfort the crying infant she cradled against her shoulder. She gave Caine a wary glance, then hurried off the escalator when they reached the second floor.

Caine moved in the opposite direction. He left the department store and headed into the open area of the mall. He had to keep moving, keep changing things up.

He walked past a kiosk that displayed a map of the mall's second floor. His trained eyes darted over the floor plan, noting the building's exits and choke points. He headed towards another set of escalators that led back down to the first floor. If he could get to the other side of the parking lot, he could steal a car, put some distance between himself and his pursuers.

Up ahead, a service corridor split off from the mall, and a sign noted the location of restrooms and an elevator. To the right of the corridor, a janitor stood in Caine's path. He wore a pair of headphones and swished a mop in a lazy circle. The wet strands of the mop wiped pink splatters of melted ice cream across the polished floor. The janitor nodded his head in time to the music as he swung the wet mop, sloshing it into a yellow wheeled bucket filled with dirty gray water.

As Caine moved closer, he could hear the muted sound of rock music blasting from the man's headphones. He watched as the janitor looked up and turned his head towards the service corridor. His eyes widened in surprise, and his jaw dropped.

Caine knew the look well... It was a gasp of fear.

They're here!

Caine surged forward, charging towards the janitor at full speed. By the time the janitor turned away from whatever had caught his eye, it was too late. Caine barreled into him at full speed, knocking him to the ground. As he fell, Caine wrenched the mop from his hands.

He spun around, facing the corridor. He saw exactly what he expected to see – armed men, storming out of an elevator and rushing towards him. There were three of them, all wearing green camouflage tactical gear, helmets, and Kevlar vests. Smoked goggles covered their faces, and white FBI patches marked their arms.

They were FBI SWAT. An enhanced team, trained to take down high-level threats.

Each member of the team was carrying an MP5 submachine gun. A variety of other small arms hung from their tactical harnesses. They were only a few feet from the exit of the service corridor. In a fraction of a second, Caine analyzed his situation. He was outnumbered and outgunned. If the men made it out of the confines of the corridor, they would flank him and take him down.

Caine moved without hesitation. He kicked the mop bucket forward. As it rolled across the floor, he stamped down on the mop, snapping the wet, soggy head off with a loud crack.

The bucket crashed into the lead officer, knocking him off balance. He stumbled, then raised his automatic weapon towards Caine. But Caine had already closed the gap between them.

He darted left with the makeshift staff, knocking aside the barrel of the lead man's MP5. The SWAT officer pulled the trigger. A spray of gunfire erupted through the air, shattering the glass barrier that ran along the edge of the second floor.

Patrons screamed and rushed away from the area. Caine continued moving, slamming the staff into the lead man's chin. As he stumbled backwards, Caine jabbed the tip of the staff into the man's Adam's apple. Even through the Kevlar, the blow was strong enough to make him drop his weapon. His hands clutched at his bruised throat.

As the other men tried to push their way around their stunned comrade, Caine dropped the staff. He drew the Glock 23 from his waistband, aimed low, and squeezed off two quick shots. The muzzle flash lit up the dim corridor as the gun roared in the confined space. The bullets tore into the officer's right leg, just above the knee.

He barked in pain and fell down, blocking the other officers as they tried to maneuver around him.

Before his target hit the ground, Caine turned and charged towards the escalators. Leaping over the stunned janitor, he sprinted forward, panting for breath. He could hear the shouts of the men pursuing him, their boots stomping across the tile floor.

The escalator was only a few feet away. Caine heard more gunfire explode behind him, felt streaks of hot air rushing past his cheek. A fire alarm rang out, the warbling siren echoing throughout the confines of the mall. Below the escalators, he saw more shoppers rushing towards the exits, fleeing from the violence that had erupted above them.

Sparks exploded to his left as a burst of gunfire hit the escalator. Smoke rose from the machine, and the smell of burning rubber stung his nostrils. Caine grabbed the handles of the moving stairs and vaulted up into the air. He landed on his back on a narrow strip of metal running between the up and down sides of the escalator.

Caine slid down the smooth metal surface, gaining speed as his momentum carried him forward. He flew off the end of the slide and landed on his feet. Bullets sparked at his heels as he darted into another large department store.

The ringing fire alarm sounded even louder within the store. Moving in a low crouch, Caine tore through the aisles. He pushed through the racks of clothes, heading towards the back of the empty store.

The alarm must have driven everyone outside, he thought. So much for losing myself in the crowd.

At the rear of the store, he found a metal door marked Employees Only. He guessed it would lead to the loading dock, where merchandise was brought into the store. He hoped he could find a vehicle there, or at least access to the parking lot.

He kicked open the door, sweeping left and right with his pistol. An alarm bell sounded, but it was drowned out by the wail of the siren. Charging forward, Caine found himself in another dim service corridor. He moved on, turning a corner, following a red arrow on the wall that pointed towards a set of swinging double doors.

He crashed through the doors and once again smelled the hot, humid Louisiana air. He was outside, standing on a raised concrete platform. The enclosed loading dock was about six feet off the ground. The garage was empty, and the parking lot beyond seemed devoid of cars. All the shoppers and employees had fled. He heard honking horns and police sirens from the other side of the mall. The dragnet was closing in.

Caine took a deep breath, then sprinted out of the dock and into the parking lot. He heard the double doors crashing open. Gunfire erupted behind him, ricocheting off the pavement.

'Federal agents... stop now!' a commanding voice boomed behind him.

Caine glanced to his left and right. He was out in the open, no cover. The vehicles at the edge of the parking lot were too far away. The next burst of gunfire would not miss.

They had him.

Caine stopped running. He set the pistol down on the ground. Then he stood up, placing his hands on his head. He turned around.

A three-man team swept into the loading dock. The lead officer raised his hand in a fist, and the two others fanned out behind him. All three kept their weapons trained on Caine.

'Stay where you are. Do not move,' the officer commanded. 'Get on your knees. Now!'

Caine paused for a second, considering his options. As far as he could see, he didn't have any. His emerald eyes glared at the lead officer, then he lowered himself to the ground.

As his knees touched the pavement, he heard footsteps racing above them. He looked up and saw a tall, athletic man wearing black jeans and a dark windbreaker. He was running along the roof of the loading dock. As the officers neared the edge of the dock, he dropped down and tossed something in front of them. There was a hiss, and a burst of white smoke filled the enclosed area.

The men stopped moving. They coughed and gasped for breath as the dense cloud of gas surrounded them.

Caine scooped up his pistol as the man on the roof drew a weapon. The man in black fired several shots into a gearbox mounted at the edge of the roof.

Sparks exploded from the mechanism. A heavy garage door rolled down and slammed into the ground with a loud clank. The barrier closed off the loading dock, sealing the FBI team inside.

As the man on the roof threw down a rappel line and slid to the ground, an engine roared through the parking lot. Caine stepped aside as a silver Land Rover SUV sped around the corner of the building. The SUV screeched to a halt as the man jogged over to him. Caine aimed his pistol at him.

'That's close enough,' he snarled. He looked the man up and down. Something about him seemed familiar. African American, tall, slim... He realized he had seen him before.

Rebecca's security detail, the last time you saw her, in DC. He was working under Josh Galloway...

'Thought you'd show a little gratitude,' the man said. He stared at Caine with cool brown eyes set in a rugged but youthful face.

'You thought wrong,' Caine replied. 'Tell your man to get out of the car.' The window of the SUV hummed down, and the driver eyed him with a sullen glare.

'Not gonna happen,' the other man said, shaking his head. 'Now, you've got about five seconds to make up your mind. You want to come with us? Or take your chances with them?'

Caine heard the FBI agents banging on the metal door from inside the loading dock. His lips twisted into a grim smile. 'Funny. I told someone the same thing yesterday.'

'They make the right choice?'

Caine stared at him over the barrel of the gun. 'Depends on how you look at it. Who are you?'

'Name's Clayton DuBose. I work for your boss. Remember her?'

'Rebecca?'

'Yeah. She'd like a word.' The banging inside the dock grew louder. The metal door groaned as the trapped SWAT team tried to force it up along its track. 'Now you got three seconds,' DuBose warned.

Caine lowered the pistol. 'Fine. But they're going to have checkpoints at the exits. They'll search your vehicle.'

DuBose opened the passenger door and Caine slid into the rear seat.

'We're making our own exit. Hold on and stay down. Ride's gonna be a little bumpy.'

The engine roared to life. Caine felt a thunk in the transmission as the driver shifted the vehicle into four-wheel drive. The Land Rover charged over the curb of the parking lot and climbed up a steep, grassy hill. The heavy-duty tires tore through the brush and shrubs surrounding the mall and gouged long track marks into the grass behind them.

The SUV skidded into a turn, exploded from the brush, and pulled onto the freeway. Other cars swerved out of the way, their horns bleating like a flock of angry geese. The noise died down as the battered SUV merged into traffic and sped off down the road.

Caine looked through the rear window. A few cars had fishtailed to a stop and pulled over to the side of the road.

'With attention like that, won't take the FBI long to find us.'

DuBose grinned back at him. 'Not long at all.' A radio on the dashboard squawked to life. Caine listened as a description of the Land Rover and its occupants blared over the airwaves.

'Police band,' Caine muttered. 'You're getting the FBI's signal. So that's how you found me.'

'They were following you, we were following them. They have a helicopter inbound, ETA is three minutes – which is why we have a switch car waiting two minutes down the road. And

I've positioned three identical decoy vehicles at various exits. Don't worry, this isn't my first time on the dance floor. Just sit back and enjoy the ride, Mr. Caine. Oh, and you get any ideas about ditching us, maybe think you're better off on your own? You go right ahead. Just tell me where to pull over and we'll drop you off curbside. The director did you a solid. You want to throw that back in her face, that's on you. But there's no more second chances after this. Get it?'

Caine stared out the window. 'Yeah, I got it.'

Rebecca... The last time he had seen her, things had not gone well. He had promised her that he would come in, that he would give up his hunt for Bernatto, and revenge. He had broken that promise, as he knew he would. He had lied to her, used her to help an ally escape custody.

It was all to protect her, to free himself to hunt down the men who had hurt her. But he knew she was hurt. Angry.

Now she had sent DuBose to free him from the clutches of the FBI. But Rebecca was the director of the CIA's Clandestine Service. Her professional pride would be on the line, and he didn't know how much she had told the agency. Did they know he was alive? Did they still believe he was a traitor? Either way, he had a feeling it would make life easier for everyone involved if he disappeared again.

Which led him to wonder... had his situation improved? Or was he even worse off than before?

10

The warehouse was dark and stank of mold and animal feces. Collapsed wooden hulls and rotting canvas sails lay in musty heaps along the walls. Caine guessed the place had been a boat storage facility, or a marine impound lot for local police. But years of wind, and rain, and the infernal Florida sun had taken their toll. Whatever the place had once been, it was now a decayed skeleton of metal and concrete. It stood in a vacant lot, perched on the edge of a weed-infested field.

A few fluorescent tubes flickered overhead. Caine leaned back in his chair and stared past the intermittent lights. He gazed through the rusted holes in the ceiling. Stars twinkled in the distance, their flickering lights set against a pitch-black sky. Droplets of water fell down to the concrete floor, marking the passing of time like a metronome.

They had driven for thirteen hours straight, taking the I-10 along the Gulf Coast, then heading south on FL-64. They switched cars several times along the way, but they never stopped for more than a few minutes. They kept their speed just above the legal limit, blending in with the other traffic as they skirted the southern edge of Alabama and Georgia. They drove past Orlando and Tampa, but Caine had no idea what small town they might be in now. The last sign he remembered seeing read Manatee County.

Their long road trip had finally ended at this abandoned warehouse. Once they arrived at the crumbling old building, Caine took a seat at a small table inside. He did not say another word, and DuBose did not seem inclined to make small talk. For a time, the falling droplets of water were the only sound echoing through the cavernous space.

DuBose filled out a series of reports with an aluminum tactical pen. From time to time, he glanced up and watched Caine with an unblinking, dead-eyed stare. Then he returned to his writing. Caine eyed the silver pen. He knew its hardened metal body could make an effective weapon, if need be.

DuBose's partner was a younger man with straw-blond hair and brown eyes. He reluctantly answered to the names Danny, Danny Boy, and Junior. He stood away from the table and practiced a series of martial arts strikes against one of the metal beams that rose from the floor.

Caine turned away from DuBose's hawkish gaze, and watched as the younger man executed a rapid flurry of punches. He finished with a dramatic spin kick that clanged off the metal beam.

'Leg's too high,' Caine commented. 'Leaves you open.'

Danny rubbed his calloused knuckles and huffed for breath. He strutted over to the table where Caine and DuBose sat. 'What was that?'

Caine looked up at him. 'Your kick. It's flashy, but it leaves you exposed. If it doesn't connect, your opponent will exploit that, use it to take you down.'

Danny wiped the beads of sweat from his forehead and

brushed back his damp hair. 'Good thing I'm fast enough to connect.'

Caine shook his head and looked away. 'Yeah. Faster than that pole, anyway.'

DuBose looked up from his reports and glared at him. Then he glanced at Danny. 'Let it go, Junior.'

The younger man puffed out his chest. 'It's all good, dawg. Hell, I hear this guy's supposed to be some kind of legendary badass, right? Maybe he can give us a demonstration.'

'I don't do tricks,' Caine growled.

Danny squatted low on his knees and stared into Caine's eyes. 'Yeah, you're an old dog, huh? But what about that trick you pulled in Afghanistan? Couple million worth of guns, big heroin score, and it all goes up in smoke. Poof... disappears. Your partner? Dead. Your asset? Dead. But you walk out of there, not a scratch on you.'

'Danny, I said let it go.' DuBose's voice cut through the air like cold steel. He set his pen down on the table.

The younger man's eyes darted towards him, then returned to Caine. 'Do you know what happens to us if the FBI finds him here? Why am I risking my ass to babysit this prick?'

''Cause the director said so,' DuBose replied, enunciating each word. 'Now go outside, get some fresh air, and cool down. I'm not asking again.'

'The director?' The younger man gave Caine a lewd grin. 'I hear things about her. too. First your sorry ass, then Galloway. Guess she's got a taste for the wild side. Hey, don't get me wrong, I don't blame you. She must have been pretty hot, before the chair.'

Caine's lips curled up, but the smile did not reach his eyes. 'Why don't you show me that kick again, Junior? If you think you're fast enough, that is.'

Danny clenched his jaw. He grunted and launched into motion, spinning his body around. DuBose leapt to his feet, but there was no time to speak, let alone stop his partner's attack.

Caine's smile never left his lips as his body made a series of small, precise movements. He angled his left foot forward, pressing down on his toe. Then he shifted his body towards his attacker. As Danny's leg swung around, Caine's left arm rose up, and his right arm crossed in front of his body, palm facing out. His head dipped down, tucking into his shoulder.

Danny's leg whipped around and the blow struck. Caine's left arm deflected the force of the kick. Grabbing Danny's shin with both hands, he locked the leg against his shoulder and launched himself out of the chair, stepping forward onto his poised left foot.

Danny staggered backwards, but he was hopelessly off balance. Caine stamped down on the inside of Danny's left ankle. The bone snapped, and Danny yelped. The leg buckled and he fell to the ground.

Caine released his hold on the man's leg and grabbed the chair he had been sitting on. Swinging it above his head, he grasped it in both hands and powered it down into Danny's face.

Danny tried to throw up his hands and block, but Caine moved too fast. The metal seat clanged against his skull and blood spurted into the air. Caine raised the chair again.

'That's enough!' DuBose shouted. Caine heard the metallic click of a pistol being cocked. He turned and saw DuBose aiming a gun at him in a steady, double-handed grip.

Suddenly, a brilliant white light filled the room. Both Caine and DuBose looked up as a series of overhead halogen bulbs blazed to life. A woman's voice echoed through the chamber.

'Nice. I can't say I'm surprised. Disappointed, yes. But not surprised.'

DuBose lowered his pistol as a shadowed figure moved into the room. Danny groaned and crawled away from the table.

As his eyes adjusted to the harsh glare, Caine could make out the fiery highlights of Rebecca's long red hair, backlit by the pools of light. The motors in her chair hummed as she rolled towards them.

'I don't know which smells worse,' she said. 'The rat piss or the testosterone overload.'

Caine looked her up and down. Her designer suit, expensive shoes and brand name handbag were all par for the course. But something about her seemed different somehow. He continued to stare, but he couldn't put his finger on it. Then he looked at the bloody chair he held in his hands, as if noticing it for the first time. He lowered it and set it on the ground.

He said nothing.

She eyed him for a moment, an uncomfortable frown marring her porcelain features. Then she turned to DuBose. 'We'll consider it a training exercise. Clayton, give us the room, please.'

'Director, are you sure—'

'And take him.' She nodded towards the younger operative, sprawled out across the floor. 'Tape up his ankle. We'll get him medical attention later. After we discuss his future career options.'

DuBose holstered his weapon and helped Danny to his feet. 'On it, Director.'

He shot the young man a rueful glance as he carried him outside to the waiting SUV. He left the heavy door open behind him. Rebecca and Caine stood alone among the rotting boat hulls and cobwebs.

'Clayton, he's one of yours, right? I've seen him before,' Caine said.

She moved close to the table and pivoted her chair to face him. 'Clayton's acting head of my security detail. I trust him with my life. He's good. Professional.' She looked up at him and cocked her head. 'Reliable.'

'And the kid?'

She shrugged. 'Good help is hard to find. I had to move fast. Seeing as you're a wanted man.'

Caine exhaled. He sat down in the chair and stared across the table at her.

'So. Here we are again,' he said.

She looked into his eyes, drumming her fingers on the table. 'You're in trouble,' she said.

He met her stare head on. 'You want something.'

'I wanted you to come in. To debrief the CIA, tell the truth about what happened with you and Bernatto. Instead, you broke a Chinese assassin out of my custody and ran off on your private vendetta.'

'You should be thanking me,' Caine snapped.

Rebecca's eyes widened and her nostrils flared in anger. 'How do you figure that, exactly?'

'I kept you from making a mistake. Lapinski was using her for his own purposes. He kidnapped her daughter. He used a six-year-old child for leverage. If you had detained them, what would have happened to the girl? After everything they went through, you really want that on your conscience?'

'Maybe you're right. But that wasn't your call to make. That woman was a killer. A double agent who executed American and Chinese assets—'

'That woman had no choice,' Caine said, cutting her off. 'She was a victim of the same people who burned me. The people who left me and my partner to die and set me up to take the fall. And the same people who put you in that chair!'

'Bernatto,' she said in a quiet voice.

Caine clenched his fist so tightly his knuckles turned white. 'Not just Bernatto. He's working with others in the intelligence community. Lapinski confirmed that. And don't forget, the only reason you have Lapinski in custody is because Jia and I tracked him down.'

Rebecca nodded. 'All right. What's done is done. So what do Bernatto and these others want? What are they planning? Do you have anything actionable?'

Caine paused. The events of the last few days raced through his mind. What did he really know? How dangerous would it be for her to get involved?

'I don't know,' he said, his voice quiet and defeated.

She squinted at him. She knew he was hiding something. He could tell by the look in her eyes.

'What happened in Louisiana?' she asked. 'You followed the Director of National Intelligence there. Is he involved?'

'Lapinski indicated that Blayne might be part of... whatever it is Bernatto is working on. I can confirm that now. Blayne was definitely compromised. He was being followed by some hired guns. I think they were working for a private security company called Delta Blue.'

She raised an eyebrow. 'Past tense. I've known you long enough to know what that means.'

Caine nodded. 'Yeah. Blayne's dead. More Delta Blue men followed us into the swamp. I tried to get him out, but...'

'The FBI considers you a person of interest in his disappearance.'

'Rebecca, come on, you know—'

'What, Tom? What do I know? You lied to me, and then you disappeared. Not the first time you dropped off the grid, I might add. I don't know where you went. I don't know what you did. I sure as hell don't know if I can trust you anymore. The only thing I do know is that you were illegally surveilling the DNI, who is now missing and presumed dead.'

Caine leaned back in his chair. A shadow cut across his face, but his emerald eyes blazed in the darkness. 'Then why are you here? Why didn't you let the FBI bring me in?'

Rebecca set both of her hands flat on the table. She stared down at her manicured nails. 'Blayne isn't the only one who went missing.'

'What are you talking about?'

'Clayton took over as head of my security detail for a reason. Josh Galloway transferred back to field ops. A couple months ago, not long after you disappeared and followed Blayne.'

'Wait, are you saying Galloway is MIA?'

Rebecca nodded. 'He was on a mission. Recently, a US drone strike in Syria took out a medical facility. We believed the facility was being used as a lab, to produce a new biological weapon agent.'

'What kind of weapon are we talking about?' Caine asked, surprised by the sudden shift the conversation had taken.

'We don't know. Ground forces inspected the wreckage. They confirmed the laboratory equipment was consistent with a bioweapons program. But no sign of the weapons themselves was recovered. SIGINT revealed that someone warned Russian forces at a nearby airbase, twenty-four hours in advance. Before the Russians cleared out, satellite imagery showed trucks leaving the medical facility. Whoever they were, they loaded something onto a civilian cargo plane at that airfield.'

'So someone tipped off the Russians, and the Russians tipped off someone else. Who?'

'That was Galloway's assignment. To track down the materials, identify the sellers, and any potential buyers. He traced the plane to a transport company connected to the Rudov family. They're a Vor family, they—'

'Thieves in law,' Caine said, his voice low and hard. 'Old-school Russian Mafia. I've crossed paths with them.'

Rebecca blinked, then continued. 'Why am I not surprised? At any rate, Galloway reported that the suspected weapon changed hands several times after that. According to his last report, he traced the materials to a Chechen arms dealer. They were last sighted in Sudan.'

'Sudan?' Caine stiffened.

Puff Adder... the voice hissed in the back of his mind. It seemed impossible, but the coincidence was too large to be ignored. Somehow, it was all connected. His fingers clutched the edge of the table in a white-knuckled grip.

Rebecca noticed his reaction and leaned forward. Her eyes narrowed in suspicion, but she continued speaking. 'Yes. Galloway believed the arms dealers were trying to sell the weapon to one of the rebel factions in the South, but he couldn't confirm the buyer. He believed the weapon had already been used in a limited capacity, a test of some kind. His last report said he was working with a local asset, a doctor named Nena Vasani. She's based in Khartoum. That was two weeks ago. After that, he went dark. No response to messages. Local contacts report no sign of him. His hotel room is empty, and he hasn't checked his dead drop locations.'

'Rebecca, look. I know you two are close. But he may have had to go dark for a reason. He may be under surveillance, or he—'

'No. Something is wrong. I sent him a message. Something... personal. He would have responded. And I can't help but feel it's my fault he transferred in the first place.'

'Why do you say that?'

He saw a tremor cross her face. A quiver of her lip, a slight flush to her cheeks. A momentary chink in her emotional armor.

'That's... that's not important right now.'

'All right. So you're the D/NCS. You run the Special Activities Group. Send in the cavalry.'

'The situation on the ground... it's complex. South Sudan is teetering on the edge of collapse. They've been mired in an endless civil war, fueled by weapons and oil money from countless other states. Civilians massacred by the thousands, refugees in the hundreds of thousands... The president is pushing the United Nations to intervene. He's ordered my boss to suspend all operations in the area until further notice. The South Sudanese president has agreed to talks with the rebel leaders. Our president is convinced any covert activity in the region is going to blow up in his face, and endanger the ceasefire.'

'More like his donors don't want to miss out on any oil rights if a coup sends the Chinese packing,' Caine muttered.

'You're familiar with the area. And as of right now, all the CIA knows about you is that you evaded the FBI Counter Intel team. As far as they're concerned, you could be anywhere right now.'

'In other words, I'm a deniable asset,' he said.

'I can get you out of the country, provide you with the intel we received from Josh. If he's still alive, you're my best shot at finding him. Tom... you're all I've got.'

'So that's what this is all about? First you want me to turn myself in, now you want me to go chase down your boyfriend?'

Rebecca stared at him for a moment, then turned her chair around. 'Forget it. I'll have DuBose drop you off on the state line. I won't report your location to the FBI, but after this you're on your own.'

Caine watched her fiery hair cascade down her shoulders.

Her chair carried her across the concrete floor, away from him. He clenched and unclenched his fist, thinking. Remembering. He stood up.

'Rebecca, wait.'

She stopped and turned the chair around. Caine saw fleeting hope flicker behind her eyes.

'Look, I'm sorry. It's just... hard.'

She brushed a copper strand of hair from her face. 'Tom, what do you want me to say? Even if you did come in now, the things that have happened to you, to both of us... There's this wall you've built up inside. You've cut yourself off from everyone. What did you think was going to happen?'

He nodded. 'I made my own decisions. I have to live with that, I know. But I've only ever wanted what's best for you.'

She sighed. 'I've made my own mistakes as well. Whatever happened to Josh, I'm responsible.'

'What do you mean?'

'He left because of me, that's all I can say. I need to make things right. Before... before it's too late. You told me once you trusted me more than anyone. Please. Can I trust you now?'

Caine stood up and walked over to her. His footsteps echoed across the cracked concrete floor.

'Yeah. You can trust me. I'll go. But Rebecca, there's something I need to know. What exactly is the priority here? Galloway? Or this bioweapon?'

She looked up at him. Her eyes were soft and damp. They glinted in the harsh overhead light. Then they hardened and met his penetrating gaze head on.

'That's why I need you to go, Tom. Because right now, I don't trust myself to make that call.'

She turned her chair around and headed towards the exit.

'Clayton will bring you all the intel and make arrangements

to get you out of the country. He'll get you an encrypted satellite phone. I'll be in touch.'

She stopped next to the door. 'And Tom?'

He looked up.

A tiny smile crossed her lips. 'Thank you.'

'You're welcome.'

The door rolled shut behind her. He was alone.

Puff Adder... The name echoed through his mind like the high-pitched cry of a wild animal. Laughing, mocking him.

Shadows surrounded him, clawed at him. For a while, he had actually believed he might be able to leave the nightmares of his past behind him. But now he knew better. He had been a fool to think he could escape the darkness. Blood still stained his hands.

The past, it seemed, was not finished with him.

But Rebecca... why didn't he tell her? If Puff Adder was active, if Josh had crossed paths with him in Sudan... Things might be even worse than she imagined. Despite all they had been through, or more likely because of it, he knew he trusted her. Trusted her more than anyone alive. So why had he kept this crucial bit of intel hidden from her?

It's like she said, he thought. You trust her. You just don't trust yourself.

11

Buri's heart thumped louder than a stampede of gazelles. He panted for breath as he raced through the grass and brush. The thin brown reeds bent and snapped under his bare feet, but he pushed himself forward. Behind him he heard men shouting, stomping after him. The grass rose almost to his shoulders, and he ducked low, trying to keep out of sight. He knew there was a dirt road to the east, but he was afraid to use it. These American men fought for money, and they were loud and clumsy. But he knew even they would be able to follow his tracks in the soft mud surface of the road.

Instead, he kept to the grasslands. He had lost track of how far he had gone. His legs were tired and covered with cuts and scrapes from the rough foliage. He had stopped to catch his breath a few times.

He remembered that the sun had just come up when he escaped. His friend, the American that Takuba called Galloway, helped him slip underneath a gap in the fence around the refinery. The hole was tight, barely a few inches wide. It looked like it had been dug by a small animal seeking the warmth of the buildings inside the fence. Buri was a slim boy, and his wiry frame was able to slide underneath. The fence's sharp edges scraped his flesh, but he had made it through.

'Go!' Galloway hissed when he was on the other side. 'I'll tell your mother what happened. Get help if you can but get far away from here!'

Buri looked back and saw one of the American guards turn and run towards them.

'Hey!' the burly man shouted. 'Get your ass back here!'

Galloway gave him a wink. He turned and walked towards the guard.

'Hey, the kid needed to take a leak. Give him a break.'

Before the soldier could react, Galloway attacked, tackling the man to the ground. Buri stared in shock, certain the soldier would shoot Galloway. But instead, they rolled and struggled in the dirt. More men rushed over to them.

Galloway looked up, his face flecked with blood and dirt. 'Run!' he shouted.

Buri ran.

As he sprinted away from the camp, he heard the men shouting. Galloway grunted as they beat him with their rifles, but he said nothing.

Now those same men were after him.

He knew Galloway was probably dead. Galloway had brought medicine to their village. Galloway had told him stories, showed him pictures of America, places Buri dreamed of visiting someday.

Galloway helped him escape.

He forced himself to run faster. He could not let the men catch him. He could not let his friend die for nothing.

Suddenly the brush ended and Buri found himself in a vast clearing. A few patches of dried grass and scrub dotted the dusty plain. Groves of gnarled, blackened trees sprang up here and there, but they were too sparse to hide in.

Buri wrinkled his nose. A rancid smell filled the air. The clearing reeked of death.

He stumbled out of the grass and walked towards a large pit, a sinkhole that led down into the earth. The stench grew worse... He peered over the edge of the chasm.

White plastic bundles littered the pit's floor. He had seen men loading them on trucks the day before. He knew what was wrapped in the translucent sheets.

He heard a buzzing rise up from the pit. A fly settled on his arm. He blinked and realized the air was full of gnats and flies. They were all around him.

He heard the men shouting... they were moving closer. They would find him any minute now. The grass rustled behind him.

Buri took a deep breath and scrambled down into the pit. The stench was overpowering, but he forced himself not to gag. He lay down and heaved one of the plastic bags over his body. He could feel the stiff corpse shifting and sliding inside the plastic. He closed his eyes. Reaching up, he pinched his nose closed.

He prayed.

Footsteps circled around the pit. He heard low voices, muffled through the plastic.

'You sure he came this way?' one man said.

'How should I know? He can't have gone far, he's just a kid.'

Buri kept his eyes closed tight. He swallowed the bile that rose in his throat.

Finally, the footsteps moved away from the pit.

'Fuck it. We'll send patrols down the road. He'll turn up. Let's get the hell out of here. This place reeks!'

The men left.

Buri waited. When he was certain he was alone, he scrambled out of the pit. He fell to the ground and retched, spilling his guts onto the dirt.

He wiped his mouth clean. Then he glanced around to be sure it was safe and darted back into the brush. He knew the men would return, eventually. They would dump more of the plastic bundles into the pit.

Galloway had told him to leave, to get as far away as he could. But his mother was still in the camp. He had promised his father he would look after his mother, no matter what.

He could not leave yet.

12

Caine wiped sweat from his brow and stared out the taxi's open window. The sun-blasted landscape along the endless road shimmered with a white-hot glare. The AC in the battered yellow Toyota wheezed and rattled. The temperature outside was already in the triple digits. A hot breeze blasted through the open window like a furnace and did little to cool the interior of the tiny vehicle.

The driver was a middle-aged man with tan, leathery skin and scattered tufts of gray hair. He seemed unaffected by the blistering heat. He wore a loose white robe that billowed around his arms in the wind. From time to time, he sang along with the Arabic disco music playing over the vehicle's tinny speakers, his head nodded to the bouncing, rhythmic beat of the tambourines and darbuka drums.

Caine checked the steel diving watch that was fastened to his wrist by a NATO strap. There were still a few hours to go until late afternoon, when the temperature would hit its peak of 105 degrees. Then it would drop into the mid-nineties once the sun settled beneath the horizon.

Caine wore a pale-blue linen shirt, khaki jeans, and suede desert boots. The clothing was as thin and light as he could find, but it was still damp and stained with sweat. After agreeing to help Rebecca, DuBose had arranged for him to catch a late-night charter into Cuba. Once there, he'd booked a non-stop flight to Egypt, and after a six-hour layover in Cairo, he'd finally landed at Khartoum International Airport.

He'd traveled light, with only a battered leather duffel bag as a carry-on. His passport was a competent forgery provided by DuBose's contacts in Cuba. It identified him as Sam Fulton, a Canadian citizen with a visa to enter Sudan.

Aside from the aluminum tactical pen in his chest pocket, he was unarmed, with no weapons of any kind in his bag. DuBose had left the pen behind at the warehouse, and Caine picked it up before he departed. It wasn't much as far as weapons went, but it could be useful as a force multiplier for stabbing and bludgeoning attacks. Its rigid metal body hid a few other useful features as well. For now, it was better than nothing.

Khartoum was the capital city of the largest Muslim country on the African continent. The CIA maintained a network of contacts and safe houses there, and could provide an operative in the country with weapons, equipment, and critical intel. But they would also report such assistance to their handlers in the US. Those reports would make their way back to Langley. This operation was off the books. Any such reports would implicate Rebecca.

He could not let that happen. So there would be no outside help. He was on his own.

The taxi drove past the Green Yard, a lush green field that served as a venue for concerts and sporting events. The driver ceased his humming and looked back at Caine. 'Allah ma'ak.

Luck is with you, my friend! The traffic is nothing. We should reach the city in twenty minutes.'

Caine smiled back and turned his attention to the rearview mirror. The driver was correct. Traffic was sparse, even though Africa Street was the only major paved road that led into the city. Normally, he would have requested the driver make several random stops and direction changes along the way. This surveillance detection routine, as it was known in the trade, would flush out any pursuers. It would force them to make obvious maneuvers that would reveal their presence.

But Sudan had achieved peace and stability in the war-torn region by exerting subtle and effective control over its citizens and visitors. Most of the popular tourist sites required special permits to visit. Photography was off-limits in many areas of the city. Caine knew that without the proper permits, he would seem suspicious if he asked the cab driver to make any sight-seeing stops along the way.

And then there was the NISS, Sudan's powerful national intelligence organization. They had saturated Khartoum with their operatives. The city was a den of spies, and for all Caine knew, his driver might belong to their ranks. He didn't want to attract that kind of attention. Not yet.

Instead, he sat back and let the scenery pass in silence. He glanced up to the rearview mirror at regular intervals, but he saw nothing that set off his inner radar.

They drove past Child City, an amusement park whose colorful rides and attractions hung lifeless beneath the stifling sun. Then, in the distance, Khartoum rose up from the dry, flat land. A mirage of heatwaves rippled around the city. The buildings on the outskirts were sparse and unremarkable – mostly apartment complexes, with a few office buildings and commercial plazas mixed in.

They entered the city proper. The apartment buildings gave way to stores and markets, parks and fountains. Caine shook his head and gave a low whistle. Even after all these years, he was still shocked by the peace and calm of the Northern capital. It was a far cry from the destruction and savagery he had witnessed in the newly independent South. It was hard to believe they had once been a single country.

They turned left onto Al Gamaa Avenue. 'Aedhami sidi. Excuse me, sir,' the driver called back to him. 'If you like, we take Nile Street to hotel, eh? There is more traffic, but the view...'

Caine nodded. 'Sure. Whatever you say.'

The driver made a quick right turn just before the domed edifice of the Republic Palace. Then they darted down a long, narrow street. He made what Caine was certain was an illegal U-turn, and they headed west along the banks of one of the most famous rivers in the world... the Blue Nile.

'Some say the name Khartoum means a place of meeting,' the driver croaked. His voice was raspy from the heat and dust of the road. 'It is here that the Blue Nile and the White Nile Rivers meet, at the Tuti Bridge. Not far from your hotel, in fact.'

Caine looked out over the vast expanse of water. The river was huge, and true to its name, the blue ribbon glowed with a sapphire brilliance. Gold highlights from the afternoon sun flecked the water's surface. He imagined history unfolding alongside the river's curves. Centuries born aloft in its undulating currents, stretching back to the dawn of civilization. Empires had sprung up along its banks and fallen beneath its silted depths.

As they neared the hotel, Caine shouldered his bag. 'Drop me off at the corner here. I'd like to walk the rest of the way.'

'Sir, are you sure? The heat is—'

'It should be cooling off a bit soon. Besides, this is the Nile. I'd like to take my time, if you know what I mean.'

The driver gave him a knowing smile. 'Of course, sir. Please remember, the intersection of the rivers is a sacred place. No photographs allowed.'

'I understand.' He looked once again over the sun-dappled water. The spires and domes of ancient mosques and temples dotted the river's far bank, silhouetted against the sinking sun.

'You can't capture something like this in a picture, anyway,' he said. 'Not really.'

The cab driver nodded as he pulled to a stop. 'No,' he agreed. 'You cannot.'

Caine handed the driver a few crisp bills, then exited the vehicle. He watched as the cab sped off down the dusty street. Then he hefted his bag, crossed the street, and disappeared down a dark alley.

* * *

Caine wandered through the Nile shopping district for thirty minutes before reaching his hotel. He made a few stops along the way, ordering a cup of mint tea from a tiny cafe, and pretending to admire the colorful woven rugs hanging outside a nearby shop. Once he was satisfied that he had not picked up a tail, he made his way back to Nile Street and the Corinthia Hotel. The shimmering white and blue structure was easy to find. At seventy-seven meters, the towering edifice of white and blue glass was one of the tallest buildings in Khartoum.

Like the Burj Al Arab in Dubai, the curved structure of the world-famous hotel was designed to resemble a billowing sail. Financed by the Libyan Government, the luxurious hotel had earned the nickname Gaddafi's Egg. Locals often used a more lewd phrase to describe it, comparing the building's bulbous shape to the infamous dictator's reproductive organs.

Despite the flow of oil from the South, and heavy Chinese investment in the city's infrastructure, the majority of Khartoum's residents lived in poverty. Caine could only imagine that to most of the city, the hotel must have seemed like an opulent monolith, a symbol of decadent luxury, forever out of reach.

Caine's room was on the fourteenth floor. He glanced left and right before exiting the elevator. The curved corridor that ran alongside a large panoramic window was quiet and empty. He followed it to his room. Swiping the key card over the lock, he opened the door with his leg, keeping his body to the right of the entrance.

His precautions stemmed years of training and habit. Normally, he would never stay in a hotel where he had a reservation. Such things were a simple matter to track. He saw no reason to give potential enemies advance notice of his location. But in this case, he wanted to be found.

The room was spacious, clean and cool. The tile floor gleamed with a polished sheen. Beams of late afternoon sunlight danced between the long, pristine white curtains. Stepping past a carved wood screen that separated the king-sized bed from a small sitting area, Caine made his way to the towering window. He brushed the curtains aside and allowed himself a quick glimpse of the stunning view.

Khartoum, in all its ancient glory, spread out before him beneath a cinnamon-brown haze of dust and sand. From this high up, the city appeared as a tapestry of stone and rock, metal and glass. It was bordered along the edges by the sapphire threads of the two Niles, joined by a pair of ivory-white bridges.

He drew the thick blackout curtains closed, cloaking the room in shadows. Reaching into his bag, he pulled out a small roll of electrical tape and tore off a piece. He covered the peep-hole in the door and wedged a carved wood chair under the doorknob.

After a scalding hot shower, and a room-service meal of beef stew and flatbread, Caine changed into a clean T-shirt and jeans. He sat on his bed, staring at a small satellite phone he held in his hand. For a moment, he hesitated.

Then he dialed a number from memory.

The phone rang several times. It's been years, he thought. What are the odds the number is still active?

A young man's voice answered the phone. 'Marhba?'

'I want to book a tour,' Caine said, his voice a low growl. 'The ruins at Jebel Barkal.'

The line was silent for a few seconds. Caine heard a distant hum, a faint clicking. He wondered if someone was listening in, but there was no way to know for sure.

Finally, the man on the other end grunted and answered. 'Jebel Barkal is far to the north. Do you have a permit to travel outside the city?'

'Sorry, I didn't know I needed one. Perhaps it would be wiser to stay nearby. What do you think of Al Kabir Masjid?'

Again, the hum filled the silence on the line.

'There are many beautiful mosques within the city, ten times more than one man could count. If you leave your number, my employer will call you back with his recommendations.'

Caine gave the man his cell number and hung up.

He took a deep breath, then tossed the phone on the bed. He did not recognize the voice on the other end of the line, but the man had given the correct responses to the code. The request to visit the Jebel Barkal ruins established his identity. His mention of the Al Kabir mosque signaled that he was not speaking under duress. The line 'ten times more than one man can count' meant that whoever was on the other end of the call would verify Caine's responses. If everything checked out, he would pass along the message.

The code was one he and Jack Tyler had used before, the last time they had worked in the city. The Puff Adder mission...

Hard to believe, Caine thought. Old Khairi is still in business, after all these years.

He assumed it would take the man some time to reach his boss and verify Caine's identity. While he waited, he stripped off his shirt and began a series of exercises on the cool, hard floor. Crunches, then push-ups, first with both arms, then one at a time. Then a series of reverse rows, hanging from his fingertips under the room's desk.

His breath became ragged and his body glistened with sweat. An electronic buzz sounded from the phone on the rumpled bed. He stood up and took a long sip of water from the bottle on the night table. Then he picked up the phone and looked at the screen. The number calling him was listed as 'unknown.'

He tapped the screen and accepted the call.

'Hello.'

'Marhba. Hello, old friend. It's been a long time.' The voice on the other end was scratchier, more raw than he remembered. But the rich, bass timbre of the man's speech was familiar.

'Is that what we are?' Caine asked. 'Old friends?'

'Well, perhaps not friends, but certainly not enemies. Not unless you know something I do not. I must admit, I am surprised to hear you call. I did not think you were assigned to—'

'I'm not here on an assignment, Khairi. Not officially, anyway.'

The man sucked in his breath as if unsure how to proceed. 'Of that, I am sure, given recent events. But why are you—'

'I need your help. Some information. Nothing your government would have a problem with. But I need to keep this quiet for now. Just you and me. Can you do that?'

Khairi exhaled slowly, as if puffing on a cigar. 'My answer to that depends. What is this information you seek?'

Caine paused. He knew he should ask about Galloway, but he was not sure yet how far he could trust his old contact. Admitting a CIA asset was operating in the country without the Sudanese government's knowledge might be a bridge too far.

'I'm looking for a woman, a doctor. Her name is Nena Vasani.'

'This woman, she is a citizen of Sudan?' Khairi asked, a guarded tone creeping into his voice.

'I swear to you, I mean her no harm. I just want to talk to her.'

'Very well. I will see what I can do.'

'There's something else.'

'*Na'am, 'ala almudiy quduman*? Yes, go on?'

'Puff Adder. I need anything you have on him. Last sightings, who he's been working with, current whereabouts.'

The voice was quiet for a long time. 'I told myself he must be dead by now. But I never knew for sure. Just salat... a prayer.'

Caine closed his eyes. For a split second, he saw the girl's face in the darkness, the whites of her eyes pleading, begging, staring wide at him...

His eyes snapped open. He realized his breath had quickened, his heart was racing. He forced himself to calm down.

'Maybe,' he said. 'But I don't think so. I think he's alive.'

The man sighed. 'This will take some time. Be underneath the Tuti Bridge early tomorrow morning, by the boats. My man will meet you there.'

'I said this was just between you and me.'

'He will bring you to me. Trust me, it is safer this way. For both of us. Be there at eleven.'

'I thought you said early?'

The voice on the other end of the line chuckled. 'I'm an old man, Thomas. For me, that is early.' Again there was a brief hiss of silence. 'Besides,' he added, his voice weak and tired, 'I very much doubt either of us will be getting much sleep tonight. To speak of that man is to invite nightmares... Shaitan jinn.'

'Tomorrow,' Caine said. 'I'll be there.'

He hung up the phone.

He lay down on the bed and stared at the ceiling. Khairi Abboud. The old spymaster had helped Caine on his operation in Sudan, years before. Could he trust him now?

You'll find out tomorrow. Get what you need and move on. The cold logic comforted him. But still, his mind was restless.

Khairi had spoken of nightmares, and the shaitan jinn. In the Islamic faith, the name roughly translated to 'evil forces.' The Christian equivalent would be 'demons.'

Caine stared at the ceiling until sleep made his eyes heavy and he succumbed to the numbing darkness. When the nightmares finally came, he did not dream of demons, or evil spirits.

He dreamt of her... Wide, frightened eyes, clawing fingers. He tossed and turned to her screams of pain in the sweltering darkness.

13

'I'll need to see some identification, ma'am.'

Rebecca looked up at the muscular, imposing man blocking the hotel room doors. Crew cut, cheap suit, sunglasses... Standard-issue FBI.

'Not exactly playing it subtle, are we?' she asked as she fished her leather ID case from her purse.

The man took the case and flipped it open. He examined her picture, then peered at her over the rims of his wraparound sunglasses. 'I'm not sure what you mean, ma'am,' he said in a monotone voice.

'No,' she muttered to herself. 'I'm sure you don't.' She heard Clayton DuBose snort and chided herself.

'Sorry, missed my morning latte,' she said, smiling at the agent. 'I do appreciate your thoroughness. Good WITSEC.'

The man in the rumpled gray suit handed her badge back and tilted his head to the mic clipped at his lapel. 'I have a Freeling, Rebecca. Requesting access to the witness, over?'

The agent's walkie squawked back to life, and a woman's

voice answered his inquiry. 'Rebecca Freeling? That's the D/NCS. She's cleared. On my way.'

The FBI agent handed her badge back to her and glanced at Clayton. He frowned. 'Your security detail will have to wait outside, ma'am.'

DuBose took a step forward. He glared down at the man and crossed his arms. 'You might want to check that again,' he snarled.

Rebecca put her hand on Clayton's arm and smiled. 'Clayton, I'll be—'

The double doors behind the agent swung open, cutting Rebecca off. Standing behind the doors was a petite, athletic-looking woman wearing a charcoal business suit. Her eyes darted back and forth behind a pair of slim rectangular glasses. A thick wave of brown hair was piled atop her head in a messy bun. Her nails were cut short, and she wore no polish.

'Director Freeling? Welcome to the Royal Suite.' She glanced at Clayton. 'I'm sorry, we weren't informed you were bringing a friend.'

Rebecca moved past the guard and held out her hand. 'This is Clayton DuBose, from Security Operations. He was assigned to me after I was attacked. We believe the people responsible may seek to harm your star witness, miss...?'

The woman blinked, then held out her hand. 'Zavala. Special Agent Zavala.'

As Rebecca shook her hand, she noticed the woman's eyes were two different colors. One was blue, and the other was a light hazel brown.

The woman nodded and gestured into the suite. 'All right, I'll get him clearance. After you, Director.'

Rebecca entered the large, tiled foyer of the Four Seasons

Georgetown's Royal Suite. The suite occupied the top floor of the dark brick building. The hotel's grounds were quiet and secluded, nestled among the historic buildings of old Georgetown.

A gold sculpture stood on a lacquered black podium in the center of the larger foyer. Rebecca looked up and saw sparkling pinpoints of light twinkling above her, Swarovski crystals set into the ceiling. The tiny gems reflected the overhead lights like a galaxy of shimmering stars.

Clayton followed her inside the opulent foyer. Rebecca turned her attention back to the woman.

'Since I'm just an observer, why don't we keep things on a first name basis. Please, call me Rebecca.'

The woman nodded. 'Fine by me. I'm Alejandra, but everyone calls me Ajay. Now, first things first, Rebecca.' Zavala gestured to a pair of agents wearing blue FBI windbreakers standing in the corner of the foyer.

Rebecca nodded and handed one of the men her purse. As he searched the voluminous Hermès bag, the other man swept her with a metal detector wand. It clicked and beeped, but the man seemed satisfied with the results.

When the man finished with Rebecca, he turned to Clayton. DuBose slipped a Glock 22 pistol from his waistband and handed it to the agent. He raised his hands over his head and allowed the man to continue. The detector warbled and chirped as it approached the hem of his right leg.

Clayton reached down and slid a tiny Ruger LCR revolver from an ankle holster.

'Backup gun,' he said with a grin. 'Forgot it was there.'

Zavala's eyes darted up and down his body, as if scanning him for more weaponry. 'Sorry, no armed guests allowed past this point. Robbins, be a lamb and get him a receipt.'

One of the FBI agents scribbled some notes on a small pad. He tore off the top sheet and handed it to Clayton.

'We'll hold them for you up here, Mr. DuBose.'

Clayton took the slip of paper. Zavala led them into a luxurious living room decorated in rich brown and cream furniture. The curtains were closed and the room was dim, lit only by a small table lamp in the corner.

Three more FBI agents sipped coffee and spoke in hushed tones. As they entered the room, Rebecca caught them staring at her. She returned their gaze. They broke eye contact and filed out of the room.

'Zavala... is that Russian?' Clayton asked, watching the men scurry out the door.

The woman laughed. 'Strike one, big guy. My father was Mexican, and my mother was from Argentina. I'm 100 percent Latina.'

Once they had the room to themselves, Rebecca glanced at DuBose, then took a deep breath. She came to a stop and turned to the woman. 'Alejandra... Ajay... I'm getting the distinct impression I'm not wanted here.'

Zavala cocked her head and removed her glasses. 'What gave you—'

Rebecca shook her head. 'Let's not waste each other's time. I get it, it's a jurisdictional thing. I pissed in the FBI's pool, and you guys don't like it.'

Zavala chuckled and sat down on a leather ottoman. She rested her chin on her hand and glanced back and forth between Rebecca and DuBose.

'Yeah, that's one way to put it.'

'And how would you put it?' Rebecca asked.

The special agent cocked her head. 'You ran an illegal CIA paramilitary operation on US soil. You stormed a farmhouse belonging to a US citizen. And you shot and killed several other US citizens in the process of executing this operation.' She arched an eyebrow and gave them a crooked smile. 'So, yeah. The FBI does get a little pissy about that stuff.'

Rebecca nodded. 'That's what I thought. But right now we—'

Zavala raised her hand. 'Not finished. According to the report, this operation also saved the life of a six-year-old girl. A Chinese national, who was being held against her will by the asshole in the other room. She was leverage, right? To blackmail a foreign agent?'

Rebecca brushed back a strand of crimson hair from her face. 'Yes. That's all true.'

'You got kids, Rebecca?' the other woman asked.

'No. I don't.'

'Married?'

'Not even dating. You?'

Zavala looked down and nodded. 'Divorced. I shouldn't say this, but as far as I'm concerned, some things... they go beyond jurisdiction. Know what I mean?'

'Yes, I do. So, are we good?'

The special agent flicked a spec of lint off her gray pants and nodded. 'Yeah, we're good. Just the same old inter-agency crap.' She checked her watch. 'In a few hours, these hearings will be over anyway. Our friend, Mr. Lapinski, will be remanded to the US Marshals for witness protection. And then we'll be out of each other's hair.'

'I've been asked to review your security protocols and the transportation plan,' Rebecca said. 'It's just a formality. I'm sure you have everything under control.'

Zavala squinted at DuBose, then looked back at Rebecca. 'Let me get this straight. You're the director of the National Clandestine Service, you oversee the Special Operations Group.

Bunch of ex-Navy SEALs, Green Berets, and other professional badasses. And whoever is after this guy has your agency so spooked they assigned you a personal bodyguard?'

Rebecca looked the woman in the eye. 'I wasn't always in this chair.'

Zavala stood and rested her hands on her hips. 'Okay then. Let's get started. We can go over our route, personnel, security precautions. I'd welcome any input you might have.'

'I'd appreciate that. But before we get started, could I ask a favor?'

'Shoot.'

'I'd like a word with Lapinski. Alone.'

The special agent closed one eye and stroked her chin. 'That's not exactly standard procedure.'

Rebecca smiled. 'Not even remotely.'

* * *

As soon as the gilded door shut behind her, Rebecca's nose wrinkled in disgust. The cavernous bedroom stank of body odor and grease. As her eyes adjusted to the dim light, she saw platters of half-eaten food scattered throughout the room. The plates covered the dresser, the nightstand... They were even tossed among the luxurious ivory sheets and gold silk pillows of the king-sized bed.

The room's air conditioner was set to full blast, yet even the constant jet of cold air could not cleanse the room of a stuffy, lingering miasma.

'Ted?' Rebecca called out. The bed sheets shifted and moved. A plate of limp French fries tumbled to the floor, sending splatters of ketchup across the cream carpet.

Ted Lapinski sat up in the bed. His skin was pale, and his

round cherubic face had turned pale and gaunt. Despite the massive quantity of food in the room, he appeared to have lost weight.

'Director Freeling. Hey, this is quite a send-off. Sorry about the mess. Didn't expect visitors.'

His voice was a flat, lifeless monotone. When Ted had been a director in the NSA's Tailored Operations Cyberwarfare unit, Rebecca had accused him of acting more like a used car salesman than a high-level intelligence operative. But now, she had to admit, she missed that touch of cocky bravado in his voice.

Don't, she warned herself. Do not underestimate this man. Lapinski hired private mercenaries to drug and kidnap you. He used an innocent child to blackmail a Chinese assassin. He forced them to execute compromised intelligence assets. And he tried to kill Sean Tyler, a CIA officer's son.

All that was true, but on some level, she knew Lapinski was a victim as well. She remembered the raid at the farmhouse, the look of sheer terror in his eyes when he realized that he was a loose end. Armed men had already tried to erase him and everyone he had been in contact with.

The question was why? What did he know? And who was pulling his strings?

'Christ, Ted, you look awful.' She looked around the room. 'Nice digs, though. Sure beats that farmhouse you holed up in. Bit rustic for my tastes.'

Ted stood up and stretched. He wore a white T-shirt, stained at the armpits, and loose boxers. He plodded a few steps forward and picked up a pair of navy-blue dress pants that lay in a crumpled heap on the floor. He struggled to keep his balance as he slid into the trousers, one leg at a time.

He gave the room a quick, cursory glance. 'Still a cage, Rebecca. Just nicer scenery behind the bars.'

He sat down on the bed. Rebecca moved closer, glaring at him. 'It's a five-star hotel, Ted. If I had my way, you'd be in a dark hole halfway across the world. Show a little gratitude.'

Ted looked up at her and chuckled. 'Gratitude? You know why they picked this place?' He gestured towards the curtains. 'It's the windows. This is one of the few suites in DC that has bulletproof glass in the windows.' He shook his head. 'Funny, I always thought that would be a common amenity here in our great nation's capital.'

'Ted, we don't have much time. In five minutes, the FBI is going to come through the doors. After that, this thing moves on rails. Senate Intelligence Committee, your testimony, witness relocation. Then, a few weeks of enhanced security. After that you're on your own.'

Ted rolled his head left and right until the bones in his neck and shoulders popped. 'You still don't get it, do you, Rebecca?'

'The US Marshals can't watch your back forever. Let me help—'

Lapinski ran his fingers through his hair. 'No, you're being way too optimistic. You actually think they're going to let me testify?'

'Who, Ted? Who is they?' Rebecca asked. 'This is your last chance. Help me! Whoever it is that wants you dead, I want to find them. The FBI is just going to play this by the books.'

'You realize any information I give you could jeopardize my immunity?'

'You just said you're worried you won't live long enough to testify. I think immunity from prosecution is the least of your concerns.'

Rebecca eyed a half-eaten club sandwich sitting on a brown tufted chair. 'That's why you're ordering all this food, isn't it?'

He hung his head. 'Couldn't decide what I wanted. Last meal, you know? Wanted it to be good.'

A loud knock thudded on the door. 'Mr. Lapinski,' AJ's voice called out from the other side. 'Ten-minute warning.'

'That's my cue.' Rebecca spun her chair around and approached the door. 'Guess you can take your chances with the US Marshals.'

'Wait!' Lapinski called after her. His voice sounded hesitant.

Rebecca paused.

Lapinski's face was calm, devoid of emotion. He stared at her for a few seconds. His pale blue eyes looked lost and confused.

'Rebecca, I just... I want you to know, I'm sorry. I'm sorry for what Bernatto did to you. For what I did to you. I always respected you, and I... I never thought...'

'I don't need your apology, Ted. I need intel. I need to find these people and stop them. If you can't help me with that... then go to hell.'

She started to turn around again, but Ted's voice stopped her.

'I know you don't believe me, but I swear, I don't know who it is. I never knew. I turned over all my information to the FBI. The texts, emails, all of it. These people were careful. There's not enough information in the file to identify them. Maybe if you can find someone else, someone like me, someone they were blackmailing, then you can corroborate, cross-reference the intel.'

'Someone like the DNI? John Blayne?'

Ted nodded. 'I can't prove it, but he must have been involved. Like I told Caine.'

Rebecca nodded. 'John Blayne is... He's missing.'

Ted swallowed. 'Yeah. I figured. The only other thing I can tell you is, this person, whoever they are, they had me use my position to access personnel files. They wanted data on potential assets. There was a file they sent me with a code name... Puff Adder. I did some digging on my own. Puff Adder was a South Sudanese rebel fighter named Simon Takuba. He was part of a black op Bernatto ran, back before he became the D/NCS. It was off-books. I think Caine may have been involved.'

Rebecca squinted at him in the dim light. 'Puff Adder? What was the op?'

Ted shrugged. 'No idea. I'm only telling you this because there was a deadline on the intel they needed.' He glanced at his watch. 'And that deadline runs out in about three days.'

Rebecca bit her lip and looked down at the spilled food on the floor. South Sudan, she thought. Josh's mission... It can't be a coincidence.

Ted's voice pulled her from her dark thoughts. 'That's all I can say. According to the terms of my immunity deal, I can only testify to the members of the committee. They want to cover their asses first, in case anything blows back on them.'

She looked up. 'What about Delta Blue? Private military company, headquarters is in Louisiana.'

'I'm sorry, Rebecca. I really am. But I can't say anything more.'

'Dammit, Ted, these people are trying to kill you. They may have already killed the DNI!'

Ted gave her a sad smile. 'I know. But until that happens... I need to have something to live for.'

14

The Tuti Bridge was within walking distance of the Corinthia Hotel. After a light breakfast of honey-drizzled yoghurt, sliced mangos and black coffee, Caine made his way outside. He crossed Nile Street, heading for the banks of the Blue Nile River.

A thick green canopy of trees hung over the noisy, traffic-filled street. Sparse eddies of sand and dust, blown in by the warm night winds, covered the pavement. A few local merchants camped out along either side of the street near the hotel. They called out in Arabic to pedestrians on the sidewalk and the slow-moving traffic that passed by.

Caine continued walking towards a suspension bridge at the end of Gamma Avenue. Two lengths of thick yellow steel cable hung from a pair of concrete support towers. They held the long, curved bridge aloft over the dark waters of the Blue Nile. The bridge had been completed in 2008 and carried traffic over the river to Tuti Island itself. It wasn't necessary to take a ferry to the small farming community on the island, but Caine knew his contact had other plans.

He stepped off the street and walked down a steep dirt

embankment to the riverbank below. A few small boats and rafts sat beached at the water's edge, their bows nestled against the dark soil of the bank.

Caine paused and examined the crowd with a wary gaze. He did not know who Khairi might have sent, nor did he know if other interested parties were present. The NISS had a reputation for ruthless efficiency. Even if Khairi proved trustworthy, Caine could not rule out his handlers acting on their own. They could have sent secondary assets to monitor the meeting.

As Caine stood alone on the riverbank, several young men lounging in their boats sat up and took notice. They walked over to him, smiling, gesturing to their rickety boats. They spoke to him in broken English. 'River cruise, sir? Picnic on Tuti Island, number one tourist spot, only 100 SDG!'

'La, utrukhu wahdahu,' a deep voice behind him shouted. 'This man is with me. I will take him to the island.'

Caine turned and saw a tall man approaching him from the riverbank. He was powerfully built, and a thin film of sweat gave his skin a sheen in the morning sun. His features looked Arabic, but his skin was almost jet-black. He wore a loose-fitting shirt with long, flowing sleeves, paired with white cotton trousers. A white skullcap covered his shaved head.

'Sabah alkhayr. Good morning, Mr. Caine. Khairi sent me. My name is Chriz.' He shook Caine's hand, then guided him towards a boat parked a few yards downriver from the others. 'These men are like wild dogs, fighting for scraps. One cannot blame them. With the bridge, fewer people choose to reach the island the old way.'

'The old way is fine by me,' Caine said, grabbing Chriz's hand and stepping into the tiny wooden boat. A canopy of woven sticks formed an awning above the small craft, blocking the intense sun. Caine sat on a bench at the stern. A light breeze blew across the water's surface, cooling the air. It carried the smell of the river through the boat, an earthy scent of reeds, peat, and fresh-cut grass.

Chriz picked up a long, narrow pole and pushed the boat away from the shore. Within minutes, they were bobbing in the current of the Blue Nile River. The craft's tiny outboard motor buzzed like a tin can full of angry bees. Soon, the steep, cliff-like edge of the flat, crescent-shaped island rose from the water ahead.

Chriz docked his boat at a small pier on the west side of the island. A tiny three-wheeled tuk-tuk waited there, and after a brief bout of haggling in Arabic, Chriz gestured for Caine to get in.

'He will take you to Khairi. I will wait here for your return. Enjoy your meal.'

Caine nodded and got into the tuk-tuk. The tiny vehicle lurched forward, then puttered down a rocky, uneven dirt road. The rough, winding path took them past long stretches of green farmland. Dozens of men worked in the fields. Their long, flowing robes glowed white in the sun, standing out amidst the verdant crops and earthy-brown rows of tilled soil. Emaciated donkeys and camels ambled past them, pulling carts piled high with bundled vegetables, fruit, and dried fish.

A few minutes later, the tuk-tuk slowed to a stop outside a small brick farmhouse, nestled under the shade of a palm tree grove. As Caine stepped out of the tiny vehicle, a middle-aged woman, her skin dark and wrinkled, approached him from the house. Her hair was covered with a pink hijab scarf, and a long linen dress wrapped around her body. She shuffled towards him with short, measured steps.

She smiled and took his arm, guiding him towards the

house. '*Min fadlika, bihadhihi al-tariqah.* Please, this way. We are honored to receive a guest of Khairi Abboud.'

Caine glanced around the property, looking for any signs of ambushers in the trees or fields. Nothing caught his eye. The building was low and flat, surrounded by rows of sweet-smelling herb gardens. It was constructed of tan clay bricks. Rows of colorful handmade pottery lined a series of crooked wooden shelves along the eastern wall.

The woman continued to smile and nod as she led him around the back of the house. There, he found a red and white striped cloth strung up like an awning, providing shade to a small wooden table and a pair of benches.

Sitting on one of the benches was a short, stocky man dressed in a cream linen suit. A shock of thick white hair swept back from his tan, lined forehead. His eyes were dark, warm, and sunken, perched above a powerful, hawkish nose. The man's bushy white mustache curled up as he smiled.

'*Assalamu alaikum.* Welcome, my friend! Thomas Caine, peace be upon you.' The man's voice boomed through the quiet, peaceful farmland surrounding them.

'*Wa'alaykum salaam*,' Caine replied, the traditional response to the greeting. 'Peace be upon you as well, Khairi Abboud.'

Caine sat down in the shade, across from Khairi, and examined the man's lined face. 'You look good. Taking care of yourself, I see.'

'Bah.' The old man frowned and sipped coffee from a small, cracked china cup. 'I am old and fat, and I do not need my vanity flattered. At least not from you.' He licked his lips as he set the cup down, then peered at Caine with dark, probing eyes.

'But you, my friend, I am pleased to say you look quite lively for a corpse. My man did some digging to verify your identity.

According to reports issued by your agency, you are a shab... a ghost. They say you went rogue in Afghanistan.'

Caine stared back at him, his emerald eyes reflecting the harsh sun beyond the awning. 'Don't believe everything you read. I was set up.'

Khairi nodded. 'Let me guess... Bernatto?'

'How did you know?'

The big man smiled, but his eyes looked tired and sad. 'You do not work in Sudan for as long as I without learning how to spot a snake in the grass.'

The woman returned and set down plates and silverware in front of Caine. She poured coffee from a long-necked metal pot. The aromas of ginger and cinnamon wafted from the cup. Caine took a sip and smiled at the woman. 'Ladhid. Delicious.'

She scurried back into the house. A robed man walked out carrying a wooden serving platter. Plates of steaming food covered the tray.

'Speaking of snakes,' Caine said, after taking another sip of the spiced coffee. 'What about the information I asked for? Puff Adder... Did you find anything?'

Khairi nodded. 'Yes, of course. But this family has spent all morning preparing this meal for us. First we eat. Then we talk business. Mutafaq?'

Caine nodded. 'Agreed.'

The man in the robe set various dishes down on the table. They began their meal by dipping wedges of warm flatbread into a bowl of ful medames. The mash of fava beans, tomatoes, and onion was garnished with herbs and a spritz of lemon.

'This family had a son,' Khairi said, in between mouthfuls of the delicious food. 'He worked for me, some years ago, before I retired. He passed away, working undercover in Iraq. I promised him I would take care of his family. So every year I buy them a cow, a sheep, some chickens. I contribute to the costs of their farm when I can. In return, they cook meals for me from time to time.'

He smacked his lips as the farmer set down a platter of grilled kofta. He speared one of the ground lamb sausages with his fork. 'Tuti Island provides most of the produce for all of Khartoum. You cannot find fresher food than this anywhere in the city.'

The kofta was served atop a thick, chunky sauce of zucchini, garlic, and parsley. Caine took a bite and felt the sting of red pepper on his lips. He washed down the cumin-spiced meat with a glass of water, then looked up at the old man.

'If you retired, why did you take my call? I was worried that code might have been deactivated by now.'

Khairi shrugged, then cut off another piece of meat. 'In our business, retirement is relative, no? When you called the old number, the agent who answered relayed your message to head-quarters. They called me. They asked me to meet with you. Find out what you want, what you are doing in Sudan.'

'And then report back?' Caine said.

Khairi nodded as he chewed. 'Of course. What did you expect? Relations between the US and Sudan may have normal-ized, but there are still procedures to follow. We provide your CIA with valuable intelligence in your never-ending war on terror. Your government is expected to alert us when an opera-tive of theirs is in our country. But don't worry. This report of mine, it may take some time to file. I must be thorough, after all.'

Caine could not help but smile. 'Thanks. You know, you don't sound so retired to me.'

They finished the small feast with a basboosa cake. The thin, golden dessert tasted of lemons and sweet rosewater syrup.

Caine took a few bites to be polite. He washed down the sugary confection with a generous helping of the warm coffee.

The woman returned and cleared their plates.

'Thank you, my dear,' Khairi said, bowing his head. 'May Allah bring fortune to you and your husband and place his blessing upon this farm.'

The woman bowed and mumbled something in Arabic. She finished clearing the table, then retired into the house, shutting the door behind her. Caine and Khairi were alone.

The old man lit a slim, pungent cigar, and leaned back in his chair.

'A lovely meal. What do you call it in America? This meeting of breakfast and lunch? It is brunch, yes?'

Caine set his hands on the table. 'Whatever it was, it was delicious. Thank you. But that's not why I'm here.'

Khairi nodded. Caine watched like a hawk as the older man reached down into a rumpled leather bag that leaned against his bench. He removed a manila folder and tossed it across the table to Caine. 'Puff Adder. Simon Takuba. The man is like you, a ghost. A ghost who has returned to life, in the South. He is still a rebel, fighting against the presidential forces there.'

Caine flipped open the file. Inside were pictures of a tall, shadowy figure. The man was a dark blur, moving through a corpse-strewn battlefield.

'He's still with the SPLM?' Caine asked as he examined the photographs.

Khairi shook his head. 'We don't think so. My sources tell me he had a falling out with the vice president. He left, along with many of his soldiers, and formed a new group. They are one of many rebel factions that have joined the killing in the South. It is chaos there, as you know. They call themselves the Army of the Chosen.'

Caine flipped a page in the file and found himself staring at a close-up portrait of an East African man. He was wearing a tattered, threadbare uniform. The jet-black skin of his face was streaked with dripping blood. His lips were curled in an angry snarl, revealing the single, gleaming diamond tooth. The picture was black and white, but Caine remembered the tooth's crimson glow.

The man's eyes were opened wide and his pupils seemed to have rolled back, leaving only the whites exposed. Caine's fingers clenched the folder in a death grip as he stared at the image of the screaming, blood-streaked madman.

It was him. Puff Adder, AKA Simon Takuba.

'So he is alive,' Caine muttered.

'Yes, although we don't know his exact whereabouts at this time. Perhaps, with a few more days...'

'We both know I don't have a few days,' Caine replied.

He flipped the page. The next picture was a woman wearing a white doctor's coat. She appeared to be working in a tented field hospital. Caine spotted UN markings on the cloth walls in the background.

'The doctor?' he asked.

'Yes, Doctor Nena Vasani. She is a graduate of the Afhad School of Medicine, in Omdurman. It is very prestigious, a private school for women only. She also studied abroad, in London. She could have left the country, opened a private practice. But instead, she manages a series of free clinics. Both here, and in South Sudan. She lives in a small apartment here, next to one of her clinics.'

Caine turned to the next picture. Doctor Vasani appeared to be in her late twenties. In the picture she was speaking at a convention of some kind. Like many in Sudan, her features were a combination of both East African and Arab descent. Her skin was the color of dark coffee, with a bronze, sun-kissed glow that suggested she spent a good deal of time outdoors. Her inky black hair was long and straight, and framed her face in two dark, flowing waves. Sharp cheekbones, and wide, cat-like eyes gave her face the appearance of an Egyptian statue.

'She travels into South Sudan alone? Isn't that illegal?' Caine asked.

Khairi grunted. 'Doctor Vasani was granted a permit to travel with an escort, a male nurse named Siddig. Anyone who travels south as much as she does is of course on NISS watch lists. But she has also spoken out against Sudan's actions in Darfur. She talked to reporters about what she saw there. And she accused the government of sponsoring violent Arab militia groups.'

Caine looked up from the picture. 'According to the UN, the lady has a point.'

Khairi raised his hands. 'Personally, I have never approved of our policies in that region. I only mention this so you understand, the woman has many enemies. I doubt my old employers would mind very much if she disappeared. To involve yourself with her could make your situation in Sudan... complicated.'

'Yeah, what else is new?' Caine muttered. He snapped the folder closed. 'May I keep this?'

'Of course. But I must ask... Why are you here? What on earth does this woman have to do with Takuba?'

Caine thought for a moment. 'Maybe nothing. She may be working with a friend of mine. Someone who needs my help.'

The old man squinted at him with one eye and rested his chin on his steepled fingers. 'I am confused. I thought you were here to kill this madman, Takuba. Or is it to help a friend?'

'It's hard to explain. Maybe a little bit of both.'

'So you wish to be both savior and destroyer? That is a difficult path, my friend.'

Caine took another sip of coffee. 'You're a good man, Khairi. Seems like your service could use you. Why did you quit?'

The old man stared past him, his dark eyes seeming to focus on the rows of crops in the distance. 'I suppose my heart was no longer in it. The things we must do, the sacrifices we must make... Perhaps it is like the path you seek to walk now. To kill in order to save. To do monstrous things, to work with monstrous men, like Takuba. You tell yourself it is for the greater good. You return home at night, to your family. You think to yourself, it is for them that you do these things. But one day you find yourself staring up at the ceiling, unable to sleep. You realize that those are lies. You do these things because it is the world itself that is monstrous. So you dance on the razor's edge, fighting to protect your tiny sliver of peace, while all around you is darkness. One step too far, one move in the wrong direction... and then the darkness has you. You become that which you fought. A monster.'

'How long till you file your report with the NISS?' Caine asked.

Khairi smiled. 'Well, this is a complicated matter. I think two days should suffice?'

'Thank you. I owe you one.'

The two men stood and Khairi held out his hand. 'Takuba... You are going to kill him, yes?'

Caine's green eyes blazed in the hot sun as he shook Khairi's hand. He said nothing. The old man nodded.

'Perhaps one less demon shall haunt my dreams. That will be payment enough. Allah be with you.'

Caine walked back to his taxi. He watched the farmhouse fade into the distance as they drove down the rocky dirt road. Khairi stood outside, waving. Soon, he was a tiny white dot, lost

among the vivid green palm trees and ancient stone buildings of
the island.

15

The motorized lift hummed as the platform raised Rebecca and her wheelchair into the passenger seat of the SUV. Once in place, Rebecca clicked on her seatbelt and pulled her cell phone from her purse.

There were no messages. She knew it was unlikely that Caine would make contact with the asset so quickly.

The asset... She caught herself using the standard agency jargon. You're talking about Josh Galloway.

A series of memories cascaded though her mind in rapid succession. Codas. Endings. A slow erosion of their intimacy.

The last time they had kissed. The last time they had made love. The last time they had spoken.

The argument, that fight...

'You're still hung up on him. Aren't you?' he had asked.

He didn't say the name, but of course she knew who he meant.

Caine.

No matter how hard she tried, she could not forget the feeling of panic those words invoked. It had felt as though she were trapped in a vacuum, the air sucked from her lungs. She wanted to say no... or even yes, anything, any answer would do, just to put an end to the question once and for all.

The next time she had seen Josh was in her office, when he turned in his transfer request. She approved it, and he returned to the field. Then there was the operation in Sudan.

And now he was missing.

Missing, presumed dead, she corrected herself.

Her driver entered the vehicle and slammed the door shut. Rebecca pulled her long hair into a thick ponytail and tied it off with an elastic band.

'Magpie One, I am in place, the director is secure, over,' the driver said into the mic of his walkie headset.

'Copy that, Magpie Two. Just wrapping things up with Special Agent Zavala. On my way. Out.'

The chatter of the walkie pushed the bittersweet memories from Rebecca's mind.

She focused her attention on a white Chevy Suburban SUV parked in front of them. To the left of the SUV, a team of four federal marshals emerged from the employee entrance of the Four Seasons hotel. They each wore armored vests under their blue windbreakers. Sandwiched between them was a pale, bedraggled-looking Ted Lapinski. He was wearing a rumpled navy suit, and his hair was a tangled mess, still wet from his shower. A Kevlar vest with FBI markings covered his blazer, adding to his disheveled appearance.

The men swept towards the SUV. Rebecca could see their eyes darting across the rooftops of the nearby buildings. They were checking for snipers.

'All clear!' the lead marshal shouted. They fanned out around Lapinski as the rear door of the Chevy swung open. Lapinski climbed into the vehicle. Even from a distance,

Rebecca could see the blank look of fear that hung across his gaunt features.

He sat down on the padded rear seats as the marshals piled in after him. He turned and looked back at her through the rear window. Her eyes met his. He nodded to her.

According to Zavala's briefing, the Chevy was modified by Streit USA, a company that specialized in armoring civilian vehicles. The white SUV was reinforced with twelve millimeters of B6 steel plating, bullet-resistant polymer windows, and Level 1 NATO floor plating. Small arms fire, up to and including most automatic rifles and grenades, would be useless against the heavily armored vehicle.

But the look in Ted's eyes... To Rebecca, he didn't look like a man about to testify at a Senate hearing.

He looks like a man being driven to his own execution, she thought.

The rear doors of the SUV opened and Clayton slid into the left passenger seat. Across from him, Alejandra Zavala entered and took a seat behind Rebecca.

'Director, I hope you don't mind,' she said. 'Mr. DuBose here told me you would be joining the convoy, so I figured I'd ride with you. Give us more time to chat.'

Rebecca turned her head and stared at her, masking her surprise. The FBI agent had traded her gray blazer for a fitted Kevlar vest. She wore a Glock 23 pistol in a holster at her side.

DuBose gave Rebecca a nervous glance. 'I told her it was up to you, Director Freeling.'

Rebecca raised an eyebrow, then smiled. 'Be my guest, Agent Zavala. This is your show.'

'Lapinski was turned over to the FBI for questioning, after your, um... operation,' Zavala said. 'But this convoy was organized by the Federal Marshal service. I'm just supervising the transfer.'

The special agent's walkie squawked to life. 'Package is secure, all convoys standing by. Over.'

She brought the radio to her lips. 'Affirmative. Standing by, you call it. Over.'

'Copy that.' The reply cut through the hiss of static. 'This is Mobile Command. All units... let's roll.'

A chorus of affirmatives crackled from the walkie's speaker. A pair of Washington DC Metro police motorcycles cruised into the parking lot. They took up the lead position in the convoy, and the line of vehicles exited the hotel grounds.

'And we're off,' Zavala said.

'What did he mean "all convoys"?' DuBose asked, glancing out the window as they drove southeast down Pennsylvania Avenue.

'Lapinski is a high-value witness. Based on your intel, we've pulled out all the stops when it comes to his security. The FBI rented three decoy suites in various hotels around the DC Metro area. And the marshals are running three identical convoys. All of them are heading to the Hart Senate Building, each taking a different route.'

'So how many people know where you were really holding Lapinski?' Rebecca asked.

'It's a short list. Myself, the marshals in this convoy, and my boss. Your director Paulis, probably, as well. And now you two, of course.'

Zavala stretched her arms over her head. A yawn escaped her lips. 'Lo siento. Sorry.' She gave DuBose a sheepish grin.

'We keeping you up, Agent Zavala?' he asked, smiling.

'No,' she groaned. 'I caught a red-eye flight last night from another operation.'

Rebecca stiffened. Something about the woman's behavior seemed contrived, as if it was a performance. She was probing, measuring their response.

DuBose and I took a red-eye as well, she thought. After the rendezvous in Florida...

DuBose didn't seem to catch on to the agent's veiled interrogation. 'They spreading you a little too thin, huh?' he asked.

'You could say that,' Zavala continued. 'I had to do cleanup on an operation of mine that went south. Rebecca, oddly enough, this one involves you as well. A rogue agent. The one who broke out of CIA custody in Virginia?'

Rebecca kept her eyes on the vehicles ahead of them. The convoy looped around the Washington traffic circle, heading south. To her left, she saw the bronze statue of George Washington mounting his horse at the battle of Princeton. To her right, a circular garden of fiery orange tulips waved in the breeze.

'Yes, Thomas Caine,' she replied. She glanced up at Zavala in the rearview mirror. The woman's two-toned eyes stared back at her.

'Quite a background on that one. Or rather, lack of background. There are so many black marks in his service record, I thought maybe the printer broke down.'

'I'm sorry, I can't comment on Mr. Caine's background, or operations he may or may not have been involved in.' Rebecca's voice was a flat, practiced monotone.

'Classified, right? Need to know. Sure, I get it. Look, I don't want to... how did you put it? Piss in your pool? But I was wondering... do you know if this Caine had any interest in the DNI?'

'Why do you ask?'

Zavala glanced toward DuBose. He averted his gaze and looked out the window. The vehicles exited the circle and motored onto 23rd Street. At each intersection, a pair of motor-cycle police roared by, their lights and sirens blazing. The police halted traffic, allowing the convoy to continue along its way without stopping.

'It's funny. We received an anonymous tip about this opera-tive of yours. We followed the intel and tracked Caine to Louisiana. Tailed him en route to the airport, but then he spooked. He must have spotted us. He changed his pattern, ended up in a shopping mall. We lost him there. He took out a few of my men. FBI SWAT, Hostage Rescue Team. They're the best of the best when it comes to our agents.'

Rebecca turned in her chair. 'Yes, I read your report. I was under the impression you had no casualties on that mission.'

Zavala pursed her lips, then nodded. 'That's true. Be a couple weeks before one of them is walking again, though.'

'I'm sorry, but I did advise your agency to let my people handle Caine. He's highly trained and extremely motivated.'

'He trusts you?'

Rebecca shrugged. 'He knows me. I don't think he trusts anyone.'

Zavala nodded and looked up for a second, as if mentally filing away this tidbit of information. 'I see. While we were there, we followed up on a crime scene report from the Sheriff's Department. Gunfire, bunch of explosions in the bayou near Honey Island. Two of the bodies were identified as mercenaries in the employ of a private military company, Delta Blue. Witnesses placed them with the DNI in New Orleans earlier the same day.'

Rebecca turned her head around to face the agent. 'What about Blayne? Was he there?'

Zavala shook her head. 'No sign of him. No body. And no

Caine. My agents on site said he must have had help. Someone got him out of Louisiana before we could close the net.'

DuBose glanced over at her. 'This is starting to sound a little unfriendly, Agent Zavala. What's your point, exactly?'

Zavala cocked her head and smiled at him. 'Just an observation. You two look as tired as I feel. And your eyes are pretty red for a guapo hombre like yourself. Want to borrow my eye drops?'

'Now wait a min—' DuBose began.

Rebecca cut him off. 'Agent Zavala, like I said, I can't comment on Caine's background or operations. But I can tell you this. If you think the DNI was murdered, and you're looking at Caine as a suspect, you're on the wrong track.'

Zavala's blue and brown eyes squinted. Rebecca knew she was a trained interrogator, and she could sense the woman trying to get into her head. She was sifting out the grains of truth hidden between her lies.

'How can you be so sure of that?' Zavala asked. 'According to what little information I could find, Caine's not exactly clean. He killed his partner and ruined a crucial anti-terrorist operation. Maybe Blayne hired Delta Blue as extra security. Maybe he knew Caine was coming after him for some reason.'

Rebecca exchanged a quick glance with DuBose. The man exhaled and shrugged.

She looked back at Zavala. 'You've got it wrong. Blayne, Lapinski, Caine's old handler, they're all linked together. The raid in Virginia, the helicopter attack... that was all part of it as well.'

'I heard the conspiracy theory. That's what Lapinski is testifying about in front of this Intelligence Committee. Little paranoid for my tastes,' Zavala said. 'But let's say you're right. How is Caine involved? He's not an active CIA operative, is he?'

Rebecca shook her head. 'No. He... he has his own reasons for seeing this through.'

Zavala thought for a moment. 'So in your opinion, this is personal. Revenge?'

'Yes. But not against the DNI. And I think it's more than just revenge.'

The convoy turned left and roared down Constitution Avenue. They were nearing their final destination, the Hart Senate Building. To their left, the ivory bricks and columns of the Smithsonian rose up above rows of marble steps. Off in the distance, the ivory spire of the Washington Monument thrust above the tree line.

'Enlighten me, Rebecca,' Zavala said. 'I trusted you with Lapinski. Now it's your turn. What the hell is going on here?'

'I believe... In his own way, he thinks he's protecting someone.'

Zavala cocked her head and thought for a moment. 'Wait, hold up. Did he go after Blayne to protect you?'

'I didn't say me...'

'You didn't have to.' Zavala smiled.

Suddenly, Zavala's walkie crackled to life. 'Mobile Command, this is Metro One, we have an obstruction ahead, over.'

The line of vehicles rolled to a stop. A jackknifed tractor trailer sat in the middle of the intersection. Traffic cops were waving cars to the north and south through side streets.

'Send civilian traffic south,' the reply hissed back. 'We'll divert to the alternate route and take Pennsylvania the rest of the way. Over.'

'I don't like this,' DuBose muttered. His hand dropped towards his shoulder holster.

'Hey, easy, big guy,' Zavala said. She rested a hand on his

arm. 'You two are just observers, remember? The marshals can handle it.'

Crack!

The retort was deafening, and unmistakable.

Gunfire.

Sparks flew from the engine block of Lapinski's SUV.

'Director, keep your head down!' DuBose shouted. He drew his pistol and scanned the street. Pedestrians screamed and ran from the congested intersection.

'Get us the hell out of here!' DuBose shouted at the driver. The man spun the wheel of their SUV, but the traffic diverting to either side of them cut off the exit streets.

Crack! Crack! Two more shots rang out.

Smoke billowed from the white SUV's front grill. Whoever was shooting at them, they were using a weapon powerful enough to penetrate the vehicle's armor plating.

Rebecca's driver leaned on the horn and pulled up next to the white SUV. He turned right, driving up onto the median of the road. Angry horns blared as he turned into the opposite lane and cut off the oncoming traffic.

'Mobile Command, I need a sitrep! What the hell is going on out there?' Zavala shouted into her walkie.

'We have shots fired, repeat, shots fired. They took out the engine, we are sitting ducks! We need backup, repeat, all decoy units, we need backup at Pennsylvania and—'

Before the man could finish his sentence, thunder roared through the air. The jackknifed trailer exploded, and a billowing cloud of fire engulfed the vehicles in the intersection.

16

According to Khairi's report, Doctor Vasani's clinic was located in Omdurman. The neighborhood was one of three urban districts that met at the conflux of the Niles. Together, they made up the greater capital of Khartoum. The address was east of Caine's hotel, across the White Nile.

As Caine's taxi crossed the Victory Bridge, they left the gleaming buildings of the prosperous Nile District behind. The streets grew darker, and potholes littered the cracked, broken pavement. Then the pavement disappeared altogether, replaced with dirt and rocks. Rows of crumbling brick houses and piles of debris lined the dark, narrow streets. Caine rolled down his window. The night air was hot and dry. He tasted dust and sand in the back of his throat.

He had the taxi drop him off a few blocks from his destination and took a long, meandering path to the address in the file. The streets bustled with activity despite the late hour. Taxis beeped and growled as they lurched through the intersection. Men haggled over slabs of lamb and beef hanging from hooks above tiny butcher's stalls. Steaming cups of coffee and tea were set out for patrons beneath the thatched awnings of the local cafes.

Caine stopped and bought a glass of hibiscus juice at one of the stands. The cool, velvety liquid soothed his dry throat as he examined the crowd. Then he made his way further down the street and cut though an alley. Above him, he could hear the sounds of running water and dishes clattering. Sitar music drifted from the speaker of a transistor radio sitting in an open window. The warbling notes echoed through the cramped space between the buildings.

The alley exited onto a dirt street. Sheets of laundry hung from the nearby buildings and fluttered in the hot breeze. A wooden barricade blocked off the center of the street. Behind the barricade, a massive pothole gaped in the pavement.

Caine remained hidden in the alley's shadows. He stared at the numbers on the building across the street. They matched the address in the file. This was Nena Vasani's clinic.

The clinic, and her adjoining apartment, were on the second floor. The ground floor housed a shoe store that appeared to be closed for the evening. A few pedestrians walked down both sides of the dark, confined street, but the crowd was sparse here. The buildings were quiet and uninviting.

Caine peered out from the darkness. He spotted a dark-skinned African man in a rumpled blue suit, pacing near the building's entrance. The man checked his watch, then pretended to examine the shoes in the window of the closed store. Caine watched as he moved on. Five minutes later, he crossed the street and circled back. Caine ducked into the shadows as the man walked past the alley.

He crossed to the other side of the street and continued loitering outside the clinic.

No way is this guy NISS, Caine thought. Khairi had

mentioned that Doctor Vasani was on a watchlist. But this man was clearly an amateur when it came to surveillance.

Twin headlights pierced the dusty air and illuminated the storefront. The man scurried off down the street. A battered pickup truck swerved around the barricade and pulled over in front of the store. The vehicle was crusted with dried mud. The windows were nearly opaque, covered by a thick film of dirt and grime.

He heard the thunk of the passenger door slamming closed. A slim, petite figure grabbed a pair of duffel bags from the truck bed. He heard a woman's voice speaking Arabic. There was some shared laughter, the woman and a man, the truck's driver. Then the vehicle pulled away, leaving a cloud of dust in its wake.

A woman dressed in olive-green cargo pants, a khaki shirt, and a floral-patterned hijab stood on the edge of the road. Her face was lit by the screen of her cell phone. Caine could not quite make out her features in the haze-filled air. She turned and walked down an alley next to the clinic.

It's got to be her, Caine thought. Khairi said she had clinics in the South. She must have just returned. And someone was waiting for her.

As she disappeared between the buildings, Caine saw the man in the blue suit reappear, followed by three more men wearing casual clothes. One of them, a tall, muscular man, wore a dark hoodie that hid his face. The men walked with a loose, confident gait. They glanced warily around the street as they crossed in front of the store. Then they turned and followed the woman's path down the alley.

Hired muscle, Caine thought. Possibly militia members from the South.

The man in blue had been the advance scout, lying in wait,

hiding in plain sight. Now the real predators had come out of the shadows to hunt.

Nena Vasani was their prey.

Caine stepped out of the alley. He checked the sparse crowd to make sure there were no other lookouts or attackers in their midst. No one paid any attention to him, or the men who had disappeared behind the clinic.

He turned to his left and jogged over to a small cart parked at the intersection. A robed woman was packing up jars of dried leaves and tea into crates. She was closing shop for the evening.

Caine slipped some bills from his wallet. 'Excuse me... aragi?' He smiled at the woman and set the money down on her cart. She flashed him a nervous smile. Her dark eyes darted left and right, looking for any signs of the police.

'No, la, asif.' I'm sorry.

Sudan was a Muslim country, under Sharia law. It was illegal to consume or sell alcohol, punishable by forty lashes with a whip. But, as always, prohibition bred demand. Aragi was a local alcoholic spirit, brewed at home by the tea ladies and others looking to make some extra cash. Caine slipped a few more bills onto the pile. 'Raja'an, please. I'm in a hurry.'

The woman shot a furtive glance down the dark street, then nodded. She produced a mason jar of thin, cloudy liquid. Caine grabbed the jar.

'Thank you,' he whispered.

The woman said nothing but whisked the money into her robes, then continued packing up her cart.

Caine opened the jar as he crossed the street. A noxious, chemical smell assaulted his nostrils. The aragi was a potent mash alcohol, made from fermented dates and yeast. Grimacing, Caine poured the foul-smelling liquor over his head. He splashed the remainder on his face and clothes.

He tossed the jar aside and let it shatter on the ground. As he reached the other side of the street, he rubbed the alcohol into his skin and clothes. He slipped the tactical pen out of his shirt pocket and clutched it in his right hand. He gave one last glance behind him to confirm no one was observing his activities. Then he hunched over and staggered down the alley next to the clinic.

The man in the blue suit and one of the other thugs leaned against the walls of an alcove, halfway down the alley. A tiny halogen bulb blazed above them. Its harsh light bathed them in a hazy glow and cast long shadows up and down the narrow brick corridor.

Caine stumbled towards them, imitating a drunken stagger.

'Hey, this the clinic?' he moaned, slurring his words. He fell against the wall, then took a few more tentative steps towards the men in the alcove.

The men stiffened at the sound of his voice. 'Go away!' the man in the blue suit shouted. 'The clinic is closed. Get out of here or we call the cops!'

Caine shuffled forward. 'Woman down there... gave me drink. I feel sick.' He bent over and pretended to retch in the alley.

The other man laughed and turned to his comrade. 'Just another pussy expat. Can't handle his aragi.'

The man in the blue suit shot a disdainful glare down at Caine. He slipped a push-to-talk phone from his pocket. 'Yiel said to call if anyone approached.'

Can't let them call upstairs, Caine thought. Got to end this fast.

The other man stepped towards Caine. 'This sod isn't worth Yiel's time.' He grabbed Caine's hair in his fist and yanked him upright. 'Eh, I talking to you! Don't you know? Alcohol illegal in

Sudan! We should call the cops. Or maybe I teach you a lesson myself.'

Caine drove the blunt end of the heavy pen into the man's ribs. The hammer-like blow struck with a dull thud, and the man's eyes bulged open. His hand dropped from Caine's head to his wounded side.

Caine's arms shot up and wrapped around the man's neck. He laced his fingers together and yanked the head down. As he locked the man's head in a clinch, he stepped backwards. The quick movement opened up the space between them. The man threw a few weak punches, but the distance and position of Caine's body left him unable to strike a solid blow.

Caine twisted his body sideways. He spun his attacker around, slamming him into the man in the blue suit. As he staggered back into the alcove wall, the phone tumbled from his hands. It bounced across the floor of the alley.

Using the clinched opponent as a battering ram, Caine kept his other adversary pinned against the wall. He drove his right knee into the locked man's face three times. The man's grunts of pain turned to a high-pitched squeal as the cartilage in his nose snapped from the punishing onslaught.

Caine released the hold and took a step back. He raised the pen in a hammer grip. His opponent looked up and snorted blood from his crushed nose. His eyes glowered with rage, and his cheeks and jaw were raw from the knee strikes. If he saw the tiny weapon in Caine's hand, he gave no sign of it. Instead, he barreled forward, swinging his fists in front of him. His left arm shot out, followed by a right hook.

Caine swung up his right forearm, diverting the punch to his left side. He kept his arm rigid and used the minimum amount of force to deflect the blow. When the next attack came, he was ready. He made another tight, controlled pivot with his arm, again knocking his target's blow off the attack line.

Caine wrapped his left hand around his opponent's bicep and clamped his right forearm on his wrist, trapping the arm. He jerked back, pulling the man off balance. Before his target could recover, Caine drew his right arm back and stabbed with all his strength. The metal pen's pointed tip tore into his opponent's neck.

Hot blood washed over Caine's hand. A plume of crimson splashed across the alcove walls. His opponent's eyes bulged wider. The thug's hands shot up to cover the gushing wound in his neck as he struggled to staunch the flow of blood.

Caine lunged forward, following up the stabbing attack with an elbow snap to the bleeding man's face. His target fell backwards and his head cracked against the concrete steps that led up to the second floor.

Caine spun towards the other man in the alcove. The man in the blue suit was reaching for the phone on the ground. Caine kicked it aside. The phone clattered along the floor of the alley as Caine slammed his forearm into the man's throat. Driving him backwards, he shoved him against the wall of the stairwell.

'Make a sound, you die,' he hissed. 'Who do you work for?'

Beads of sweat dripped down the man's face. His panicked eyes darted left and right as he gasped for breath. Caine pressed his arm tighter against his windpipe. 'Now is the part where you talk,' he growled.

Before Caine heard a sound, he knew... Something about the way the man clenched his jaw, or the way his eyes stopped their nervous jittering...

The man was going to cry out.

His cheeks puffed with air. 'Yiel—'

Caine drove his knee into the man's solar plexus. His hoarse cry turned into a sputtering cough as the wind exploded from his lungs. Caine yanked him forward by his collar, letting him collapse to the ground.

As he fell to his hands and knees, Caine spun the tactical pen around in his fingers. The blunt end of the cap was a knurled hammer tip, designed to break auto glass.

Caine slammed it down on the back of the man's skull. A fleshy thud echoed around the tiny alcove. The man stopped struggling and went limp.

Caine struck him again, this time on the side of his temple. He stood up and glanced around the corner. The alley was still empty. At the far end, he saw a couple of late-night pedestrians walk past. No one looked down the dark, foreboding corridor.

He looked back at the stairs. The man he had stabbed wasn't moving. His dark skin had taken on a gray pallor, and his clothes were soaked in a growing pool of blood.

Using the pen's glass breaker, Caine reached up and shattered the light bulb. The alcove was cloaked in darkness. He grabbed the man in the blue suit and dragged him next to the other body. If anyone cut through the alley, the shadows would hide the two corpses from view.

Two down, two to go...

Caine paused for a moment, letting his night vision adjust. Then he ascended the stairs, disappearing into the pitch-black darkness above.

The stairs ended at a splintered wooden door. The faded paint on its surface looked like pale, teal green, but it was difficult to tell in the dim light. Caine listened for a moment. The only sounds he heard were the muted traffic outside and distant music from the nightclubs on the busier streets.

He turned the knob. The door opened with a soft creak. Caine stepped into a narrow corridor. Moths and flies fluttered around dim fluorescent lights hanging from the ceiling.

The corridor was empty, but Caine heard muffled voices behind a door about halfway down the hall. He stalked closer to the door. A sign on the wall read 'Eiada' in red Arabic letters. The English translation, 'Clinic' appeared underneath. An arrow pointed to the door. It was cracked open, and Caine could hear the voices clearly now. A man was shouting in an East African dialect, possibly Nuer, but he could not be certain.

He heard the sound of breaking glass. A woman screamed.

Keeping his back against the wall, Caine peered through the cracked door. The lights in the room were dim, but distant street lamps glowed through a pair of windows on the opposite wall.

Medical charts and posters hung from the other walls. Glass and metal cabinets lined the room, filled with cotton swabs, bandages, and medicine bottles. A wheeled stretcher stood in the middle of the clinic beneath a hanging light fixture.

One of the men from outside stood with his back toward Caine, facing another door. The door was closed, and the voices were coming from the room on the other side.

Caine moved silently across the tile floor, the muscles in his body coiled and taut. He raised the tactical pen, focusing his gaze on the back of the man's neck.

Suddenly, the buzz of a tiny engine raced outside the windows. A motorbike sped past the clinic, its headlamp filling the windows with light. The moving beam cast a shadow across the opposite wall.

Two shadows.

The guard grunted in surprise as he realized he was not alone in the room. Caine lunged forward, but the man was already spinning around.

The guard blocked Caine's strike with his forearm. He launched a counterattack with his right hand. Caine saw the glint of a blade. The man was armed with a knife of some kind.

Caine leapt back, but the knife's tip sliced across his side. He heard his shirt tear and felt the burning sting of the blade as it grazed his flesh.

The man swung the blade again.

'Yiel, come quick!' he shouted.

Dammit! The curse of frustration echoed through Caine's mind. He brought up his hands in a defensive position. He kept his eyes on the man opposite him, watching his arms and shoulders.

The man swung wide, angling the blade towards Caine's wounded side again. Caine pivoted his torso and knocked the strike aside. Using his left arm, he locked the man's arm. Then he stabbed the pen down on the back of his attacker's knife hand.

The man yelped in pain and the knife clattered to the floor. Behind him, the other door exploded open and the fourth man barreled into the room. Caine caught a glimpse of bulging muscles and snarling lips. The man was tall and towered over Caine's current attacker. The hood of his sweatshirt was pulled back, revealing a painted white skull that covered his face.

He raised a pistol in his giant fists.

Caine moved on instinct, swinging the pen back and slamming the blunt end into his target's face. The man howled in pain and struggled to pull away, but Caine locked the hold on his arm tighter. He swung the man's body to the left, using him to block the bigger man's shot.

The gun roared twice. Orange muzzle fire flashed through the dim room. Caine's target jerked as the bullets thudded into his body. Tossing the corpse at his new attacker, Caine dipped low and dropped the pen. His fingers wrapped around the hilt of the discarded knife.

He darted forward as the bigger man shoved his partner's corpse out of the way. The big man raised the gun again, but before he could get a clear shot, Caine was upon him.

Caine's left arm swung out, knocking the gun to the right as the man pulled the trigger. The noise was deafening at such close range, but the shot went wide. The bullet struck the hanging light fixture. A shower of sparks cascaded into the room.

Caine yanked the barrel down, pointing it at the floor between them as his right hand sliced up with the knife. The bigger man snapped up his left hand and blocked the strike. His meaty fingers curled around Caine's wrist in a crushing grip.

Bellowing an angry roar, the hulking brute shoved Caine backwards. The two men fell onto the stretcher, their momentum sending the rolling platform careening across the room.

They slammed into the wall, the thin plaster crumbling from the impact. Caine felt medical equipment tumble and fall from the shelf above them and winced as it pelted his face and shoulders. A plastic cord curled around his right arm, but he ignored it. His opponent was larger and stronger than him... It would take all his focus to keep the man from regaining control of his pistol.

The big man wore a collection of gold and silver necklaces. A large gold pendant, shaped like the letter Y, hung above his broad chest.

'You must be Yiel,' Caine gasped. Keeping his grip on the barrel of the gun, he slammed a knee into the man's stomach. The blow seemed to bounce off the hard, smooth muscles of the man's torso.

The big man smiled. 'You die with my name on your lips,' he snarled. He began to force the gun up.

In the dim light of the room, Caine saw a faint red glow illuminating Yiel's face. He looked up. A plastic box covered with knobs and dials hung from the wall just above his head. The coiled cable that wrapped around his arm led up to the box. A red LED light on the console flashed on and off, next to a black switch.

Yiel's gun fired again. A cabinet next to Caine exploded, sending shards of glass across the floor. Caine struggled to keep the man at bay.

Yiel slammed Caine's knife arm into the wall, battering his fingers against the crumbling plaster. Caine's grip on the weapon grew weak. He released the blade, letting it fall to the floor. The big man relaxed his grip. It was only for a second, but that was all Caine needed.

He twisted his elbow up, striking the side of the man's face. The blow was weak, but it caused Yiel to flinch. Caine used the momentary distraction to yank his arm from the man's grip. He reached over his head and pounded the switch on the machine.

A droning whine filled the air. As it grew louder and louder, Caine felt for the dangling cord. He grabbed a rod-like handle attached to the end of the cord.

His fingers curled around a plastic trigger on the inside of the handle. He was holding a defibrillator paddle.

Caine gritted his teeth and pulled his knees up to his chest. The big man grabbed his gun in both hands and yanked it upwards, freeing it from Caine's hold. Caine kicked forward, pinning the man's gun arm against his chest. He hissed with exertion as he used his feet to lever the bigger man's weight off him.

Reaching back, Caine grabbed the other paddle mounted to the side of the machine. The high-pitched whine went silent, replaced by a loud beep.

Yiel jerked his gun arm up, pulling it from under Caine's foot. Before he could aim the weapon, Caine leaned forward. He slapped the two paddles on either side of the man's bulbous, glistening head and depressed the trigger.

The crackling hum of electricity filled the air. Yiel's eyes bulged and his limbs went stiff. One thousand volts of electricity surged through the man's skull. Only the rubber soles of Caine's boots touched the man's twitching body, insulating him from the high-voltage current.

The lights in the room pulsed then dimmed again. The machine went silent and Yiel fell backwards.

Caine panted for breath, then slid off the stretcher. He bent over Yiel's smoking body and checked for a pulse.

'Ya ilahi...' It was a woman's voice, low and quavering in shock. 'Oh my God. Is he...'

Caine looked up. A shadowy figure stood in the doorway, silhouetted by the light from the other room. It was the woman, Nena. She rested her hand on the doorframe as she surveyed the carnage in her clinic.

'Dead,' Caine said. He pried the pistol from the man's stiff grip. He glanced at the weapon as he stood up. It was a Chinese-made Norinco Type 54, chambered in steel-jacketed 7.62 mm. A knockoff of a Russian Tokarav, it was a common firearm in the region. He patted the body down and found a spare magazine in the man's front pocket.

He took the spare mag and slipped the gun into his waistband. Then he grabbed the tactical pen and shoved it back in his pocket. The woman backed up, glancing at him with wide, frightened eyes. As she stepped back into the light of the other room, Caine saw her features clearly. Dark, liquid eyes. Thick black hair. Flawless ebony skin... It was her.

He spoke in a calm voice. 'Doctor Vasani. It's okay, I'm here to help. I saw these men follow you up from the street. I thought you might be in trouble.'

Her wide, cat-like eyes narrowed. 'Who are you? How do you know my name?'

A loud squawk crackled from Yiel's body. Caine turned and rolled the corpse over. A push-to-talk phone was clipped to his belt. A voice squawked through the speaker, speaking in the same dialect as Yiel.

He pulled the walkie off the man's belt and held it up. 'Do you understand what they're saying?'

The voice repeated. The woman listened for a moment, then

nodded. 'He is asking if they have... if they have me. He says if he does not get a response, they will send more men.'

Caine clipped the phone to his belt.

'I promise I'll explain everything, but we have to leave now. Do you have a car?'

She nodded. 'It's parked in a garage down the street.'

Caine glanced over her shoulder. The room behind her was in shambles. Clothes were strewn across the floor. What little furniture there was had been smashed to splinters.

'These men were looking for something. Did they find it?'

She shook her head. 'No. What they were searching for... it is not here.'

He nodded. 'Okay,' he said. 'For now, that will have to do. Let's go.'

She looked down at his bloody shirt. 'Oh, you are injured.'

'It's nothing. Come on.'

She shook her head and grabbed an empty tote bag from the floor. She began throwing first aid supplies into the bag.

He gently took her arm. She looked up at him but did not pull away.

'It will only take a second,' she said.

He pulled her towards the open door. 'We don't have a second.'

He glanced left and right, making sure the hallway was clear before they moved through the doorway. He locked the door and shut it behind them.

She sniffed the air. 'You reek of aragi! Are you drunk?'

'Not yet,' he muttered. 'But a drink is sounding better and better.' They descended the stairs to the dark, lonely streets below.

18

Nena gasped as they sidestepped around the bodies he had left in the dark stairwell. He looked back at her and grasped her hand in a reassuring grip.

'Careful, watch your step,' he said in a low voice as he guided her down the stairs.

They emerged into the alley. She brought her hand to the bruise on her face, wincing as she touched it. Caine saw the look of shock and fear disappear from her eyes, replaced by an angry glare.

'These men, they came here to hurt me, maybe kill me. I know the NISS has been watching me, but—'

Caine looked her in the eye. 'It's not the NISS.'

'Yes, I know that now. But what I don't know is, who are you?'

'My name is Tom. We can figure out the rest later. You said you had a car?'

'Yes, it's a few blocks away. Follow me.'

Nena turned and walked out into the street. All traces of the timid, scared woman from the apartment above were gone now.

She moved with the confident stride of someone who was no stranger to violence and danger. Khairi said she operated clinics in South Sudan, and Darfur... Hellish war zones, where death, or worse, could come at any second.

The walkie at Caine's belt crackled to life. He couldn't understand the words, but he was familiar with the urgent, clipped tone of the man's voice.

'Nena, wait!'

As Caine hurried after her, a motorcycle roared around the corner. The growl of its engine drowned out Nena's reply. She turned and froze, like a deer in headlights.

The rider raised his arm towards her. He was carrying a submachine gun of some kind. Caine could make out a cruel sneer on the man's lips as he aimed the weapon.

Caine charged into the street. He grabbed Nena by the collar of her shirt and yanked her backwards just as a barrage of automatic weapon fire streaked towards her. Puffs of dirt kicked up at their feet, and the explosive chatter of the weapon echoed through the street.

As the bike screamed closer, Caine grabbed the wooden beam of the barricade and lifted it from the two sawhorses. He ducked behind a parked car. The engine noise was deafening now as the rider charged closer. He aimed his weapon at Caine, preparing to fire another burst.

Caine charged into the street and swung the beam like a baseball bat.

Crack!

Caine's arms and shoulders shuddered as the blunt weapon made contact. The wood splintered and cracked, snapping in half against the rider's chest.

The rider fell backwards and tumbled to the pavement. The

bike surged forward, dipping down into the pothole. As the wheel struck the edge of the depression, the entire bike flipped and careened into the air. Sparks flew from the motorcycle as it skidded across the pavement and struck a parked car.

Caine ran over to the bike and lifted it from the dusty ground. It was a Kawasaki KLR 650, with off-road tires and dusty, neon-green fairings. Caine sat on the bike and kicked the starter. The engine roared to life.

More chatter squawked from the walkie. He turned to Nena.

'Get on.'

Nena gave him an incredulous stare. 'On that? But my car is—'

Again, the roar of motorcycle engines rose up in the distance. More bikes were closing in.

'They're almost here,' Caine snapped. 'Get on!'

Nena hurried over and straddled the rear of the Kawasaki.

'I hate these things,' she muttered. 'They are noisy and dangerous.'

'Yeah, so are submachine guns.'

Caine shifted into first gear and gunned the throttle. They tore away from the building. Nena yelped and wrapped her arms around his waist. Caine leaned into a turn and sped around the corner. Glancing down, he saw a series of headlights reflected in the Kawasaki's side mirrors. A Jeep, or an off-road vehicle of some kind, was pursuing them, flanked by two more pairs of motorcycles.

'Hold on tight,' Caine shouted to Nena. 'Whatever you do, don't let go!'

His words were almost drowned out by the engine's roar. But he felt Nena nod, and her grip around his waist tightened.

Caine turned again and sped down a crowded market street.

The throng of pedestrians parted as he hammered at the bike's horn. Behind them, the lead rider raised his weapon and fired.

Gunfire ricocheted through the street. A metallic twang sounded from the back of the bike as a bullet struck its exhaust pipe.

The crowd panicked as pedestrians dove for cover behind parked cars.

Nena gasped and gripped tighter still as Caine leaned the bike into another turn. They zipped down an alleyway, the roar of the engine echoing around them in the tight, confined space. Two other riders followed, their tires chirping as they skidded across the pavement. The Jeep and remaining motorcycles sped past the alley's entrance.

Caine's bike exploded from the alley and turned onto another crowded street. The smells of cumin, garlic, and other spices filled the air. Colorful tents lined each side of the street. Thick, aromatic smoke billowed from slabs of meat cooking on long, flaming grills.

He skidded to a stop as a group of men in green robes ran into the center of the street. Their cloaks and beads billowed around them as they danced and spun in circles. Arabic music blasted from speakers inside the tents.

'It's the spice market,' Nena said. 'They close the street here at night.'

The other two bikes shot out of the alley behind them. Caine gritted his teeth and gunned the throttle. He swerved the bike left, circling around the spinning, dancing men. He tore through several silk curtains and found himself riding through the rows of tents.

He pulled the pistol from his waistband and waved it at the merchants in his path.

'Taharrak! Move! Get out of the way!' he shouted.

A dark-skinned Arab dove into a stack of spice jars as Caine's bike roared past. Clouds of red and yellow powder ballooned into the air.

The other bikes tore down the center of the street. One of the riders lashed out with his right leg, kicking a green-robed dancer out of the way. The man yelped as he collided with a sizzling grill and his robes caught fire.

Caine glanced to his right. The two bikes were gaining on them, racing along the other side of the tents. He extended the pistol and took aim.

His gun roared twice as he sent a double tap towards the closest pursuer. The rough terrain and the bike's speed made accuracy almost impossible. The bullets sparked off the enemy bike's fairing. The two men veered off, disappearing behind a long row of carpets hanging between the tents. Caine heard the roar of their bikes on the other side. They were neck and neck.

Up ahead he saw a group of men sitting around a large, circular grill. Flames danced over the red-hot coals as thin strips of lamb cooked on the grill's surface.

'Keep your head down!' he shouted to Nena.

'Down where?' she yelled back.

Caine gunned the throttle and angled towards the sizzling grill.

'Min al-tariq! Out of the way!'

The men surrounding the grill dove off to the side as the motorcycles charged towards them.

As they cleared the row of carpets, Caine maneuvered the bike alongside the grill. He swung out with his right foot, kicking the flaming platter towards the enemy riders.

The burning oil and hot coals struck the leg of the closest

pursuer. The man roared in pain as the inferno crawled up his leg, and the sickly-sweet smell of charred flesh filled the air. His bike wobbled and swerved left, crashing to the ground in front of Caine.

The flames leapt to the cloth tent surrounding them. Smoke clouded the air. Caine cursed and leaned right. Using a wooden crate lid as a makeshift ramp, he launched the Kawasaki up and over a stack of produce crates. The studded tires of the bike tore through rows of squash, tomatoes, and dried beans. A shredded paste of mangled vegetables sprayed behind the bike.

They reached the end of the crates and slammed back down into the middle of the street. Caine gunned the throttle and the bike leapt forward, pulling ahead of their remaining pursuers.

They turned off the market street and merged into the heavy traffic on Omdurman's Nile Street. To their right, the city lights reflected across the dark, rippling surface of the Nile River. They were north of Tuti Island, and the two Niles had joined into one single, massive stretch of water.

Caine heard tires squeal behind him. He glanced at the side mirror. The Jeep had returned, flanked by the remaining motorcycles.

With a silent curse, Caine glanced to his left, searching for an opening in the traffic. Cars swerved behind them as the Jeep scraped against a three-wheeled delivery truck. The rickety vehicle careened off the road. The Jeep surged forward, closing the gap between them and Caine.

Caine leaned left and cut in front of a row of yellow taxi cabs. The bike's powerful engine roared as he leapt up and over the narrow strip of grass and palm trees that divided the two lanes of traffic. Nena's fingers dug into the fabric of his shirt as the bike slammed down into the opposite lane and sped towards the oncoming traffic.

As he wove the tiny bike between the headlights rushing towards them, he heard honking horns and screams behind him. The motorcycles had jumped the divider and continued to give chase.

Then the crack of snapping wood and crumpling metal rose above the traffic noise. Caine looked back. The Jeep had plowed through a row of palm trees and skidded into the street.

A loud airhorn howled in front of them, and Caine jerked his head back to the road. He swerved right, narrowly avoiding an oil tanker truck hurtling towards them. The three motorcycles split up and veered around the lumbering vehicle. Gunfire roared through the street. Caine felt trails of hot air streak past his ear.

'I need a clear shot!' he shouted. Nena hunched low, tucking her head under the crook of Caine's arm. He gave one last glance at the road, then spun around, aiming the pistol behind him.

He squeezed off a single shot. The lead rider jerked back in his seat. His bike wobbled, then fell, crashing the ground. Sparks rose from the pavement as it skidded forward.

A neon-pink van swerved around Caine and bounced over the fallen motorcycle. The shriek of crumpling metal drowned out the rider's cries. The van dragged the bike's wreckage across the pavement. Caine allowed himself a quick grin of satisfaction, then turned his attention back to the oncoming traffic.

His victory was short lived. More gunfire sparked across the pavement, inches from his leg. Glancing in the mirror, he saw the Jeep closing in. Its body was battered and dented, but it was still operational. A man leaned out from the rear seat and aimed an AK-47 rifle towards them. The remaining motorcycles had dropped back, allowing the Jeep to take point.

They were heading towards an intersection. Caine swung the bike left and hurtled through the stop light. Brakes squealed as more traffic skidded out of their way. The Jeep spun around the turn, followed by the motorcycles. The bikes charged forward and closed in.

Caine darted down a smaller street but the bikes swerved after him. They streaked past a row of parked cars. More gunfire erupted behind them. The cars' windshields exploded as they drove past, showering them in shards of broken glass.

Caine glanced at his pistol. There was only a single bullet left in the Norinco's chamber. No time to reload.

One shot, two bikes...

He looked up and swung the bike into another tight turn. More gunfire ricocheted off the pavement. Caine glanced to his right and spotted a squat metal pipe studded with valves. It was painted white and poked up a couple feet from the sidewalk.

That's it! he thought.

The bike engines roared as they followed him through the turn and straightened out. Once again, they were closing the gap.

Caine's eyes darted across the sidewalk. There had to be another one somewhere in the city...

There!

He shot around a tight bend. As he straightened out, he aimed the pistol at another of the strange metal pipes. The men behind them fired again. Sparks flew off the tail pipe of the Kawasaki. Nena gasped and clutched him tighter. Caine gritted his teeth, but he did not flinch.

He pulled the trigger.

Blam!

The 7.62 steel-jacketed slug tore into the valve of the fire hydrant. As Caine streaked past the hydrant, a jet of pressurized water exploded from the pipe and shot straight across the street.

The high-powered jet struck the riders behind him with the

force of a firehose. One of the bikes wobbled, then slid sideways. It slammed into the other bike, and both motorcycles skidded to the ground in a shower of sparks.

Caine felt the Norinco's slide snap back, and the trigger went loose. The weapon was empty. He tucked the pistol back into his waistband. Behind them, the Jeep charged through the spray of water.

Caine heard the roar of a new engine... Another motorcycle jumped up onto the sidewalk.

'There's more of them!' Nena shouted.

The new motorcycle sped around the fire hydrant, avoiding the powerful jet.

'I know somewhere they cannot follow,' Nena shouted. 'Turn right, up there!'

Caine swerved right as the Jeep's AK-47 fired again. Palm leaves fluttered down around them as the wild shots tore through the trees lining the street.

Nena pointed to a sign up ahead to the left. A tan industrial building with a white aluminum roof stood in the distance. The building was surrounded by smaller sheds and a few abandoned construction vehicles. Caine could make out the words 'Al-Manara' written in red Arabic letters on the sign.

'There!' she said. 'It's the water treatment plant. Narrow walkways. Their Jeep will not fit!'

Caine sped into the building's driveway. He could hear the men in the Jeep shouting behind them as they reloaded their weapons. He spotted a narrow gap between the main building and a smaller gray metal shed. He jerked the handles left and drove through a row of green hedges, then sped between the buildings.

The Jeep screeched to a halt behind them. He heard the

shriek of metal scraping against metal as the vehicle slammed into the side of the shed.

The motorcycle exploded through the hedges and followed behind them. The concrete path between the two buildings ended in a narrow staircase. It loomed before them in the spotlight of the Kawasaki's headlamp.

'Brace yourself,' Caine shouted as he yanked up on the handlebars. The bike whined as its off-road tires dug into the concrete. The bike bounced up and down on its suspension as they raced up the stairs.

Caine felt the shock of each impact vibrate through his aching body. Finally, they reached the top and sped along an elevated walkway. Long rows of blue pipes flanked them on either side.

Beneath them, the rumble of rushing water rose above the motorcycle's engine. In the moonlight, Caine could see vast pools on either side of the walkway. Huge pumping stations forced water from the Nile into the treatment tanks. Filters removed impurities and made it safe to drink.

Gunfire sparked off the pipes to their left as the motorcycle roared behind them. Caine shifted and revved the throttle, but there was nowhere to go but straight ahead.

As they neared the end of the walkway, yellow safety tape blocked their way.

'They are expanding the plant,' Nena shouted. 'It has been under construction for months.'

Caine's bike tore through the thin plastic tape as if it were tissue paper. They dropped onto a rough dirt embankment and raced into the darkness. To their right, a deep channel carved through the earth. It was lit at regular intervals by clusters of halogen work lights.

Another volley of gunfire streaked past them.

'Hold on!' Caine shouted. He darted the bike right and dropped into the channel. He felt the shockwave in his legs as the bike's suspension struggled to compensate for the impact. Dirt and debris fell from the sides of the trench as the rider above continued firing at them.

The channel ended in a large section of pipe buried in the earth. The deafening roar of the Kawasaki's engine engulfed them as they plunged into the pipe. Behind them, Caine heard the whine of the other bike as it dove after them, following them into the pitch-black metal tunnel.

Muzzle flash lit the darkness. Gunshots ricocheted off the curved metal walls of the pipe. Caine swerved left and right. He rode up the sides of the tunnel like a race car shooting through a banked curve.

Up ahead he saw a circle of light... the tunnel was ending. More halogen beams gleamed in the darkness, their bright glow outlining the far bank of another trench. It cut a horizontal slash in the earth across their path. The ground sloped down, and the opposite bank was lower than the pipe's exit.

'Nena, your bag... Do you still have it?' Caine shouted.

'Yes, I have it.'

'When I give the word, throw it at him. Try to hit his face, if you can.'

'But our supplies—'

'Do as I say or we're dead!'

He swerved the bike one more time, then straightened out and raced along the center of the pipe. Gunning the throttle, he charged ahead at full speed. The headlamp of the pursuing bike reflected off the curved walls. It was gaining on them.

The exit of the tunnel grew larger as they sped towards it. He could see the far side of the trench clearly now. The lights glinted off long stacks of smaller pipes, and Caine could see piles of earth dredged from the new channel.

'Nena, now!'

He felt her spin around, but he did not take his eyes off the looming exit. Behind him, he heard the engine of the pursing bike warble and dip in volume... Her bag had struck the rider, forcing him to slow down.

She turned back around and clutched him tight. The bike shot out of the tunnel like a bullet. The Kawasaki's engine wailed like a banshee as they flew through the air. Caine looked down and saw the dark gorge of the channel pass beneath them.

A second later, he felt his bones rattle as the bike slammed into the ground on the other side. As Caine struggled to control the motorcycle, a second wail sounded behind them. The other bike roared out of the open mouth of the pipe.

Caine skidded to a stop. The other motorcycle arced into the air, then began to drop. Nena's last-minute distraction had cost the rider speed and balance. He had not been able to regain control in time. He wasn't going fast enough to make the jump.

The bike plunged towards the bank of the channel, then dropped out of sight. They heard a loud crash and the screech of crumpled metal. The motorcycle collided into the dirt wall, then tumbled to the floor of the trench.

Caine took a deep breath. His arms and legs were shaking. He wasn't sure if it was from nerves, or the shocks and impacts of the ride.

Nena's breathing was shallow and ragged. Her arms were still clamped around his waist in a tight embrace. He could feel her chest heaving, trembling against his back. She stared into the darkness, panting for breath. She did not let go.

He turned and looked back at her.

'What was that you said about getting drunk?'

She laughed, a quick, sharp exhale. But her eyes were dark and pensive. She did not look up from the black gorge.

'A drink would be good, yes,' she said. 'Then, you and I... We need to have a long talk.'

'We'll talk on the road,' Caine said. 'We can't stay in the city.'

He flipped the ignition switch and the Kawasaki rumbled to life. They sped into the darkness, hurtling across the rough, ancient earth towards the twinkling lights across the river.

19

Rebecca turned and covered her head as the blinding fireball exploded next to them. Agent Zavala screamed. Her walkie tumbled to the floor. The rear window of the SUV shattered as a powerful shockwave rippled through the street. The back wheels of the vehicle flew into the air, then crashed back to the pavement.

Rebecca's head slammed into the dashboard. She felt blood drip down her face and her vision went hazy. Amidst the blaring car alarms and sirens, she could hear screaming. Then another sound rose above the panic – a low, mechanical growl, moving closer and closer. A vehicle was approaching the wreckage at speed.

The rear end of a metro DC garbage truck crashed through the smoking remains of the semi-trailer. The hulking metal truck slammed into the front of the marshals' SUV, the impact shunting it back into the car behind it. Rebecca saw Ted's head snap back from the collision.

The marshals in the rear car exited the vehicle and took

cover behind the doors. They pumped their Remington shot-guns, preparing the weapons to fire. The marshals in Ted's SUV followed standard procedure and stayed put. They trusted the vehicle's armored plating to protect them.

A hydraulic whine came from the garbage truck. The rear gate raised up. Rebecca lifted her head. Her vision was still blurry and her ears were ringing, but she could make out shadowy figures darting out of the truck. The group charged through the billowing smoke. The blurry shapes resolved. They were men, dressed in black tactical gear. They were carrying automatic weapons.

They swarmed towards the damaged SUV. The high-pitched cough of silenced gunfire hissed through the air.

Two of the armored men fired at the downed motorcycle cops. Their bodies jerked on the pavement, then stopped moving.

The rest of the team advanced forward. Another pair stopped alongside the armored SUV. The remaining four fanned out around the back and opened fire on the marshals at the rear of the convoy.

The federal marshals returned fire. Their shotguns seemed to have little effect on their attackers' body armor. Rebecca watched as puffs of smoke exploded from the barrels of the men's weapons. One of the attackers staggered backwards. He recovered within seconds and opened fire with his submachine gun.

The compact weapon spat a stream of high-powered auto-matic fire. A series of holes riddled the metal door of the rear SUV. The marshal jerked as the slugs tore through the door and struck his body. He fired one more wild blast with the Reming-ton, then dropped to the ground.

'Driver, get us the hell out of here!' DuBose shouted. The driver turned the key in the ignition, but the engine sputtered and stalled.

Another marshal collapsed to the ground. The attacker's armor-piercing ammunition sliced through the SUV's doors as if they were tissue paper.

'They're outgunned, we have to help them!' Rebecca shouted.

'Director, your safety is—' DuBose began.

There was another sharp crack. A high-powered rifle shot pierced the driver's side window of their SUV. The driver's head snapped sideways, a fine red mist spattering the windshield as he slumped over the wheel.

Rebecca's face went pale. She swallowed, fighting the bile rising in her throat.

'Sniper, driver's side,' she said. 'We're not safe in here. Help the marshals. That's an order!'

She threw open the passenger door and activated her chair lift.

DuBose turned to Agent Zavala as she drew her Glock. 'You ready for this?'

Zavala gave him a nervous smile. 'I got a choice?'

DuBose kicked open the side door and leapt to the pavement. He charged towards the rear of the marshals' truck, a line of gunfire nipping at his heels. The pavement chipped and cracked as the bullets from the attackers traced his path. He dove behind the truck, and the bullets sparked and ricocheted off the side of the bumper, just missing his leg.

He looked back at Zavala. 'Move your ass! I'll cover you!'

She sprinted towards the truck. DuBose popped around the side and sent three bullets into the nearest attacker. The man staggered, but the pistol could not penetrate the thick Kevlar covering his chest.

Zavala made it to the rear of the truck. She huddled behind the cover, along with DuBose and the remaining two marshals.

Another pair of armored men stalked towards the driver's side of Rebecca's SUV. As her chair lowered to the pavement, she reached under the seat and slid a Glock 26 pistol from a concealed holster. Taking a deep breath, she maneuvered her chair to the front of the vehicle. She kept her head and shoulders low, taking cover behind the hood.

Bullets ricocheted off the sheet metal above her head. She stifled a scream and tightened her grip on the pistol.

There was a lull in the gunfire.

They're reloading, she thought. Move, now!

A tremor of fear ran through her body. She took a deep breath and the shivering ceased. She popped up and saw the two men in black advancing on her position. She fired twice. One shot missed, the other thudded into one of the men's shoulders.

She heard the metallic clank of the other man's weapon as he reloaded. From the corner of her eye, she saw him slide a long box mag into the top of the squat, short-barreled weapon. He slapped it down and raised the gun towards her.

Rebecca ducked back behind the hood as the weapon chattered once again.

FN P90... she thought. What the hell? Fifty rounds of high-velocity armor-piercing bullets, fully automatic. Whoever these men were, they were well-equipped.

The federal marshals were hopelessly outgunned. Backup would be on the way. According to the information Zavala had shared in the hotel room, response time was estimated to be three to five minutes.

Might as well be five hours. They would be lucky if they survived another minute against this kind of firepower.

Rebecca heard the men pivot and fire behind them as DuBose and Zavala lay down covering fire. She rolled around the front of the vehicle. Raising her pistol, she steadied her grip and took aim at the closest attacker. The man was clad in a thick Kevlar vest and a black helmet.

She fired again, striking him in the center of his back. The man dropped to one knee, but the Kevlar absorbed the impact. He staggered back to his feet.

She took a deep breath. Get it together, she ordered herself. Don't panic. Remember your training!

After her attempted kidnaping, Rebecca had forced herself to put in regular hours at the firing range. In her mind, she could hear the voice of her shooting instructor, drilling her in the Mozambique Drill. The shooting pattern was designed to take down armored attackers.

'Two in the chest, one in the head. First you stop 'em, then you drop 'em.'

The armored man spun around, raising the short, lethal submachine gun to his shoulder.

Rebecca's pistol roared again.

Blam! Blam!

The two shots struck the man center mass. Even through the heavy Kevlar, the impact was enough to throw off his aim and force him to stumble backwards. The submachine gun fired, sending a trail of sparks across the hood of the SUV. Rebecca didn't move. She kept her eyes on her target and used the man's split second of pain and distraction to line up her third shot.

Blam!

The man's head snapped back. A stream of crimson

exploded though the air, jetting from under the rim of his helmet.

He collapsed to the ground.

As Zavala and DuBose engaged the other man, Rebecca saw movement to her right. Another pair of armored attackers squatted next to Ted's SUV. The marshals inside huddled around Ted. So far, the attackers' weapons seemed unable to penetrate the vehicle's armor plating.

The Kevlar-clad men stood about ten feet from the passenger side of the vehicle. One of them set up a small tripod. The other removed a thick white canister from a ballistic plastic case.

Rebecca squinted. Something about the device looked familiar.

Oh my God!

One of the marshals rolled down the rear passenger window a couple of inches. He aimed his pistol through the gap.

Crack!

The men outside the SUV did not even flinch as another high-powered rifle shot rang out. A hole appeared in the glass. The marshal slumped down. Ted's terrified face stared back at Rebecca through the rear window. The other marshal pulled his head down.

Sniper, she thought. He's still out there.

She ejected the partially used magazine and slammed in a fresh one. She rolled towards the men, firing a pair of double taps into each of them.

The men dropped their equipment and raised their weapons. Rebecca fired again, dropping one with a head shot. The other opened fire, jogging backwards away from her. Rebecca had no cover. Bullets ricocheted off the pavement next to her wheelchair.

She kept firing, but her shots ricocheted off the man's helmet.

He stopped shooting for a fraction of a second and adjusted his aim.

The chatter of high-velocity bullets tore through the air. Rebecca winced but then gasped as she saw the attacker jerk and stagger backwards. A collage of holes ripped through the man's armor. He fell to the ground. Rebecca turned around and saw Agent Zavala standing behind her. She had scooped up one of the fallen attacker's weapons. The armor-piercing bullets had penetrated the man's Kevlar vest with ease.

Rebecca heard muffled shouting from inside the car. She turned and saw Ted holding up his cell phone. He pressed it up to the cracked glass window and stared at her. She rolled closer to the window, ignoring the danger of the unseen sniper.

She squinted as she noticed movement on the other side of the glass. Another pair of men. Another white canister.

'EFP!' she shouted. 'Zavala, get—'

The explosion shook the SUV. As Rebecca raised her arm to cover her face, she saw the interior of the truck balloon outwards. She caught a brief image of Ted's body hurtling towards the window. Then he vanished in a cloud of smoke and dust.

In a fraction of a second, the explosion tore through the side of the truck. The force impacted against the rear passenger door. The sheet of metal tore free from the vehicle's frame and exploded outwards.

The heavy metal door shot straight towards Rebecca. It slammed into her chair, throwing her backwards and knocking her to the pavement. As her head struck the ground, Rebecca felt her consciousness slipping away, all her senses reducing to a single point of pale white light.

She remembered Ted staring at her from the back of the truck, His blue eyes calm and bright in that brief second before oblivion.

His quivering lips had mouthed words to her, behind the shattered glass window. Before the explosion obscured him in darkness.

'I'm sorry...'

Then the white light receded and the black rushed towards her, like the tide on a moonlit night.

20

Caine and Nena drove south on the Jabal Awliya Expressway, one of the few major roads that led into South Sudan. Nena's truck looked like it had been driven hard. Its tubular steel frame was dented, and the front right fender was torn clean off. A thick crust of dried mud and caked sand obscured whatever color paint had once decorated the exterior.

But the engine chugged at a steady pace, and Nena swore by the vehicle's reliability. The air conditioning managed to keep the cabin somewhat comfortable as they bounced along the road that led south from Khartoum. Their route ran parallel to the White Nile, although Caine could see no trace of the river in the distance. It was a couple miles away, to the west of the long, narrow stretch of pavement. Instead, the view outside the windshield was nothing but flat brush and desert, lit by the pale silver glow of the moon and stars above.

Caine winced as the vehicle bounced over a patch of cracked, broken pavement. The road conditions were harsh, and his side ached where the thug's knife had cut him earlier. He reached through the tear in his shirt and touched the bandage

Nena had applied before they left the city. It was dry. She had managed to stop the blood flow.

'You'll still need stitches.' Nena's voice was low and groggy.

Earlier, as they left the lights of Khartoum behind, Caine had watched her slump against the passenger window. He was familiar with the after-effects of violence. The adrenaline rush of fear had ebbed from her body as he drove into the warm, black night. She had passed out within minutes.

Now, she was awake. Caine handed her a bottle of water as she sat up in the passenger seat and adjusted her hijab.

'I've had worse,' he said. 'It can wait until we cross the border.'

'We've only been driving a few hours. We have many more to go. You need stitches. Doctor's orders.'

He could feel her eyes peering at him in the darkness.

'Who are you?' she finally asked. 'How did you know my name?'

Caine winced again as he slipped his phone from his pocket. He scrolled through the pictures until he found one of Josh Galloway. He handed her the phone.

'We have a mutual friend,' he said. 'He sent word that he was working with you, in South Sudan.'

'This is Jason... Mr. Carter. He works with the World Health Organization. I met him in Malakal, in the South. He said he was investigating a possible outbreak, a new strain of Ebola. His equipment was stolen, so I offered to run some tests for him at my clinic there.'

'Is that what those men were looking for, in Khartoum?'

She shuddered. 'The big one, he grabbed me... hit me. He kept asking me where the case was. The samples Mr. Carter gave me, they were in a small silver case. I assume that's what he meant, but I can't be sure.'

A pair of headlights appeared in the rearview mirror. Caine glanced up to confirm no one was following too closely. The road behind them had been long, dark and empty. Now, a trio of three large trucks followed them on the narrow lane of pavement. Caine slowed and let them pass. The trucks each pulled blue cargo trailers, marked by the letters AHA. They rumbled past and disappeared into the distance.

No other vehicles appeared behind them. Caine turned his attention back to Nena.

'How would they know this Carter gave you the case in the first place?'

She was silent for a moment. She reached up and tucked a strand of black hair into the scarf wrapped around her head. She took a long sip of water, then handed the bottle back to Caine.

'I have no idea. You say Mr. Carter is your friend, but you don't seem concerned about him. He sounds like a stranger to you.'

Caine kept his eyes on the road ahead. 'It's complicated.'

'Please, I am no fool. Who are you? I mean, who are you really?'

Caine lifted the bottle to his lips. 'My name is Thomas Caine, and I'm looking for your friend, Mr. Carter. But I'm also looking for someone else. Does the name Simon Takuba mean anything to you?'

He heard her sharp inhale of breath and turned to look at her. Her eyes were wide, her nostrils flared.

'I have heard of him. In the South, once the civil war began, many rebel groups sprang up. The SPLM, the Nuer White Army, the Arrow Boys. Even the LRA was active in the region. Some of these people are considered freedom fighters. Others are little more than thieves and terrorists.'

'It's usually a fine line,' Caine said, keeping his eyes on the road.

Nena modded. 'A few years ago, a new militia group formed, one people say is worse than all the others. The Army of the Chosen. They attack villages at night. They steal whatever food or medical supplies the people have. They kill the men, take the children. And the women...' Her voice trailed off.

'I understand,' Caine said.

'This man you speak of, Takuba. They say he is their leader. Some of his men fight for food, or merely to survive. Others were taken as children, they know no other life. But he has a small group of bodyguards who worship him like a god. They believe he controls the spirits of the dead, that he can speak to their ancestors. He claims to have the power to prevent these spirits from crossing into the afterlife.'

'Every cult needs a messiah,' Caine said.

'They call these men "Ghost Jackals". They wear red scarves and armbands in battle. They paint their faces... The mark of the skull.'

She mumbled something in Arabic. Caine could not understand the words, but her hands clasped together as if she was praying. When she finished, she looked up at him. 'Like the man in my apartment. The one you killed.'

Caine glanced over at her. 'I don't want to frighten you. But if what you say is true, Takuba is obviously after you and these samples.'

'And what are you after?' she asked. 'Do you work for the oil companies? Are you private security, a mercenary of some kind?'

'What makes you say that?'

She looked out the window at the stark, empty landscape. Pale and gray, the desert was as smooth as a silk sheet billowing in the wind.

'You know how to fight,' she replied. 'You are a killer. And you are white.' She turned back to him. 'If you are here, you must be getting paid. What else is there of value here but oil?'

'Nena, I can't tell you everything. The more you know, the more danger you will be in. But I promise you, I don't work for an oil company, or anyone else. I'm here for my own reasons. This man, Takuba... In a way, he's my responsibility.'

'I don't understand.'

Caine was silent for a moment. 'I'm not sure I do either,' he finally answered. 'It's a long story. You said you left your samples at your clinic?'

'Yes, in Malakal.'

'Can you take me there?'

She nodded, and Caine again saw the determined glare light up her eyes. 'Yes. If Takuba's men are after those samples, we must get to them first. They could be dangerous. We cannot let a monster like that get his hands on them.'

The truck lurched as they bounced over another pothole in the road. Caine hissed in pain and dropped his hand to his side. The look of determination in Nena's eyes softened to one of concern.

'Pull over,' she said.

'What's wrong?'

'I need to check your bandage.'

'I don't want to lose the time. I've been hurt much worse than this, trust me.'

'Don't be a fool. If you bleed out before we reach the border, what good will you be then?'

Caine shrugged. 'You've got a point.' He pulled over to the side of the road. Nena threw open the passenger door and hopped out into the warm night air. They switched places, and Nena turned the key in the ignition. She let the car idle, and the

AC blow, as she reached over Caine's lap and opened the glove compartment. She removed the paper bag of bandages and iodine they had purchased back in the city.

She looked up at him. 'Take off your shirt.'

'Excuse me?'

'I'm going to change your bandages. When we reach my clinic, I'll stitch you up. Until then, I don't want to risk infection.'

'Nena, trust me, it's—'

'Doctor's orders,' she snapped in a commanding voice.

'Fine,' he grunted. He shrugged out of the torn shirt, wincing in pain with each movement of his arm and shoulder. Nena used a tiny pair of scissors to cut off the old bandages, then she began wrapping fresh white linen around his torso.

She made a clucking sound and squinted. Her eyes traveled over the patchwork of old scars and wounds that traversed Caine's toned, muscular body. Her fingers brushed over a small white scar beneath his shoulder blade.

'This is a bullet wound. I was right, you are a soldier.'

'I've seen combat,' Caine said.

'What were you? Army? Marines?'

Caine shook his head. 'The uniform doesn't matter. The bullets are always the same.'

He raised his arm and she reached across his chest, tying off the fresh bandage. In the close confines of the truck, Caine could smell her skin and hair... a combination of essential oils and shampoo. And beneath the light, sweet fragrance, a perfume of dirt and sweat. The lingering hint of adrenaline.

She leaned back and examined her handwork. 'This will do for now.' She looked up and saw him staring at her. 'What are you looking at? You like my hijab?'

Caine laughed. 'No. The shampoo you use... It smells nice.'

She blinked, then smiled. 'Thank you. Unfortunately, you

smell like a dog who fell in the river.' She tossed his shirt at him. 'Put this back on. After we cross the border, you need a shower.'

Caine slipped the shirt over his shoulders. Nena put the car in gear and pulled away from the shoulder of the road.

'Doctor's orders?' Caine asked with a grin.

She smiled but kept her eyes locked on the road. 'You are finally learning.'

Rebecca's eyes fluttered open, but all she could see was a dark blur. She felt numb. She blinked, and the black opiate haze of the painkillers receded. A bright light shone down on her from above. She moved her head side to side. She tried to see past the blinding white circle of illumination, tried to make out some detail. Where was she? What had happened?

Details and memories snapped into place. A jolt of adrenaline flooded her body, replacing the liquid warmth seeping into her limbs. The convoy... the explosion. Ted.

She opened her mouth and tried to speak. All she could manage was a murmured groan.

She felt a soft pressure on her shoulder. A face came into view, blocking the light above her. 'Director? Director, can you hear me?'

She blinked again. The room seemed to spin around her. With each revolution, details began to sharpen and come into focus. She could make out sterile white walls, and she heard the electronic beeping of the EKG machine. Nurses and doctors rushed past the glass panels surrounding her room.

She was in a hospital.

The face above her resolved into a familiar sight.

'Clayton,' she murmured. 'Is that you?'

DuBose smiled. 'Welcome back, Director.' He shook his head. 'Doctor Corrigan said you were alright, just in shock, but... You gave me a scare. It's good to hear your voice.'

Rebecca wrapped her fingers around his arm in a weak grip. 'Sitrep,' she murmured. 'The convoy... Ted?'

DuBose frowned. 'They hit us hard. I've never seen anything like it. Right in the middle of Georgetown, for God's sake. Whoever they were, they were well-armed and highly trained. Cool under fire, precise.'

She forced herself to focus on his face. 'I remember... there was a sniper?'

DuBose clenched his jaw. 'We never put eyes on them, wherever they were hiding. That's how they stopped the convoy. We pulled the slugs from the engine block of Ted's SUV.'

He reached into his jacket and pulled out a squat, deformed lump of metal. Rebecca squinted as he held it up to the light.

'A 50 BMG, better known as 12.7x99 NATO,' he said in a quiet voice. 'The slugs in Ted's SUV had armor-piercing cores. Boys in the lab checked the striation patterns on the bullets. Results show they were fired from an Accuracy International AX50 Anti-Material rifle. That's some serious hardware. Designed for snipers to take out armored vehicles and military equipment. I haven't seen an AX50 in the wild since Iraq.'

He shook his head. 'You combine this kind of firepower with the ground team's FN P90s... Body armor's worthless against those suckers. The federal marshals didn't stand a chance.'

'And the explosion?'

DuBose leaned closer to her. 'You called it in the field, Director. EFPs – explosively formed projectiles. Shaped charges with multiple detonators, mounted behind a concave metal disk. The detonators go off in a precise pattern and mold the disk into a giant seven-pound slug. That thing hit the SUV at over Mach 6.'

She nodded weakly. 'I recognized the canisters they were using from an old briefing. They're popular with insurgent groups all over the world. Cheap, easy to make, and very effective.'

'Yeah, just one of those things took out everyone in that SUV. And they had a second one ready to go.' He shook his head. 'The sniper team had to be at least two people, and there were eight more on the ground. Four men arming the EFPs, and four providing cover fire. That means whoever set this up was able to get at least ten men, armed with heavy military hardware, in and out of the area. And in under five minutes. Rebecca... that intersection was less than six miles from the goddamn White House!'

Rebecca shivered as she remembered the explosion rippling through the SUV. She bit her lip in concentration. She was missing something...

Ted's face, in the car. His pale blue eyes, that blank, emotionless stare. His phone... pressed against the cracked glass.

He was trying to tell me something, she thought.

Rebecca's arm flailed and her fingers reached for the leather strap of her purse.

'Clayton, my purse. I need my phone.'

DuBose grabbed the heavy leather bag. He fished around inside, looking for her cell phone.

'Were the other convoys hit?' she asked.

DuBose looked up and shook his head. 'Negative. Special Agent Zavala said we were the only ones attacked.'

Rebecca exhaled. 'Then we have another leak. Someone in the FBI, or the Federal Marshals. Or someone closer to home.'

'You mean internal? CIA?'

She nodded. 'The attackers knew Ted was in that car. Someone tipped them off. Until we know who, we have to assume anyone could be the leak.'

DuBose pulled out her phone and handed it to her. She grabbed it and scrolled through the messages.

'Here.' She held up the phone. 'Ted sent me a text, before the explosion.'

DuBose took the phone and read the message on the screen. 'Blackwing Capital. What the hell is that?'

She thought for a moment. 'I don't know. But I looked him in the eye before... before it happened. He knew he was going to die. This must be important. You need to look into it.'

He handed her back the phone and raised his eyebrows. 'Director, I need to be here. I promised Josh I'd protect—'

Before he could finish his thought, the door to the room swung open and Doctor Corrigan walked in. He consulted a series of medical charts on a large tablet he cradled in his hands.

'Rebecca,' he snapped, 'what part of "take it easy" did you not understand?'

Rebecca gave him a weak smile. 'Told you I was no good at following orders.' Her expression turned grim. 'How serious is it? Does this mean I won't... I can't...' Her voice cracked, and she let the unfinished question hang in the air.

Corrigan swiped the screen and examined the next chart. 'I can't say for sure, but it looks like the chair took the brunt of the impact. There's definitely some bruising and blunt force trauma involved. I'll have to remove shrapnel fragments from your left thigh and abdomen.' He looked up at her. 'But it doesn't look like your previous injury was affected. Rebecca, that wheelchair of yours may have just saved your life.'

Rebecca nodded. She began to speak but found herself

unable to form words. Her eyes glistened in the harsh light of the hospital room. 'Good,' she finally muttered. 'That's good.'

Corrigan glanced at DuBose. 'She has to be prepped for surgery. I'm afraid you need to leave. Now.'

DuBose looked down at Rebecca. She squeezed his hand. 'It's okay. I'll be fine. Go ahead, you have work to do. Don't you?'

He took a deep breath and nodded. 'Okay, okay. I'm on it.'

Corrigan tapped some information into the tablet, then slid it into a holder on the door. 'The nurses will be here any minute. With any luck, we'll have you in the operating room within the hour. Try not to engage in any guerrilla warfare while I'm gone.'

He smiled at the two of them, then left the room. DuBose turned to follow.

'Clayton,' Rebecca called after him. He stopped in the doorway and looked back at her.

'Remember, Zavala said only a few people knew which convoy Ted was in. The Marshals, her superior at the FBI, and Director Paulis. We have to keep this between us, for now. We're on our own.'

He nodded. 'Yeah. I got it.' He shut the door behind him.

* * *

DuBose paced down the long sterile corridor outside Rebecca's room. A storm of dark thoughts clouded his mind. Was Rebecca right, was there another leak? And if so, with so many federal agencies involved, who could he trust?

It all sounded like a paranoid delusion, the deranged product of Ted Lapinski's imagination. But he couldn't rule out the possibility that it was true.

The men, the military hardware, the EFPs... That attack was

no delusion, he reminded himself. Someone wanted Lapinski dead. And whoever it was, they got their wish.

DuBose turned and continued toward the elevator. He slipped his cell phone out of his pocket and stared at it for a moment, hesitating.

You better figure out who your friends are...

He had seen the FBI agent, Zavala, risk her lift to help Director Freeling. His gut told him she was one of the good guys, maybe the only person he could trust right now.

But could he be sure?

He made his decision and dialed a number.

A woman's voice answered. 'Special Agent Zavala.'

DuBose stepped into the elevator. 'Zavala, we have to talk. Alone. I'll text you.'

The elevator doors slid shut, and the call went dead.

22

It was just past 4 a.m. when Caine and Nena crossed the border into South Sudan. There was no town or village to speak of, just a faded green sign written in both Arabic and English. The writing warned travelers to stop and present their documents. A pair of clay brick towers flanked the road. Sagging razor wire fences extended from each tower and ran along the border for a few hundred meters, until they came to an abrupt end. The border continued in the distance, open and unguarded as far as Caine could see.

A soldier shuffled from one of the towers and approached the car. His green beret and blue shoulder patch marked him as military police. He cradled an HK G3 assault rifle in his arms. He tapped on Nena's window with the barrel of the rifle. She rolled it down and presented her travel papers. The soldier lowered his weapon and clicked on a tiny flashlight. He gave the papers a cursory glance, then turned the light into the car at Caine.

'Who is he?' the man grunted. His eyes looked heavy and tired, but they held a wary glint.

'Al-amn al-khass'. Private security,' Nena answered. 'He is my bodyguard.'

The soldier nodded. 'Passport.'

Caine reached over with a slow, non-threatening motion and handed the man his passport. The soldier flipped it open and glanced at the picture. He turned the page and slipped out the folded hundred-dollar bill with practiced ease.

He handed the passport and papers back to Nena. 'Be careful, Doctor Vasani. The rebels have been active in the South. Much fighting. Much shooting. Allah be with you.'

He waved them forward. They drove through the checkpoint and left Sudan behind them.

As Caine slipped his passport back into his pocket, he glanced over at Nena. She tugged her hijab off her head, letting her thick, dark hair spill out around her shoulders. She looked over at him and noticed him watching her.

'In Sudan, I am a Muslim, because my father was a Muslim,' she said. 'Even though my mother was Christian, I must follow Sharia law. I can be arrested for apostasy, for marrying a non-Muslim. I can be beaten or whipped for refusing to fast during Ramadan...' She glanced down at the scrap of fabric she clenched in her fist. 'Or for not wearing a hijab. These things, and more.'

'And here, in South Sudan?'

She set the scarf down on the seat next to her.

'Here, my faith is my own concern. I need not discuss it with you, or anyone else.'

Caine nodded. 'Fine by me.'

Nena watched him from the corner of her eye but said nothing. They continued down the long road in silence, driving into the purple twilight that separated night from dawn.

* * *

The first sign of Malakal was a sparse cluster of tents and shelters scattered on the grassy plains. The paved roads that had carried them out of Sudan had long since given way to dusty trails of packed earth. Malakal County bordered the banks of the White Nile. Here, a slick of wet mud and clay covered the soft ground.

Caine looked out the window as the truck bounced and clawed its way across the uneven terrain. 'Sure you don't want me to drive? It's pretty rugged out here.'

Nena clenched the wheel tighter in her small hands. 'I have driven throughout most of South Sudan, Mr. Caine. I can manage just fine, thank you.'

'I'm sure you can. I thought you might be getting tired.'

She glanced over at him and smiled. 'Sorry. I didn't mean to sound defensive. But we will be stopping soon. Look.' She pointed to a cluster of buildings in the distance.

'Malakal,' Caine said.

'What is left of it,' Nena added.

As they cleared the tents, the dirt road widened and the buildings grew closer. They were a motley assortment of shacks, warehouses, and municipal buildings. Half the structures were burned-out husks. Those that remained standing were badly in need of repair.

They drove past a stone and brick church near the center of town. Wood scaffolding surrounded its bell tower, and workers swarmed around the base. They patched holes in the tower's walls with a mix of rocks and cement. The heat outside was already brutal, and the workers' clothes were stained by dark patches of sweat.

'South Sudan's government says that peace has finally come

to Malakal,' Nena said. 'Officially, they signed a ceasefire with the rebels a few years ago. But the truth is, neither side ever really stopped fighting. Each group blames the other when there is shooting, but the killing never stops for long.'

'The city is in a strategic location,' Caine said as he stared out the window. He watched a group of children, only a few years old, splash in a pothole filled with stagnant green water. The collapsed frame of a charred school house leaned against the trees behind them.

He looked back to the road. 'There are oil fields to the north.'

'Yes,' she said. 'And where there is oil, there is always blood.'

Nena spun the wheel and turned down a bumpy side street. She smiled as they drove towards a cluster of colorful buildings. 'Here we are—'

The smile on her face melted away, replaced by a grimace of fear.

Caine heard her gasp. He stared out the windshield. Ahead of them, another burned-out shell of a building sank into the soft ground.

Nena opened the door and stepped towards the charred ruins.

'Nena, wait.' Caine glanced around the street. A few local women walked along either side of the dirt road, carrying jugs of water. A man in a pink polo shirt pushed a wheelbarrow filled with sacks of cement.

Caine exited the vehicle and pulled out his shirt tails, allowing the fabric to cover the butt of his pistol. He jogged over to Nena, who stood in front of the charred wood beams, staring. Her face was frozen, as if in shock.

'Nena, are you okay?'

'This was my clinic,' She said.

Caine put a hand on her shoulder. 'I'm sorry.'

A pair of South Sudanese soldiers rounded the corner. They spoke in low voices and laughed, despite the sweat and exhaustion that lingered around their faces.

Nena ran over to them. Caine stayed where he was, keeping an eye on her and the pair of armed men.

'The clinic,' she cried out. 'I was here the other day... What happened?'

One of the men took off his green beret and wiped a slick sheen of sweat off his shaved skull.

'Sorry, Doctor Vasani. There was a fire. We think it was rebels, hiding in the city.'

'Just a small group, Doctor,' the other soldier added. 'We find them soon. There is no more fighting here. You can reopen clinic, keep helping the sick.'

Caine stepped through the blackened archway of the ruins and prodded at a pile of debris with his foot.

'But what about my staff?' Nena continued speaking with the soldiers behind him.

'I'm sorry, Ma'am. We give them proper burial. We will catch the rebels, I promise. Good day, Doctor.'

Caine bent down and examined a speck of metal embedded in a charred wood beam.

As the soldiers continued down the dirt road, Nena joined Caine in the ruins.

'My clinic... the people who worked here...' Her voice was distant, as if describing a half-remembered nightmare. She looked around at the other buildings on the street. 'Why would rebels burn down my clinic, but nothing else?'

'I doubt they did,' Caine muttered.

'What?'

Caine pulled out his tactical pen. He inserted the tip into the piece of wood and pried out the shiny sliver of metal. He held it up to the light.

'This is a 5.56 NATO round. The rebels in this area mostly use Chinese AK-47 knock-offs.'

'So what?'

'Those guns don't fire this kind of bullet.'

'How can you be so sure?' she asked. 'Maybe they just got different guns.'

Caine shook his head. 'Not likely. But either way, we already know Takuba's men targeted you in the north. It only makes sense they would have searched here first.'

'Then Takuba must have taken the samples. What do we do now?'

He looked up. A few men stood at the corner, staring at the crumbled building. Caine scanned the rest of the street. A group of women glanced at him and Nena and spoke in hushed whispers. They were starting to attract attention.

The city's population was almost completely East African. Nena's mixed heritage allowed her to blend in as a local. Caine knew the same could not be said for him.

'We should get off the street,' he muttered. 'Takuba's men may still be in the area.'

He felt the eyes of the crowd follow him as they walked back to the truck.

23

Special Agent Zavala wrinkled her nose and grimaced. 'God, what is that smell?'

DuBose took a sip of cold coffee and stared out the window of his rental car. 'We're on the Black River. Wastewater Treatment Plant is less than a mile away.'

Zavala sipped her own coffee and shuddered. 'Asqueroso. Disgusting.'

Across the street, a crumbling brick warehouse perched above the riverbank. A thick mist filled the air, and a cool breeze blew across the dark water, sending ripples across its surface. DuBose watched a homeless man in a tattered raincoat push a shopping cart along the sidewalk. The rusty metal cart creaked and rattled as he moved past them. In a few minutes, he was gone. There was no other movement or sign of life around the dark, abandoned building.

'We've been here for hours,' DuBose muttered, keeping his eyes focused on the warehouse. 'No trucks, no security guards. Hell, even the crack addicts seem to avoid this place. You sure your intel is good?'

Zavala raised her eyebrows. 'After what happened today? I'm not sure of anything. Blackwing Capital is like a financial black-hole. Dummy corporations, proxies, forged documents... My friend in the Financial Crimes Investigation unit said she's never seen anything like it. Other than CIA front companies.'

'It's not one of ours. At least, not one the director knows about. This friend... You sure you can trust her?'

Zavala glanced at him. 'I'm still not sure I trust you. Anyway, of all their holdings, this warehouse was the only one she could find in the DC Metropolitan area. And speaking of your director, she dodged my question before all hell broke loose.'

'Yeah? What question was that?'

'Louisiana. This rogue operative, Caine. You helped him escape the FBI dragnet, didn't you?'

DuBose stared at her. 'You still won't let this go? What do you want from me?'

'The DNI is still missing. My guess is he's not gonna turn up alive anytime soon. Caine is our number one suspect. I want to know why you helped him escape custody.'

DuBose shook his head. 'Look, I don't know Caine very well, but I do know he's not some domestic terrorist, or a gun for hire. The guys he's after are connected to the guys who killed Lapin-ski. And who tried to kill us, by the way. Besides, he's not the FBI's problem anymore.'

Zavala squinted at him. 'Why? You mean he's out of the country?'

DuBose nodded. He took another sip of coffee. 'Yeah. He's on mission. So trust me. Let this go. Caine's not your guy.'

Zavala smiled. 'Well, you did come to me for help, so I guess I should trust your judgment of character.'

DuBose nodded. 'Now that's what I'm talking about.' He set down the coffee and opened the car door.

Zavala glanced at him in surprise. 'What the hell are you doing?'

DuBose stepped out of the car. 'Look, there's clearly nobody here. Either there's something useful inside or not. Either way, we're not gonna find out sitting in this car.'

He shut the door and walked across the street. Zavala hurried after him. They approached a pair of rusted metal doors on the front side of the building. There were no streetlights on the industrial road, and the entrance was shrouded in darkness. Zavala pulled a small flashlight from her belt and clicked it on.

DuBose tugged at the door. It was locked. He glanced behind them. The street was empty.

'Stand back,' he said. He drew his pistol from a shoulder holster and aimed it at the door.

Zavala grabbed his arm. 'Take it easy, big guy. I have a better way.' She reached into her purse and removed a slim metal tension bar, along with a plastic tool that resembled a staple gun. A long, thin needle extended from the tip of the device.

DuBose stood behind her as she inserted the tension bar into the door's lock. She twisted the bar and slid the needle-like device into the lock above it. She pulled the trigger on the plastic gun several times. After a series of loud clicks, the tension bar rotated freely, and the lock popped open.

She pulled on the door. It opened with a loud, rusty creak. She turned and flashed DuBose a smile.

He laughed and gestured inside. 'You always carry a snap gun in your purse?'

'Comes in handy when I forget my keys.'

Their footsteps echoed through the dark warehouse. A musty, chemical smell filled the air. Zavala traced the walls of the building with her flashlight. A set of metal stairs climbed up the southern wall, leading to a catwalk which ran around the sides of the building. The narrow walkway terminated at a metal door high above them. Beyond the door, a row of offices hung over the warehouse floor. Their windows were opaque with dust and cobwebs.

Her flashlight's beam settled on an enormous pile of trash and rubbish gathered in the center of the building. 'Looks like whoever was here cleared out in a hurry.'

DuBose picked up a torn, crumbling file box. A fine layer of brown, powdery dust fell to the ground. Zavala coughed.

'What the hell is that?' she asked. 'Smells like rotten eggs!'

DuBose tipped the box over. Old papers and manila folders cascaded to the floor. 'Anyone ever tell you you've got a sensitive nose?'

He looked up. More boxes were piled high in the center of the warehouse. The stacks almost reached the second-level catwalk. The same brown dust covered every flat surface. Particles shimmered in the air, caught by the beam of Zavala's flashlight.

The special agent picked up one of the crumpled pieces of paper. She unfolded the sheet and studied it.

'Numbers. It's just rows and rows of numbers.' She held the sheet out to DuBose. 'It must be some kind of code.'

DuBose swept the brown dust off another box and dumped it to the floor. 'Same here. More numbers.' He lifted up another sheet. 'There's a letterhead on this one. AHA.'

'Let me see that!' Zavala snatched the sheet of paper and held it under her flashlight. 'Tienes razón. You're right. AHA... African Hunger Alliance.'

'What's that?'

Zavala stood up and coughed. The particles of dust swirled around them. 'African Hunger Alliance is a nonprofit organization. They just began operating in the last couple years or so. Here's a list of donors.'

She ran her finger down a typed list of company names. 'Clayton... all of these companies showed up in the financial investigation of Blackwing Capital. They've each been making regular monthly donations.'

DuBose dumped another box of papers to the floor. He looked up at Zavala. 'So Blackwing is behind AHA? But why? What are they doing with all that money?'

She flipped to another page. 'According to this report, AHA was founded to provide relief and support to the people of South Sudan, and other African nations. They've been making monthly food shipments there since they opened their doors.'

DuBose stood up. 'South Sudan?'

She nodded. 'Yes, there's a terrible famine there.'

He grabbed her arm. 'Come on, we have to go.'

'What? We still need to search all these boxes!'

He pulled the special agent towards the door. 'Remember when I said Caine was out of the country, on mission?'

'Yes?'

DuBose looked her in the eye. 'I'll give you three guesses where he is.'

Zavala tilted her head. 'Wait... you don't mean—'

'Yeah. South Sudan. This must be connected. We have to get to the director, let her know AHA is involved somehow.'

A loud crash echoed through the dark building. The metal doors shook as if a great weight had slammed into them.

'Ajay, run!' DuBose sprinted towards the exit. He smashed into the doors with all his weight, but they would not open.

Zavala added her weight to his, throwing her shoulder against the rusty metal.

'Damn, they're stuck!' she said, gasping for breath.

DuBose kicked at the doorknob one more time. It shook and rattled, but the door remained closed. 'Something's blocking them from the other side. Something big, a car or a truck. Someone's trapped us in here!'

'Shhhh.' Zavala spun around and swept the darkness with her flashlight. They heard the tinkling of breaking glass. A soft buzzing sound filled the air.

'What the hell is that?' Her flashlight swung around the room.

'Point it up,' DuBose hissed as he drew his pistol. 'Show me the skylights.'

The beam swept up. A small, dark form flew into the circle of light. It swooped towards them, whirring like a giant mechanical insect.

DuBose fired. Sparks flew from the object as his shots hit home. It dropped from the sky and crashed into the concrete a few feet away.

'Cover me!' DuBose whispered.

Zavala drew her pistol as he stalked towards the wreckage.

In the shifting beam of her light, he caught a glimpse of smashed blades and twisted mechanical arms. The machine looked like a mechanical spider, suspended beneath miniature helicopter rotors.

'Some kind of drone,' he called back to her. 'It's carrying a payload.'

He pried a small metal cylinder from the mangled claw mounted beneath the tiny machine. 'Come closer with the light, I can't see.' He turned the object over in his hands.

Zavala moved closer and stepped aside so her body did not cast a shadow over the cylinder.

'What is it?' she asked.

More glass fell from the ceiling. The buzzing sound returned, louder this time.

DuBose stuffed the object in his pocket.

'The stairs!' he shouted. 'Run!'

The two of them charged toward the metal stairs. 'What the hell is going on?' Zavala panted.

'It's an incendiary grenade. The powder on the boxes, it's not dust. That smell, the rotten eggs? It's sulfur. This whole place is covered with thermate powder! It's like thermite, but the sulfur makes it burn even hotter!'

Three more drones dropped through the skylights. DuBose and Zavala raced up the staircase. Their footsteps clanged against the metal. As she neared the top, Zavala spun around and opened fire.

Her gun barked three times. One of the tiny drones sparked and fell from the sky.

The other two swooped low. DuBose grabbed her and pulled her the rest of the way up the stairs.

'There's no time,' he shouted. 'We have to get out of here!'

There was a click, and one of the silver canisters fell from the drone. It struck the piles of boxes. Zavala shielded her eyes as a blinding red flash erupted from the debris.

Within seconds, roaring flames raced across the concrete floor below them. The glowing pyre of papers and boxes crumbled to ash, and the flames began to lick at the walls.

DuBose and Zavala ran down the catwalk, choking and gasping as smoke filled the air. The metal catwalk jerked and swayed. Zavala screamed as she stumbled and fell to her knees.

DuBose spun around and held out his hand. Zavala reached out, but the catwalk was tilting, bending down towards the floor. She looked over her shoulder, her eyes wide with fear and panic. The flames were consuming the metal stairs behind them. The metal rods and planks glowed red-hot, liquefying in the intense heat. The glowing metal dripped to the floor, forming pools of molten steel.

The catwalk groaned and dipped lower. It tore away from the wall as the white-hot flames licked at the metal support beams. Zavala began to slide toward the hungry inferno below.

'Ajay!' DuBose threw himself after her and grabbed her hands. Sweat dripped down his face as the heat continued to rise. Digging his heels into the metal floor of the catwalk, he pulled her back up to safety. The narrow platform shook again. Gasping for breath, the pair continued to run around the edge of the building.

The second drone dropped its payload. Another bloom of fire exploded beneath them.

They reached the door that led to the offices and threw it open. Coughing and gagging for breath, DuBose pushed his way forward. Thick white smoke filled the beam of Zavala's flashlight. The windows that overlooked the inferno outside cracked and shattered. Another blast of heat billowed up from the floor.

DuBose squinted at a dim red light shimmering through the smoke and heat.

'Fire escape!' he shouted. He pointed towards the light. 'That way!'

They raced through the burning haze. Particles of glowing ash drifted through the broken windows. Flames burst to life and began to eat at the molding industrial carpet beneath their feet.

They reached the emergency door. DuBose yanked at the handle.

The door wouldn't budge.

'It's locked! You still got that snap gun?'

Zavala covered her mouth and nose with her sleeve and bent

down to examine the lock. She shook her head. 'No good,' she shouted. 'It's a deadbolt!'

DuBose removed the canister from his pocket. 'Okay, step back! Cover your eyes!'

He wedged the grenade into the door handle and pulled the pin. He took a few steps back. Behind them, the flames grew higher. A sea of fire roared up the walls and across the ceiling.

Whoosh!

An orange lance of flame hissed from the incendiary device. It cracked and sizzled as it melted through the steel door.

DuBose grabbed Zavala's arm. 'Okay, when I open this door, there's going to be a rush of oxygen heading straight outside. The fire is going to follow, and I mean fast. So we have to be faster. Got it?'

She nodded. 'Got it!'

'Okay... go!'

DuBose charged forward and kicked the door open. They continued running as the flames howled and roared even louder behind them.

They found themselves perched on a fire escape high above the Black River.

DuBose moved without hesitation. He grabbed Zavala, charged forward, and jumped off the metal platform.

As they fell toward the water, a fireball exploded out the door behind them. The water lit up orange, reflecting the bright light of the inferno. They struck the river with a loud splash and sank beneath the glowing water.

DuBose surfaced first. He wiped his eyes and spat water from his mouth. He looked left and right. 'Zavala?'

He heard a splash. He spun around, treading water. Zavala surfaced behind him, gasping for breath.

'Zavala!' DuBose paddled over to her. 'You okay?'

She nodded. 'Yeah... yeah, I'm okay.' She was pale and her pupils looked dilated. She gave him a nervous smile. 'You worried about me?'

DuBose grinned. 'Well, you did call me handsome. Come on, let's get out of here.'

They swam towards the riverbank. The remains of the warehouse crumpled into burning rubble, leaving behind a glowing skeleton of steel and iron beams.

24

The sign for the Harmony Inn towered over the dirt road that ran through the center of Malakal. It looked like a motel sign from fifties America, but its neon bulbs had been reduced to a mosaic of shattered glass and hanging wires. The inn itself looked more like a military bunker than a guesthouse. Coils of razor wire topped the two-story building's stark concrete walls. The entrance sat a few yards back from the main road, hidden behind a weed-infested courtyard and a shattered stone fountain.

Caine parked the truck around the back of the building. He left the shocked doctor in the vehicle, then walked around the corner and stepped under the archway that led into the hotel.

Inside, the curtains were drawn, and the blazing sun outside was reduced to a dim, soft glow. A TV was mounted to one of the walls, and a local newscaster reported on the upcoming peace conference.

A Turkish carpet covered the concrete floor. Old, threadbare sofas sat against three of the walls. Five girls, dressed in cutoff shorts and miniskirts, reclined on the couches. They were fanning themselves with rolled-up newspapers and sipping tea from glass cups. A pair of them looked up at Caine and smiled.

Caine ignored the invitation and walked over to an older woman sitting behind a desk. She wore a colorful sarong, and she looked up at Caine with a knowing glance.

'You like room, sir?'

'Two rooms, please.'

The woman clucked her tongue and nodded towards the girls. 'Two rooms? You here with friend? You want pretty girl to stay with you? Or you here with your wife?'

'No, I'm here with my doctor,' Caine said with a smile.

The woman squinted and gave him a confused look. Caine slid a hundred-dollar bill across the desk.

'Two rooms please, close to each other. And no questions.'

The woman shook her head. She handed him two keys and gestured towards a shadowed staircase at the rear of the building.

'Whatever you say. Rooms upstairs, to the right. Good rooms, good view.'

Caine took the keys, thanked her, and went back to the truck. He carried what little baggage they had, and led Nena to the hotel, keeping an eye on the foot traffic in the sprawling dirt road. As they walked up the stairs, she glanced at the young girls lounging in the front room and bit her lip. She was silent as she followed him up to the second floor.

A pair of squat potted palms flanked the end of the staircase. Caine looked left and right down the hallway. It was empty and quiet.

'Are we the only ones here?' Nena asked.

'I doubt they get much tourism. I think the working girls downstairs are the primary source of revenue.'

He opened the door to one of the rooms. Nena started to

walk in, but Caine held her back. He drew his pistol and made a quick sweep of the tiny chamber's bathroom and closet. They were clear. He drew the curtain aside and looked out the window. True to the old woman's word, the room had a view of the street and the colorful, rickety buildings that surrounded the town square.

'It's clear. Come in,' Caine called to Nena. She followed him into the room, collapsed onto the bed, and moaned.

Caine looked over at her, then glanced around the room. It was a tiny, cramped square, with a white tile floor and a stained wood door that led to a toilet and shower. The bed lay in the center of the room and was covered with a faded floral sheet. White mosquito netting hung from the ceiling overhead. It fell around Nena's body like a veil.

'Hope the room is okay,' Caine said. 'I doubt we'll find much better here.'

'I have lived in tents and UN refugee camps,' Nena said. 'This is paradise to me.' She propped herself up on her elbows and gave Caine a suspicious look. 'But where do you plan to sleep?'

Caine smiled and dangled the other key in his fingers. 'I'm right next door. I have to make a call. You should get some rest. We can't stay here long. We should leave after dark.'

'Leave for where?'

'That depends,' Caine said as he walked towards the door.

'What does it depend on?'

'On my call. Try to get some rest. Lock the door, don't open it for anyone.'

Nena lay back down on the bed and closed her eyes. 'Don't forget that shower,' she said in a sleepy voice. 'Doctor's orders.'

Caine smiled and quietly shut the door behind him.

* * *

Caine's room was almost identical to Nena's, with the same furniture and the same view out the window. The only difference he could spot was a torn, faded poster tacked to the wall. It was a photograph of the South Sudan flag – black, red, and green stripes, and a single star in a blue triangle. Below the flag, the words 'Happy Independence Day!' were written in English. The bottom of the poster was ripped off, leaving only the top half of the letters.

He sat down on the bed and ran his fingers through his sweat-slicked hair. His instincts were buzzing, sending adrenaline through his jangled, road-weary nerves. Takuba, Galloway, Nena... Like the poster on the wall, he felt like something had been torn away. A piece of the puzzle was missing. Every muscle in his body felt taut and alert. The old familiar tingle on the back of his neck was a constant, muted presence.

They were in danger here. He was certain of it.

He tuned on the satphone Rebecca had given him and dialed her number.

A series of long, intermittent beeps sounded from the earpiece. The satellite network encrypted the call's signal, preventing others from listening in. Finally, he heard a click, followed by the soft, buzzing static of an international connection.

'I was wondering when you'd call.' It was Rebecca. She sounded tired, strung out. Just like he felt.

'You sound exhausted. You okay?'

'I'm better than Lapinski.'

'What? Did something happen?'

Rebecca paused. 'Whoever is behind this – Bernatto, Blayne, someone else – they made their move. They took him out. Tom, I... I've never seen anything like it. Georgetown was a war zone.

They had men, weapons. They had goddamn EFP devices on a public street.'

'What?' Caine's voice snapped like cold steel over the phone. 'Are you sure you're okay?'

'It was close. I... I'm in the hospital now. But I'm fine, honestly. I was lucky. Once they hit their target, they disappeared. The FBI is looking for them, but there're no leads so far. The men left behind... they're ghosts, their records have all been doctored.'

'Firepower like that can't be too hard to trace.' Caine thought for a moment. 'Lapinski must have known something. Something big.'

'I spoke to him before... before it happened,' Rebecca's voice crackled back. 'He swore he didn't know who was blackmailing him. I believed him.' She was silent for a moment. 'Tom, he did have one name. It was a code name. An asset, someone involved in an old operation of yours.'

Caine clenched his teeth. It can't be, he thought. But he knew what she would say before the words left her mouth.

'Puff Adder.'

You should know better, he thought. You should have told her!

He silenced the guilt that slinked through his mind. 'Rebecca, I—' He froze. He had no idea what to say.

'You knew, didn't you? Before I sent you, you knew. Did John Blayne tell you?'

Caine said nothing. Empty static crackled over the phone.

'Tom, answer me!'

'Yes. Blayne told me. When I found him, he was in a meeting of some kind, a video conference call. I didn't see who was on the call. I think Bernatto was one of them. And I think 'Puff

Adder' may have been on as well. His real name is Simon Takuba. He's a rebel leader in South Sudan.'

'Why the hell didn't you tell me? After all we've been through, you still don't trust me?'

'It's like you said. I trusted you. I didn't trust myself.'

'Trust yourself to do what?'

'You sent me here to find Josh. I know... I know what he means to you, and I meant what I said. I want you to be happy. But Takuba... He and I have unfinished business.'

'Meaning, putting a bullet in his head was more important to you than helping an agent under fire.'

'Maybe, before. But now...' His voice trailed off.

'Now what? Do you know where Josh is? Do you know if he—'

'I don't, Rebecca. I swear, I don't. But I think he was right about his bioweapon theory. I've made contact with Nena Vasani. Galloway left some samples at her clinic, in Malakal. That's where I am now. There's no sign of him here.'

'And these samples? Were they the material from Syria?'

'I don't know. They're gone. Her clinic was burned to the ground. And armed men tracked her north, to Khartoum.'

'Takuba's men?'

Caine gritted his teeth. 'I think so. But something doesn't feel right. The weapons the men used, their organization. Hell, even this bioweapon, whatever it is... It all feels too sophisticated for Takuba.'

'What about Delta Blue?'

Caine's head snapped up. 'What about them?'

'Lapinski gave me another lead, before... before they took him out. I had DuBose do some digging. Delta Blue is part of a portfolio of private security companies. Intelligence brokers, private militaries, arms dealers, satellite communication networks. The holding company is called Blackwing Capital. We haven't been able to track down who owns it yet. But with resources like this...'

'They could back someone like Takuba. But why?'

'I don't know, but like I said, Delta Blue is only part of it. There was another company in the portfolio that stood out. It's a nonprofit, an NGO that works in Africa. It's called Africa Hunger Alliance. They send food, medical supplies, infrastructure support. Billions of dollars in aid, and no one seems to have ever heard of them.'

'AHA... I've seen their trucks here. It can't be a coincidence. I'll look into it.'

'You sound tired.'

Caine sat down on the bed. 'I am.'

'Get some rest. Call me if you hear anything about... about the situation.'

'I will.' He blinked and realized there was more he needed to say. 'Rebecca, I'm sorry. I should have told you.'

He heard her sigh. For a few seconds, there was only crackling silence between them.

'Keeping secrets isn't exactly new for you, Tom,' she finally said. 'With everything that happened, trust is hard for you, I get it. But sooner or later, you have to make a decision.'

'I know.'

'We're either in this together, or we're alone. You can't have it both ways.'

There was a click, and she was gone.

Several minutes passed. He rose from the bed and staggered to the shower. He stripped down, leaving his dirty clothes on the floor, and leaned under the pulsing jet of water.

He closed his eyes and let the lukewarm spray wash away whatever sweat, grime, and pain it could.

25

Caine's eyes shot open. The room was dark. The ceiling fan spun overhead, a soft whisper in the quiet room.

He sat up in bed. Something had woken him. Something was wrong. He glanced at his watch. It was a few minutes past midnight. His hand slipped under the pillow and gripped his pistol. He stood up and slinked over to the window. Using the barrel of the gun, he parted the curtains just enough to view the street outside. It was dark, empty, and silent.

He walked over to the door and listened. Again, he heard nothing. He unlocked the door and opened it an inch. The hallway outside was quiet as a tomb. A thin sliver of light spilled from the door of Nena's room. It was open just a crack.

He heard a man's voice, whispering. Then he heard Nena scream.

Caine darted into the hallway and sprinted towards her door. Pressing his body against the side of the frame, he took a deep breath. Then he kicked the door open, raising his pistol in a steady grip.

A tall, lanky man stood over Nena. She was lying on the bed

beneath a thin white sheet. Her eyes were wide with shock and fear.

The man looked up at Caine. His jaw dropped, and his hands shot up in surrender.

'Please, don't shoot!' he cried out.

Caine kept his pistol aimed at the man. 'Who the hell are you?'

'It's okay,' Nena said. 'He's a friend. He startled me, that's all!'

'I work in the clinic,' the man said, his voice stuttering with fear. 'I was there when it burned down. I escape, I hide.'

Nena sat up in bed, clutching the sheet to her body. 'Close the door! I need to get dressed.'

Caine kicked the door closed with his foot. Nena grabbed some clothes off the floor and padded into the bathroom.

Caine gestured to the bed with his pistol. 'Sit down.'

The man did as he was told. He looked to be in his early twenties. His hair was short and neatly trimmed. A thin goatee and mustache framed his trembling lips.

'What's your name?' Caine asked.

'I am Rafael. I worked in the clinic with Doctor Vasani. There are girls here, downstairs. One of them knew my sister. She told her Doctor Vasani come back to town. I come here to warn her.'

'Warn her about what?'

The bathroom door opened. Nena stepped out wearing jeans and an olive-green shirt.

'It's okay, Tom, he's telling the truth. He goes to medical school in Juba and works as a nurse at my clinic during his free months.'

'Doctor Vasani, thank God you are alright!' The man stood up and embraced her. Nena hugged him back for a moment, then pushed him away.

'Please, Rafael, get a hold of yourself. What were you saying about warning me?'

Rafael paced in front of the window. 'The men who burned down the clinic... It was the Army of the Chosen!'

'Takuba's men?' Caine asked.

Rafael nodded. 'Two of the men bore the mark of the Ghost Jackals... the armbands, the white faces. But the others, they kept their faces hidden under black hoods. I could see the skin around their eyes. And the way they spoke, they were not from here.' He turned to Caine. 'They spoke English, like you. American.'

Caine thought back to the slug he had pried from the wreckage of the clinic. 5.56 NATO. The same caliber used by the IWI Tavor rifles the Delta Blue mercenaries had carried in Louisiana.

He knew many guns used that caliber of ammunition. It could just be a coincidence. But still...

'How did you escape?' Nena asked the panicked man.

'I was in the bathroom when the men came in. I heard them shouting. Then I heard gunfire. I ran out the back door before they set the building on fire.'

He looked into Vasani's eyes. Pain and guilt contorted his features. 'I heard the other staff. They were crying, begging the men. And then, when I ran out of the building, I saw the flames. I should have gone back... I should have helped. But I was scared.'

'Hush, there is nothing you could have done.' Nena gave him a gentle smile, and the man's ragged breathing slowed down.

'These men, they were looking for you,' he said. 'They say an American gave you property that belongs to them.'

'The bioweapon samples,' Caine said.

'Did they get the samples, Rafael? The case Mr. Carter gave me?'

The man shook his head. 'No. The samples were not there. Mr. Carter came back the day before. He took the case and the test results. He said he was going to wait for you in Kanfar.'

'Where's that?' Caine asked.

Nena sat down on the bed. 'Kanfar is southwest of here, along the river. It's a small town. Conditions are bad... even worse than here.'

'Do you have a clinic there?'

She shook her head. 'No. There is no infrastructure there at all. But Rafael and I would travel there in the truck and deliver medical supplies. Your friend, Mr. Carter, knew I visited there often.'

'Then that's where we have to go next.' Caine tucked the pistol in his waistband. 'Rafael, if I were you, I'd take your family and head back to Juba. Get as far away from here as you can.'

The young man continued his frantic pacing. 'My whole family? But my mother is old, she cannot travel to Juba. What am I going to do?'

'I don't know, but Takuba must have men near Malakal. He could come back, or—'

Before Caine could finish his sentence, the crackling of automatic gunfire burst through the room. The window exploded into shards of broken glass. Rafael danced and jerked as bullets tore through his body.

'Nena, get down!' Caine shouted. He dove through the air, knocking her off the bed and onto the floor.

Rafael's bloody corpse collapsed next to them.

Nena screamed. She reached out for him but yanked her hand back as more bullets ricocheted through the room.

Caine pressed up against the outer wall and peered around

the corner of the shattered window. A pair of headlights lit up the street. Three men crouched behind a battered pickup truck across the from the hotel. Caine ducked back as one of them sent another burst through the window.

The gunfire ceased. Caine snapped out from his cover and opened fire. His gun roared three times. As he ducked back behind the wall, he saw one of the men fall to the ground clutching his shoulder.

He turned to Nena. She lay on the floor of the tiny room, her body shaking. She stared at Rafael's corpse and muttered an unintelligible prayer.

'Nena, look at me. Look at me!' He stared into her panic-stricken eyes. 'We have to move. On my signal, we go for the door. Stay low. Crawl. Do you understand?'

She nodded her head.

More gunfire burst through the window. Caine returned fire again, sending a double tap of bullets at the truck. The two remaining men charged towards the front of the hotel. A second vehicle rumbled down the road and skidded to a stop. It was another pickup truck, painted in brown and tan camouflage. A soldier in a tattered uniform stood in the flatbed, manning a pole-mounted W-85 heavy machine gun.

As he swiveled the weapon towards the hotel, Caine dropped to the ground.

'Move!' he shouted. 'Go now!'

The chugging machine gun sounded like fireworks erupting through the air behind them. Thick slugs tore through the concrete walls, sending a shower of debris onto Caine and Nena. They scrambled across the floor towards the door.

A dusty haze filled the room. 'Stay low!' Caine ordered, coughing in the thick, chalky air.

He reached up and swung open the door. Grabbing Nena's

shirt, he herded her out into the hallway. Behind them, the room's walls continued to crumble under the onslaught of the heavy weapon.

He heard shouting in the lobby downstairs. More gunfire sounded from below. Heavy footsteps stomped up the stairs.

'Stay here,' Caine hissed. He jogged towards the staircase, keeping as low as possible as he moved through the dim corridor. He ducked down behind the bannister as a pair of men ascended into view. His hands wrapped around the trunk of a potted palm.

As the soldiers reached the top step, Caine leapt up and swung the tree in front of him. The heavy pot slammed into the nearest man, throwing a spray of dirt and dried leaves into the air.

The rebel soldier staggered backwards. He cried out as his feet shot out from under him and he tumbled down the staircase.

Caine hurled the potted plant after him as the other soldier advanced towards him. Before he could fire, Caine grabbed the barrel of the man's assault rifle in both hands and shoved it straight up. Muzzle flash exploded from the weapon, but Caine was already out of the line of fire.

As the confused soldier struggled to regain his balance, Caine stomped the edge of his foot into the man's shin. The soldier took a step back, dropping his rear foot down the stairs.

Caine released the barrel with one hand and drew his pistol. He fired, sending two shots into the man's gut at point blank range.

The soldier gasped as a crimson stain spread across his uniform. Caine yanked the rifle from his weakened grip. The man's eyes rolled into his skull and he tumbled backwards.

Caine stuffed his pistol in his waistband and quickly grabbed spare magazines from the soldier before advancing further down the stairs, swiveling the rifle towards the other soldier. The man cursed as he threw the heavy plant off his chest and rolled to his feet. Muzzle flash lit up the dim lobby as Caine cut him down with a quick burst. Moving with a swift, precise stride, he took up a position next to the archway that led to the front courtyard.

Out in the street, the soldier in the back of the truck unleashed another barrage from the W-85. Caine watched as more glass and chips of concrete exploded from the hotel's second floor.

He dropped into the open doorway and took aim with the rifle. The soldier was so engrossed in firing the heavy weapon that he didn't notice Caine lining him up in the rifle's sights.

Caine squeezed the trigger and a three-round burst barked from the Tavor. The soldier jerked backwards and ceased firing. His confused gaze dropped to the entrance of the hotel. Caine squeezed the trigger again. The soldier collapsed, his body toppling over the edge of the pickup bed.

Caine darted back behind the entrance. 'Nena, come down,' he shouted. 'Get behind me!'

He heard her footsteps rushing down the stairs. Suddenly, a high-pitched whistling sound cut through the air. It warbled louder and louder, closing in on their position.

Caine cursed and darted back into the lobby. He grabbed Nena as she reached the first floor and dragged her behind the front desk.

'Cover your head!'

There was a tremendous whoosh, and a rush of air blew in from the front of the hotel. An explosion rocked the street, sending a plume of dirt into the night sky. Nena screamed as the building trembled around them.

More whistles screeched across the sky, this time in the distance. The ground shook as a wave of explosions rippled through the city.

'What are they?' Nena gasped.

'Mortars,' Caine shouted back. 'Takuba's men aren't just attacking this hotel. They're attacking the whole city!'

26

Caine dragged Nena back as another explosion shook the building. The arched entrance collapsed behind them. Bricks and rubble cascaded down from the second floor.

Nena froze in her tracks as the groan of twisting wood and metal echoed from the staircase. Caine kicked open a door marked *Laundry* and pushed her through. A shower of dust and wood chips rained down from the second floor. The staircase creaked and moaned as it snapped loose from its moorings. Caine darted through the door as the second floor collapsed behind them.

They ran past a row of battered old washing machines as another explosion rattled the building. One of the machines toppled over behind them. The metallic crash rang like a gong as it struck the floor. Nena screamed and covered her ears.

'Don't stop, keep running!' Caine shouted. The laundry room was located in a screened rear porch. Caine heard gunfire and shouting in the distance. He threw open the rear door of the porch and they charged out into a muddy field that lay behind the building. Clusters of palm trees separated the hotel from the street where their truck was parked.

Caine and Nena dashed across the field towards the truck. He saw a crowd of civilians flee from a row of burning buildings across the street. The families scrambled along the mud-slicked road, carrying their wailing children in their arms. Behind them, fire burned bright, casting a hellish orange glow across the town.

An engine roared from down the street. Caine grabbed Nena's arm and pulled her behind a grove of trees. Two more of the rebels' pickup trucks barreled around the corner, heading towards the center of town. The men in the back aimed their heavy machine guns at the scattered cars parked along either side of the dirt road. The weapons spat bright bursts of muzzle fire into the darkness.

Glass pelted Caine and Nena as the gunfire blew out the windows of the parked cars. One of the rebels tossed a Molotov cocktail from the back of their pickup. A fireball engulfed Nena's truck and several other nearby vehicles. As the pickups roared past, Caine smelled smoke and burning rubber.

'My truck!' Nena shouted.

Caine peered out from behind the trees. A group of armed men in ragtag uniforms jogged down the street, following the path of destruction left by the pickup trucks. They sprayed gunfire through the street, targeting the civilians who straggled behind the crowd.

'The truck's gone. Forget it. Stay behind me,' Caine ordered.

Caine darted into the street. A wounded man in a bloody, tattered T-shirt staggered into him. The man looked into his eyes and pleaded with him in words he could not understand. Caine shoved him aside and raised the rifle. He targeted a squad of rebels as they opened fire on a burning house a few yards away. Three women burst out of the house. Their clothes and hair were on fire and they were howling in pain. Their flaming bodies writhed and their skin hissed as they fell into the muddy street. The rifle-toting men laughed and aimed their weapons at the smoking bodies.

Caine gritted his teeth and opened fire. The gun jumped and rattled in his hands. One man fell. The rebels swung their rifles towards Caine, but they were too late. Caine pivoted to his next target. He sidestepped across the street, sweeping his fire across the gang.

Only one of the rebels managed to return fire with his battered AK-47. His shots kicked puffs of dirt into the air and ricocheted off the mangled wreckage of an old Jeep. Caine ducked behind the Jeep and fired another short, controlled burst. The rebel jerked backwards, then dropped his rifle. He fell face-first into the dirt.

Caine gestured to Nena. She joined him in the street, and they ran towards the front of the hotel. Bodies darted around them... dark, desperate shapes, silhouetted against the flames of the burning buildings.

As they rounded the corner, another whistle sounded through the air. Caine looked up and watched as a smoking mortar shell struck the stone church tower. A cone of bricks and stone exploded out from the impact zone. Caine pulled Nena into the doorway of an abandoned building as the heavy chunks of debris pelted the street behind them.

'This is insane!' Nena shouted.

'This is a war zone,' Caine answered. 'Takuba's men have penetrated the government force's perimeter. They're advancing on the city. We have to get out of here.'

'But how?'

'Wait here. I'll see what I can find.'

Caine started to move, but Nena grabbed his arm. He looked

down at her. Her eyes were wide with shock and fear. A fine gray dust covered her dark skin, giving her a deathly pallor.

'You can't leave me here!' she screamed.

Caine grabbed her shoulders. His emerald eyes burned into her dark, dilated pupils. Her body was trembling. He moved his hands up to her cheeks and pulled her face close to his.

'I'm not leaving you, understand?'

She shook her head.

'Say it! I'm not leaving you. I'm coming back.'

'You... you're not leaving me,' she stammered. 'You're coming back.'

He nodded. 'Doctor's orders, right?'

A trembling smile crossed her lips. 'Hurry.'

Caine let go and slapped a fresh magazine into the Tavor. 'I'll be back as quick as I can. Now stay here and stay down. Got it?'

She nodded and stepped back into the building. Caine watched as she hid behind an overturned table. Then he turned and continued jogging down the street towards the front of the hotel. He spotted the Ghost Jackal's trucks still parked in the middle of the intersection. He ran towards them, but a line of gunfire cut though the street in front of him. The shots were coming from above.

Pivoting around, he spotted shadows moving along the roof of an empty building. Dark figures popped up from behind the roof's low wall and took potshots at the fleeing civilians. Caine squinted in the dim light. He sprayed the roof with automatic fire as he jogged towards the abandoned trucks. The shadows scrambled back from the edge of the building, shouting in panic. Caine continued laying down suppressive fire until the weapon clicked empty.

Caine pressed himself close to the first truck and ducked down as bullets tore through the street. Another mortar round whistled above him. Caine followed the sound with his eyes. A concrete building to the east of the town square crumbled as the explosive round slammed into its roof. Men in uniform scurried for cover amidst the shrapnel and debris.

South Sudanese forces, Caine thought. They must have been using the building as a garrison.

The squad of soldiers took cover behind a barricade of heavy rubber tires at the end of the street. Caine watched as a bullet twanged off one of the men's helmets. The soldier flew back from the barricade as if jerked by an explosive force.

Bullets ricocheted off the side of the truck. Caine covered his head with his hands. The window above him exploded into a rain of sparkling glass shards. He ejected the empty mag from the Tavor and used his last spare to reload the weapon.

He heard more shouting and saw dark figures approaching from the opposite side of the street. Before he could react, another of the rebel pickups skidded through the town center. It swerved left, and one of the men onboard tossed a bottle stuffed with a lit rag towards Caine.

Caine charged away from the trucks, running towards the group of shadowy figures who had fired on his position. The Molotov cocktail shattered, spreading a burning slick of fire across the roof and bed of the first vehicle. The flames spread quickly in the hot night wind, and thick smoke billowed up into the dark sky.

Caine raised his rifle as the advancing rebel squad came into view. He watched as their faces were lit by the flames of the burning truck.

He saw wide, terrified eyes reflecting the orange glow of the flames. Small mouths twisted into snarls of rage and fear, baring tiny, gritted teeth. Baggy, scavenged clothes hung from their malnourished limbs. Their lanky arms could barely support the weight of the heavy rifles they carried.

They're children.

Caine froze. He watched as the child soldiers pivoted their weapons towards him. One of the boys wielded a machete. He shook the bloodied weapon in the air. They were shouting, yelling. The words were in their native tongue and Caine couldn't understand what they were saying. But after a lifetime of violence and conflict... a lifetime spent dealing death, both on the battlefield and in the dark allies and streets like this... Caine knew exactly what those sounds were.

War cries. Chants meant to exorcise their own fear. That was how the killing got done. In a place like this, if you couldn't rise above your fear, if you couldn't make yourself kill... then you became the prey.

The children moved towards him. They were shaking their rifles now. They pointed them into the air, fired bursts to frighten and intimidate him. A pair of them ran off into the darkness, overcome with fear or revulsion.

Caine's finger froze on the trigger of his rifle.

Children. The word echoed through his head, over and over.

One of them, an older boy maybe fourteen years old, bit his lip. He raised his rifle towards Caine and took aim. Caine took a step back and lowered his gun. He stared at the boy.

'It's okay,' he shouted. 'It's not your fault.'

Suddenly, a heavy shell streaked through the air and slammed into the burning truck. A thunderclap echoed around them as the truck exploded. The shockwave knocked them both to the ground. Caine rolled through the mud, trying to get as far away from the wreckage as he could.

He looked down the street. An armored personnel carrier rolled up behind the barricade of tires. The heavy vehicle was backing up the South Sudanese soldiers' position. It was armed with a 30mm automatic cannon.

Caine staggered to his feet and blinked, clearing the haze from his vision. His ears were ringing. The battle around him sounded muted, like a television playing behind a closed door.

He watched as the boy picked himself up and shook his head. Blood seeped from a gash across his cheek, and his clothes were soaked with mud. His rifle was wedged in the soft earth a few feet away from him. He stared at it for a second, then glanced up at Caine. Then he turned and bolted. He ran between two nearby buildings and disappeared into the shadows.

'Tom!'

The voice sounded distant, but he jumped as he felt hands touch his shoulder.

He spun around. It was Nena.

'I told you to wait—'

'They were shelling the building, I had to run. Look, there!'

She pointed north, towards the opposite side of the street. The pickup that had driven past him earlier had crashed into a row of parked cars. The men on board were now corpses, littering the mud-soaked streets, cut down by the soldiers' weapons.

The heavy cannon thumped again. The air seemed to crack in half around them as another shell tore past. Behind them, the building that had housed the snipers exploded. Heavy chunks of concrete tumbled to the ground.

Caine grabbed her hand and pulled her away from the debris. They raced across the street towards the truck. More rebels whooped and hollered as they poured out of the darkness. The armed men surged toward the soldiers' barricade.

Their crackling rifles sent a curtain of death flying through the streets.

As they made their way to the truck, two rebels scrambled out of a nearby building and took up a position in the street. They were wearing red armbands and Caine could see white smeared across their faces. Long, painted fangs streaked down their cheeks.

Ghost Jackals...

One of the men dropped to his knees and lifted a long, tube-like barrel onto his shoulder. The other shouted orders into a walkie-talkie.

Rocket-propelled grenade, Caine thought. These rebels have been well-supplied.

He hopped into the rear bed of the pickup truck. One of the rebels sagged against the mounted gun. His lifeless eyes stared unseeing into the darkness. Caine shoved the corpse out of the bed and grabbed the handles of the heavy machine gun.

'Drive!' he shouted to Nena.

She climbed into the driver's seat and slammed the door shut. The keys were still in the ignition. The engine sputtered for a second, then it turned over and roared to life. Nena shifted into reverse and hit the gas. The twisted metal of the truck's front bumper screeched as it tore loose from the mangled cars.

The men in the street spun around at the noise. Caine saw the man with the walkie squint, then point in their direction. The man with the RPG spun around. The truck lurched to a stop as Nena shifted into drive.

Caine pivoted the gun towards the Ghost Jackals. He pressed forward on the handles, locking the gun's bolt mechanism into the firing position. He knew the RPG was unguided, but he could see the man lining them up in the weapon's sights.

He squeezed the trigger on the handle, punching the air with a barrage of heavy slugs. Puddles of mud splashed into the air as the line of death swept towards the Ghost Jackals.

The man with the walkie staggered backwards as the projectiles tore through his body. The gun vibrated in Caine's hands, and he saw the other man fall sideways and crash into the mud. A plume of red-hot exhaust fired behind him... He had fired the rocket launcher! The explosive projectile lanced into the air, streaking sideways into an abandoned building on their left side.

'Nena, punch it!' Caine shouted.

Whoosh!

Every window in the building exploded out into the street. A wave of super-heated air tore through the structure's interior. The rippling heat ignited the peeling paint and decayed wood floor. The explosion lit up the street. A cloud of dust and smoke billowed from the wreckage, glowing orange and red against the black sky.

The truck picked up speed as the building collapsed behind them. The rumbling drowned out the sounds of the battle.

Caine let go of the gun and let its barrel drop. As they left the buildings of Malakal behind them, a thumping roar swooped overhead. A pair of government helicopters soared past them. Their searchlights cut through the dark streets of the town. Caine stared at the burning pinpoints of light in the sky as their gunfire swept through the distant buildings.

They raced on into the night. A stray shot rang out from the darkness and struck the side of the truck. Caine didn't even flinch.

He remembered Jack's words from that night, years ago.

Sooner or later, you'll learn... You have to fire and forget.

Fire and forget...

27

It was still dark when the truck's engine sputtered to a stop. Caine jerked awake as the vehicle lurched off the side of the road. A final smoking gasp wheezed from under the hood. The vehicle rolled a few more feet, then ceased moving.

Caine shook his head. He did not remember falling asleep, and for a moment, he forgot where he was. The cut in his side ached and throbbed. The hot night air was thick with haze. He heard the chattering of insects all around him. A high-pitched shriek rang out in the distance. He assumed it was a baboon, or a monkey of some kind.

'Nena, you okay?' He checked his Tavor rifle and flipped on the safety. He hopped out of the truck bed. The moonlight cast silver highlights across a vast plain of tall grass rippling to the south. Beyond that, clusters of dark, shadowed trees curved up against the purple night sky. To the north, he could detect the earthy smell of the Nile River waters. It was familiar to him now, scenting the air like the exotic perfume of a lover.

'Nena?' he called again. He walked to the driver's side of the truck cab. She sat ramrod straight behind the wheel. The whites of her eyes were wide and unblinking. She stared straight ahead, fixated on the darkness.

Despite the heat, she was shivering.

'You fell asleep,' she said. 'I drove as far as I could. We ran out of gas.'

Caine reached through the window and rested his hand on her arm. 'Nena, it's okay. We made it.'

'I... I have seen violence before,' she said, her voice a quivering whisper. 'War, fighting. The aftermath... but never like that. Not all around me...'

'I know,' Caine said. 'I'm sorry.'

She looked up at him. Her eyes seemed to reflect the moonlight back at him. 'What about you?'

Caine said nothing.

'You have seen such things before?' she asked.

Caine looked at her for a moment. Then he turned and peered into the darkness surrounding them. 'We have to keep moving.'

He opened the door and held out his hand. After a few moments she took it, wrapping her cool, slender fingers around his. He helped her out of the truck. She looked up at the sky. A thin line of red cut across the horizon, like blood seeping from a fine cut.

'The sun will come up in a few hours,' she said, her voice regaining a trace of strength and confidence. 'I think we are maybe fifteen, twenty miles from Kanfar. We should cover as much ground as we can before sunrise.'

Caine searched the back of the truck. He found a canteen of water and a canvas sack filled with rations tossed among the machine gun parts and debris. He slung the meager supplies over his shoulder and handed the canteen to Nena.

'We'll have to conserve water. Take a small sip every hour.'

A low growl rumbled across the grass. Caine spun around and raised the rifle. Nena grabbed his arm and froze. The sound was deep and primal. It vibrated in the pit of his stomach.

'What the hell was that?' he asked in a low voice.

'We are on the edge of the Ez Zeraf game reserve,' she whispered. 'Many animals live in the protected area south of here.'

'What kind of animals?'

She glanced at him and gave him a nervous smile. 'Elephants, buffalo, giraffe... lions.'

Caine eyed the dark splotches of forest with a wary stare.

Nena pulled at his arm. 'It would be best to head north,' she whispered. 'Follow the river.'

'Lead the way, Doctor.'

They hiked off into the moonlit night, heading towards the crimson sliver on the horizon.

* * *

After a few hours of walking through the grassy plains they came to the banks of the White Nile. They followed the serpentine curve of the river west, towards their destination. As they walked, Caine shook the canteen. The sloshing of the water inside sounded weak and miniscule. He doubted they would get more than another few sips each.

A pair of long-legged storks marched across the muddy banks in front of them. They bent their long, graceful necks down to the rippling surface of the water. As they drank, Caine scanned the terrain ahead of them. He spotted a small, dark shape in the distance. They walked closer. It was a tiny shelter, a lean-to built from lashed sticks and brush, perched near the water's edge.

As they walked past the storks, the birds spread their enormous wings and took silent flight. They were barely visible against the dusky sky.

The shelter was abandoned and showed no signs of recent use. A makeshift raft sat on the damp ground next to the tiny hut. The water craft was a collection of scavenged lumber fastened to rows of old rubber tires. A long, crooked stick lay next to the rickety craft.

'You said Kanfar is near the river, right?' Caine asked. Nena nodded but eyed the raft suspiciously.

'Yes, but—'

'Water travel will be faster. And the more distance we put between us and Malakal, the better.'

Caine grunted as he lifted the edge of the raft and dragged it into the water. He squinted in the dim light and examined the surface for leaks. A few droplets of murky water bubbled through the cracks between the wood beams, but the craft bobbed and floated above the surface of the dark river.

'I hope whoever made it doesn't mind,' Nena replied.

She splashed into the water. Caine held the raft steady for her as she lifted herself up onto the damp planks of wood. He stepped up after her and stood near the rear of the craft. Using the crooked stick as a pole, he pushed the raft away from the bank. They began to float downriver.

Nena sat near the front of the craft. Caine watched the breeze rustle through her hair. She tilted her head and looked up at the canopy of stars above them. They grew dimmer as the light on the horizon increased. It was now a heavy orange glow, pushing back the velvet curtain of night.

The pair of cranes circled overhead, then peeled off and flapped their wings. They glided in a precise, straight line towards the distant trees.

'It is beautiful here,' Nena said in a breathy voice. 'So peaceful. It is almost enough...'

'Enough for what?' Caine asked.

'Enough to forget.' She looked back at him. 'You have many scars. You must have many things you would like to forget, yes?'

Caine drove the stick down into the dark water, pushing the raft along. 'I've tried. Tried to forget the past, move on. But somehow the past keeps finding ways to remind me.'

Nena lay down on the raft and looked up at him. 'Give me a rag to wipe away the past, a rose to sweeten the present, a kiss to greet the future.'

Caine smiled but he kept his eyes on the river. 'I've never heard that.'

'It is an old Arab proverb,' Nena said. Her voice was heavy with exhaustion. She closed her eyes.

'Get some rest,' Caine said quietly. 'It's been a long night.'

Her breathing became a soft sigh. As she slept, Caine continued driving the pole into the water.

They floated along, drifting onward into the darkness.

28

Caine sensed danger before he saw the dark object in the water. A tingling sensation crawled up his spine, lingering on the hairs behind his neck.

They were being watched. He was sure of it.

He glanced left and right but saw nothing along the banks of the river. There were still a few minutes of darkness left before the sun pierced the night sky. The rising orange glow was just enough light to see by. The surface of the water was smooth and flat. The dim horizon cast shadows of reeds and trees across the river's glassy surface. All was quiet and still.

Suddenly, a loud thud sounded from under the raft. The wood platform bobbed up in the water, then settled back down. Caine heard a splash a few yards away.

Something had struck the bottom of the tiny craft.

The sudden motion stirred Nena. She moaned as she lifted her head. Her hair fell over half her face, revealing a single, sleepy eye.

'How long was I out?' she breathed.

'There's something in the water,' Caine whispered. 'It hit the raft.'

Nena scrambled to her feet. The raft dipped up and down as her weight shifted.

'Where is it?' she whispered.

Caine was silent as he scanned the placid river's surface. He spotted a ripple to their right side. A dark shape floated in the water, moving alongside them.

He pointed with the stick. 'There.'

Nena peered into the darkness. 'I don't see...'

The shape bobbed up the water. In the dim glow of dawn, Caine saw a pair of massive eyelids peel up, revealing two dark orbs. The eyes were the size of a man's fist, peering up at them from the waterline. The creature's body was submerged, but Caine caught a glimpse of smooth gray skin, mottled with patches of pink.

Nena brushed her hair from her face and looked closer. Her eyes grew wide and she gasped. She grabbed the pole and pushed it down into the water. 'We have to get to shore! Now!'

'What the hell is it?' Caine asked as the two of them guided the raft towards the south bank of the river.

Before she could answer, a louder splash sounded in the water, only a few feet away. Caine spun around and saw the massive dark shape launching towards them. He pulled Nena away from the edge of the raft as the tiny craft listed in the churning water.

The bulbous creature surfaced, lifting the raft up into the air. Nena screamed as the two of them tumbled into the water with a splash.

Nena surfaced and spat a stream of water from her mouth. Caine gripped her hand and began kicking towards the shore. 'Can you swim?' he shouted.

She yanked her hand away and ignored the question. Caine could see she was moving at a swift pace, using a powerful breast stroke.

He heard the crack of splintering wood behind him. He turned and saw a massive hippopotamus slam its girth down onto the raft. Its cavernous mouth yawned open and released a bellowing roar. Caine felt his innards shake as the powerful noise vibrated through his body. The beast's gaping maw sported a series of thick, bony tusks. It plunged them into the raft, piercing the wood beams as if they were mere twigs. The creature shook its head and the raft flew apart, scattering debris across the water.

The hippo snorted angrily and lurched through the water towards them. Caine swam between the behemoth and Nena. As she crawled up onto the shore, the creature rose up in front of Caine. Three tons of blubber and sinew loomed before him in the dark water. He felt a blast of stagnant air as the animal once again opened its massive jaws.

Up close, the hippo's wet bellow was deafening. The pink flesh and white teeth of its gaping maw filled Caine's vision, blocking out the dark river and the orange sky.

The pole they'd been using as a punt floated nearby. Caine thrust forward with the long stick, jabbing it into the creature's mouth. The animal bit down, snapping the rod in two. Its head lurched sideways, sending a wave of water cascading over Caine.

He spun around and paddled towards the southern bank of the river as fast as he could. Behind him, he heard the animal splash and roar. It turned its attention to the floating debris surrounding it in the river. The massive jaws clamped onto one of the raft's rubber tires. Long, curved tusks pierced the thick rubber with ease. The hippo shook its inanimate prey back and forth, sending a cascade of droplets through the air.

Then, with a final, triumphant snort, the animal sank back under the water.

Caine crawled out of the river and scrambled to the shore. He collapsed on the ground next to Nena, panting for breath. He turned and saw the bulbous head of the hippo floating next to a smaller, identical shape. The pair of animals touched snouts, then floated away into the distance.

'Hippopotamus,' Caine said between lungfuls of air. 'Didn't expect that.'

'They are very dangerous,' Nena gasped. 'They kill more people in Africa than any other large animal.' She panted for breath. 'They are especially aggressive around their young. We are lucky she didn't come on land...'

They lay silent, letting the wave of adrenaline wash over them. Caine turned towards her. Her wet hair trailed behind her like a shadow, and her translucent clothes clung against her dark skin.

Without thinking, Caine reached out and touched her face. 'Are you alright?' he asked in a soft voice.

She stared at him. Her wide, cat-like eyes glinted in the dim early light. She said nothing. Her breathing slowed to a low, heavy pant.

Caine pulled his hand away and looked down. 'I... Sorry, I just—'

She grabbed his hand and pulled it back to her. She closed her eyes as she pressed the rough skin of his palm against her soft cheek.

Caine was silent. She opened her eyes. 'Why do you not kiss me?'

Caine gently removed his hand.

She tilted her head. 'Is there another woman that you love?'

Caine looked away. 'It's not that simple.'

She stared at him, then sighed. 'It never is.' She stood up and tied her wet hair into a dripping ponytail.

'Perhaps it is just as well,' she muttered as Caine stood up next to her. 'Hippos defecate in the water to mark their territory.'

'Great,' Caine said, sniffing his soaked clothes.

Nena scrunched her nose and pursed her lips. 'Now we both need a shower. We should keep moving. Kanfar is close, but the terrain is difficult. We'll be lucky if we can make it by morning.'

Caine followed her along the riverbank as the rippling orange sun began its slow ascent.

29

Caine staggered forward. His foot splashed down into the soft grass and sank into the marsh below. His tan skin flared with sunburn and beads of sweat rolled down his cheeks. His short hair was plastered to his scalp.

Nena panted for breath and splashed after him. They were traversing the northern edge of the Sudd, a vast swampland that stretched for miles to the south. The terrain was brutal, and their travel was slow going. Every step through the muck and mire of the soft earth was like trudging through quicksand.

The blazing sun rose higher above them. Caine lost track of the hours. He could not remember the last time either he or Nena had spoken. The deeper they penetrated into the thick marsh, the quieter they each became. Every yard gained was a battle, every mile a war. They were struggling, fighting their way through the thick mud and tangled vegetation. They had no more energy left to speak.

Flies and water bugs buzzed around his face. There were so many creatures flying through the air, it seemed like a dense black cloud hovered around them. He was too tired to swat them away. He watched Nena from the corner of his eye. She swung her arm in a listless arc. The insects parted and buzzed away, but they returned in seconds.

The knife wound in Caine's side throbbed with a dull ache.

Should have listened to the doctor, he thought. You need stitches.

A loud hiss sounded from the river's edge. Caine kicked at the weeds and whistled. He knew their best bet was to try to frighten away hostile animals by making as much noise as possible. To appear weak and tired was to accept a death sentence... to mark themselves as prey.

A long, sinewy crocodile slithered from the brush. Sunlight gleamed off its thick, armored scales. The huge reptile cruised away from them and disappeared into the water.

Nena paused and watched it swim, then glanced over at Caine. Her eyes had glazed over. To Caine, it seemed like she was looking right through him.

'Here, take my hand,' Caine spat the words out, his voice thick and dry.

The doctor grabbed his arm and leaned against him. Caine's muscles ached in protest. He continued plodding forward, supporting her weight against his shoulder.

At one point, Caine swore he saw tiny huts, brown domes of reeds and straw. The dwellings perched above floating islands of swamp grass far in the distance. He blinked, and his vision wavered... The brown dots vanished in a sea of rippling heat-waves. He looked down at Nena. Her eyes fluttered but remained fixed ahead of them.

He took a deep breath and continued the march forward.

* * *

The sun reaches its zenith overhead. The terrain is dry now and more stable. The swamp-like marsh is replaced by long, waving brown grass and scrub.

Caine feels a surge of energy. He moves faster through the grass, lowering his hand to feel it graze the tips of his fingers. The reeds brush the dry, cracked skin of his palms.

He hears another growl in the grass up ahead... deep and guttural, it shakes his bones and sends a primal rush of adrenaline through his loins.

Predators ahead, he thinks.

The voice in his head whispers back a reply. You're a predator as well...

He stalks through the grass. The savannah parts, revealing an endless stretch of cracked, rocky desert. The hellish terrain stretches as far as the eye can see. It vanishes in a crimson haze at the foot of dark, distant mountains.

Caine stands alone in the desolate expanse. He glances left and right... Nena is nowhere to be seen.

Something's wrong, he thinks.

She was slowing you down, the voice answers back. You have work to do.

He sees more tiny brown dots in the distance... huts, sprouting from the arid landscape, like blisters on sun-scorched skin.

He walks towards them. As he moves closer, he notices a flickering glow rising from their thatched roofs.

The huts are burning.

Children run from the collapsing structures. Caine listens to their high-pitched cries of terror and pain. He is in the village now. They are all around him, darting past him, disappearing into the billowing clouds of smoke.

One boy stands in his path and raises a rifle. His feet are

shoulder-width apart on the cracked, parched earth. His legs tremble in fear. Caine stares down the long, black barrel of the gun.

'It's okay,' he whispers. He holds out his hand. 'It's not your fault.'

No, the voice in his head hisses. It's your fault. All of this is your fault.

Puff Adder...

The black circle of the rifle barrel splits open. A serpent's eye stares back at him, looking down the barrel of the gun. He watches the eye blink. A clear membrane slides back and forth over the slit reptilian pupil.

He spins around, peering through the smoke and flames of the devastated village.

'Takuba!' he shouts.

The boy drops the rifle and scampers off. Caine picks up the gun. The bolt action clicks with comforting precision as he yanks back the lever and chambers a round.

'Mr. Caine... Tom. Nice of you to come, good sir.'

Caine whirls around and raises the rifle to his shoulder. He peers above the notched sights. A dark figure emerges from the swirling clouds of smoke.

It is him... Simon Takuba.

He looks older now. His hair and stubble are flecked with gray. Long, deep lines cut into his gaunt face. But when he smiles, there is no doubt. The blood-red diamond tooth reflects the hellish glow of the inferno around them.

He hunches over and drags something across the dusty rocks. It is the girl... His long, bony fingers clutch at the tangled mass of her hair. He pulls her struggling body behind him.

'Why are you here, Tom? This place... you don't belong here anymore.' His voice is high-pitched... almost a giggling laugh.

'I came here to kill you,' Caine shouts. 'Like I should have done before.'

He pulls the trigger of the rifle. Nothing happens.

'Tom...' It was the girl. She looks up at him, and he remembers the fear, the pleading... God, her eyes. How can he ever forget those eyes?

But this time it is not her. It is Nena. Takuba's fingers grow through her hair, like the roots of a malignant tree.

'Don't leave me,' she gasps. 'Please, you can't leave me.'

The gun shakes in his hands. He roars in frustration. No matter how hard he tries, the trigger is frozen. He cannot fire. He hears the kiss of metal sliding against leather.

Takuba draws his machete. He holds it above Nena's head.

'You cannot kill me, Tom. I told you before. My spirits protect me.'

And they curse you...

The smoke thickens around him. Caine pushes forward, gasping for breath.

'Nena? Are you there?'

He hears the hiss of the blade slicing through the air. The sound is so intimate, so familiar...

His coughing grows more intense. He is staggering, falling. He can't breathe. The red haze surrounding him blots out the light and mutes her cries to a strangled sob.

He feels hands lifting him up, pulling him away. He reaches out, but his fingers touch nothing. Everything fades to black. He hears a voice calling to him. It is an echo, far away and yet whispering in his ear.

We're weapons, Tom.

You have to fire and forget...

Fire and forget...

30

Caine gasped and sat up. Something cold and wet slid off his face. He grabbed it in his hands and held it up. It was a rag, soaked in water. His eyes darted around the tiny, dark room. The surroundings were new and unfamiliar.

He was lying on the dirt floor of a tiny shack. It was a patch-work dwelling of plastic sheets, scavenged timbers, and other random materials. A narrow beam of sunlight pierced the tattered curtains hanging over the entrance to the room. He smelled smoke and heard low voices drifting in from outside.

The burning pain in his side had dwindled to a dull throb. He reached down and felt fresh stitches. His shirt had been washed and was folded on the ground next to him.

He stood up, dressed, pausing for a moment to listen to the people beyond the curtains. He recognized Nena's voice speaking an African dialect of some kind. He parted the curtains and stepped outside.

Nena sat on a small bench next to a cooking fire. She held a chipped plate in her hands and was dipping her fingers into a thick white ball of paste. She swished the paste through a ring of watery tomato sauce on the edge of the dish and licked it off her fingers.

She looked up. Her eyes widened with surprise as she saw Caine standing there.

'Tom! You're awake... You slept the entire day. You must have been exhausted!'

She gave him a sheepish grin and wiped her fingers on her jeans.

An elderly local woman sat next to a clay pot suspended above a small fire. She smiled at Caine and ladled another mass of the white porridge onto a plate of sauce. She held it out to him.

Caine ignored her and took a few steps forward. He blinked as his eyes adjusted to the harsh sunlight. Based on the high position of the sun, he knew it was late in the afternoon. He had a dim, feverish memory of the sun in the same position as they trudged through the Sudd swampland. Was what Nena said true? Had he slept an entire day? Takuba, the burning village... Had it all been a feverish nightmare?

The shack sat on a flat, muddy plain. In the distance, he could see the tall grass, and beyond that, the wetlands they had crossed.

'Where are we?' he asked, his voice dry and raspy.

'Tom, sit down, rest. We made it.' Nena gently tugged at his arm. 'This is Kanfar.'

Caine stared at the ruins surrounding them.

The shack he was standing in was one of the few buildings left intact. Everywhere he turned, he saw scattered timbers, piles of rubble, jagged pipes sticking from the ground. Scraps of burned tents flapped in the breeze. Families huddled beneath them, desperate for whatever tiny patch of shade they could find. In the distance, he saw a stretch of barren land covered with rusted, empty bed frames. Their mattresses and bedding had been burned away, and they were now only useful for scrap metal.

He heard children crying, women sobbing. He saw a young girl in the distance take a few trundling steps as she emerged from under one of the flapping tents. Her tiny legs looked like burned twigs. Their skin and flesh had dwindled to a dry sheath, revealing the outline of bones and joints beneath. She sat on a sun-bleached patch of baked earth and rested, exhausted from the short burst of energy.

Kanfar was a wasteland. Whatever it had once been, it was a desolate husk of a town now. A trio of mangy birds hopped through the shimmering heat distortion in the distance. One of them spread its wings, and a buzzing cry pierced through the wind.

Vultures, waiting for their chance to feed.

Caine swallowed, then clenched his jaw. 'What happened here?'

The wrinkled old woman gestured with the plate of food. Nena took the plate from her and stood next to him.

'You had to carry me the last couple of miles. We were both suffering from heat exhaustion, and your wound was infected. You had a high fever.'

'I don't remember...' His voice faded to a hoarse whisper. He couldn't tear his eyes away from the devastation surrounding them.

'I'm not surprised. This woman's name is Saynab. She took us in and found me some basic medical supplies. She says conditions were bad here before, even worse than Malakal. But a few days ago, a rebel militia group attacked. Painted faces, white skulls. Ghost Jackals.'

'Takuba,' Caine muttered. 'The Army of the Chosen.'

Nena pulled Caine back under the awning.

'Tom, they are sharing this food with us. It is all they have. Do you understand?'

Caine blinked and took the plate in his hands. He suddenly realized how hungry he was. He sat down next to Nena and began to shovel the paste into his mouth.

Nena gave him a relieved smile. 'It is called asida. It's made from wheat.'

Caine scooped more of the paste into his mouth. 'Please, thank her for me.'

Nena spoke to the old woman, and she smiled. They continued to speak in low, hushed tones. Nena turned back to Caine.

'She says Takuba himself was here. They took your friend, Mr. Carter. They were looking for something, searching the ruins after the attack.'

Caine nodded and continued eating. 'The samples. And your test results.'

Nena coughed. 'Do you think... they did all this? Because of...' Her voice trailed off.

Footsteps approached the front of the shack. Caine looked up as a shadow crossed in front of the porch. A tall, muscular man stood before them. His left hand was severed at the wrist. Tattered, stained rags bandaged the stump.

'I know what they were looking for.' The man spoke English with a deep, powerful voice. His eyes traveled from Nena's face to Caine's. They squinted at him with a disdainful stare.

Caine stood up. 'You know what they wanted? Is it still here? Did you keep it hidden?'

The man glared at him, then looked away. 'I did not know when they came. If I had... I would have gladly given it to them.

Takuba and his jackals... They took my wife, my son. Girls from the village as well.'

'You're hurt. Did they...' Nena glanced at the man's severed hand. He nodded but said nothing.

'Who are you?' Caine asked. 'This thing Takuba wanted, do you have it on you?'

The man shook his head. 'No, but I can take you to it. My name is Nhial.'

Caine and Nena exchanged a worried glance. Caine set down his plate of food and looked up.

'Alright, Nhial. Lead the way.'

* * *

Nhial led them on a meandering path through the decimated village. They circled around the rusted chassis of a bombed truck, then squeezed down a narrow, muddy alley between two abandoned tents. Finally, on the outskirts of the village, they came to another shack.

Like Nhial's dwelling, this one had been left somewhat intact after the fighting. Nhial knocked on the door, an old, crooked slab of wood, fastened to the shack by two mismatched hinges.

'Talak... let us in.'

The door creaked open, dragging a path in the dirt and mud. A wrinkled East African man stood in the shadows, leaning against the doorframe. His face was gaunt, and his beard and hair were gray as ash.

The man looked up at Caine and stared for a moment, then turned to Nena.

'Doctor Vasani, word has spread that you were back in Kanfar,' he said in English. 'Please, come in.'

Nena smiled, ducked her head, and stepped into the tiny shack. Caine and Nhial followed.

The old man gestured to a small table and set down some clay cups. He spooned cold tea into the cups and served them to Nena and the others. 'You have done much for the people of Kanfar, Doctor Vasani. I am ashamed that I have no food to offer you.'

Nena sipped the tea and smiled at him. 'This is wonderful, thank you. Your name is Talak?'

The man nodded. 'Yes. I was at Nhial's home when the Army of the Chosen attacked. Your friend, Mr. Carter, he told me you would be returning. He gave me something for you, told me to keep it safe.'

Nhial slammed his fist on the table. 'You knew what those men were after the whole time?' he snapped. 'While they took my wife and son, you scurried back here and hid the white man's treasure from them! My family is gone because of you!'

Talak blinked. 'I was a soldier once, Nhial. I am sorry for what happened to your family. But if what Mr. Galloway said was true, then many more lives are at stake.'

'Who is Galloway?' Nena asked.

'Carter's real name,' Caine answered. 'He was undercover.' He glanced at Talak. 'He told you?'

The old man nodded. 'He did. He also told me where he hid the case Takuba's men were looking for. There is an old minefield, left from the last civil war, a few kilometers north of here. Galloway hid the case there. He made a map, a safe passageway through the unexploded mines. After the attack, I went back and retrieved it.'

He hefted a dusty canvas sack onto the table, then stepped away. Caine opened the sack and slid out a silver metal case, followed by a manila folder bulging with papers. He dropped the bundle onto the table and opened the case. Several vials of liquid lay nestled in protective foam.

'It's the samples!' Nena gasped. She flipped open the folder and examined the charts and papers inside. 'These are the results of the tests I ran!'

Caine set down the case and slid it towards Nena. 'Nhial, Talak... do either of you know where Takuba is now?'

The men glared at each other, then Nhial shook his head. 'No. I tried to follow their tracks after they left, but I lost them west of here. They could be anywhere by now.'

Caine clenched his fingers into a fist but said nothing. He turned from the table and walked towards the door. Nena grasped his arm as he passed, but her wide eyes did not look up from her papers.

'Tom, it's going to take me some time to analyze the data here, but this looks bacteriological, not viral.'

'Knock yourself out,' he grunted. He pulled away and walked out the door. Nena looked up and followed him with her eyes. She stood, but Talak reached out and touched her arm.

'Let him go, Doctor.'

'But he—'

'There are some paths a man must walk alone,' the old man said.

'I don't believe that,' she replied in a soft voice.

Talak held up one of the vials. He turned it around in the dim light, watching the reflection on the curved surface of the glass.

'That is because you are a doctor, a healer,' he said. 'You fix what is broken, you heal people and take away their pain.'

He looked up at the door where Caine had exited. Beams of light fell through the gaps in the crooked frame.

'But there are some wounds that only heal when they are ready. For some men, to take away their pain is to remove their soul. And your Mr. Caine... he has the look of such a man.'

31

Caine sat on a dry patch of land and surveyed the desolation around him. Tiny plumes of smoke rose from the cooking fires of the tents and shacks. The blood-red sun hung low on the horizon. The vultures, black shadows that hung suspended in the air, were silhouetted against the crimson and orange clouds. One by one, they peeled off and circled overhead.

Caine heard footsteps crunching on the sand behind him. His eyes remained locked on the horizon.

Nena sat down next to him. She rested her chin in her hand and stared at him.

He dragged his eyes to her face. She had changed out of her filthy clothes and draped her body in a colorful cotton sarong. The dress flapped and billowed in the hot breeze.

'What are you looking at?' she asked.

'Nothing,' he answered. 'I was thinking about that saying you told me, on the raft.'

'Is that why you came here? To wipe away the past?'

Caine looked away. One of the vultures cried out and swooped to the ground. It landed a few feet from a collapsed tent and paced back and forth on the ground. The inhabitants of the tent huddled under the scrap of cloth. They were too tired to shoo away the hunched, squawking bird.

'When we first met, in Sudan, you said Takuba was your responsibility,' Nena said. 'What did you mean by that?'

Caine looked down at the ground. 'A long time ago, I came here on a job. It was a joint operation, Sudan and the United States. They called it "normalizing relations." We shared common interests.'

'So I was right. You are a soldier.'

Caine shook his head. 'No, not then. Soldiers fight wars. They look their enemy in the eye when they pull the trigger. The men I killed that night... I stabbed them in the back.'

'Were you here to kill Takuba?'

'No. I was sent here to protect him. Back then, Takuba was working with South Sudan's vice president, and the SPLM rebels. Technically, the United States supported South Sudan's independence. But somewhere along the way, the US oil companies got cold feet. Between the human rights protests and security concerns, most of them pulled out of the area. And I guess the powers that be realized they had just handed control of 75 percent of the region's oil over to the Chinese.'

Nena ran her fingers through her hair and looked away. 'Oil. It always comes back to the oil, here.'

'The Sudanese government in the north had intel my people needed: movements of radicalized terrorists, financing sources, that kind of thing. And of course, they weren't too keen on negotiating lower prices with South Sudan for the use of their pipelines. The vice president offered them a bigger cut, if they helped oust the sitting president.'

'So your country and mine joined in support of the rebels?'

Caine picked up a twig and dragged it through the dirt.

'Nothing that official. It never is. Certain parties close to both governments set up some introductions for the rebel forces. Arms dealers, weapons manufacturers, mercenaries. The meetings were held in secret, in Khartoum. Takuba was sent as the SPLM rebel's representative. But there was a leak.'

'A leak to who?' she asked.

'The CIA had intel that someone in the VP's inner circle leaked the meeting's location to the president's forces. They were planning to follow Takuba into the city, kill him and his contact before he could close the deal. My partner and I were sent to deal with the assassins, neutralize them before they got to Takuba. It was a close call... One of their snipers had Takuba in his sights. I was there. I... I stayed on mission.'

'Neutralize? You mean kill?'

Caine stared at her. 'I knew what kind of man Takuba was. I had seen him kill, loot, and worse. I hesitated. I had my orders, but I knew the world would be better without Takuba in it. I froze up. I almost let the sniper take his shot. But my training kicked in. I followed my orders. I slit two throats. I watched two men bleed out. And then I watched Takuba walk out of his arms deal, smiling.'

Nena rested her hand on his shoulder. 'Back in Malakal, I saw you hesitate as well. Those boys had guns, they could have killed you. But you did not give in to fear. You risked your life to spare them.'

A bitter laugh escaped Caine's lips. 'That night, we met up with Takuba's forces and our Sudanese contact to debrief. Takuba's men had already used the weapons to raid a village nearby. They were Dinka, the same tribe as South Sudan's president. Takuba killed all the men and kidnapped the children. There was a girl... She was barely a teenager, maybe thirteen, fourteen years old. Takuba took her. I tried to stop him, I tried...'

'Tom,' Nena whispered. 'You can't blame yourself. Men like Takuba...' her voice trailed off. She shuddered, despite the hot wind blowing across the plains. 'They are monsters. I will never understand them. But they have always been with us. They are like a plague, or—'

'Or a curse,' Caine muttered. 'Takuba told me that he was protected by evil spirits. And that he had put a curse on me.'

'Surely you do not believe in such things,' Nena chided him. Her dark hair fluttered around her face in the wind.

'No,' Caine admitted. 'I don't. But when I look back on every-thing, the years that followed, the things I've done...' He paused and looked at her. A shadow moved across his face as the vultures swooped overhead.

'The past hasn't been so easy to wipe away. If I had stopped him, if I had let those men take their shot, maybe none of this would have ever happened. Maybe these people, those boys back in Malakal...'

They were silent for a few moments. Caine watched as another of the vultures landed on the ground. Its pink head and hooked beak pecked at the sand. It looked towards the inhabitants of the billowing tent and squawked with impatience.

Caine picked up a rock and tossed it at the bird. 'Get the hell away from them,' he hissed.

The bird cocked its head and gave him an annoyed glance. It hopped up onto an overturned plastic bin and screeched in anger. The bin was a pale blue color, and Caine could make out some markings stenciled on the side, half-buried in the soft earth.

AHA... African Hunger Alliance.

He realized he had not had a chance to follow up on Rebec-ca's lead.

Too busy sitting on your ass, throwing rocks at birds, he thought.

Time to get back to work.

He turned to Nena. 'Did you find anything useful in the samples?'

She crossed her arms and gave him a concerned look. 'Yes, but keep in mind, our clinic was not designed for infectious disease research.'

'Is that what we're dealing with here? A weaponized bacteria of some kind?'

She shook her head. 'I'm honestly not sure. Mr. Car—I mean, Mr. Galloway, your friend, gave us two sets of samples. The vials in that case, and a small blood sample he said he got from an infected oil worker somewhere south of here.'

'You said the samples looked like some kind of bacteria?'

She nodded. 'Yes, but the worker's blood showed signs of viral infection. So at first, I thought the two samples might be unrelated.'

Caine narrowed his eyes. 'And now?'

Nena's brow furrowed. 'Like I said, I can't be sure. But I think we may be dealing with a bacteriophage here.'

'Something man-made?'

'In this case, yes. A bacteriophage is a virus capable of infecting and replicating within bacteria. In nature, they spread DNA from one microbe to another, causing mutations in successive strains of bacteria. Things like spontaneous antibiotic immunity.'

'But these specimens don't appear to be natural?'

'I'm not sure about the virus itself. But the bacteria samples they were inhabiting are definitely man-made. They had an unusually thick cell wall, and they appear to be hyperthermophiles. They can survive in extremely high temperatures.'

'How hot are we talking here?' Caine asked.

'In the wild, thermophilic bacteria have been found near geothermal geysers, deep-sea volcanic vents, even on the exterior of spacecraft. But the cell wall of this bacteria is unique. For my dissertation at Omdurman Medical School, I studied cells created by companies like Synthetic Genomics in California. They created an organism that was controlled by man-made DNA. It was designed to consume large amounts of hydrocarbons and then die off. It was developed to clean oil spills and other chemical disasters.'

'Oil-eating bacteria... You said the infected blood sample was from an oil worker, right? Could these bacteria have come from an oil refinery?'

She nodded. 'I think so. The cell walls are similar to the samples I viewed for my dissertation. These bacteria were definitely engineered to survive in crude oil. And their thermophilic properties mean they could even survive through the refining process. If that's true, and the cell wall is eaten away during that process, it could release the virus inside. That could mean this bacteriophage is capable of infecting workers at the refineries.'

Caine stood up and dusted off his pants. He held out a hand to Nena.

'Come on,' he said. 'This isn't over yet.'

She took his hand and he pulled her up. 'What do you mean?' she asked.

'You need to identify this virus, figure out if it really is a weapon of some kind.'

'There's no way I can do that here. I need special equipment, a laboratory.'

Caine walked back towards Talak's shack. 'Where do you need to go?'

She bit her lip as she followed him. 'Mmmm... Juba,

perhaps. The university. Rafael's medical school should have what I need.'

Caine nodded. 'Okay, let's see what we can do.'

He opened the crooked door and stepped into the shack. Talak and Nhial still sat at the table. Talak appeared to have dozed off, and Nhial stared at him in sullen silence.

'Alright, listen up,' Caine commanded as he walked over to the silent men. 'Doctor Vasani has to get to Juba. How far is that from here?'

Talak's eyes fluttered open. 'The capital? That's two days' travel, at least!'

Nhial rocked in his chair. 'Not necessarily.'

Caine looked over at the younger man. 'Go on?'

'The United Nations has a camp not far from here. Perhaps a half day's walk. A helicopter delivers medicine and emergency supplies there each day. As a doctor, she might be able to convince them to take her to the capital.'

'I will convince them,' Nena said in a determined voice.

'Can you take her to the camp?' Caine asked.

Nhial glared at him. 'What about you? Where are you going?'

'I'm going to find Takuba.'

'If you know where he is, then I must go with you. I must find my family.'

Caine shook his head. 'Nhial, you are a brave man, I'm sure. But I must do this alone. I have training, experience. And the truth is, I don't know where he is. But I have an idea on how I might find him. Trust me, if your family is still alive, I'll do whatever I can to help them. And if not... I promise you, I'll make Takuba pay for what he's done.'

'And just how do you plan to find Takuba?' Talak asked.

Caine pointed out the open door of the shack, towards the plastic bin where the squawking vulture perched.

'That bin says African Hunger Alliance. Do their trucks come through here?'

Talak shook his head. 'No. But I have seen them on the road east of here, near Bentiu.'

Caine looked him in the eye. 'I have to take a look at one of those trucks. Up close.'

Talak thought for a moment. 'Perhaps there is a way... I know a man, from a village not far from there. He runs a shelter.'

Nena raised her eyebrows. 'A shelter? You mean for refugees?'

The old man nodded and scratched his chin. 'Of a sort, yes.'

'Haven't these people suffered enough? Now you want them to fight for you?'

Talak smiled. 'Well, miss, I did not say this was a shelter for men.'

32

Caine felt vibrations rattle though his bruised and battered body. He peered out from under a grass-covered tarp and watched as six massive African elephants took long, slow strides down the road near Bentiu.

The road, like most of the roads he had traveled on recently, was a long unpaved line of packed sand and earth that stretched off into the rippling, heat-distorted horizon. Every step the giant animals took pounded the earth with a force of over five tons. One of the creatures raised its six-foot-long trunk into the air and trumpeted.

Talak and his associate, a man who went by the name of Paul, spoke to the elephants in soothing tones. They patted their legs, gently guiding the lumbering creatures down the road. Paul ran the Sudd Area Elephant Sanctuary. The large swath of protected swampland served as a safe haven for the animals. The creatures' previous habitats had been decimated by war and poaching.

The two men were old army friends. Paul was keen to help

out as long as Caine could assure none of the elephants would be harmed in their plan.

Caine had positioned himself 150 yards from the road. The tarp covering his body was hidden under a layer of reeds, grass, and scrub the men had gathered from the surrounding area. The camouflaged cloth acted as a makeshift ghillie suit. Caine was confident he could not be spotted from the road.

Cradled in his arms was the nicked, battered wood stock of a bolt action rifle. The Lee Enfield No. 5 Jungle Carbine was an antique. When Talak had pulled the canvas gun bag out of a dusty old footlocker, Caine had assumed it would hold an AK-47. Instead, Talak proudly displayed the carbine in one hand and a small cloth pouch in the other. 'This rifle is not old,' Talak said when he noticed Caine's skeptical expression. 'It is like me... classic!'

The pouch held five loads of .303 Brit, the obsolete caliber used by the British-made rifle. As far as Caine knew, the ammunition had not been used in a mass-produced firearm since the fifties. But the antique weapon was the best he was going to find in the ruins of Kanfar.

Now he was grateful for the short-barreled, lightweight rifle. The bolt action was smooth, and the gun's design included cutouts in the receiver body and barrel to keep the weight down. After a couple of hours lying under the heavy tarp, with the sun beating down overhead, Caine was thankful that the weapon was light. It was easy to keep the rifle sighted on the road before him.

Another low bellow rumbled through the air. The elephants' tails swished back and forth with short, rapid strikes. It was a gesture of annoyance. They were restless, uncomfortable in this foreign terrain. Caine glanced down at the glowing luminescent numbers on his watch. Beads of sweat rolled down his forehead, but he ignored them. He lined up the simple notch sight of the rifle on a patch of road and waited. It was almost time.

According to Paul, an AHA truck had cleared border customs in the early morning. It was driving in from Uganda, in the south. The truck would turn east on this road. As the ground shook from the elephants' thundering steps, Caine saw movement on the horizon.

The tiny dot grew larger. It kicked up a cloud of dust as it moved towards them. Caine tightened his grip on the rifle. The vehicle came into view, driving through the curtain of heat and haze. He saw the familiar logo painted on the side of the light-blue cargo trailer. African Hunger Alliance.

The herd of elephants blocked the truck's passage, and the vehicle groaned to a halt. The driver leaned on the air horn, and a loud blast echoed through the hot air. One of the elephants trumpeted back in return, but the creatures obeyed Paul's commands. They did not move out of the way, and even a big rig truck was not going to plow through almost forty tons of animal.

'Come on,' Caine whispered to himself. 'Get your ass out of the truck.'

He needed at least one man to exit the vehicle, but both would be ideal.

The truck sounded another blast of its horn. The animals remained where they were, swaying in place. Talak raised his arms in an exaggerated shrug.

Caine was facing the passenger side of the cab. He heard a distant metal thunk as the driver opened the door. A man jumped to the ground and stepped into view, pacing between the front of the truck and the clustered elephants. Caine's eyes narrowed. The man was Caucasian and wore gray body armor over a black polo. He waved an automatic rifle at the men and shouted in a garbled African dialect. The rifle had the distinctive bullpup design of the IWI Tavor.

Mercenaries, Caine thought. Delta Blue...

Talak and Paul argued with the man. He spoke in English when he realized they spoke his native language. Their voices were muted and distant. Caine shifted his rifle sight to a second man sitting in the passenger seat. He wore similar clothes, and wraparound sunglasses shielded his eyes from the intense sun.

The Lee Enfield was unfamiliar, and Caine knew the bolt action rifle had a reputation for a 'wandering zero'. It could not be sighted in and reliably hit the same spot twice. He waited, hoping the man would leave the cover of the truck and present a larger target. If his first shot missed he would have to quickly eject the cartridge and line up a second shot. A head shot with this weapon was far from a sure thing.

He heard another clunk... The door was opening.

Caine held his breath.

That's it... Go help your friend.

The second man hung from the side of the truck and raised his rifle in the air. He fired a short burst.

'Get these fucking animals out of—'

Crack!

Caine's rifle fired. The echo of the gunshot exploded from the brush. The second man fell from the open passenger door and collapsed to the ground. He clutched his leg and howled in pain. Blood streamed from a wound just above his knee.

Even as the gun fired, Caine was already moving. Keeping the butt of the rifle pressed against his left shoulder, his right hand shot up under the bolt, slapped it up, and pulled back. The spent shell clinked to the ground next to him as he slid the bolt forward and down, loading another .303 round.

He had already lowered the sight as the bolt locked into

firing position. Settling his right hand under the barrel, he zeroed in on the fallen man's head.

As the mercenary in the road spun around towards his fallen comrade, Caine fired again.

Crack! The second shot rang out barely a second after the first.

The fallen merc's body jerked, then slumped back to the ground, motionless.

The other man pivoted towards the brush where Caine was hiding. He raised his rifle and opened fire, sending a barrage of wild shots into the grass. Caine winced as a few bullets thudded into the earth next to him.

Talak and Paul crouched low as the gunfire echoed around them. At the sound of the mercenary's automatic fire, the elephants stomped the ground and bellowed even louder. The angry beasts flapped their ears and raised their long, curved tusks in the air.

Their bellowing cries were so loud, they even drowned out the explosive gunfire. The mercenary swung around and aimed his weapon at the herd. His face was pale with panic and fear. The massive creatures stomped towards him.

At the sight of the weapon, the lead elephant emitted a bone-shaking growl and reared up on its hind legs. Thirteen feet and five tons of enraged animal loomed over the terrified man. Sunlight glinted off the pointed tips of the animal's ivory tusks.

Caine leapt up from under the tarp and stalked towards the mercenary. He cycled another shot and fired. The bullet kicked up a puff of earth near the merc's feet. The man turned again, confusion and uncertainty flashing across his terrified face. Caine saw defeat in the man's eyes. He had hesitated, and now he was surrounded by multiple enemies. The ground shook as the massive elephant dropped back to all fours. The animal shook its head in a display of aggression.

Caine chambered another round as he moved closer to his target. He kept the rifle pointed dead straight at the man.

'On your knees. Drop the weapon!'

The man hesitated. His eyes darted back and forth between the animals and Caine.

Caine moved closer. 'I won't tell you again. And if those elephants stampede, you don't have enough ammo to take them out.'

The elephant bellowed again, and the man muttered a curse. He knelt in the dirt and set his rifle down next to him.

'Very good. Hands on your head.' Caine nodded towards Talak. 'Get the gun. Check him.'

The old man hurried over and grabbed the Tavor. He patted the mercenary down and removed a pistol and knife from the man's tactical harness. A key ring jangled from the man's belt. Talak tossed aside the weapons and grabbed the man's keys.

He grinned and held them up for Caine to inspect.

Caine kept the rifle aimed at the mercenary.

'Tie him up. Then we check the truck. Let's see why Africa Hunger Alliance hires professional mercenaries to deliver food and water.'

* * *

Caine turned the key in the master lock and let it drop to the ground. He and Paul rolled up the heavy rear door of the trailer and peered into the dark space. A faint buzzing sound drifted out from the dark container. As the wind around them picked up, it carried a rotting stench from inside.

Caine hefted himself up and stepped inside the trailer. He

felt a soft fluttering brush against his face, and the buzzing grew louder. The smell of rot and decay was overpowering. Bile rose in his throat.

He swatted at his cheek and felt a tiny insect squish against his flesh.

Flies...

He blinked as his eyes adjusted to the dim light. Open crates of food surrounded him. The wooden boxes were piled high with fruit, grain, and vegetables.

Caine moved closer to one of the boxes. The fruit inside was shriveled and brown. Patches of green mold crept across the surface of the food. The air around him hummed with swarming gnats and flies.

He glanced over at a pallet of large sacks. One had burst open, spilling its contents across the floor. Worms and maggots writhed in the pile of grain.

Talak followed him into the truck. He wrinkled his nose in disgust.

'All this food, gone to waste. They never even delivered it!'

Caine tipped over the box, letting its decayed contents splatter on the floor. Another crate sat beneath it, and he emptied that one too. The flies swirled around them, drawn to the sickly smell of the rotted fruit.

He examined the bottom of the empty crate. 'My guess is, this food was rotten before they even got here,' he said. Using his knife, he pried at the wooden planks on the bottom of the crate. 'The smell discourages customs agents and throws off dogs.'

The wood splintered and pulled away. A narrow compartment was concealed in the bottom of the crate. Caine dragged the box out into a beam of sunlight. A thick green metal tube lay exposed between the wooden beams. Yellow writing was stenciled across the curved barrel.

Talak gazed at the bottom of the crate. 'What language is that?' he asked in an astonished whisper.

'Turkish,' Caine answered. 'This is a MANPADS. Man-Portable Air Defense System. FIM92 Stinger missile. They were developed in the United States, but the technology was licensed to weapons manufacturers in Türkiye.'

Caine slid the crate back into place, then hopped down out of the truck. He extended a hand and helped Talak climb down.

'Air defense?' the old man said, shaking his head. 'I've never seen weapons like these.'

'The South Sudanese forces' major advantage over the rebels are helicopters,' Caine replied. 'They have an armed air force that can assault rebel positions from above. These missiles will level the playing field.'

'But these trucks have been coming into South Sudan for months.' Talak eyed the rows of crates in the shadowy trailer. 'Someone must be spending a fortune on these missiles.'

'Not just missiles. Modern rifles, pistols, RPGs... Someone's been arming Takuba and his followers to the teeth. Whoever they are, they must be planning a major offensive of some kind.'

'And these samples that Doctor Vasani examined, they are another weapon? A biological one?'

Caine nodded. 'That's what I'm going to find out. Wherever this truck was going, that's the next step. I'll either find Takuba there, or someone who knows where he is.'

He paced around the truck to where Paul stood next to the trussed-up soldier. The elephants sauntered a few yards away. The enormous creatures eyed the men with suspicious glances.

Caine kicked the mercenary in the side. The man sputtered and coughed.

'Where were you taking these weapons?' Caine glared at the

prisoner. The man met his emerald gaze for a moment, then turned away and spat in the sand.

'Go to hell,' he muttered.

Caine smiled. 'Have it your way.'

He hefted the man's rifle and pulled back the charging handle.

At the sight of the weapon, the lead elephant again reared up on its hind legs.

'Whoa, whoa,' Paul called out. He rushed to the animal's side and patted the beast's leg. The massive creature dropped back down. Caine felt his legs wobble as the ground trembled beneath him. The elephant gave Caine a disdainful look and snapped his trunk side to side. Then it turned and rubbed up against another member of the herd. Its angry roar turned to a soft, gentle purr.

'These animals' homes were turned into a war zone,' Paul explained in a quiet voice. 'They saw members of their herd shot and killed. First, by accident. Later, from poachers, on both sides. The guns... They remember the guns. Loud noise makes them angry.'

'Then you better move the herd away from here,' Caine said, his voice low and cold. He crouched down next to the mercenary and again stared him in the eye. He placed the barrel of the rifle against the man's knee and flipped the firing selector lever to single shot.

'This man has some talking to do. And I promise, he will tell me what I want to know. But it might take a while. And there might be some screaming.'

33

It took about three hours to drive the big rig south from Bentiu to a narrow dirt road that branched off the main strip. The truck shook and rattled along the uneven path. Caine struggled to keep the large vehicle under control. The tiny road headed east, back towards the Ez Zeraf preserve.

The blurry, scorched terrain streaking past the windows of the truck was bleak and desolate. To the north, the oil fields of Thar Jath had been a site of constant fighting and bloodshed. While under the rule of Sudan, their neighbor to the north, the region's civilians had been forced off their land. Government troops had burned their homes to the ground.

The roads Caine traveled were built by American oil corporations. They no longer operated in the area. After several attacks by rebel forces, they had ceded their territories to French and Malaysian consortiums. As far as Caine could tell, this region was no different than the rest of the country. The land changed hands frequently, and the only constants were fighting and bloodshed. And of course, the oil. There was always the oil.

Another twenty minutes passed. The silver tower of a

refinery pierced the thick, hazy air in the distance. The mercenary's directions had been accurate. The man had been too terrified to lie. Caine had made sure of that.

Let's hope the rest of his intel is good, Caine thought.

A rusted fence, covered in withering vines and weeds, cut
across the road. Caine drove the truck through a narrow gate in
the fence. The truck's airbrakes hissed as he slowed down and
brought the rig to a stop.

He was dressed in the mercenary's uniform and carrying the
man's weapons and equipment. Another man, wearing similar
clothes, emerged from a tiny gatehouse. He sauntered towards
the truck. Caine slipped some folded paperwork from a pouch
on his vest and handed it to the guard, along with an ID badge.
In Kanfar, there was no way to find the proper tools to doctor the
badge, but the picture on the ID was old and faded. Caine was
wearing a black cap and sunglasses. He was a close enough
match, as long the guard didn't look too closely.

The man eyed the badge for a second, then turned his attention to the paperwork. Each page contained row upon row of
numbers and letters. Caine assumed it was a coded manifest of
the contents hidden in each shipment.

The guard flipped through the pages. 'You're late. We
expected this stuff yesterday.' He looked up and squinted at
Caine. 'Where's your other man?'

Caine smiled. 'Truck started overheating outside Bentiu.
Had to stop in the village for water and repairs. That idiot you
paired me with took off with one of the local girls. I left his ass
behind.'

The guard shook his head. 'Bloody amateur. Pull up to the
loading dock, behind the main tanks.'

The guard returned Caine's papers and ID badge. He
pointed towards a row of circular gray tanks in the center of the

complex. A distillation tower, flanked by columns of long, slim pipes, rose up between the tanks. All the refining equipment appeared to be inactive.

'Report to the foreman's desk inside. He'll send a team to unload and direct you to your assignment.'

Caine nodded and smiled. 'Copy that. Thanks.'

The truck shuddered as he shifted into drive and pulled into the complex. As he drove around the tanks, he spotted rows of South Sudanese men, dressed in the ragtag uniforms of Takuba's rebels. They stood in a field beyond the tanks, training under the guidance of Delta Blue mercenary leaders. Several groups were practicing MANPADS deployment. Other men were firing Tavor automatic rifles at practice dummies lined up in a firing range.

Takuba's setting up a nice little army here, Caine thought. Modern weapons, top of the line training. But who's footing the bill?

The dirt road curved around the tanks and widened out into a large rectangular lot. A squat gray building sat at the end of the field, and three trucks were already backed into loading bays. A group of lanky, bedraggled men and women unloaded crates from the other trucks. They labored under the watchful eyes of more Delta Blue mercenaries.

Their faces were flushed and dripping with sweat. Caine watched as a group of four young men stumbled in the mud. They struggled to move one of the heavy crates into the loading dock. They wore torn, ragged clothes and their bodies were malnourished.

Prisoners of war, Caine thought. Slaves taken by Takuba's raiding parties.

Smoke rose from the bright red tanks of an industrial incinerator that stood next to the building. More men were dumping the crates of rotting food into the device, and the smoke gave the air a pungent smell.

An elderly man tripped in front of Caine's truck and keeled over in the mud. His crate tumbled to the ground and split open. Automatic rifles and ammo containers spilled out onto the soft ground. Caine slammed on his brakes and the truck ground to a halt.

'Hey, watch it, asshole!' the supervisor shouted through a megaphone. 'Those things aren't cheap! You four, get over there and clean off those guns!'

The group of young men set down their crates and hurried over to the spilled weapons. They gathered them up and wiped off the muck with their tattered clothes.

Two mercenaries grabbed the barely conscious man by his arms and hauled him to his feet. His head lolled and his eyes rolled back in his head. They dragged him towards a concrete building near the edge of the fence that ran around the complex.

A mercenary wearing a blue hard hat jogged over to Caine's truck. He rapped on the door. Caine opened it and lowered himself out of the cab.

'I'll back it in for you,' the man said. 'You can go ahead inside. The locals will help unload.'

Caine forced himself to return the man's grin. He took a few steps towards the loading dock, then paused. When the truck started reversing, he changed direction, following the two mercs as they dragged their prisoner through the mud.

* * *

Whatever the building's original purpose, it now served as a dungeon for Takuba's prisoners. The small sitting area where the two mercs entered was clean and functional. It contained a desk, a refrigerator, and some computer equipment. But beyond that, the dank interior reeked of human body odor and waste.

A rebel soldier sat behind the desk. The mercs walked past him and threw the old man on the floor. Caine stood behind them, pretending to wait patiently. He glanced up at the ceiling but saw no surveillance cameras in the room.

'This one's used up,' one of the mercs snarled. 'Time to put him down.'

The rebel soldier looked down at the man and sneered. 'He can work a bit more, eh? We shall find ways to motivate him.'

The men laughed. 'Suit yourself,' one grunted. 'But we're not carrying his ass anymore.'

The rebel soldier stood and kicked the man in the ribs. 'Move, you lazy bastard! Back in your cell!'

The man yelped and tried to pick himself off the floor. He fell back down, moaning in pain.

'Least you know he won't go running,' the merc said, chuckling as he shouldered past Caine. He gave Caine a suspicious glance. Caine smiled. The man nodded, then he and his partner left the building.

The soldier turned and glared at Caine. 'What you want?'

Caine's mind raced. His first instinct was to ask for Galloway, but he had no idea if the man was being kept here or not.

Nhial's family, he thought. His wife, Aya...

'I'm looking for a woman. Name's Aya,' he said. 'Your men took her in Kanfar.'

The rebel grunted. 'Why you want to see her?'

'Interrogation,' Caine said.

The man stared at him. 'Takuba already interrogated that bitch.'

Caine shrugged. 'Guess he enjoyed himself.'

The man laughed, then tilted his head towards the corridor.

'Yeah, okay. She's in unit fifteen. Give me a hand with this one, then I open it up for you.'

Caine followed the rebel as he bent down and grabbed one of the old man's arms. The soldier turned his back to Caine. 'Take his other arm,' he grunted.

Caine lunged forward and looped his arm around the soldier's neck. The man gasped as Caine pulled the arm tight. He clawed and scratched at the flesh of Caine's forearm, but he could not free himself from the chokehold.

Caine took a step backwards and dropped to one knee, pulling the rebel down to the floor. The man kicked and struggled as Caine twisted the hold even tighter, cutting off the flow of oxygen to his brain. As his struggles weakened, Caine let go with one arm and slipped a folding knife from a pouch at his belt. He flicked it open with one hand. The curved, serrated blade glinted in the light.

'Here,' he whispered into the struggling man's ear. 'Let me give you a hand.'

He plunged the blade into the man's thigh, severing his femoral artery. A jet of crimson gushed from the wound. The rebel's eyes bulged. He gave a few last kicks, then his eyes closed as his consciousness faded. Blood puddled on the floor beneath him.

Caine searched the man's body. He wrapped his fingers around a yellow plastic key card attached to the corpse's belt. He yanked it off and stuffed it in his pocket. Then he tore off the man's shirt, dragged his body across the floor, and shoved it under the desk. Working fast, he used the shirt as a rag and mopped up the blood as best he could. He opened the fridge and pulled out two bottles of water.

He opened one and kneeled next to the prisoner. He placed the open bottle in the man's hand.

'Here,' he said in a quiet voice. 'You're dehydrated. Drink.'

Leaving the old man behind, Caine paced down the dark corridor. A series of industrial metal doors lined the concrete walls. Numbers were sprayed on each door in red paint: 12... 13... 14...

He located the one marked 15. He banged on the door. 'Aya?' he called out as loud as he dared. 'Are you in there? Nhial sent me.'

'Nhial?' It was a woman's voice, weak and muted behind the metal barrier. 'He is alive?'

'Yes, he's alive. Give me a minute.'

The door rolled up along a track, but a yellow padlock blocked it from opening. Caine grabbed the key card from his pocket and held it up to the lock. A tiny green light blinked, and the lock clicked open. He rolled the door up.

The dank smell in the corridor grew stronger. Caine's eyes blinked as they adjusted to the dim light. At first, he thought the room was empty... then he realized the shadows hid a sea of bodies. They were so still they seemed almost dead. There were no windows, and the heat in the room was staggering. Sweat swelled up on his forehead as he entered the stifling chamber.

'Aya?' he called again.

A woman limped to her feet. The other bodies began to moan and stir. Caine put a finger to his lips. 'Shhhh... we have to stay quiet.'

A few of the bodies parted, revealing a Caucasian man slumped against the far wall. Caine barely recognized him. He had lost weight, and his skin was burned and covered with bruises.

'Josh Galloway?'

The man turned and glanced at him with one eye. His other

eye was black and swollen shut. 'Yeah,' he croaked. 'Who the hell are you?'

'Rebecca sent me. We have to get out of here.'

The man stood up. 'Wait... Caine? Is that you?'

'Have you seen my son, Buri?' Aya whispered. 'He escaped the compound. He is all alone outside.'

Caine shook his head. 'No, I haven't seen him. How many people are in these cells?'

'About half are out in the yard now, unloading,' Josh answered. 'The other half are in here.'

Caine clenched his jaw. 'And Takuba?'

Josh nodded. 'He's here. Or at least he was.'

'Doctor Vasani has your samples,' Caine said. 'She's taken them to a lab in Juba. I know about the bioweapon.'

'Takuba calls it "Gemini." The man is psychotic. And he's not alone.'

'What do you mean?'

Josh looked him in the eye. 'Allan Bernatto is running the show here.'

Caine's jaw clenched and his nostrils flared in anger. 'Bernatto? Are you sure?'

'Saw him with my own eyes.'

Bernatto... The name echoed through his mind. Caine's muscles stiffened. He felt his blood boil as memories of his betrayal bubbled to the surface.

Aya looked up at him with pleading eyes. 'Please... I have to find my son. We must leave this place!'

He nodded. 'You will. I promise. But this facility is crawling with Takuba's men. Not to mention a small army of professional mercenaries. We have to wait for the right moment. Let me scout the area, figure out our next move. In the meantime, lay low. And stay quiet.' He handed her the other bottle of water.

Josh limped over to him. 'I'm coming with you.'

Caine stared at him. 'You're in no condition to fight, Galloway. You should wait with the rest of them.'

Josh glared at him. 'Go to hell. What are you doing here anyway?'

'I told you, Rebecca sent me to find you.'

'Mission accomplished. You found me. Now let's get on with it.'

Caine thought for a moment. The longer he stayed here, the more likely they were to be caught. And despite his weakened state, Josh had a determined glint in his eye.

'Fine,' Caine muttered. 'But if you slow me down—'

'I can manage. Let's go.'

Caine wiped his bloody knife clean on his pants.

All right, he thought. Bernatto and Takuba, working together... Time to wipe away the past for good.

34

Nena squinted as she looked through the microscope. On the slide below the lens, she could see several translucent blobs, drifting in a diluted oil solution. She watched as the undulating bacteria cells bumped into the hydrocarbon molecules in the liquid. The circular pools of oil began to break up where they contacted the cell walls of the bacteria.

A shadow drifted in front of the slide, obscuring her view. Nena lifted her head from the lens and whispered a curse in Arabic. She pulled her hair behind her head and fastened it with a rubber band.

Nhial stood behind her, glancing around the laboratory with an anxious look in his eye.

'This virus, you say it eats oil?' he asked.

Nena looked back at him and smiled. 'The virus itself doesn't eat the oil, but the bacteria it's hiding in does. The virus is too small to see with this equipment.' She glanced down at the microscope and frowned. 'I can see the inclusion groups on the bacteria cells, but not the individual viruses themselves. Too bad there's no electron microscope here.'

'We're lucky they let us come here in the first place,' Nhial said, puffing out his chest. 'This place may not rival your schools in the north, but it is the greatest university in South Sudan.'

Nena lowered her head back to the microscope. The University of Juba's teaching hospital consisted of a series of small brick and concrete buildings, near the city center. Like everything in the country, she knew the hospital had been affected by years of civil war. Constant fighting made acquiring supplies and a stable faculty a challenge for the university.

The laboratory facilities were tiny, and far from sterile. Her microscope looked like it had come from a high school science class. But she had to admit, in a few hours here, she had accomplished more than she ever could have in Kanfar, or even at her clinic in Malakal.

'You're right,' she said in a soft voice. 'And thank you.'

'Why are you thanking me?'

'For coming with me. After everything that's happened... I am grateful I didn't have to travel alone.'

Even though she could not see him, she could almost hear his smile. He shuffled behind her.

'You have helped our village, our people, many times, Doctor Vasani. This is the least I can do.'

Nena slid a second slide under the microscope. She grabbed a pen off the counter and made some notes on a yellow pad. 'These facilities have been extremely helpful. I've been able to confirm these bacteriophages are capable of hibernating in crude oil for months. Possibly longer.'

She turned to a sealed glass cabinet sitting on the lab counter. Inside the cabinet, a round-bottomed flask hung from a wire rack over a Bunsen burner. A long glass column sat above the flask, and a narrow, piped tube ran from the top of the column to a nearby beaker.

'What is in there?' Nhial asked, squinting at the cabinet.

Nena slid her arms into a pair of black rubber gloves mounted to the side of the cabinet. The interior of the glass box was airtight. Using the gloves, she picked up an eyedropper inside and sucked up several drops of liquid coating the bottom of the beaker.

'This is a fractional distillation column,' she said. She placed a drop of the solution on a glass slide. 'It simulates the oil refining process. The burner heats the liquid in the flask. The chemical compounds inside have different boiling points. They are captured by different trays in the column. That's how oil refineries separate crude oil into different products, such as gasoline, kerosene, or diesel.'

Nhial walked closer to the case and peered inside. 'You are very knowledgeable, Doctor. But are you sure this is safe?'

Inside the case, Nena picked up a can of pressurized liquid nitrogen. She gave the sample on the slide a quick spray.

'Conditions here aren't ideal. But this should freeze and kill the pathogens, if there are any. But of course, there is a risk.'

Nhial stepped back from the case.

Nena took the slide and deposited it into a smaller box jutting from the side of the cabinet. She closed off the box from the rest of the apparatus and removed her hands from the gloves.

She took a deep breath and bit her lip. 'Okay. Now we see...'

She opened up the box, removed the slide, and slid it under the microscope. She bent down and adjusted the lens. 'Najah, success! Again, the bacteriophage survived the refining process.'

As she scribbled more notes on her pad, Nhial stared out the small window in the door at the far end of the room. A nurse wearing a pink uniform stood outside, consulting a clipboard of charts. Two men approached the nurse and smiled at her. They began talking and gesturing around the corridor.

Nhial took a step closer to the door. Something about the men looked familiar...

'Intazir. Wait a minute. Something is different here.' Nena's brow furrowed as she pressed her face closer to the microscope. 'These samples didn't just survive... their cell wall has barely decayed.'

'Is that important?' Nhial asked, not taking his eyes off the door. The nurse turned and pointed through the glass window.

'The other samples delivered the virus during the refining process. Their cell wall decayed, and the virus was released into the surrounding areas. These samples are different. The cell walls are weakened but still intact. The virus is still trapped inside.'

One of the men outside turned and looked through the glass window. His smile vanished from his face, replaced with a cold, determined stare. Nhial glanced at the other side of the room. Another door in the opposite wall led outside to the campus.

'Doctor, we must leave. Now!'

Nena tilted her head and gave him a surprised look. 'What? We can't leave. I still have work to—'

She was cut off as the men opened the door.

'Doctor Vasani,' one of them called out. 'You must come with us. We are with the Juba police.'

Nhial grabbed her hand and pulled her to the opposite door. 'Move,' he whispered. 'Quickly!'

As he dragged her out the back door, Nena saw the men draw pistols from their waistbands. Nhial slammed the door behind them. They ran down a narrow dirt path between two of the medical buildings.

'Who are they?' Nena gasped.

'They were with Takuba the day he came to Kanfar. The day he took my family!' Nhial shouted back. 'They are Ghost Jackals!'

The two cleared the building and sprinted across the dirt square in the center of the campus. As they neared the stone arch of the entrance, a Jeep roared into the square and skidded to a stop. More men leapt out and marched towards them.

Nhial clutched Nena's arm and jerked to a stop. 'This way!' They turned and ran between more buildings.

'The city is on high alert for the peace conference,' Nena huffed between breaths. 'How did they get in here?'

'Takuba must have already had men in place,' Nhial muttered. 'Like I said, this is the biggest medical center in South Sudan. He knew we would come here. I was a fool to bring you—'

As they raced around the corner he collided with a nurse wheeling a cart of IV bags. Nhial and the woman fell to the ground and the cart toppled over in the dirt.

Nena ran a few more feet, then looked back. She skidded to a stop. 'Nhial!'

The Ghost Jackals rounded the building. They opened fire and bullets ricocheted off the wall behind Nena. The nurse screamed. She struggled to disentangle herself from Nhial's sprawling body.

'Go!' Nhial shouted. 'Run!'

Nena's eyes darted left and right, searching for an escape route. But more of the armed men emerged from a nearby alley and fanned out around them.

There was nowhere to run.

One of the Ghost Jackals approached her, aiming a pistol at her head.

'That's enough, Doctor,' he snarled.

Nena froze. The man smiled as she glared up at him with defiant eyes.

'Very good. Now, you will come with us. Mr. Takuba would like a word with you.'

35

Caine led Josh across the compound. The battered agent's wrists were cuffed behind his back, but Caine made sure they were loose enough to slip off if need be. The prison guard's pistol hung in Josh's waistband, covered by his tattered shirt.

'Somehow I don't think you showed up here out of the goodness of your heart. You came to kill Takuba, not to find me,' Josh muttered as they stalked toward the main building. 'Am I right?'

'Keep your voice down,' Caine snapped. 'What are you doing in the field, anyway? I thought you were heading Rebecca's security detail. And the last time I saw you, your arm was broken.'

'Just a fracture,' Josh whispered. 'I transferred to field ops as soon as it healed. Rebecca told me what you said before you disappeared again. That I let things get too personal. Well, maybe you were right. Soon as you showed up, she changed. I saw it in her eyes every time your name came up. And I'm not wired to be second best.'

'Drop it. I told Rebecca I was happy for you, and I meant it. You're better for her than I was. That's a fact.'

'Jesus, you really are an idiot, aren't you?'

'Shut up. Are you sure this is the right building?'

They moved around the corner towards a large industrial building at the center of the complex. Caine looked up at the distillation columns rising from the roof. A pair of small satellite dishes protruded from two of the columns.

'Yeah,' Galloway whispered. 'That's where I saw Bernatto. The second floor has offices, computers, electronics. Best bet to find communications equipment is up there.'

Caine found a side door and twisted the handle. It was unlocked. He swung open the door and led Josh into the dark stairwell.

'You know,' Josh continued, 'the irony is, I never wanted to work in the field. I chose the security branch because I already knew guys like you. I saw how they ended up. Burned out. Cut off from everyone they might give a shit about. And anyone who might give a shit about them. Guys like you, Caine... they die alone.'

Caine turned and slammed Josh against the wall of the stairwell.

'We don't have time for this. You got a problem with me, Galloway? If you have something you want to say, say it now!'

Josh glared into his eyes. 'Well, well... looks like there's a human being in there after all. So wake the fuck up. I asked her, Tom, I asked her point blank if she was over you.'

Caine stared back at him in silence.

'She couldn't say it. She couldn't say anything. That's when I knew.'

'Christ, Galloway, that's not an answer.'

Josh shrugged. 'Sure it is. Just not the one I wanted. Maybe you should ask her yourself.'

'Are you finished?'

Josh grinned. 'Yeah. Just wanted to get that off my chest. Didn't want there to be any unresolved hostility between us.'

Caine squinted, then released him. 'You got a strange way of showing it.'

Josh gave him a crooked grin. 'Nah, just pushing your buttons, that's all. Come on, comms should be this way. Stop wasting time.'

Josh resumed walking up the stairs. Caine shook his head, then followed him up into the darkness.

* * *

Caine pushed Josh across the catwalk over the refinery floor. Two mercs stood looking over the railing, examining the floor below. On the ground floor, groups of prisoners organized the guns and weapons into various piles. It looked like the work was almost finished.

Caine knew it was only a matter of time before someone noted the missing prison guard and got suspicious.

The mercenaries paid them no mind as they walked past. Caine's disguise appeared to be working, and Josh's battered appearance marked him as a candidate for interrogation. As they cleared the catwalk, Caine glanced at the control panels and gauges along the walls. They all appeared to be instruments and monitors that controlled the refining equipment. The stations were dark and unmanned.

They moved through a metal door and entered a corridor lined by rows of offices and cubicles.

'Last time they dragged me out this way, I saw something through an open door. Looked like a VSAT terminal, but I couldn't be sure.'

Caine nodded. VSAT, or very small aperture terminal

systems, were a common communication solution for industries operating in remote areas, with no cell towers or other infrastructure. It made sense that an oil refinery like this would have a terminal somewhere, with a link to the satellite dishes outside.

'You better be right. If we can't get through to Rebecca, then all of this is for nothing.'

'At least we get a star on the wall at Langley,' Josh whispered.

'Yeah,' Caine muttered. 'What an honor.'

Finally, they found a door marked 'COMMS.'

Josh opened the door. 'We're lucky this place was an oil refinery and not a military installation. Takuba doesn't seem too worried about security.'

Whoop! Whoop! An alarm blared to life, and spinning red lights flooded the corridor with a crimson glow.

'You were saying?' Caine muttered as he pushed past Josh into the room.

'Lock must have a proximity alarm or something,' Josh shouted. 'Anyone without a security badge triggers it when they open the door.'

'Cover the entrance!' Caine ordered. He examined the communications equipment sitting on the desk as Josh quickly slipped out of his handcuffs and grabbed his pistol.

The VSAT box was a small rack of electronics that resembled a computer server. A series of cables ran into a computer on the desk. A second cluster of cables ran up through the roof, presumably to the satellite dishes outside. Caine tapped on the keyboard and the computer screen lit up with a soft glow.

A text message popped up on the screen.

VSAT COMMUNICATIONS RESTRICTED. AUTHORIZED PERSONNEL ONLY. ENTER LOGON.

A cursor flashed below the message.

'Damn it!' Caine hissed. 'The system's locked down.'

The alarm continued to blare, but no one entered the corridor. Josh kept his pistol trained on the door that led from the catwalk.

'If they know we're here, where the hell is everyone?' he shouted.

The alarm's wailing ceased. A loud crackling echoed through the room. 'Put down your weapons. Hands on your head. Do it now, please.'

Caine looked up and gritted his teeth. The voice was familiar. 'Bernatto,' he snarled.

He stormed into the hallway and raised his rifle, ready to target any mercenaries that tried to breach their position.

'We're going to have to fight our way out,' he said.

Josh glanced over at him. 'That's crazy. We're outnumbered and outgunned.'

The speaker blared back to life. 'You should listen to him, Tom. I always told you, don't let things get personal.'

Caine looked up at the ceiling. He couldn't spot any obvious cameras, but Bernatto could obviously see them. 'Allan! I told you I'd find you eventually,' he shouted.

'Yes, you did. And I believed you,' the voice boomed from overhead. 'That's why I was prepared.'

A thunk sounded from the door ahead of them.

'Electronic locks,' Josh whispered. 'He's trapped us in here.'

'I control the ventilation system as well as the locks, Mr. Galloway. Now, you have ten seconds to lower your weapons and place your hands on your heads. After that, I flood the area with the refined Gemini virus. You've seen the effects up close, you know what it can do.'

Josh looked at Tom and shook his head. 'It's not pretty. What do we do?'

Caine looked up at the ceiling once more. He lowered his weapon to the ground. 'The only thing we can do. We survive.'

The door swung open, and a squad of mercenaries stormed down the corridor.

'Hands on your heads! Kick your weapons over here. Easy.'

Caine obeyed, then placed his hands behind his head. Josh did the same. They were cuffed and hustled out of the corridor.

'Take that one to the pit,' the lead mercenary snarled, nodding towards Josh. He turned to Caine and grinned. 'You're coming with me. You must have really pissed someone off. You just won yourself an audience with the man behind the curtain.'

36

Allan Bernatto looked up from behind a desk as the Delta Blue mercenaries marched Caine into a large, circular office. The curved windows behind Bernatto looked out over the refinery and the field beyond. To either side of Bernatto, a series of large screens and televisions stood on chrome metal stands. The dark black rectangles were still and lifeless.

Bernatto leaned back in his chair. He did not smile or frown. His expression was inscrutable behind his wireframe glasses.

'Hello, Tom.'

Caine felt an involuntary tremor run through his muscles. Every fiber of his being longed to throw himself at Bernatto. To attack him, to kill him, to tear into his flesh with his bare teeth if that was what it took to kill the man. But his arms were cuffed behind his back, and he was surrounded by a half-dozen armed men.

Instead, he forced himself to stare out the panoramic window in silence. He watched as a large cargo helicopter landed in the center of the field. The powerful rotors of the Mil

Mi-17 helicopter thumped through the air. He could hear it even through the thick glass.

'I knew you'd come, Tom,' Bernatto finally said, breaking the silence. 'Like I said, I took your threat seriously. A man like you, with your skills and training... I'd be a fool not to. But I have to admit, I thought we'd get you in Khartoum, or Malakal. I never thought you'd make it all the way here.'

Caine narrowed his eyes. He watched as a trio of dark figures emerged from the helicopter and walked towards the building.

Bernatto glanced back at the windows. 'Mr. Takuba will be joining us shortly. He intercepted your doctor friend in Juba.'

Caine tensed but said nothing.

'You know, it's funny,' Bernatto said, his dark, beady eyes half-closed behind his glasses. 'For the first time, I'm not sure who you'd rather kill. Me, or that madman.'

'Madman?' Caine stared at Bernatto. 'He's your partner.'

The older man stood and shrugged. 'Thanks to you and Rebecca, friends are hard for me to come by these days. I knew someone who was looking for an asset in East Africa. I remembered our old operation here. Takuba was willing to play ball in exchange for a seat at the table.'

'Takuba's insane,' Caine replied. 'If you've thrown in with him, you're more desperate than I thought. What's this all about, Allan? Oil? Whatever it is, I guarantee you Takuba will go down in flames and take your plan with him.'

'Takuba will serve his purpose. After that, he's expendable, the same as any of us. And just for the record, it's not my plan.'

'So who's pulling your strings?'

Bernatto picked up a small remote from the desk.

'You never could see the big picture, Tom.' He pressed a button and the dark screens blinked to life.

A blurry, distorted face turned towards the camera. Caine

squinted, but he could not make out any details of the man on the screen. Something about the face looked familiar, but he could not quite place it.

'Thomas Caine. Been a long time, son. Lot of water under the bridge, but you still look fit. Still got that look in your eyes, too.'

The voice was masked but the speech patterns, the Southern drawl... Could it really be him, Caine wondered, after all these years?

'What look?' Caine asked. 'Do I know you?'

'Sure you do. The look I told you I saw in your eyes. Years ago, when you were recruited for the Special Activities Division. I told you your talents would go to waste running agents, analyzing signals, working behind a desk. You're a natural born predator, son. A killer. Just like me.'

'Is that why you're afraid to look me in the eye?' Caine asked, staring at the screen, struggling to mask his disbelief.

'Shit, son, we taught you better than that. You don't look a man in the eye when you kill him. Not unless you have to, anyway. You stab him in the back. Or you shoot him from a hundred yards away. Hell, you bomb his house from another country if you can. You do whatever you have to, to get the job done. We didn't train you to fight fair. We trained you to win.'

'Grissom,' Caine said. 'It's really you.'

The distorted blur on the screen dropped away, revealing a craggy, wrinkled face. Pale, sunken skin and bushy white brows framed a pair of baby-blue eyes. The man smiled. His lips were thin and dry, a hard slash set below a bulbous pink nose.

'Nice to see you remember me after all, Tom,' Grissom said.

'How could I forget?' Caine glared at the screen. 'Walter Grissom. Former director of the National Clandestine Service. And Allan Bernatto's old boss.'

37

Josh winced as the truck bounced over rough, uneven terrain. He was battered and bruised. The muscles in his arms throbbed in pain from being tied behind his back for so long. Darkness surrounded him. His head was covered by a black, sweat-stained hood.

He estimated they had been driving for about twenty minutes. Based on the turns the vehicle made, he believed they were heading north, but it was impossible to be sure.

Finally, the truck lurched to a stop. He heard the driver's door open, then slam closed. Another door opened, and hands grabbed his legs, yanking him off the seat. He groaned in pain as he fell to the ground and rolled a few feet from the truck.

Someone tore the hood from his face, and he squinted in the sudden, harsh light of day.

'Get up,' a deep voice commanded.

Josh stumbled to his feet. As his eyes adjusted to the light, he glanced at the surrounding terrain. Scrublands, brown withered grass, as far as the eye could see. A few flat-topped trees stood in the distance. Their gnarled black trunks were silhouetted against the burning sun.

A buzzing sound filled the air. Black shadows circled overhead, birds of some kind.

One of Takuba's rebel soldiers stood a few feet away from him, an AK-47 rifle hanging in a loose grip from his right hand. His left hand held a jingling key ring.

'Turn around.'

Only one man, Josh thought. They think I'm too injured, too tired to fight back.

They might be right.

Josh turned around. Before him, a deep depression gouged the earth. The pit was about fifteen feet deep, and a thin layer of glistening mud lined the sloped edges. The bottom of the pit was filled with bundles of plastic sheeting, tied off at the ends with cord or duct tape. There were over a hundred of them, each one about the size of a man.

Josh blinked. Behind the translucent plastic, he could make out the blurred outline of a human face. Its pale, gaunt features were frozen in a look of stark terror.

The buzzing grew louder. Tiny black dots swirled around him. He realized they were flies.

They were standing before a mass grave.

'I take off these cuffs. Then you work,' the rebel grunted. 'Unload the truck. You try to run, try to escape, I kill you.' The man hoisted his rifle and took a step towards Josh. 'You go in pit. Understand?'

'Yeah, I got it,' Josh muttered, rubbing his wrists.

The soldier lowered the rifle. He unlocked the cuffs that bound Josh's wrists and shoved him forward.

'Work. Now.'

Josh stumbled to the back of the vehicle. More bodies lay in the truck bed, all wrapped in plastic.

'Who are they?' he asked.

Keep him talking, waste time. Get your strength back.

'Doesn't matter. They go in the pit.'

The soldier paced over to a tree and leaned against the trunk. He fished a toothpick from his pocket and stuck it in his mouth.

Josh heaved one of the bodies over his shoulder. He trudged towards the pit, as slow as he could without arousing suspicion.

The sun beat down overhead, and the heat was brutal. Beads of sweat dripped from his hair and stung his eyes. He tried to control his breathing, tried to recover some energy. He knew his survival was unlikely, that these could be his last moments on earth. But he had to try.

He dumped the body into the sinkhole and watched it tumble and slide to the bottom of the pit. He recognized a few of the men through the plastic wrapping. They were prisoners who had grown too exhausted or injured to work. A few of them bore festering, pock-marked sores on their faces and arms. Test subjects for the Gemini virus.

After about an hour of work, the last body toppled down the hill. Josh stood at the precipice, panting. He wiped the sweat from his battered face. He heard a clink as the soldier stood up and paced towards him.

This is it, he told himself. Go time. Do or die.

He turned around and raised his hands. He shuffled towards the advancing soldier.

'Come on, man. I did as you asked. How about we call it even?'

'Turn around,' the soldier barked. 'Hands on your head. Walk to the pit.'

Josh lowered his hands a bit and took another step forward. The distance was too far; there was no way to reach his attacker before the man fired. But better that than let Takuba's men shoot him in the back like a sick dog. He shifted his weight onto his right foot.

Before he could lunge forward, a figure exploded out of the brush behind them with a high-pitched scream. The soldier whirled around. A young child careened towards him. The boy clutched a sharpened stick over his head. He yelped another war cry and drove the stick into the soldier's leg.

It was Nhial's son... it was Buri!

The soldier backed towards Josh, grunting in pain.

Now, dammit! The command roared through Josh's brain. Adrenaline shot through his aching muscles and flooded his weary nerves.

As the soldier raised his rifle to fire at the young boy, Josh clamped his left arm around the man's neck. His right arm darted over the man's shoulder, grabbed the barrel of the rifle, and yanked it straight up. The gun fired into the air, startling the circling vultures above. They screeched and peeled off into the blue sky.

Josh squeezed tight with his left arm, but he was too weak to complete the sleeper hold. The soldier threw his head back, slamming his skull into Josh's battered face. Pain shot through his nose and eyes. The soldier broke free from the hold and spun around. Before he could fire, Buri jabbed him again with the stick, impaling the man's thigh.

The soldier howled and shoved the boy to the ground. He tore the small spear from his leg and tossed it aside. Then he turned back to face Josh, his lips curled in an angry snarl.

Josh used the momentary distraction to his advantage. He darted right and shot out his left hand. His fingers curled around the barrel of the rifle and yanked the gun to his side. Then he swung up his left leg in a savage groin kick.

The soldier's eyes bulged as the powerful blow made contact. He doubled over, yelping in pain.

Josh shifted his weight and threw a right hook. The punch connected with a loud crack. The man's head snapped back. Keeping his grip on the rifle, Josh tore the weapon free from the reeling soldier's grip.

'Buri, get down!' he shouted. The child dropped into the tall grass. Josh kicked the soldier, sending him staggering backwards.

Josh took aim and pulled the trigger. The gun shook and rattled in his hands as he fired a quick burst. The sound echoed across the plains. The soldier fell to the ground. Blood stained the fabric of his shirt, just above his chest.

Josh stood panting, still aiming the gun at the dead soldier. After a few moments, he lowered the rifle. Buri stood up from the brush and jogged towards him. 'You did it, Mr. Carter, you kill him!'

Josh held up his hand. 'Buri, stay there!'

The boy did as he was told. Josh bent over, heaved the dead soldier over his shoulder, and carried him to the pit.

He tossed the corpse in and watched as it tumbled down the slope.

One more body to join the others, he thought.

He turned around and walked over to Buri, who sat trembling in the grass. The boy looked up at him and gave him a nervous smile. 'You move so fast,' he said. 'You great fighter!'

Josh looked down at the boy and laughed. 'You're not so bad yourself. You saved my life, Buri. You are one brave kid.'

'Don't tell my father,' the child said, shaking his head. 'He say fighting is bad. Evil spirits make us fight. Good spirits make us study.'

'Your father sounds like a smart man. I'm going to make sure you see him soon, but there's one thing I have to do first. Do you know how to get back to the refinery from here?'

'Yes, it is not far. I hid here after I escaped from that place. Is my mother still there?'

'Yes, she is,' Josh replied.

The child stood up, a determined look on his face. 'Then we must go back to get her. I must fight some more, before I study.'

Josh laughed and rubbed the boy's head. 'How about you leave the fighting to me this time.' He glanced at the truck parked near the edge of the pit. 'You wait here. I'm going to get that truck and drive it over here. I want you to stay away from that pit. Do you understand me?'

Buri gave him a pensive look. 'I saw the men come here yesterday. I know what is inside the pit.'

Josh looked the boy in the eye. 'You do?'

The child's eyes were wide. 'Yes. Ghosts. Angry spirits.'

Josh nodded. 'You might be right, son.'

He turned and stalked across the sun-bleached earth towards the truck. He had to get word back to the CIA monitoring station, let them know what was going on.

And he had to leave word for Rebecca. Let her know he was still alive.

Maybe it was too late for either message to do any good.

But he had to try.

38

Caine glared at Bernatto. 'I should have guessed you'd go running back to the old man, Allan. You always were Grissom's dog.'

The man on the screens chuckled. 'I know you got a chip on your shoulder, son, but you gotta stop and think things through. You've been chasing poor old Allan halfway around the world, all for what? Revenge?'

Caine flicked his eyes back to the screens. He forced himself to smile.

'It's a long list, Grissom. Operation Big Blind is right at the top. Bernatto framed me, left me to die. I was captured, tortured. And Jack... He didn't make it out at all.'

The images of Grissom nodded in unison. For Caine, it was surreal to see the man's face spread across all the different sizes and shapes of screens in the room. Like a sinister reflection in a hall of mirrors.

'Sure, sure. I know all about Operation Big Blind,' Grissom said. 'But what on earth makes you think Allan had a choice in the matter? He was just following orders, after all.'

'What are you talking about? Big Blind was after you resigned. The D/NCS at the time had no idea what we were doing there, he didn't order—'

'Condor Group was my baby,' Grissom snapped. 'Always was my baby. And I told you when we brought you into the fold. The operations we ran, the missions you undertook... the stakes were high. Higher than you could imagine. And when the stakes get that high, everyone is expendable. Everyone. Allan, Jack, you... there's no room for special snowflakes in this game.'

'It was you.' Caine stared at the screen. 'You framed me, left Jack to die. You were still pulling the strings, behind the scenes. Even after you resigned.'

'I may have resigned, but I didn't slink away with my tail between my legs,' the old man on the screen snapped, his withered lips curling into a scowl. 'The Senate Intelligence Committee... It was all just politics as usual for those idiots. But I knew what was coming. And I was ready.'

'Ready for what?' Caine demanded.

'Allan and I, we could see the world was changing. The old ways weren't working anymore. Oversight committees, budgetary cutbacks, congressional hearings... you can't fight the war America has to fight now, not under those conditions. Our enemy doesn't play by those rules. It doesn't fight fair. So neither could we.'

'Now I know where Bernatto gets his line of bullshit,' Caine snarled.

'This planet isn't getting any bigger. Every day, people slaughter each other all across God's green earth for a slice of the pie. You think fighting over oil and gas is bad? Wait till it comes down to drinkable water. Clean air. Hell, a square foot of empty space to grow food. That's the war that's coming, son. You're either king of the hill, or someone's boot is in your face.'

Caine turned his stare back to Bernatto. As usual, the man's face was blank and unreadable.

'I've heard all this before, Grissom,' Caine said. 'But Bernatto didn't betray me out of principles, or some paranoid delusion about a coming war. It was money. Guns, drugs... just money.'

'What do you think paid for all this, Tom?' Grissom replied. 'If there's one thing I know, it's war. I've seen all kinds. Short and quick. Long and bloody. Cold, hot, and everything in between. I learned long ago, the only way to win this kind of war was to fight it outside the system. And that takes money. Vast sums of it. Condor Group was the first step. Men like you and Jack helped me secure valuable intel. Resources. Funding. Equipment. But I always knew that sooner or later, the powers that be would step in. I was an embarrassment to them. I was winning, and they weren't even in the game yet.'

'That's why you kept our group off-books. So you could use them to continue to fund this insane private war of yours.'

'Condor Group was just a nickname. Officially, you and the men you worked with fell under the umbrella of Operation Blackwing. The D/CIA at the time saw the need for a unit like yours. A deniable team. A secret cell, recruited from within the ranks of the Special Activities Division and other paramilitary units. But after a few operations, the higher ups got cold feet. They ordered me to disband the unit. Well, that was just a waste of good material, as far as I was concerned. They tried to bring me up on charges, but none of those old fools had the stomach to get in the trenches with me. I left on my own terms and continued doing the work that had to be done. Privatization, Tom. It's the way of the future.'

Caine thought for a moment. 'Blackwing Capital. You own it. You own Delta Blue, the African Hunger Alliance. You own all of it.'

'I can't take all the credit. I have people like Allan here helping me with the day-to-day details. But thanks to Blackwing Capital, and the revenue it's accumulated over the years, I have my own private army. My own intelligence sources, a satellite and communications network. And now, I'm about to have my own damn country.'

Caine laughed, a short, cynical bark. 'You're planning a coup? With Simon Takuba in charge? The president and the rebels have been squabbling over power here for years. Dozens of nations and oil conglomerates have their fingers in the pie. No way a psycho like Takuba can hold it together.'

Grissom smiled. 'Takuba may be crazy, but at least he's got some fire to him. The man has vision. And sometimes, that's all it takes. Takuba doesn't have to hold the country together, he just has to take the major oil fields and hold them long enough for Gemini to do its work.'

'You're planning to release the Gemini virus into the oil pipelines? Once the death toll begins, you'll shut down oil production in this entire country!'

'Only temporarily. You see, while the United States has backed South Sudan in its struggle for independence, we ended up getting the short end of the stick. That son of a bitch we put in charge, President Kiir? He drives around in a limousine with his black cowboy hat and designer suits. Owns a multi-million-dollar house. Has lunch with the president of the United States at the goddamn White House. And what the hell has he done for us?'

Caine was silent. He stared at the screen and let Grissom continue his rant.

'Right now,' the old man sputtered, 'China controls over 75 percent of oil investment in South Sudan. The few US companies that were here pulled out due to security concerns and human rights violations.'

'And you think a military coup, backed by a biological weapon, is going to make things any better?' Caine replied.

A new image blinked across one of the larger screens. It was a map, showing the key oil fields of South Sudan. Red lines ran from each oil field to a point at the northern border of the country.

'These are the five largest oil fields in South Sudan. Adar, Block 5A, Fula, Palogue, and Unity. Chevron spent over a billion dollars exploring Unity alone. Now it's owned by a Chinese consortium. All that oil flows north, through the Greater Nile Oil Pipeline. Also controlled by the Chinese.'

'I doubt China is going to pack up and leave just because you ask nicely.'

Grissom chuckled. 'No, it's going to take a bit more than that. Takuba and his men, backed by my hand-picked military advisors and armed with state-of-the-art weaponry, are going to take control of these oil fields.'

Caine squinted at the map. He thought back to the crates of weapons he had discovered in the truck. 'Rebel forces have attacked these oil fields before, but they could never hold them. The South Sudanese armed forces have aerial support, helicopters.'

Grissom's face wrinkled into a smug grin. 'My MANPADS will even those odds. And like I said, Takuba only has to hold the fields long enough to pump the Gemini virus into the pipeline. Once that happens, it will grow and multiply inside the oil.'

The map zoomed into the pipeline, following its twisting curves north to Khartoum.

Caine stared at the screens. 'Any oil that runs through the

pipeline will become worthless. It can't be refined without unleashing the virus and infecting the workers. China and the others will be forced to abandon their holdings.'

Grissom smiled. 'Oh, it might take them a minute. But after enough men die, they'll go running home, all right. Leaving Blackwing Capital to take control of all oil production in South Sudan. You see, I don't just have the Gemini virus. I have the compound that can neutralize it and allow the oil to be processed normally. And once the oil starts flowing again, no one is going to risk upsetting the balance. The rest of the world will bend over backwards to support Takuba's regime. He can call himself president, emperor, supreme leader, whatever the hell he wants. But I'll control the oil. And with Delta Blue contracted to provide security, we can ensure the region remains stable.'

'What about the thousands that Gemini kills before China pulls out? All the soldiers and civilians that burn in your little coup? What about the hell a man like Takuba will unleash on the people of this country?'

Grissom gave an exaggerated sigh. 'Look around you, Tom. Every day in this country, thousands die. Millions starve or are displaced from their homes. Villages burn, women are raped and mutilated. This place sits on top of trillions of dollars in oil wealth. Meanwhile, the rebels are slaughtering each other over stolen cows and tribal feuds a hundred years old. Now, a few thousand more lives, in exchange for peace and stability? Sounds like a good deal to me.'

'It's always a good deal when you're not the one paying the price.'

On the screens, Grissom glanced down at his watch. 'You may be right about that. But like I said. It's not about fighting fair. It's about getting the job done. Anyway, let's not get ahead of ourselves. In six hours, the vice president in exile, leader of the SPLM forces, is going to gather together the leaders of all the other rebel groups in this region. They'll sit down with President Kiir himself, at a UN Camp just outside the Unity State. One more round of bullshit peace talks. Only this time, things will be different.'

The door behind Caine swung open. Takuba marched into the room, flanked by a pair of his Ghost Jackal soldiers.

Bernatto gave him an annoyed glance. 'Mr. Takuba. You're late.'

Takuba glared at him. 'I had some last-minute things to take care of. Besides, we were waiting for our guest to arrive. Now I see he is here. Soon, he can join his pretty doctor friend, yes?'

Caine lurched towards Takuba, but the Delta Blue men held him back. One of them slammed the butt of his rifle into the back of Caine's neck. Caine fell to his knees.

'Easy, Tom,' Grissom said. 'We all have a part to play today. Even you.'

'Go to hell,' Caine growled.

'Once this peace conference begins, the vice president will give a speech. He's going to propose another ceasefire. God only knows why, nobody followed the last one. But this time... Let's just say he's gonna set the world record for the shortest ceasefire in history.'

Caine looked up at the screens. He staggered to his feet. 'You're going to kill him.'

Grissom nodded. 'Bingo. One Sniper. One fifty-cal shot to the head. One dead vice president. And our man, Mr. Simon Takuba, giving a rousing speech to unify the remaining rebel leaders. Later, after we control the oil fields, authorities will find a dead body in a Juba hotel room. A former CIA officer, wanted by his own government for treason. With a hundred thousand dollars of President Kiir's money in a Swiss bank account, under his name. Your name, Tom.'

'You never did go in to debrief, did you Tom?' Bernatto asked. 'I knew you wouldn't. You don't trust anyone. You've been working on your own. Alone. That makes you vulnerable.'

'You're setting me up again,' Caine said. 'Framing me for killing the vice president.'

Grissom chuckled again. 'You have to admit, with your background you're the perfect fall guy. The narrative is flawless. A corrupt president. A disgraced killer, paid to assassinate a political rival on the eve of peace? Well, hot damn! Now that's how you run a coup, son.'

Takuba walked over to Caine. They stood face-to-face, his cold, dark eyes meeting Caine's emerald stare head on.

'It was a mistake to come back, my friend. I warned you. My spirits protect me.'

Caine did not look away. 'The only mistake I made was letting you live. But I won't make the same mistake twice.'

Grissom's smirking face looked down at them, multiplied across the screens in the room. 'Well, what's done is done. I won't say I'm sorry, Tom. We both know that's not true, and I won't insult you with cheap sentiment. But I want you to know, what happens here today will bring peace to this country and security to the United States. Your sacrifice will not be in vain. I thought that might bring you some comfort.'

Caine turned to the screens. 'You know what will bring me comfort, Grissom? Adding your name to my list.'

Grissom cleared his throat. 'Takuba, take him to the helicopter,' he ordered. 'Wait until the peace conference begins. Then finish it.' The screens blinked out and went dark.

Bernatto dropped the remote on the desk and shoved his hands in his pockets. He stared at Caine. 'You never should have crawled out of Thailand, Tom. You should have put the past behind you. You should have stayed dead.'

Two of the mercenaries dragged Caine to the door. Takuba smiled and gave a slight bow to Bernatto. Then he followed them out of the room.

39

Caine felt the helicopter shudder as they flew through a patch of turbulence. He sat on a metal bench in the cargo bay. His hands were cuffed behind him, attached to a steel pole behind the bench. An identical bench ran along the opposite wall, and two Delta Blue mercenaries sat facing him, their assault rifles resting in their laps.

Nena was cuffed to the bench next to him. A black hood covered her head, and judging by the muffled sounds coming from under the cloth, Caine assumed she was gagged as well. She huddled against the curved metal fuselage of the helicopter, trembling in terror. He longed to reach out to her, to give her some sort of comforting touch, anything to let her know she was not alone. But she was just out of reach.

'Nena, I'm here. It's going to be all right,' he had whispered to her when they first boarded.

She had stopped her struggling, and her hooded head gave a tiny, imperceptible nod. They spent the rest of the flight in silence.

Behind them, towards the rear of the sloping cargo bay, sat a pallet stacked with blue barrels of oil. A tight netting of yellow nylon straps held the barrels firmly in place on top of the wheeled pallet. A heavy-duty winch mounted to the side of the aircraft locked the pallet in place with a taut steel cable. A small stack of ballistic cases, unloaded from the AHA trucks, completed the chopper's load.

The stacked barrels almost touched the roof of the cargo bay, and each one held fifty-five gallons of unrefined crude oil. Caine stared at the barrels as they rattled with each vibration of the helicopter. The oil inside was laced with the Gemini virus. If those barrels were refined in a populated area, the virus would be unleashed.

People would die.

A row of portholes ran along the side of the helicopter. Caine glanced outside and watched the tan brush and parched earth rise up as the helicopter dipped. The craft dropped suddenly as it hit an air pocket. Caine felt his stomach lurch. The two mercenaries exchanged surprised glances and turned to look out the windows. The ground grew even closer. The helicopter was landing.

With a metallic thunk, the cockpit door slid open and Takuba stepped into the rear bay. He grabbed hold of a frayed cord that ran along the roof and steadied himself as the helicopter dropped again. One of his Ghost Jackals followed close behind. The man balanced on the balls of his feet as the craft dipped and swayed.

'Hey, what the hell is going on?' one of the Delta Blue men snapped. 'We weren't supposed to land until we reached Unity State.'

'It's okay, no problem,' Takuba said, grinning at the two men. 'Slight change of plans. We refuel here, at a local airfield. Then we continue our journey.'

'We fueled up before takeoff,' the man said. 'If we're going to land here, I need to clear it with Bernatto.'

The merc lifted a radio from his belt. Takuba stepped aside as the Ghost Jackal raised a pistol.

The roar of gunfire echoed through the aircraft. Blood splattered against one of the portholes as a crimson hole opened in the mercenary's forehead. A muffled cry escaped Nena's mouth. The Ghost Jackal pivoted and fired again.

The second mercenary's eyes bulged as he slumped over on the bench and fell to the floor.

Takuba's grin grew wider, and he laughed like a hyena. He slid open the side door of the helicopter. Wind exploded into the cargo bay and whipped through Caine's hair.

'No room for dead weight,' Takuba shouted over the rushing vortex. He jerked his thumb towards the open door. The Ghost Jackal soldier grabbed one of the dead men and rolled him across the floor. The corpse tumbled out of the aircraft and plummeted off into the distance.

After the second body flew off the helicopter, Takuba slid the door shut. The wind noise was silenced and only the thumping hum of the rotors vibrated through the cargo bay.

'I warned Grissom and Bernatto they couldn't trust you,' Caine said. 'You're a rabid dog, Takuba. You can't resist biting the hand that feeds you.'

'Those men... Ha!' Takuba chuckled. 'They think they can seduce me with empty promises of freedom. Buy my loyalty with scraps of power.' He tugged at the skin beneath his right eye. 'But I see the truth. Their lust for oil has turned their hearts and souls black. Their greed blinds them. They think I am like our president, or the leader of the rebels. Corrupt, foolish men, holding out their hands to be bribed with what their people have fought and bled for. But make no mistake, old friend.

Bernatto and Grissom have served my purpose, my glorious cause. Not the other way around.'

He stood over Nena and yanked off her hood. She glared up at him with defiant eyes. Takuba smiled and caressed her chin.

'She is beautiful, Tom. Just like that girl all those years ago.'

Nena jerked her head away from his slim fingers. Takuba laughed and turned to Caine.

'Ah, and the temper on this one! What do you think? You want to fight me over this pretty as well?'

Caine's lips curled into a grim smile. 'If we had fought, you wouldn't be standing here now. You'd be dead.'

Takuba chuckled. 'You came all this way to kill me. But you do not know my secret. You see, I have already died once. But the spirits, they were not done with me. There was still work to be done.'

'Listen to yourself, Takuba. You're insane.'

'It is true. It happened a few years after you left South Sudan. I was fighting with the SPLM rebels, just outside Juba. A bullet struck me right here...' He pointed to a faint scar, just above his ear. 'It kissed my skull. One moment I was shooting my rifle, killing my enemy. There was a white flash. And then... nothing. I knew time was passing, I could sense it. But all around me there was emptiness. No sun, no moon. Not even dreams. Only darkness. Finally, I woke up in a small hut, outside the city. A local doctor had found me, cared for me. I don't think he knew whether I was a rebel, or a government soldier. He did not care. He was a good man.'

'Sounds like he made the same mistake I did,' Caine said. 'He saved your life.'

'No, good sir. That man cared for me, but it was the spirits that kept me alive. They whispered to me while I slept, spoke to me of my great purpose.'

'Yeah? And what purpose was that? More killing? More genocide?'

Takuba smiled. Sunlight glinted off his red diamond tooth and reflected around the interior of the cargo bay.

'Soon, you shall see, old friend. Nothing here is as it seems.'

The helicopter dipped lower. Takuba turned to the Ghost Jackal standing behind him. 'We will be landing in a few minutes. Take them off the helicopter while we transfer the cargo. If he causes any trouble... shoot the woman.'

He tilted his head and flashed Nena another leering grin. Then he stormed back into the cockpit and shut the door behind him.

40

The helicopter set down on a flat patch of land outside the Unity State borders. The only thing that identified the clearing as an airfield was a wooden shack standing in the distance. A lone windsock flew from a pole on the roof and fluttered in the scalding breeze.

The cargo bay's ramp lowered on hydraulics. Caine and Nena were marched out onto the airfield. Nena's hood and gag had been removed, but their hands were still cuffed behind their backs.

A hydraulic whine rose above the howling wind. Caine watched as the cargo pallet, stacked high with the infected oil barrels, was lowered down the ramp. The helicopter's heavy-duty winch chugged and hummed. It released its spool of cable at a slow, controlled pace.

One of Takuba's soldiers stood guard over them. The other stood next to Takuba, near the helicopter. The two men scanned the horizon. A cloud of dust moved towards them, growing larger in the distance.

'What the hell are we doing here?' Caine muttered. 'Why is he unloading the virus?'

'I have no idea,' Nena whispered back. 'There is no pipeline access here. But back in Juba, at the medical school, I was able to finish my examination of the samples. The bacteriophage has been altered. It is not the same as the original sample.'

'Who altered it?' Caine asked.

She shook her head. 'I don't know. But the new organism will not release the virus when the oil is refined. The cell wall is too thick. It will survive the distillation process intact.'

'Nothing is as it seems...' Caine's voice trailed off as he repeated Takuba's words.

The Ghost Jackal eyed them with a wary glance and raised his rifle. 'Shut up! No talking!'

The dust cloud moved closer. A small convoy came into view. The vehicles burst through the swirling air and heat distortion and parked near the helicopter. The convoy consisted of a small flatbed truck flanked by a pair of filthy, battered Jeeps. Takuba exchanged some words with the men inside. It sounded like they were speaking in English, but Caine detected a slight accent to the men's voices. They sounded Russian.

No, not Russian, he realized. Something else...

'These men are Chechen,' he whispered to Nena. 'Galloway was following a group of Chechen arms dealers. He said they acquired the virus from a lab in Syria.'

The Ghost Jackal slammed the butt of his rifle into Caine's back. Caine stumbled forward and dropped to his knees.

'I said no talking,' the man growled.

As he fell to the ground, Caine's fingers brushed against the tops of his leather boots. The tips of his fingers wrapped around a small length of aluminum tucked into the left boot's shaft. He staggered to his feet and continued to watch the men work.

The Chechens unloaded another cargo pallet from the truck. The helicopter's winch groaned as it pulled the new load up into the cargo bay. The pallet appeared to be identical to the old one. The same number of barrels were stacked on board, held in place by an identical mesh webbing. The only difference appeared to be a red band painted around the center of the new barrels.

Takuba paced over to them as the Chechen men locked the wheels on the cargo pallet inside the helicopter. Then they began loading the old pallet onto their truck.

'Get them back onboard,' Takuba shouted. 'We take off now.'

The Ghost Jackal shoved Caine. As he stumbled towards the helicopter, his hand wrapped around the tactical pen he had removed from his boot. Takuba's men had missed it in their weapons search. He slid the slim metal barrel down the back of his waistband, making sure his fingers could reach the cap.

Takuba followed them up the ramp of the helicopter and grinned as they were once again cuffed to the bench. He glanced at a rugged watch strapped to his wrist.

'Your time is almost up, my friend. In thirty minutes, the peace conference begins. As your life ends, a new era begins for my country.'

The hum of the rotors filled the air. The helicopter shook as it prepared for takeoff. Takuba turned his leering stare on Nena. She glared back at him for a moment, then looked away.

'Thirty minutes... less than an hour,' he said, his eyes wide above his shimmering smile. 'I wonder how we shall spend the time?'

41

Sweat rolled down Josh Galloway's face as he crouched behind the metal fence. Using the bolt cutters from the guard's truck, he snipped another length of wire. He heard the roar of an engine and looked up. Takuba's helicopter lifted off from the complex's landing pad and soared into the blue sky above them.

Caine and the oil barrels were onboard. He had watched Takuba's men load them before takeoff.

Gemini, he thought. It has to be in that oil.

Whatever Takuba and Bernatto were planning to do with it, time was running out. He had to get a message out, get someone to intercept the chopper.

But first, he had to keep his promise to Buri.

The boy huddled next to him, watching the complex through a pair of binoculars.

'A guard is coming this way... only one man,' he whispered.

Josh snipped one more wire in the fence, then ducked in the thick grass. They waited in silence.

The lone guard ambled along the perimeter of the fence. He

moved past them and disappeared behind a building. Josh sat up and continued working.

He cut a few more wires and tugged at the hole in the fence. The opening was larger now, big enough for him to slip through.

'There are fewer men now, less guards,' Buri whispered. He continued peering through the binoculars. Josh looked down at the boy and smiled. The lenses looked comically large against his tiny face.

'Thanks for the recon,' Josh whispered back. 'Judging by all the trucks that rolled out of here a few minutes ago, I'd say it's all hands on deck. Hopefully, that will make things easier.'

Buri lowered the binoculars. 'What are you going to do?'

'I have to get a message to my friends. Warn them about what's happening here. But first, I'm going to free your mother and the others.'

'I want to come with you, I want to help you!'

Josh shook his head. 'Buri, you are the bravest kid I ever met. You've already helped me... you saved my life. Now, I need you to wait here. Your mother will be looking for you. Can you do that for me?'

Buri nodded.

'Okay, stay hidden in the grass and keep your head down. If you hear any shooting, run as far away as you can, got it?'

'Got it.'

Josh took a deep breath. 'Okay. Here we go.'

He slid under the large opening in the fence. The wires bit and tugged at his tattered clothes, but he was able to make it under. He crouched inside the complex, cradling the AK-47 in his hands.

He turned and gave Buri one last smile, then stalked towards the bunker that held the prisoners.

Inside, the building was dark. The office was empty, and the body Caine had left earlier had been removed. The heat in the dim concrete box was stifling. Josh heard low moans and murmurs from the cells in the back.

Buri was right, Josh thought. This place is on a skeleton crew now. They're pulling out, and they just left these people here to die.

He rummaged through the desk and grabbed a yellow key card. Jogging back to the rows of metal doors, he swiped the key card over the locks. One by one they clattered open and fell to the ground. The doors began to shake and rattle as the prisoners inside stirred.

He reached his old cell, number fifteen. He swiped the lock and rolled up the door. The crowd of bodies inside looked up at him with dull, listless stares. They were weak from hunger and exhaustion.

'Aya, are you in here?' Josh shouted.

The woman staggered to her feet.

'I... I am here.'

'Good. Buri is outside the camp. He's alive.'

The woman clasped her hands together. Tears spilled from her eyes. 'Oh, thank God. Thank you, Mr. Carter, thank you for coming back!'

'Don't thank me. It's my fault you're here in the first place.'

A crowd formed behind him as the prisoners spilled out into the corridor.

Josh turned and addressed the crowd. 'Everyone, listen to me. I've made an opening in the western fence. It's tight, but it's large enough for a man to slip through.'

One of the prisoners pointed to the front of the building. 'There are guards heading this way! Two of them!'

'Get back in the cells,' Josh ordered. 'We can hide, let them move on before we escape.'

The men began to grumble and whisper.

'No! I don't care if they have guns,' a lean, elderly man hissed. 'I don't care if I die... These men caged us like dogs. I am not going to run and hide. I am going to fight!'

The mumbles rose to angry shouts and chanting. The men surged toward the entrance of the building.

Josh grabbed Aya by the arm and led her towards the exit. 'Aya, whatever happens, go to the fence. Get outside. Buri is waiting for you.'

The woman gave him a frightened nod.

The crowd of men uttered a bloodcurdling war cry and charged out of the building. Josh kept a tight hold on Aya, protecting her from the rushing mob. He heard gunfire from outside.

Josh pushed her away. He pointed to the western edge of the fence.

'That way... go!'

Aya turned and sprinted for the fence. Bullets nipped at her heels.

Josh whirled around. The crowd of men had brought one of the Delta Blue guards to the ground. They were beating him to a pulp as he thrashed beneath them.

Another mercenary staggered from the throng of men. He was firing at Aya with his rifle, but his shots went wild, sending puffs of dirt into the air.

Josh fired back, striking the man in the leg with a three-round burst. As he fell to the ground, more of the prisoners piled on top of him. They beat and clawed at his face.

Josh rushed over and began pulling men off the wounded soldier. 'Wait, don't kill him! I need him alive!'

The crowd parted. Josh kicked the man's rifle aside. The soldier's face was battered and bruised, but he was still breathing. He groaned as he tried to sit up. Josh planted his foot on the man's chest and forced him back onto the ground.

He turned back to the prisoners. 'Everyone, go! Get to the fence! I promise these men will pay for what they did to you.'

The men in the crowd exchanged a few glares, then turned and jogged toward the fence after Aya. The rest of the prisoners filed out of the building after them.

Josh reached down and tore a security badge off the wounded mercenary's vest.

'Okay, asshole. One question. Do you have access to the VSAT system?'

The man nodded. 'Yes... yes, I do. I can get you in, I swear!'

Josh smiled. 'Good answer.'

* * *

INCORRECT LOGON – VSAT ACCESS DENIED

The VSAT terminal beeped as the error message flashed on the screen.

The mercenary quickly typed in another code. Josh pulled back the charging handle on his rifle. 'If you can't help me, you're dead weight. Got it?'

'They... they rotate the code!' the man stuttered. His words were slurred by his swollen lips and mashed teeth. 'They must have changed it after you were captured.'

Josh glanced toward the door of the communications room. It was closed and locked behind them. The battered mercenary claimed he had shut down the cameras in the room, but Josh had no idea if he was lying. They had made it into the main building without incident, but if he couldn't get a message out soon, it wouldn't matter.

'How many of you are still in the complex?' he asked.

'I... don't know. Less than ten. Plus Bernatto. Everyone else is heading to the oil fields with Takuba's men.'

'It's about to be less than nine if you don't access this system ASAP,' Josh growled.

The man typed in another code and hit enter.

INCORRECT LOGON – VSAT ACCESS DENIED. YOU HAVE EXCEEDED LOGON ATTEMPTS.

The alarm whooped to life. Spinning red lights flooded the room with a crimson glow.

The mercenary looked up at him. 'I can bypass the lockout, but I can't stop the alarm... Bernatto will know we're here! He'll flood the room with the Gemini virus! We have to get out of here!'

Josh hefted the rifle. 'No. Try again. You want to live? Access the system. Now!'

The man turned back to the VSAT terminal. Beads of sweat dripped down his forehead. He entered another string of letters and numbers on the keyboard and pressed enter.

LOGON VERIFIED. ACCESS GRANTED.

The logon screen dissolved away, leaving a blinking cursor.

The door to the room shook and rattled. Men pounded on it from the other side.

Josh prodded the man with the rifle. He slid a piece of paper in front of him and gestured towards it.

'That's the VSAT link for the CIA station house in Juba. Start the connection. Now.'

The mercenary stood up. 'This is over. My men are outside, there's nowhere to run!'

Josh stepped back and aimed his rifle at the man. 'You're right, there is nowhere to run. And you're stuck in here with me. Start typing. Now!'

The man moved towards the door. 'Hey, I'm in here!' he shouted. 'It's Galloway, he—'

The men outside opened fire. Gunfire tore through the office door. Josh threw himself to the ground as the mercenary staggered backwards. He fell back into the chair. Bullets thudded into his body and ricocheted off the table.

Josh grabbed the leg of the chair. He pulled the man's corpse in front of the VSAT terminal. More slugs thudded into the man's body. A few shots struck near the communications equipment, but the mercenary's corpse shielded the terminal.

The gunfire stopped. Josh muttered a curse and knelt in front of the table. He typed in the link information and waited. The satellite signals suffered from minor latency, and it took a few seconds before the cursor blinked back to life. A progress bar flashed on the screen, counting down.

VSAT CONNECTION INITIATED.

More gunfire perforated the door. Josh threw himself back to the ground. He scurried away from the table and rolled over onto his back. He aimed the rifle at the door and returned fire.

He saw movement through the holes in the flimsy panel. Men fell to the ground. Josh kept firing. His muzzle fire flashed bright orange in the dim room. The rifle clicked empty. He tossed it aside and staggered to his feet. Leaning over the terminal, his fingers raced across the keyboard.

PRIORITY ONE:
UNMARKED MIL-17, OUTBOUND NEAR THAR JATH.
DESTINATION UNKNOWN.
BWLIBRA – REPEAT, BWLIBRA.

He paused. The brief cryptonym BWLIBRA would alert the station house that the message concerned an imminent biological attack.

He heard the men moving into position behind the door. The mercenary had been right... there was nowhere for him to go.

Rebecca...

There was no time. No time for regrets or last words. No time to even think. He typed a few more words.

ALERT D/NCS: CAINE ONBOARD. HOPE YOU'RE SMARTER
THAN HE IS. SORRY I CAN'T BE THERE FOR YOU.
GALLOWAY OUT.

He reached for the enter key.

Another hail of bullets exploded through the door. Josh grunted as he felt red-hot pain lance through his shoulder.

He dropped to the ground. More bullets struck his legs and stomach. He felt warm blood seeping through his shirt.

The men began pounding on the door again. The flimsy barrier buckled under the onslaught.

Josh groaned in pain. Reaching up, his trembling fingers grabbed the edge of the desk. He pulled himself up to his knees.

His message blinked on the screen. He stabbed his bloody finger down on the enter key.

SENDING MESSAGE.

A progress bar appeared on the screen, counting down the latency period of the VSAT connection.

The door burst open. Another hail of gunfire ripped into Josh's back.

He fell away from the table, onto the floor.

Five Delta Blue men stormed into the room. They covered him with their rifles but said nothing. Josh spit blood onto the floor. He looked up at the terminal.

MESSAGE SENT flashed on the screen. Josh grinned and rested his head on the floor.

The men parted as Bernatto stepped into the room. He looked down at Josh and shook his head.

'Galloway. I warned Grissom we should have killed you days ago. You were his fallback in case we couldn't pin things on Caine. He underestimated you.'

Josh gasped for breath. His eyes fluttered in his head. 'Bernatto... tell you... something...'

Bernatto pulled a pistol from a shoulder holster. He held it at his side.

'Tell me what?' he asked.

A tremor ran through Josh's body. 'There... there will be a reckoning. Caine... He'll never stop. He'll... he'll come for you.'

Bernatto stared back at him. He pushed his glasses up the bridge of his nose. 'Caine will be dead soon. Just like you.'

Josh looked into his eyes. 'T-tell yourself what you... what you like, Allan. But you know. I see... in your eyes. You know he'll find you again.'

Bernatto raised the pistol. 'Coming back here was stupid, Galloway. We beat you. You should have accepted that and ran. You could have escaped, made it to safety.'

Josh shook his head. 'Not... not wired to be second best.' He smiled. 'See you... in hell.'

Bernatto fired.

Josh's head snapped back. His body slumped to the ground, eyes closed.

42

The helicopter swooped low across the plains. Takuba paced back and forth, bracing himself with the cord that ran across the roof. As the minutes ticked down, the man seemed consumed with nervous energy. His eyes darted around the interior of the cargo bay. He glanced out the windows at the parched landscape below, then his manic gaze settled on Nena. She glared at him as he ran his fingers through her long, dark hair. His lips curled into a sadistic grin.

'Such lovely hair. Do you remember her, Tom? That beautiful girl?' He glanced over at Caine.

Caine remained silent.

Takuba waved a finger at him. 'I can see in your eyes, you do. You remember what I said to you?'

'You said your spirits would protect you,' Caine said.

Just keep him talking, he thought. The fingers of his cuffed hands darted to his waistband. They brushed against the cap of the tactical pen.

Takuba nodded. He slid his fingers down Nena's cheek.

'Yes. And they put a curse on you. Now, years later, here we are. So you see, I was right.'

'What have you done to the Gemini virus?' Caine asked. 'You changed it, mutated it somehow.'

Takuba dragged his eyes from Nena's face and looked over at him. 'The Chechens work with the Russian Mafia. They traffic in women. I made a deal with them, behind Grissom's back. My men and I provided them with prisoners. Young girls, taken from the villages I liberated. In exchange, they modified the Gemini virus to my specifications.'

'You're not a liberator,' Caine snapped. 'You're just another madman who blames mass murder on the voices in his head. You pimped out your people, innocent children, for what? To be Bernatto and Grissom's errand boy?'

As he spoke, his fingers made tiny, precise movements behind his back. The bottom of the pen turned a fraction of an inch.

'Bernatto and Grissom know nothing,' Takuba boasted. 'I stole their greatest weapon from under their noses and made it my own.'

'But you rendered it useless,' Nena said, inching away from him. 'The new cell walls will survive the refining process intact. The virus will not be released from the bacteria.'

Takuba laughed. 'So, she is both smart and beautiful! You are right, my lovely. The virus will not be released when the oil is refined. Gemini will live, hibernating within the gasoline. The kerosene, the diesel... any product made from South Sudan's oil will hold the kiss of death inside, waiting to strike.'

Nena gasped and her eyes opened wide. 'No... the bacteriophage will survive, but the cell walls will be weakened.'

'What do you mean?' Caine asked. 'I thought you said the virus wouldn't be released?'

The bottom of the pen rotated another fraction of an inch. His probing fingers felt the threads of the screw become exposed. Almost there...

'The virus won't be released in the refineries,' she said, staring in horror at Takuba's grinning face. 'It will be released all over the world. Anywhere the refined products are sold and burned, the cell walls will finally decay, and the virus will escape.'

'Europe, China, America,' Takuba snarled. 'A cloud of death, choking the entire world. A world that has stood by and watched while my country is defiled by war and bloodshed. All for a taste of the black blood that flows through her veins. In Sierra Leone, men kill for diamonds. In the Congo, it is timber. Here, it is oil. Everywhere in Africa, there is wealth and resources. But it is the foreign powers who grow rich, while Africans starve and die.'

'You may be right, Takuba. But your hands are just as bloody as anyone else's,' Caine said.

Takuba nodded. 'Yes, yes, this is true. When you first met me, I was a monster. How could I be anything else? As a child, I was taken from my home by monsters. Beaten, tortured by monsters. I was forced to murder my father, my own flesh and blood. The horror of it all... it weighed on my soul. Left me an empty shell, a vessel for evil. But now? Now, I am a savior.'

'You are insane,' Nena whispered. 'You will kill millions of people!'

'When I woke from my coma, I was reborn. I had a new purpose. I cared nothing for this rebellion. The squabbling between tribes, the feuds between governments... It is all a farce, a silly joke. The only way to free my people is to end foreign meddling in my country once and for all. If the oil is the root of all evil, then I will turn the oil itself into a poison. Once my men take the key oil fields, we will flood the pipes that lead into the north. Gemini will grow and thrive within the pipeline, and soon it will be too late to stop it.'

Caine felt the bottom of the pen slip off into his fingers. Underneath, a short, knobby length of metal protruded from the pen. Working quickly, he maneuvered the metal key into the lock of the handcuffs. The cuffs had been applied by the Delta Blue mercenaries and Caine had recognized them as US law enforcement models. They used a standardized lock and key system.

The key in the top of the pen would be able to open them, if he could manipulate it without being noticed.

'Even if your plan works, you're dooming this country to starvation,' Caine said. He stared into Takuba's wild, manic eyes. 'Without oil profits to prop up its economy, South Sudan will fall into chaos. Famine, disease, riots... You're not setting anybody free. You're just burning the whole country down.'

'The LRA taught me one thing, Tom. War can be a holy act. It is the healing hand of God. Those who die are the rotten flesh he cuts from an infected land. The survivors... they are the pure. They are his chosen. When crops become diseased, overgrown with corruption and sickness, then you must burn them down. You must start over with fresh seed.'

Takuba reached behind Nena's back and unlocked her handcuffs. She screamed as he yanked her to her feet.

Caine's eyes followed him as he dragged her to the center of the cargo bay.

'Like me, my country must be reborn. And for that, it has to die first. Only then will my people be free.'

'Leave her alone, Takuba,' Caine shouted. 'It's me you want! I'm the one who came here to kill you!' His fingers worked out of sight, twisting the key back and forth in the cuff's locking mechanism.

'No, my good friend. You are not here to kill me. The spirits brought you for a different purpose. Just as they did years ago. When I was taken as a child, the LRA marked me. They cut the sign of the holy cross into my flesh. They told me if I anointed my cross in blood, before each battle, the spirits would protect me. God would make me invincible. That night, Tom, after I killed that girl, I traced the cross in her blood across my beating heart. And they were right. The spirits saved me. God shielded me from the bullet that should have killed me.'

Takuba threw Nena to the ground. She groaned as she struck the metal floor of the helicopter. The madman stood over her and drew his machete from its leather sheath. Reaching up to his collar, he tore open his shirt. Caine stared at the crisscrossed scar that ran across his flesh. The mark of the cross cut across his chest and ran down his stomach.

'Now, it is time once again. Before I go into battle, I will mark myself with the blood of this half-breed bitch. And once again, you shall bear witness.'

He raised the machete into the air.

Caine struggled to fit the end of the pen into the lock. His face flushed red, and his eyes blazed with emerald rage.

'Takuba!'

Suddenly a high-pitched beeping came from the open door to the cockpit. The helicopter tilted to the right, and Nena rolled across the floor. She slammed into the cargo pallet and groaned in pain. Takuba reached up to steady himself as the aircraft swung in the other direction.

He turned to the cockpit. 'What is happening?' he bellowed.

The pilot turned and looked back. 'Helicopters, sir, two of them! South Sudan Air Force!'

Galloway! Caine thought. He must have made it back to the

refinery, sent out a warning. South Sudan Air Force is moving to intercept!

The helicopter swung through the air again. Gunfire screeched across the left side of the cargo bay. Heavy slugs tore through the metal fuselage of the aircraft and buried themselves in the floor.

'Lower the ramp!' Takuba ordered. 'We must shoot them down. Quickly!'

One of the Ghost Jackals lurched past Caine. He flipped open the latches of a long plastic case that lay on the floor. Caine watched as the soldier opened the case and removed one of the MANPADS missile launcher systems. Moving to the back of the aircraft, he slammed his fist against a red button mounted to the wall. The hydraulic hum once again whined through the cargo bay as the rear ramp lowered down. Wind billowed through the aircraft.

Caine squinted as sunlight flooded into the cargo bay. Turning his head, he caught a glimpse of another helicopter swooping past the open ramp. The tall, narrow-bodied craft was unmistakable, even from a distance. Russian-made MI-24P gunships, sold to South Sudan by Ukraine. A pair of short, slanted wings were mounted to either side of each attack helicopter. Rockets and guns peeked out from under the wings. The gunships were fast, maneuverable, and heavily armed.

Caine gave the key a final turn, and the cuff popped loose. He shook one of his hands free. The cuffs were still attached to his other wrist, but he was no longer bound to the bench. He slid the key into his pocket and looped the fingers of his right hand through the metal circle of the cuffs.

Takuba turned and threw open the side door. Another attack helicopter hovered to their right. He grabbed the handles of the heavy machine gun and swung it into firing position.

'Bring us alongside,' Takuba shouted to the pilot. 'I will swat them out of the air like mosquitoes!'

He turned his back on Caine.

It's time. Take him out...

The voice in Caine's head was calm, precise. Seductive. His killer instinct, honed by years of experience, took over. Caine leapt to his feet and charged at Takuba. He wrapped his arm around Takuba's neck and yanked him away from the machine gun.

Takuba's eyes bulged and a hissing gurgle escaped his lips. Caine tightened his grip, crushing his thrashing target's windpipe in the crook of his arm. Using the cuffs as a makeshift pair of brass knuckles, he drove his fist into Takuba's right side. The man gasped as the blow pummeled his liver.

The second Ghost Jackal stormed out of the cockpit. Takuba reached towards him with a feeble hand. The soldier raised his rifle and bellowed at Caine, but before he could fire. Caine pivoted, stacking Takuba between him and the rebel's gun.

The helicopter swung to the right. Caine and Takuba both flew away from the open doorway and slammed into the cargo pallet. Caine lost his hold and Takuba slithered away from him.

Explosions rumbled through the air around them. Looking back through the open ramp, Caine saw trails of white smoke streak towards them from the rear helicopter.

Rockets!

He dropped the cuffs and grabbed the cargo net to steady himself as one of the explosive projectiles slammed into the left side of the aircraft.

He heard the shriek of tearing metal, and smoke billowed into the cabin. The helicopter lurched sideways again. Nena rolled toward the rear of the bay.

Caine felt himself moving towards the side door. Sparks flew from the edge of the cargo pallet. The wheel locks had been damaged by the rocket's impact. The slab of metal broke free and skidded across the cargo bay floor.

The heavy load slammed into Takuba. He flailed at the nylon straps as the towering pallet slid towards the open door, pushing him and Caine with it.

With a horrendous crash, the pallet crashed into the machine gun and sheared it off its pole mount. Caine and Takuba hung on to the cargo net for dear life as they both found themselves dangling out the open side door, thousands of feet above the ground.

43

Caine's stomach lurched as the helicopter dove closer to the ground. He held on to the nylon straps of the cargo net with a white-knuckled grip while his feet flailed in the air. He and Takuba both struggled to find footing on the helicopter's landing skid. The aircraft pitched and rolled in a sickening series of evasive maneuvers.

The buffeting wind around them muted the chugging roar of the gunship's cannon fire. Caine ducked his head as a row of slugs cut across the side of the helicopter, inches above him. A series of two-inch holes burst open in the exposed oil barrels. The thick black liquid sprayed into the air, stinging his eyes.

The helicopter leveled out and flew straight over the brush and scrub below. Caine's feet found solid purchase on the landing skid. He heard Takuba bellow a war cry to his right. Caine let go of the straps with one hand and swung his body sideways, just as Takuba struck with his machete. The long, shimmering blade clanged off one of the oil barrels, narrowly missing Caine's hand.

Caine shuffled closer to Takuba. He raised his arm to block

another swing of the machete and slammed his right knee into the man's abdomen. Takuba grunted in pain and tried to shimmy back on the skid. Caine grabbed the back of the man's head and slammed his face into the oil barrels. Takuba reeled from the impact. His feet fell away from the helicopter, but he did not lose his grip on the net.

Before Caine could strike again, he heard the whine of the rotors increase. The helicopter banked left as more rockets streaked through the air around them. Caine's body flew off the skid... He grabbed at the straps with both hands as he swung in the air, hanging off the side of the helicopter.

Below them he could see shimmering metal towers and steel pipeline gleaming in the harsh sun. He knew they had not yet reached the oil fields in the Unity State. This was a smaller natural gas factory.

The cargo helicopter dove straight for the towering silver tanks.

As they leveled out, Caine's body crashed back into the barrels, and his feet made contact with the skid. He kicked Takuba, sending the man flying away from him. The attack left Caine off balance, and Takuba swung by one hand from the cargo net. His feet scrabbled against the skid as he struggled to regain solid footing.

The helicopter shuddered as canon-fire grazed the tail. The aircraft flew into a dizzying spiral. Caine felt gravity and centrifugal force tugging at his body. It was all he could do to maintain his grip on the net as the helicopter whipped around in a tight circle.

The pilot regained control and swung around one of the towers. Caine saw the wall of steel pass behind them, missing their hanging bodies by inches. The attack helicopters in pursuit ceased firing. As they sped away, Caine caught a glimpse of the warning symbols stenciled on the tank in bright red letters.

Liquid natural gas... If those gunships fire again, they might hit the tanks, Caine realized.

The chopper tilted to the left and swooped over the gas plant. The heavy cargo pallet groaned and slid away from the door, pulling Caine and Takuba back into the cargo bay.

Caine dropped to his feet. His legs were shaking, and he felt nauseous from the dizzying spin of the helicopter. He forced himself to keep moving, keep attacking.

He closed in on Takuba as the man swung his machete. Caine got inside Takuba's reach and threw up his left arm, blocking the downward strike. He grabbed Takuba's shoulder with his free hand and pulled the man forward. His knee exploded upwards, driving the air from Takuba's lungs in a savage blow to the gut.

Caine sensed the Ghost Jackal soldier moving towards them. He dropped to the ground and rolled away as automatic weapon fire sparked across the floor of the helicopter. Takuba stumbled backwards, moving out of the man's line of fire.

Caine moved to intercept the soldier but froze in place. He heard the rapid pulse of their pursuers' auto-cannons firing at them. He threw himself to the ground as the heavy slugs sliced through the side of the helicopter. The Ghost Jackal's body jerked and spun as the massive 23mm slugs ripped into his flesh. As his corpse fell, his rifle tumbled across the floor and flew towards the open side door.

Sparks flew from the cargo winch as the cannon fire swept across the machinery. Caine heard a high-pitched beeping from the rear of cargo bay... the other Ghost Jackal had locked on with the MANPADS missile system.

'Fly level!' the soldier shouted. 'I have missile lock!'

Caine covered his ears and stayed low on the ground as the soldier fired. A plume of smoke shot above him. The powerful exhaust from the portable missile filled the cargo bay. He heard a loud hiss as the projectile streaked towards their pursuers.

Orange fire lit the sky behind them. The explosion was deafening, and the helicopter shook from the vibration. Caine looked back and saw the wreckage of the gunship hanging suspended in the air. A plume of fire shot out from the rotors, and the tail section flew away from the cabin. The burning debris dropped from the sky.

The Ghost Jackal raised his fist in the air. He kneeled and grabbed another missile from the case.

Caine slid towards the fallen rifle. He reached out with grasping fingers. The helicopter shook again. The rifle jumped and clattered another few inches across the floor. It flew through the open side of the helicopter and fell out of reach.

The Ghost Jackal steadied himself, then slid the long white missile into the MANPADS launcher. Before he could finish reloading, a slim figure stood over him. Nena had picked herself up from the corner of the cargo bay. She raised a heavy steel wrench above her head.

Screaming like a banshee, she swung the grimy hunk of metal like a club, striking the Ghost Jackal's head with a dull thud. The man's eyes rolled back and blood gushed from his forehead. His body fell onto the open ramp. His fingers clawed at the smooth metal surface, but he could not stop himself from sliding backwards. The wind gusted and lifted him from the ramp's surface.

His panicked cry echoed through the cargo bay as his body spun away and fell to the ground.

Caine staggered to his feet. He squinted, struggling to make out Takuba in the hazy, smoke-filled air.

He heard the pilot shouting from the cockpit. 'They coming around again!'

The helicopter began to climb. Sparks flew from the damaged winch. Caine heard the hiss of rushing metal as the cable went slack. The cargo pallet slid backwards, toward the open ramp.

Nena screamed.

Caine whirled around, just in time to see the pallet tumble out the back of the aircraft. The steel cable spooled out behind it, hissing through the damaged winch.

There was no sign of Nena... She was gone!

The helicopter dipped as the cable snapped taut. The weight of the cargo pallet swung beneath them, throwing the aircraft off balance. Caine's head slammed into the roof of the cargo bay. He fell back to the floor as the aircraft recovered from the sudden jolt. He lifted himself off the floor.

He heard coughing. Footsteps clanged across the bay. He scrambled to his feet and spun around, raising his right arm in front of his face in a defensive block.

The smoke cleared. The rushing wind whipped through his clothes and hair.

Takuba stood before him. He pointed at Caine with his machete. 'Now, my old friend,' he croaked. He held up his other hand. Blood dripped from his fingers. He painted the crimson liquid over the scars that ran across his chest.

'Now, nothing can stop me.'

He raised the machete over his head and uttered a bloodcurdling scream as he lunged towards Caine.

44

Nena watched Takuba's soldier soar out of the open cargo bay. Before she could recover her breath, she heard the crackling pop of the winch exploding at the far end of the cargo bay. The helicopter lurched into a steep climb. The high-pitched wail of its radar detection system blared though the cabin.

She leaned against the wall and took a step back from the open cargo bay. The rushing wind blew through her hair and whipped at her clothes. She heard the harsh rasp of metal scraping against metal. She spun around and saw the towering pallet of oil barrels rushing towards her.

She threw up her arms and screamed. The heavy pallet slammed into her, knocking her backwards towards the open ramp.

She looped her arm through the mesh webbing as the pallet skidded down the ramp. For a brief moment, she could hear the metal cable twang as it rushed out of the winch. Then the heavy load flew out of the helicopter, dragging her with it.

She felt a dizzying rush as her body plunged through the air. She forced herself to hold her arm tight, locking her grip on the nylon straps. Suddenly, the pallet jerked to a stop. The weight snapped up from the impact, and her arm slid loose from the strap. Her fingers clawed against the mesh as she grabbed hold with her other hand. She hung beneath the swinging pallet, hundreds of feet above the ground.

She felt her stomach lurch again. The helicopter dove lower, flying toward the metal towers of a natural gas plant. Looking up, she could see brief glimpses of the attacking helicopter. Crimson streams of cannon fire arced from its underbody, but the only sound she could hear was the rushing wind.

The towers and pipes of the refinery loomed closer. The helicopter swooped low, heading for a gap between two towers. The ground rushed up towards her. As the helicopters maneuvered between the gas towers, the pallet swung like a pendulum below. She tightened her grip as the metal walls of the tanks loomed closer.

Clang!

The metal oil barrels collided with the side of the tank, sending a shockwave through the mesh. Nena gasped as her grip slipped. She clawed at the next row of webbing and managed to grab hold. Her legs swung beneath her as the impact sent the pallet spinning in circles.

The helicopter swooped back around. More gunfire traced the air above her. The gas tanks loomed on either side of the spinning pallet. If she struck one of them, she knew the impact would crush her or, at the very least, send her falling to her death. She reached up and grabbed another strip of webbing. Grunting with exertion, she pulled herself up the side of the dangling pallet.

As she reached the top, she saw the helicopter swoop above two tall, narrow distillation towers. The cable slipped between the structures, but the gap was too narrow to allow the pallet to pass. As she swung forward, the curved metal walls loomed closer.

She scrambled over the top edge of the pallet and threw one arm around the cable. She grabbed at the netting with her free hand and dug her feet under the mesh as best as she could.

She closed her eyes tight and braced for impact.

The edge of the pallet crunched into the two towers. The steel cable snapped taut as the heavy weight wedged between the structures.

The helicopter bucked and swayed at the end of the cable, like a dragonfly caught by a thread. The attacking gunship veered off, barely avoiding a collision as the Mi-17 stopped short in midair.

The helicopter was trapped. The pallet wedged between the twin structures acted as an anchor. There was no way they could pull free...

* * *

Caine pivoted on his feet, letting Takuba's machete swing through empty air. He moved in close as Takuba swung again. Blocking the strike with a raised forearm, he threw a quick jab with his free hand. The blow snapped into Takuba's jaw and he stumbled backwards.

Caine pressed forward, stomping his foot into the man's shin. He moved in for a punch, but the swooping dive of the helicopter threw off his balance. He staggered back, moving out of Takuba's attack range.

Takuba snarled and charged at him, raising his machete over his head in a two-handed grip. Before he could strike, the shriek of the pursuer's autocannon burst through the air. Caine threw himself to the ground as more slugs perforated the walls of the cargo bay. The roar of the other helicopter's rotors drowned out the rushing wind as it veered off from its attack run.

Caine rolled over onto his back as Takuba loomed over him, the madman's tattered shirt whipping behind him in the wind. He swung the machete through the air. Caine rolled left. The blade clanged against the metal floor of the helicopter, sending sparks into the air.

Caine kicked his left leg into Takuba's knee. The man's leg buckled, and Takuba fell face first to the ground. The other helicopter swooped back behind them. Metal shrieked and groaned as more heavy slugs flew overhead.

Caine straddled Takuba's back, using his knees to pin the man's legs to the ground. He grabbed the rebel leader's head and slammed it into the deck of the helicopter. He heard a grunt of pain. He slammed it again and felt Takuba go limp. He looped the handcuff that dangled from his wrist under the man's throat. Then he grabbed the other side and pulled the chain tight against his neck.

Takuba gasped for breath and clawed at the metal cuffs.

Caine shifted his weight and drove a knee into Takuba's back. He pulled tighter. The chain bit deeper into Takuba's throat.

Caine's vision blurred as the muscles in his arms and shoulders pulled taut. He could feel blood pounding through the veins in his forehead.

He closed his eyes. For a moment, he caught a glimpse of her in the fog and haze of his adrenaline-fueled rage. The girl from years ago. Her pleading eyes, her hand reaching out to him...

Nena's final scream echoed through his mind.

Caine's eyes snapped open. His vision cleared. He clenched his jaw and pulled the chain tighter. The metal edge of the cuff dug into his wrist, but he ignored the pain.

A violent jolt shook the helicopter, throwing Caine forward. He rolled across the cargo bay floor and came to a stop by the side door. He could hear the metal cable twang and scrape against the ramp. The aircraft hovered in place, bobbing up and down like a boat buffeted by a typhoon.

We're stuck, he thought. The cargo pallet must have hooked on to something... The cable got tangled!

The aircraft yawed left and right as the pilot struggled to dislodge the pallet. Caine felt himself rolling closer to the open door. He threw out his arm to stop his sliding movement.

'Now, Tom... now you will see!'

Takuba!

The man's voice was a hellish croak. He stood over Caine as the entire helicopter tilted sideways. Caine rolled to his right. The machete blade clanged where his head had been a second earlier.

Another body slid next to him in the doorway. It was the Ghost Jackal, the soldier who had been cut down by the gunship's autocannon. Caine noticed the bulge of a parachute strapped to the man's back. He must have put it on earlier, when the helicopters first attacked.

Caine rolled back to face Takuba. The man's lips twisted into a hateful grin. Blood and spittle dripped from his mouth, and his eyes fluttered in their sockets.

'Now you will know what it means to be cursed,' the madman gasped.

He swung the machete again, but his motions were slow, predictable. He was growing tired.

They both were.

Caine threw up his arms and blocked the clumsy strike. He raised his knee and slammed a kick into Takuba's chest, knocking the man away from him.

Before he could get up, the helicopter dipped to the right again. Caine felt his upper body scrape against the floor and slide towards the open door. He grabbed the edge of the doorframe with his left hand to steady himself. His flailing right hand gripped the corpse to his right.

The wind outside whipped through his hair. Looking up, he saw the blur of the heavy rotors churning above them. The engine whirred and groaned as it struggled to pull the helicopter free. Smoke poured out of the motor. The metal cable snapped taut again and the helicopter shifted to the left.

Caine pulled himself back in the door just as Takuba fell towards him. He let go of the doorframe and grabbed the man's weapon hand, stopping another attack. Reaching out with his right hand, he snapped the open end of the handcuffs around the strap of the parachute.

'I was cursed long before I met you,' Caine snarled.

He felt the helicopter wobble. It was leaning to the right again. Loose debris fell towards him, pelting his body.

He let go of Takuba. The man swung the machete up over his head, preparing for another attack. Caine punched with his left fist. He felt bone and cartilage snap, and Takuba roared in pain.

Caine used the moment of distraction to pull the handcuff key from his pocket and slip it into the cuff that was still attached to his wrist.

Takuba recovered and leaned forward. He slammed a fist into Caine's stomach. Red-hot pain lanced through his body as the blow struck the stitches of his knife wound. Caine gritted his teeth, but he could not hide the searing agony that flashed across his face. Takuba grinned and pummeled him again. Caine shook as another spasm shot through his nerves.

The grinning madman raised the machete again as Caine gasped.

'You cannot win!' Takuba shouted. 'My spirits will—'

Caine's right arm shot out and slapped the open cuff around Takuba's belt.

The helicopter groaned and tilted right again. Caine and Takuba slid towards the doorway. The pipes and tanks of the gas refinery yawned beneath them. The black shadow of the rotors whirled over their heads.

Caine reached under the corpse. His grasping fingers wrapped around the parachute's ripcord.

He grabbed the doorframe with his free hand and yanked the cord.

Takuba's eyes bulged as he watched the white cloth of the chute explode into the air outside the helicopter. Before he could even move, the trail of silk fabric billowed up as it was sucked into the spinning rotors. Caine felt Takuba fly away from him, yanked up by the tremendous force of the helicopter's engine.

He heard a brief shriek of terror, cut short by a metal grinding. A crimson spray misted the air.

Takuba was gone.

Caine staggered to his feet. More smoke billowed from the damaged engine. A loud, chirping alarm filled the cargo bay, and a red light flashed on the roof.

The helicopter's engine was failing.

Caine slid the door closed and panted for breath. He struggled to keep his balance as he jogged to the open ramp at the rear of the bay.

The winch line was about a hundred feet long, and it stretched taut behind the helicopter. Looking down, he could see the pallet, wedged between two distillation towers. He saw a figure crawling on the top of the lashed barrels.

It was Nena... She had survived!

The helicopter dropped suddenly. Caine staggered backwards as he regained his balance. The line went slack for a moment, then tightened again as the aircraft gained altitude.

This thing is going down any second, Caine thought. And there's only one way off...

He whipped his belt from his pants and slid a few feet down the ramp. He looped the length of leather around the bucking cable.

Holding both ends in his hands, he took a deep breath. The helicopter dipped. The engine wheezed, and it began to climb again...

Caine slid off the ramp.

He flew through the air, zip-lining down the steel cable as the helicopter bobbed behind him.

Nena looked up and gasped. She moved away from the cable and tightened her grip on the mesh. Caine slammed into the pallet. He fell forward and rolled towards the edge. His fingers grabbed at the mesh. Nena tugged at his waistband, stopping him from tumbling over the side.

Caine scrambled to his feet. Nena threw her arms around him. He hugged her back, then held her face in his hands. 'Nena! You made it! I thought—'

He stopped himself. The second helicopter roared above them. The crackling fire of its autocannon blazed through the sky. It veered off again, as smoke streamed from the pilot's cabin.

Caine looked to their left. A metal ladder ran down the side of one tower. It was about three yards away, out of arm's reach.

'We have to get down,' he shouted. 'Now!'

Nena looked over the edge of the pallet. Her eyes were wide

with fear, and her face was pale. Caine was sure she was in shock after all she had been through.

'Someone will come. It's safer if we wait here,' she stammered.

Caine shook his head. 'No. These tanks are filled with liquid natural gas. It's highly flammable. If that helicopter hits...'

Nena bit her lip, then nodded. 'Then I will do as you say.'

'We have to jump. Follow me.'

Caine stood up, took a running leap, and jumped off the edge of the pallet. The metal creaked and groaned as his weight struck the ladder. He grabbed hold of the side rails and turned to Nena.

'It's not that far! You can do it,' he shouted.

Nena kneeled near the edge and looked down. 'Tom, I don't know, I...'

The metal cable scraped against the side of the tower. Caine looked up and watched as the helicopter listed sideways. It began to circle around them. The cable was pulling it in closer as it wrapped around the tanks.

'Nena, there's no more time. We have to go now!'

She stood up and took a few steps back. The steel cable flew over their heads and slapped against the tank as it wrapped tighter. The noise of the spinning rotors grew louder as the helicopter was pulled closer.

'Nena, jump!'

She leapt off the edge of the pallet and sailed towards him.

Not gonna make it! he thought as he watched her body drop towards him.

She reached out... Her fingers missed the metal rung of the ladder by millimeters. Her mouth gaped open in fear...

Caine's arm shot out. He grabbed her outstretched hand. She

slammed against the ladder. Caine's other hand slipped down a rung, but he managed to hold on.

'I've got you... Let's go!'

Panting for breath, she found her footing and climbed down the side of the tank.

Above them, the cable continued to wrap around the tanks. The helicopter spun around them. Its engine buzzed in protest, but it was now hopelessly tangled. A stream of smoke trailed behind it as it looped around the tanks.

'Nena, go faster,' Caine shouted. 'We're close enough, slide the rest of the way!'

They both slid down the remaining distance and rolled to the ground. Caine scrambled to his feet and pulled her forward as they sprinted away from the tanks.

The metal cable snapped around the tanks one more time. The spinning blades of the chopper were only a few feet away...

Caine looked back. A shower of sparks burst through the air as the spinning rotors tore into the tanks. The helicopter crumpled as the sudden impact and centrifugal forces tore it apart.

There was no time to speak, no time to think. Caine threw Nena to the ground and dove on top of her.

The explosion was deafening.

The earth shook and rumbled beneath them. Caine closed his eyes tight as a tremendous ball of fire blossomed into the sky. The heat was like a physical force bearing down on them, pushing them into the ground. A curtain of fire rippled overhead, singeing their clothes and burning their lungs with superheated air and vapor.

Then, with an echo like distant thunder, the wave of heat receded. The earth was still.

Caine staggered to his feet. He helped Nena up. They both

choked and coughed as a thin film of ash floated down around them.

Caine looked her in the eye. 'Are you okay?'

She nodded. 'Yes... I... I think so.'

Caine checked his watch. The peace conference was starting in six minutes. Looking up, he saw tiny figures running towards them in the distance. He put a hand on Nena's shoulder. 'I have to get word to Khairi. We have to warn the conference, a sniper is targeting the vice president. Wait here. I'll be back, okay?'

She nodded.

Caine put his hands up and marched towards the other men. As they ran closer, he could see they carried rifles and wore helmets. They were soldiers, or private security of some kind.

Caine stopped and turned back to Nena. Dust and wind swirled around her. Flames flickered in the background, distorting the air with their rising heat. She stared back at him with a pale, uncertain expression.

'I'm not leaving you here,' he shouted. 'I'm coming back.'

She gave him a tiny smile. It was a small, enigmatic grin, but it brought color and life back into her face. 'I know. You always do.'

He turned and continued walking towards the men in the distance.

45

ONE WEEK LATER

Caine stood behind a gnarled wood railing and looked over a vast green savannah. The Mihingo Eco Lodge in Uganda was built into the side of a rocky, forested hill known as a kopje. His spacious bungalow looked out over Lake Mburo National Park, and the view was spectacular. In the distance, herds of impala leapt towards the dark surface of a watering hole. A few zebras strutted between the bounding animals, calling to their young with high-pitched yelps. The sun hung low in the sky, casting an orange glow over the land and water.

Earlier in the day, a low mist had clung to the valley. In the quiet, still twilight of dawn, he had seen a leopard stalk towards the pool and lower its head to drink. Then the big cat had slinked away into the shadows, resting before the evening's hunt began.

The bungalow was mostly open space. A warm breeze rustled the white netting that hung from the rafters. To Caine, the stained wood and simple white fabrics that decorated the room were relaxing. It was a far cry from the luxurious suite he had rented in Khartoum, but he felt more at home here. The sounds of the grasslands at night lulled him to sleep, and he awoke to watch the animals gather in the mornings. For now, he was at peace.

An electronic chirping disturbed his thoughts. He walked over to the nightstand and picked up the satellite phone Rebecca had sent him. He looked at the display and smiled. He recognized the number and country code.

He answered the call. 'Khairi.'

'Hello, Thomas,' Khairi said. The deep rasp of his voice sounded warm and full, even over the digital satellite uplink. 'After all that has happened, I was not sure we would have a chance to speak again. I take it you are no longer in South Sudan?'

'No, my people got me out through Uganda. Things are a little hot there right now.'

Khairi chuckled. 'That is quite an understatement. But I'm glad to hear you still have people looking out for you. That's something I miss in my retirement.'

'Retired, huh? You seem pretty active to me. How did your people get into the peace conference to take out that sniper?'

'Well, it's a delicate matter, but of course I trust you implicitly, Thomas. Like any intelligence agency, the NISS has double agents in place. People inside South Sudan's government and military. I pressured one of my former colleagues for the identity of one such agent, a high-ranking lieutenant in the armed forces. Since it was in both our governments' interests to stop the attack, he ordered his man to intervene. They searched the perimeter of the UN camp and found your sniper. And then he... how should I put it?'

'Made the problem go away?' Caine replied.

'Yes, quite. To announce such a thing publicly, it is in no one's best interests in these turbulent times, yes?'

'Whatever you say. Frankly, I'm surprised. I would have thought your government would welcome more turmoil in the South.'

Khairi sighed. 'Do you remember what I told you all those years ago? Governments, their policies, their people... Everything is always changing. These days, I believe Sudan realizes its future is intertwined with the South, for better or for worse. Even those who opposed the South's independence don't want a collapsed nation of refugees on our border. For now, peace and stability are in everyone's best interests.'

'You played a part in that peace, Khairi. Thank you.'

'La shay. It was nothing. After a lifetime of working with questionable men in dark places, it feels like a blessing to do some good in the world. It was the least I could do to atone. And what of your atonement? I take it Puff Adder is dead?'

'He is,' Caine said. 'For good, this time.'

'And how are you sleeping?'

Caine thought back to his hallucination in the Sudd. He could only remember brief flashes, snippets of images and sounds. Takuba, his eyes wild with madness and hate. The children toting their guns. The girl, looking up at him, pleading, begging...

He shook his head and forced the demons of his past back into the dark recesses of memory.

'Thomas, are you still there?' Khairi asked.

'Yeah. I'm here.'

For a moment, there was only crackling silence. Then the old man spoke again. 'It will take time. Time to heal, time to forget. For now, please know that Takuba, the things he did... I have many regrets. In the name of my government, I have done many things that haunt me. But he tipped the balance for me, from light to shadow. I am an old man, weak, tired. You had to come here, you had to slay the shaitan jinn, kill the demon. Now that you have done so, you have set me free. For me, the shadow has lifted. I thank you.'

'Khairi, I need to ask one more favor.'

'Of course, anything.'

'Doctor Vasani. She'll be returning to Khartoum tomorrow. She's been through a lot. She risked her life to save people in both countries. I know she has enemies in your country. I'm hoping I can count on you to look out for her.'

'Mmmm, I did not realize you and the doctor had become so close.'

'Khairi...'

'Heh, I joke, of course. And do not worry. I understand Doctor Vasani possesses valuable scientific information regarding this so-called Gemini virus. I am confident my government will be able to overlook their issues concerning her. They must work with her to make sure our pipelines are protected from such attacks in the future. I may be retired, but I still have some influential friends. It is always good to have friends, Thomas.'

'You still don't sound retired to me. But thank you.'

'As I said, it is nothing.'

A loud knock echoed through the room. Caine turned towards the stairs that led to the ground floor entrance. 'Khairi, I have to go now.'

'Of course,' the old man said. 'I hope you enjoy Uganda while you can. It is a beautiful country. Ila al-liqa.'

'Until we meet again,' Caine translated. 'Goodbye, old friend.'

He hung up the phone. Footsteps ascended the curved stone

steps that led to the second floor. Nena rose into view. Caine raised his eyebrows and took a deep breath.

She wore a short orange dress that contrasted perfectly with her dark skin. A thin tunic of red and gold silk was cinched at her waist and fluttered open around her long, shapely legs. It was a modern take on traditional Ugandan dress. The colors reminded Caine of the sunset painted across the sky outside.

Her hair was long, thick, and shimmering. She had pulled it back from her face, and it hung behind her like a sleek, inky black waterfall.

'Wow... You look different!' he said.

She laughed. 'You mean, I'm not covered in mud and filth?'

'No, the dress... I mean, you look beautiful.'

'The lodge had a few of these for sale. The designer works here, in Uganda.'

Caine checked his watch. 'Maybe I screwed up the time, but I thought we said—'

She laughed again and waved her hand at him. 'No, no, I am early. But it has been so long since I could wear a dress like this, I didn't want to wait any longer. They're playing local music in the restaurant. There is dancing. Let's go and have some fun.'

Caine gave her a sheepish grin. 'I'm not much of a dancer, I'm afraid.'

She took his arm and pulled him to the stairs. 'Yalla, come on. All those fancy fighting moves, and you cannot dance? What good are you then?'

Caine laughed and followed after her. 'At least we can finally get that drink.'

She leaned against him. Her perfume smelled of jasmine and orchids.

'You may drink,' she said. 'I am going to dance until I am too tired to move. If you will not join me, you can just watch me have all the fun.'

'You've got yourself a deal,' Caine said.

They left the open bungalow and walked down the stone path that led to the lodge. The molten, fiery sky was reflected in the waters of a long infinity pool that ran alongside the path. Their dark, laughing figures entwined arms in the placid mirror of the water's surface.

* * *

Later, after dinner, they stopped at Nena's bungalow for a drink. Inside, the bungalow was identical to Caine's but was decorated with vases and jars of fresh flowers. She led him up the stairs to the bedroom. Trails of leopard orchids, lilies, and African roses lined the stairs. The mosaic of colorful blossoms sweetened the warm night air with their fragrance.

'I ordered champagne, the bottle's over there.' She nodded towards the balcony as she removed her earrings. 'I'll just be a minute,' she murmured.

She entered the bathroom and Caine heard the sound of running water. He stepped over to the ice bucket, removed the chilled green bottle, and popped the cork. He poured two bubbling glasses and took a sip. Again, he looked out over the grasslands below. They were now shrouded in darkness and mist.

He heard footsteps behind him. Nena emerged from the shadows. Her orange dress was gone, and the red tunic hung open from her shoulders. Sweat glistened on the dark slash of naked skin revealed between the slivers of fabric. Her long, coffee-brown legs parted the slight covering further as she moved towards him.

'Nena, I—' Caine paused. He felt the pull of her intoxicating scent, the gravity of her dark onyx eyes.

'That day, by the river,' she said, her voice low and husky. 'You never told me why you would not kiss me. I am not a naive girl, Tom. I know you wanted to. I know you want to now. I can feel it. I ask you again... is there another woman you love?'

Caine blinked. Up close, her sleek flesh, her intoxicating scent... her sudden raw sensuality was overpowering.

'To be honest, no. Not now. But there is someone. Someone I might want a future with.'

Nena stepped closer. He grabbed her waist in his hands. She reached up and caressed the rough stubble of his cheek.

'If she is your future, then she may love you tomorrow. Tonight is for us. We are here, we are alive. Tomorrow, I go back north. But tonight, I am still free. Here, no one may tell me what to believe, or who I may spend my time with. And no one can tell me what pleasures I may taste.'

She looked up into his eyes. With a roll of her shoulders, she shrugged out of the red sheath. It fell to the floor with a quiet rustle. 'No one but you.'

Caine could resist no longer. He pulled her close and pressed his lips to hers. There was no more room for thought, no time for objections. She groaned softly as she kissed him back. Her breasts pressed against him through the thin linen of his shirt. He bit her lip, and she gasped as she felt the heat build between them.

They fell back onto the bed, her fingers scratching across his back and tugging at his clothes. She tore open his shirt and ran her fingers across his chest. He let her roll him over on the bed and gazed up at her as she straddled his waist.

'You must be careful,' she whispered. 'You'll tear your stitches. Do not exert yourself. At least, not too much...'

Caine slid his fingers up her abdomen. Her skin felt like warm silk. 'Doctor's orders?' he said with a grin.

She giggled and lowered her mouth to his neck. 'Oh, quiet you.' The soft, moist caress of her lips slid down his body.

Their talking and laughter ceased. The sounds of their pleasure carried over the grasslands below and mingled with the cries of the other nocturnal animals.

* * *

In the morning, she was gone. Caine sat up in bed and glanced around the room. The dim glow of dawn crept over the balcony and illuminated the bungalow. He could see that she had taken all her things. Only the colorful dress remained, crumpled on the floor where she had left it.

He turned and stared at the sheets next to him where she had slept. A single rose lay above the covers. Its petals matched the colors of her dress – fiery orange, tipped with crimson highlights.

Once again, Caine thought back to her words on the raft.

A rose to sweeten the present...

He stood up and padded over to the balcony. The evening mist was receding. The tapir herd was already moving towards the watering hole, as they had done the day before. As they did every day, long before humans saw fit to perch their wooden dwellings on the rocks above.

The lodge was far south of the White Nile. Caine knew Nena would soon be traveling alongside the river's curves as she made her way north to the spice markets and mosques of her ancient home. He hoped Khairi was right, that peace and stability awaited her there.

The past had been put to rest. And for now, the present was as sweet as he could remember in recent times.

That only leaves the future, he thought.

He got dressed and returned to his bungalow. Then he grabbed a chair, pulled it to the edge of the balcony, and picked up the satphone. He dialed a number.

Rebecca.

'Tom?' Her voice was slow and heavy with sleep. She sounded like she had just woken up.

'Hey. Sorry if I woke you,' he said.

'No, it's fine. All I do is sleep these days.'

'Are you still in the hospital?'

'Yes. Tom, there's something... something I didn't tell you before. I'm scheduled for an operation. Spinal surgery.'

He felt his pulse quicken. He clenched his fist. 'What's wrong, are you okay? Did the attack—'

'No, no, it's nothing like that,' she said. 'They think... if the surgery is successful, they think there's a chance I could walk again. The operation is in a couple weeks. At first I was worried my injuries from the attack might have made things worse, but my doctor said everything is still on track.'

'Rebecca, I don't even know what to say. That's incredible news.' He felt a lump in his throat, and his voice dipped low. 'I'm happy for you.'

'Thank you. I don't know what to say either, to be honest. I'm afraid to get my hopes up, in case... well, you know.'

Caine thought for a moment. 'That was the message you left for Josh, wasn't it. That was how you knew he was in trouble.'

'Yeah,' she said quietly.

'I'm sorry. I wish he could be there for you now. I never wanted...'

He heard her swallow. 'I know, Tom. I know. They're adding

his star to the memorial wall next week. If the operation is—no, when the operation is successful, that's the first place I plan to walk to.'

There was crackling silence.

'I understand the man who helped you, Nhial, was reunited with his family,' she finally said.

'Good. They deserve some peace,' Caine replied.

'Speaking of which, the peace conference moved forward. There was some fighting at the oil fields, but without Takuba and his coup to fan the flames, the military routed his men easily. Maybe now the president and the other rebels can craft a ceasefire that actually sticks.'

'I hope so,' Caine said. 'Even Sudan, in the north, seems ready for peace. Maybe everyone's just too tired to keep fighting. But there's still all that oil. All that money. Takuba was right about that, at least. The oil is the root of all the killing here.'

'It's not just the oil, Tom. It's human nature. There will always be some who see more profit in war than peace. We have to be better than that. We have to hope for the best, even as we prepare for the worst...' Her voice began to drift and fade.

'Rebecca, there's a reason I called... I want to come in.'

'What?' She snapped to attention. 'I've heard that before from you.'

'I know. But I'm serious. What you said to me in Malakal, you were right. We're in this together. I can't do it alone. Not anymore.'

'If the intel you gave me about Walter Grissom is true, then we need you, Tom. More than ever. Grissom is in a league of his own. He's a lifetime cold warrior, with a black ops file longer than yours. He was notorious for running unsanctioned ops, and he taught Allan Bernatto everything he knows.'

'Yeah, I know. And now he's running wild, setting up his own new world order.'

'With his experience, connections, and resources, he can do it. He's probably the most dangerous enemy this agency has ever faced.'

'He gave the order, Rebecca. He told me straight to my face, he ordered Bernatto to burn me in Afghanistan. He got Jack killed. And Josh...'

'Tom, this is bigger than you and me. I want you to come in, but it has to be for the right reasons. It's not going to be easy now. Not after what you pulled in Louisiana. The DNI's body is still missing, and you put two FBI agents in the hospital. And we still don't know who leaked the convoy intel. Paulis is going to want a full debrief, by the book, before he trusts you.'

'I know.'

'They're going to dig into all your old ops. Full interrogation, psych evaluation, the works.'

'Whatever it takes.'

'Are you sure about this? Are you sure you can work with Paulis, work with me? I need to know we can trust you. And more importantly, that you can trust us. Are you really prepared to forget the past?'

Caine thought for a moment. He pictured the rose lying on the rumpled bed in Nena's bungalow.

'I can't forget,' he said. 'I never will. But I'm ready to move forward.'

'Alright. I'll let Paulis know. We'll make the arrangements. And Tom?'

'Yes?'

'When I'm out of my surgery, when you're back... maybe you can walk with me. To see Josh's star.'

'I'd like that,' he said.

'I'll see you soon, then.' Her words were almost a whisper. She hung up.

Caine set down the phone and turned back to the balcony. He watched the morning sun explode above the horizon. It burned away the last vestigial traces of darkness and mist.

Once again, the balance had tipped from shadow to light.

46

A cool mist hung in the air above the still waters and rolling grass hills of Boston's Public Gardens. The famous wooden swan boats were lashed to their green-steepled dock. They bobbed in the dark, still water of the lagoon. It was early morning, and the park was not officially open. A small crowd of joggers and businesspeople gathered on the bank of the lagoon, under the bowed branches of a weeping willow tree.

The crowd muttered amongst themselves in low, hushed tones, as a pair of police officers in rubber coveralls waded out into the water. A few snapped quick pictures with their cell phones. A dark shape floated a few yards from the grassy shore. The officers dragged the bloated mass back towards the water's edge.

The crowd gasped as they moved closer. The men were pulling a body, facedown, through the water.

A uniformed officer blocked the crowd. 'Everyone, you need to get back. Move it, people, move it.'

He gestured for them to move back. A pair of black and white police cruisers skidded to a stop on a paved road that ran through the park. Their flickering lights bathed the crowd in a red and blue glow. Their sirens were muted, as if they did not wish to disturb what little peace remained in the quiet, dewy morning.

The doors of the cruisers swung open. More police officers hustled out. They escorted a pair of men toward the lagoon. The men wore blue windbreakers and carried plastic cases of forensics equipment.

The officers in the water finally reached the shore and dragged the corpse onto the grass. The water in the lagoon was cold, and the body appeared to be fresh. It was a male in his early fifties. Strands of wet hair were plastered against his pale forehead. The damp locks hung down over the body's glazed, blue eyes. A neatly trimmed goatee decorated the corpse's chin. A series of ragged, red holes pierced its water-logged clothes. The bloodstains were concentrated around the heart and lungs.

One of the police officers patted down the body. 'No ID. No wallet.'

The forensic techs began to snap pictures of the corpse's wounds.

'Alright, show's over. Let's get back and let these people do their jobs!' The officer on crowd control waved his arms towards the park's exit. 'Come on, move back. Let's show some respect, people!'

The crowd began to disperse. A tall, muscular man broke away from the onlookers. He wore a long navy-blue trench coat and sipped steaming coffee from a white Styrofoam cup. His face was tan and leathery and lined with the deep, worn crevasses of one who spent too much time in the sun.

He walked up a gentle, grassy hill, exited the park grounds and walked along Charles Street. As he sauntered past the rows of brick buildings and blossoming cherry trees, he slipped a phone from his pocket. His bright blue eyes darted left and right – one last check to make sure he had not been followed. Then he tapped a number on the phone and waited while the call connected.

A series of beeps indicted the phone had made a secure connection.

'Blackwing One reporting,' he said.

'Good to hear from you,' a gruff voice responded. 'Did you go to see the doctor?'

'Yes, Mr. Grissom. Corrigan has been taken care of,' he said in a low voice. 'He made the dead drop last night before he suffered an accident in the park. The police will report it as a mugging. And I recovered our material.'

As he spoke he slipped a tiny clear pouch from his pocket and held it up to the light. A microchip lay nestled inside the bag. The chip was stained with what appeared to be dried blood.

'Paulis can run around in circles chasing after his mole,' Grissom said with a chuckle. 'I wonder how long it will take him to figure out that his own D/NCS led us straight to his star witness?'

'Whatever your leverage on Corrigan was, it worked,' the man replied. 'Once he inserted the tracking chip during his exploratory surgery, I was able to activate it remotely on the day of the hearing. Burst transmission, short duration. Identified the real convoy. I shut down the transmission after I took care of Lapinski's SUV. There's no chance anyone else detected the signal. Corrigan removed it during her operation. It's in my possession now. I'll dispose of it shortly.'

'At least one goddamn thing went right,' Grissom muttered. 'Look, there's something else I need you to take care of. I've booked you on a flight to Geneva. I'll brief you when you get here. You leave this afternoon.'

'What's the new job?' the man asked in a monotone voice.

'Bernatto,' Grissom snapped. 'He disappeared in the aftermath. Better than the authorities finding him, I suppose. But his asset, Takuba... That lunatic almost ruined everything. Poor judgment on Bernatto's part. Allan is a loose end now, just like Lapinski was. And we both know I can't have that. Not with what we're trying to build. Everyone is expendable.'

'I understand, sir.'

'Then there's Caine... You worked with the man. What do you think?'

'Caine will be a problem, sir. He won't let this go. You and Bernatto took him apart, put him back together again. Just like you did to me, Tyler, and the others. But Tom... he's missing a piece. He forgot the most important part of this job.'

'Yeah? What's that?'

'He forgot how to be a weapon, sir. He never could get that through his head. He can't let go of the past. It will eat away at him until there's nothing left.'

Grissom was silent for a moment, then grunted into the phone. 'Well. First things first. Get your ass to Geneva. We'll deal with Caine later.'

'Yes, sir.'

He hung up the phone and slipped it back into his pocket. The mist was thinning as the morning sun came up. The streets were growing crowded with businesspeople, tourists, children running to school.

He eyed the people rushing past him. No one paid him any mind. He was just another face in the crowd. Invisible. A ghost. He continued walking down the scenic street. His dark, flowing coat became a shadow, weaving between the bodies.

You didn't listen, Tom, he thought.

You didn't see me, but I was there... That night in Sudan,

years ago. Jack tried to warn you. I heard him clear as day, through my earpiece.

He told you the same thing I told him, when we were back in the Unit. The only way to survive in this business... You have to be a weapon.

You have to fire and forget.

* * *

MORE FROM ANDREW WARREN

Another book from Andrew Warren, *Code Green*, is available to order now here:
    https://mybook.to/CodeGreenBackAd

ACKNOWLEDGEMENTS

This book could not have been written without the gracious help of the following:

Thank you to Diane Sievert, whose early editorial guidance and encouragement were critical in bringing my first book to the finish line.

Thanks to Sam Carver, for sharing his insights into Sudan/South Sudan's complex history and politics. Mr. Carver also gave me some expert recommendations for the military firepower wielded by the Delta Blue assault team.

Thank you to fellow authors Matt Fulton and Aiden Bailey. Mr. Fulton is a research guru, and he kindly shared some details with me about the CIA headquarters building and the D/CIA's office within. Mr. Bailey directed me to some African proverbs that helped me focus on the theme for the book. He also connected me with his colleague, Dr. Ben Dearman, whose information regarding oil-eating bacteria started me down the path to creating Gemini.

To paraphrase the great Stephen King, what I got right is thanks to them; what I got wrong is thanks to me.

I'd also like to thank my editor Vic Britton and the entire Boldwood Books team. They've helped take the Thomas Caine series to the next level, and I couldn't be more thrilled.

A very special thanks to my wife, Mimi, who believed from the beginning...

Finally, thanks to you, the reader, for taking the time to read this book. Without you, none of this means anything! I hope you will join me on Thomas Caine's next adventure.

ABOUT THE AUTHOR

Andrew Warren is the international bestselling author of the Thomas Caine thriller series. Andrew was born in New Jersey and has over a decade of experience in the television and motion picture industry, where he has worked as a writer, story producer, and post production supervisor. He currently lives in Southern California with his wife and trusty dachshund sidekick.

Sign up to Andrew Warren's mailing list for news, competitions and updates on future books.

Visit Andrew's website: www.andrewwarrenbooks.com

Follow Andrew on social media here:

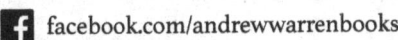 facebook.com/andrewwarrenbooks
instagram.com/andrewwarrenbooks
bookbub.com/authors/andrew-warren
bsky.app/profile/aawarren.bsky.social

ALSO BY ANDREW WARREN

THE *Hit* LIST

Every crime has a story...

THE HIT LIST IS A NEWSLETTER DEDICATED TO PULSE-POUNDING, HIGH-OCTANE ACTION THRILLERS!

SIGN UP TO MAKE SURE YOU'RE ON OUR HIT LIST FOR EXCLUSIVE DEALS, AUTHOR CONTENT, AND COMPETITIONS.

SIGN UP TO OUR NEWSLETTER

BIT.LY/THEHITLISTNEWS

Boldwood

Boldwood Books is an award-winning fiction publishing company seeking out the best stories from around the world.

Find out more at www.boldwoodbooks.com

Join our reader community for brilliant books, competitions and offers!

Follow us
@BoldwoodBooks
@TheBoldBookClub

Sign up to our weekly
deals newsletter

https://bit.ly/BoldwoodBNewsletter